# RELICS II

## THE HONOBIA REMNANT

A NOVEL BY
### JOHN VANDEVENTER

Printed in the United States of America

ISBN: 978-1-0880-1197-3

10 9 8 7 6 5 4 3 2 1

EMPIRE PUBLISHING
www.empirebookpublishing.com

Cover Illustration credit goes to Debbie Hefke

# DEDICATION

*Dedicated to my sons, Travis and Thomas Vandeventer*

Few men have their courage truly tested.

Your courage never failed.

# ACKNOWLEDGEMENTS

First, I'd like to thank my wife, Monica Vandeventer. You were the one who first told me of the Nephilim and planted the seed to this story. You were also the first one to explain scripture to me in a way that brought it to life. You didn't try to lead or drag me down the path of salvation; you simply showed me its beginning. For that, I am eternally grateful. To my children, Thomas, Donald, Jessica, and Trevor. Thanks for listening to all my book talk with a straight face.

To all my new friends in Gillham, Arkansas, who gave me my very first author meet-and-greet in August 2018. Especially Michelle Bohannon, Hal, and Dee Pettigrew, Gene and Queta Bryan, Suzie Shelton, and JeriAnn Kelly Ybarra. Your hospitality and kindness on that afternoon will never be forgotten, and your friendship is always cherished.

I'd also like to thank the many new friends I've made in various Oklahoma Bigfoot Research Groups and Bigfoot enthusiasts and fans of the first book. Your stories and experiences have provided fuel for my writing. Troy Hudson, Evans Bailey, Steven Byrd, Larry James, Chuck Schlabs, Tim Jones, Lance Hightower, Kurt Stanley, Barry Coy, Rick Ezell, Jim and Melinda Chidester, Jack and Jodi Foster Chism, Lauren A. Smith, Michael Humpherys, and Sharrie Sanders. Also, a special thanks to Judy Korten of the Talihina Chamber of Commerce and Tanya Kordek the operator of Chutay Ranch Project, Bigfoot Museum in Talihina, Oklahoma. In Honobia, I want to give a big thank you to Shawna Cline, who has so graciously allowed me to sell the first book in The Honobia Creek Store and use it as a location in this book. I'd also like to thank Artie and Theodora Carnes, the directors of the Kiamichi Christian Mission (Christ's Forty Acres) here in Honobia. Thank you for allowing me a table to sell the first book during the 2019 Honobia Bigfoot Festival.

I also want to mention that I appreciate the encouragement of longtime friends from my work, school days, as well as my Air Force brothers. Beth Adams, Johnna Sue Asher, Renee Tynes, Cinde Hosick Guant, Marion Cunningham, Sherri Pedigo Veach, Kelly Graham Jones, John and Sharon Takerer, Brian Stanley, and Roger Davies. New friends John and Tereasa West, Dyanna

Wilson and Arthur and Natasha Carnes. I'd also like to mention my cousins Nolen Brown and Ellen Brown Livingston and my new cousins in El Paso, Yvonne Apodaca and Rowena Garcia. Thank you all for your encouragement.

A huge thank you to my friend Joseph Beirer and his wife Kim. Joe, we still need to figure out that thing in Long Pool.

A very special thank you to my friend and favorite Fighter Pilot, Lt Col. Duane "Blood" Artery USAF Ret. Your knowledge of the F-4 Phantom and your experience as a career fighter pilot were a huge blessing when it came to writing the flying sequences in this book. I'm forever grateful, Sir.

Also, a big thank you to Empire Publishing; I was ready to throw in the towel, you guys made writing enjoyable again.

# A LETTER TO MY READERS

As a boy roughly 12 years of age, my cousin Ann Vandeventer gave me a book. Its title was Flying Saucers Serious Business. The author was Frank Edwards. Mr. Edwards published this book in 1966, just about a year before his death in 1967. The book captured my young imagination. Although I was curious about UFOs, this book cemented a lifelong interest in the subject. I believe UFOs were the perfect paranormal subject for me since I've also been a lifelong military aviation fan. I was already looking skyward, hoping to see a military fighter plane, so if I'm looking up already, it just seemed natural to keep an eye out for UFOs. To be honest, I was never a huge Bigfoot fan, and the publishing of my first edition of Relics in 2017 came as a big surprise to me as anybody else. It also surprised me I even considered writing a novel, though I must admit, had it not been for my sister Molly, "Relics" would never have happened.

In 2016, I'd written a novel and was about to publish it. I was already encouraged to write a sequel to Relics but was not sure the subject would hold up to another large novel. There are only so many Sasquatch stories you can write before they become repetitive. Then inspiration hit again from an unexpected direction. During one of my earliest conversations with the woman who is now my wife, Monica. She asked me about the book I had written and not yet published. Feeling a little embarrassed, I told her that it was a Bigfoot novel. Expecting a less than positive reaction, she calmly said, "I think if they exist, they may be a form of Nephilim." I admit having dodged church and the Bible my whole life up to that point; I did not know what a Nephilim was. She gave me what's known as the Angel view of the story of Genesis Six from the Bible. I was extremely interested in learning more, so I started reading the Bible, looking for answers. Next thing you know, I'm in church regularly, and then in 2017, I was baptized.

My novel series has taken on the viewpoints and opinions of some Christians. I'd like to add not all Christians will agree with the ideas I use for the storyline. In my church, we have people who do not believe the Angel Theory of Genesis 6 and subscribe to the Line of Seth Theory. I may end up being taken to task because, through my research for the second book, I've come across theories and opinions many find uncomfortable. Things like

Fallen Angels mating with human women to form the Nephilim. Demons are not Fallen Angels but the spirits of dead Nephilim. UFOs are not interplanetary - they're interdimensional. UFO occupants are not aliens but Angels or Fallen Angels. I ask all readers to remember that this is a novel written to entertain. Yes, there are quotes from the Bible; yes, there is information and theories found in other ancient texts such as the Book of Enoch. The story told in this, the second in the Relics series, covers a lot of theories. It also uses dramatizations of some famous and not-so-famous UFO encounters reported since the late 1940s and into the 1960s.

It also covers more recent tales and legends, such as the Giant of Kandahar and the Siege at Honobia. As I stated earlier, the entire purpose of this book is to entertain you with the continuing adventures of the characters, so many folks fell in love with reading the original novel Relics. So, the bottom line is… Fear not! If you're not a Christian, there's no agenda to secretly covert you within this book. However, there is every intention to entertain you. If you are a Christian, it doesn't matter if you believe the "Sons of God" mentioned in Genesis 6 are Fallen Angels or merely human males from the Lineage of Seth. You know neither influences your salvation, as that is only achieved through our Lord and Savior Jesus Christ and nothing else. So relax, put your feet up, turn the page and enjoy the ride. It's going to be a wild one.

# HONOBIA BRIDGE ENCOUNTER

By Sharon Takerer, Tucson AZ'

# Table of Contents

# PROLOGUE

"Civilization is like a thin layer of ice upon a deep ocean of chaos and darkness." ~Werner Herzog

## Thursday, 17 November 2016, 9:55 PM CST, Hwy 71 South of Gillham, AR

The small town of Gillham, Arkansas, lies in the Southwest part of the state. The area, originally known as the Silver Hill community, prospered during the first of the county's mining booms, around 1874. There was never any silver found in the area. However, antimony was found. This metal is useful in alloys with lead or tin, so some mining carried on until World War I, which caused the town to continue growing. In 1897, a new town on the Kansas City, Pittsburg, and Gulf Railroad was developed immediately to the Southeast of Silver Hill; They named it for Robert Gillham, chief engineer of the railroad. The town was incorporated in 1902 with an estimated population of four hundred. The timber mill at Silver Hill and the proximity of the Bellah and Antimony Mines provided prosperity for the area until the Great Depression, which devastated the town's economy.

World War II finished off what little remained of the community's economy, which had faltered when the Great Depression had begun. The war took almost all of Gillham's young men off too far-flung parts of the globe, with some never to return. Most of those who did return were in no mood to settle back into the homes and lives they had lived during the depression. Most scooped up their sweethearts, hurriedly planned and executed weddings, and headed off to build new lives in the excitement and endless possibilities of postwar America. A few stayed and continued working the family ranch or found work in the timber industry. Others found work in the larger towns of Mena, to the north, or De Queen, to the south. By 2016, Gillham, Arkansas, was simply another small town nestled alongside Hwy. 71 as it snakes from The Missouri border near Bella Vista to Texarkana, Texas.

Two seventeen-year-old boys, Curtis Downs and his best friend Paul Archer, were living it up. Curtis was feeling on top of the world as he gunned the engine of his 2005 Dodge Ram pickup, climbing the rolling hills and maneuvering around the sharp turns of Hwy. 71 as they raced away from their hometown of De Queen. Both young men wore their black and gold De Queen Leopards letter jackets. Their season had been a disappointment, as they had only won two of their ten-game season. The successful teams were presently winding their way through the second round of the state playoffs. Curtis and Paul were trying to forget their miserable season and the reality that neither of them would ever play organized football again. Even though both were gifted athletes, neither young man had the size or speed to advance to the college level. Boyhood dreams of running out onto the field at Razorback Stadium in Fayetteville or War Memorial Stadium in Little Rock, wearing the cardinal and white jerseys of the Razorbacks, were fading fast.

It looked as if their future Razorback gear would be nothing more than tee-shirts purchased at the local Walmart in De Queen. Their future playing field would be the Weyerhaeuser timberlands in the local Kiamichi or Ouachita Mountains or, even worse, a Tyson Chicken plant. Both boys tried to push these thoughts to the back of their minds and concentrate on their newly found freedom. No more football meant no more football coaches, no more football practice, and best of all, no more football curfews. As they sped through the chilled November night, they had a couple of things on their minds: girls and guns. A week ago, Curtis had hit it off with a young lady from Gillham, located a few miles north of De Queen. Janis Burke was eighteen, and everything young Curtis thought a woman should be. More importantly, Janis lived in a trailer with her single mother, who worked nights at the Tyson Chicken plant in Grannis, Arkansas, about 10 miles north of Gillham. Normally the plant closed at 11:00 PM; however, with the holiday season fast approaching, the plant was running twenty-four hours a day. The mother of young Janis had volunteered to work overtime through the night because she needed the extra money to get herself and her daughter through the winter.

Janis promised her mother she would do her homework and go to bed early. Well, Janis got her homework done. However, knowing her mother would not return from work until after 8:00 the next morning, she invited her new boyfriend Curtis to come for a visit. She knew Curtis had a cute friend, Paul, who would be perfect for her best friend, Lisa. Janis had the evening perfectly planned, or so she thought, as she and Lisa waited for the two boys. Curtis was doing his best to live in the moment as he and Paul rocketed north along Hwy 71.

2

"Tonight's the night!" he said, smiling at Paul, who was busy examining Curtis' new Judge Pistol, a recent gift from his father.

Looking up from the pistol, Paul asked, "The night for what?"

"I'm going to get busy, my man."

"You'll be busy getting slapped and told, no," Paul said, laughing.

"No way, man, tonight is the night! There won't be any saying, 'No' tonight," Curtis exclaimed, producing a bottle of Jack Daniels.

"It could work," Paul said, momentarily losing interest in the pistol. "So, what's her friend look like? Have you seen her?" He inquired.

"No, but Janis says she's a hottie."

"They all say that when they want to hook up their ugly friends with one of their boyfriend's buddies," Paul said with sarcasm.

"I wouldn't worry about how she looks if I were you, Paul. You have bigger worries than that."

"Yeah, what would that be?" Paul asked, walking right into the trap Curtis had laid. "You better hope she's blind and doesn't have a sense of smell or you'll be sitting on the porch all night."

Holding the pistol out of the passenger window, Paul said, "How about I just toss this in the weeds, smart guy?"

"Don't even joke like that, man," Curtis said, seriously.

"Don't worry; I wouldn't do you that way. Besides, I'll be loving up both women tonight while you sit around and rub your pistol," Paul said confidently as he rolled up the window. Both young men burst into laughter. They knew the best they could hope for was some topless fondling if they got that lucky. "You got ammo for this?" Paul asked.

"In the glove box," Curtis answered. Digging in the glove box, Paul produced a box of four-ten shells. "Just four-ten shells, no forty fives?" He asked with mild disappointment.

They didn't have any at Walmart. Dad's going to take me to the Academy in Texarkana Saturday, and I'll get some then. Those four-ten shells are slugs, though; they will do some serious damage to whatever we shoot at."

"Cool," Paul said, eyeing the box of shells with newly found respect.

As the boys neared Gillham, Curtis slowed the truck as he came upon a sharp curve just before going under a railroad bridge. The bridge had been upgraded several times over the years. The last upgrade left sizeable walkways between the concrete bridge pylon and the natural rock structure, which were as much a part of the bridge's foundation as the concrete pylons themselves. When the headlights of the Dodge truck filled the bridge area

3

with light, both boys saw an enormous figure with glowing, orange eyes blinking against the glare of the headlights. The figure was wedged in between the bridge pylon and the natural rock. It was holding something to its chest and appeared to be covered in blood.

"What the hell?" Paul exclaimed.

"Was that what I thought it was?" Curtis asked, nervously looking back at his friend.

"It was eating a sheep!" Paul screamed. "It was a Sasquatch, and it was eating a damn sheep!"

"Load the gun!" Curtis said, slamming on the brakes.

"I don't know man, maybe we should just keep going," Paul said, nervously, even as he loaded the gun; his hands were shaking violently.

"Don't be a wimp, man. You know what that is?" Curtis asked his friend.

"That thing is a monster and will probably do to us what it did to that poor sheep," Paul answered.

"Wrong! That's our ticket out of here, man! No lumber mill, no chicken plant, no job at the Walmart changing tires. Man, that's money and freedom. All you have to do is shoot it in the face with those slugs," Curtis said as he turned the truck around to head back toward the bridge.

"Why do I have to shoot it?" Paul asked.

"Because I have to drive. Don't worry; if the thing looks like it's going to attack us, I'll just speed away. Come on man, this is the chance of a lifetime. We have to take it."

"I guess so," Paul said, nervously.

"Roll your window down and get ready. I hope it didn't run off," Curtis said as they approached the bridge. As the lights of the truck illuminated the area of the bridge, Curtis was elated, and Paul was deflated. A tall reddish-brown figure stood in the middle of the highway directly on the center line, fifteen feet in front of the railroad overpass. Blood covered the area around its mouth, as was its chest. It clutched a dead sheep in its hand as it stared unblinking at the truck. It didn't move a muscle. Its expression was vacant as if it didn't care that the two young men in the truck were approaching it. It continued to gaze passively in their direction, almost as if curious. "Damn, he's huge," Curtis said with a nervous laugh.

"Curtis, throw this rig in reverse and let's get the hell out of here," Paul pleaded.

"No way, Paul. This thing is dumber than a box of hammers. It's going to let us roll right up on it and shoot it. Roll your window down Paul and get ready."

"No way man, I'm not rolling down my window."

"Paul, if it wanted to get us, the window wouldn't keep us safe. It would go right through it; the damn thing must be ten feet tall."

"Yeah, and bullet proof too," Paul snarled, upset by his friend's lack of concern with the threat right in front of them.

"Paul, we're seconds away from being rich men. Do you want to be known as the guy who killed Bigfoot, or do you want to pluck chickens for the rest of your life? This time tomorrow you'll be shopping for a new truck." Paul was warming to the idea of being rich, plus the creature wasn't exhibiting any threatening behavior. He decided he was stuck here anyway, so he might as well play his hand. "Okay man," he said, rolling down the window and nervously extending his arm forward with the pistol pointed in the general direction of the creature.

"Let me ease up a little closer," Curtis said as he took his foot off the brake, allowing the truck to inch forward slowly. The creature remained motionless, illuminated by the headlights, continuing to look passively at the vehicle and its occupants. Paul again saw the orange glow of the eyes, which caused him to shiver. The truck was ten feet from the creature, and Paul had to hold the gun upwards at a forty-five-degree angle in order to point it toward the face of his intended victim. Both boys had to lean forward and look up through the windshield in order to see its face. There was the slightest of changes in the creature's facial expression.

For a moment, Curtis and Paul both thought they saw a slight smile on the creature's face and saw it nod its head, almost imperceptibly. A moment was all they had to register that thought. Suddenly, a blinding white light illuminated the vehicle from above. Both teenagers squinted their eyes to see through the immense glare. At the same moment, they heard very heavy and fast running feet approaching from their right. Then there was a furious explosion of glass and metal as the truck was turned on its side. Paul's world went black; he never knew what hit him. Curtis could only register surprise at the attack from their flank as he lay on his side against the driver's window. The last thing he saw was the truck's windshield as it smashed, spraying him with shards of glass. Then sweet darkness took away his fear. Janis and Lisa spent the rest of the evening confused and wondering why Curtis and Paul never showed. It never occurred to them that the distant sound of emergency vehicle sirens had anything at all to do with their missing guests.

### Thursday, 17 November 2016, 10:25 PM CST, Hwy. 71 South of Gillham, AR

The accident site surrounding the area of the Dodge pickup was a mystery to the First Responders. There was a dead sheep in the road, a bashed-in windshield, and evidence that at least two occupants had been in the truck. They questioned the original motorist who came upon the scene. He said he never saw a driver, only the overturned truck. Sevier County Sheriff's Deputies and Arkansas State Troopers discussed several plausible scenarios. Did the truck strike the sheep? Did somebody throw the sheep from the railroad bridge onto the truck's windshield? None of it made sense. There were no skid marks indicating a high-speed rollover. It was as if the truck had simply been turned on its side. There was no blood or evidence of the truck's occupant or occupants other than an unopened bottle of whiskey. There were, however, two sets of tennis shoes neatly lined up next to the road, as if the owners of the shoes had removed them and placed them neatly beside the road. A Taurus Judge pistol was rested in one shoe.

Arkansas State Trooper, Jennings, had been the first to notice the shoes. A Sevier County Sheriff's Deputy said to him, "That's weird, have you ever seen anything like it before?"

"Yeah, once," Jennings replied.

"What do you make of it, then?"

Jennings moved away silently. I don't even want to think about it, he thought, putting distance between himself and the shoes. The truck was registered to a man in De Queen, and a unit was sent to that address. Following questioning the owner, they discovered the truck was being driven by his teenage son, Curtis, and there was a good chance his best friend, Paul, was with him. Now, the parents of both boys were at the accident scene, and the wailing of two worried mothers was more than Jennings could take. Determined to find answers and put distance between himself and the grieving mothers, Trooper Jennings kept moving and searching. A couple of other law enforcement officers had moved further away into the darkness as well. They, too, were affected by the sorrowful sounds of the mothers as they reacted to the accident scene, which held no sign of their children.

Since the arrival of the parents, he and the other officers knew they were looking for two teenage males. Beyond the truck itself and the whiskey, the only other evidence at the scene was the remains of a dead sheep. The sheep didn't appear to have been hit by the truck. It looked as though something had torn it open with brute force. Jennings came upon a low area that was covered in soft, damp soil with no grass. As he looked down, his heart sank. This wasn't what he had expected to find. A huge, bare, humanlike footprint was embedded in the soft soil. The footprint sent chills down the spine of the Trooper. Things were getting a little too creepy now. The footprint appeared to be at least eighteen inches long and seven to eight inches across. It brought back the memories of an incident he had been trying to forget for over two years now.

In July of 2014, he had responded to a military aircraft crash at Queen Wilhelmina State Park in the Ouachita Mountains near Mena, Arkansas. He and another Trooper, along with a Game Warden, had come upon a group of National Guardsmen who had discovered three charred remains. Remains of what? He had been asking himself for the past couple of years. He knew they weren't people, and he knew they weren't local black bears as the Game Warden had claimed during the discovery. There was a National Gur Sergeant who seemed to suspect they were the corpses of something else which had gotten caught in the fireball of the crash. He remembered the young NCO and his passionate argument with the Game Warden. He also remembered how the Game Warden had taken command of the situation and ordered the Guardsmen out of the area before the NCO had a chance to explain his theory.

Those weren't bears, he reminded himself. Bears would not have been the subject of such a heated debate. Nor would they explain the debrief he and his fellow Troopers were given by the Game Warden and a Special Agent with the National Forest Service, who swore both troopers to secrecy. He had never received any plausible explanation for the scene which he'd witnessed or why it was so important to keep it all quiet. Then again, he didn't need to be told. A Park Ranger had come to the scene to assist the Game Warden in guarding the bodies until they could be removed. On their way out of the area, he and the other State Trooper had come across footprints in a creek bed, which led straight to where the corpses were lying. They were large prints of bare feet, exactly like the one he was staring at now, except this one had six toes. Although he found the number of toes confusing, the growing fear in his stomach soon made it just a confusing detail. His mind was racing; he did not want to encounter whatever left this print, much less on a dark night like this.

He and the other Trooper couldn't wait to get out of the woods and back to their vehicles which were parked at the Lodge. They never spoke about the prints to each other, but they both knew there were things in those woods they didn't want to encounter. It reinforced their fears after dawn the next morning when they saw the Game Warden and Park Ranger in the medical tent. Both were injured and in shock. They claimed to have been attacked by assailants who threw large logs and rocks with incredible accuracy. When asked why they didn't shoot, they explained the attackers were hidden from view inside the wood line.

Trooper Jennings had some law enforcement friends in Oklahoma whose border was only nine miles away to the West. He'd heard tales from some of his Oklahoma buddies about the troubles in and around Talihina, Oklahoma, which also occurred two years ago. How could you keep something like this quiet? He thought to himself. He didn't want to believe any of this could have happened to those two boys who were missing from the truck, but the evidence was staring him in the face. As much as he didn't want to admit it to himself, he knew what left the print on the ground. He caught himself shivering; it wasn't so much because of the print. It was because of the shoes at the accident scene. All they'd ever found of the F-16 pilot two years ago were his boots. Those boots had also been neatly aligned on the side of the road, exactly like the tennis shoes here. The print pointed west toward Oklahoma, which added to his unease. Wherever these kids are, I'm afraid we're never going to find them, he thought to himself.

Keying the microphone on his lapel, he said into the radio, "Base, this is seven; we're going to need Fish and Game out here. And you'd better wake up the boss; he'll need to see this." The other State Troopers and a couple of County Deputies heard his transmission and made their way over to him. As they walked up to him, he looked at the Deputies and said, "Better get your brass out here. They'll tear you a new one if you don't let them know about this. They'll want to get ahead of it before it hits the media." Then he directed his light on the print.

8

# CHAPTER ONE

# Rising Darkness

*"And do not fear those who kill the body but cannot kill the soul. Rather fear him who can destroy both soul and body in hell."*

*~Matthew 10:28*

## Saturday, 19 November 2016, 9:45 PM CST, Redstone Ranch, two miles North of Talihina, OK

The Beast stepped from the creek onto the western bank. It stopped for a moment, fatigue from its journey causing it to be slightly disoriented. It had been a long journey, not long in miles but vast in dimensions. The November moon cast the Beast's dark shadow on the sand and light-covered rocks which lined the creek bed. It sniffed the air as if it could smell past the stench of sulfur, feces, and rot that emanated from its body. The longer the Beast stayed in this area, the less pronounced its scent would be, but for now, its stench was overpowering. This odor was a warning of the creature's presence to every living thing within 400 feet of it. For hundreds of feet in all directions, the forest went silent in the darkness. The stillness and eerie shadows cast by the moonlit trees would have put concern into the heart of any man who might stalk the Kiamichi Mountains this night.

Yet, there were no men in the forest this cold, lonely night. Only the forest creatures reacted to the Beast. Armadillos and raccoons stopped their foraging and went silent. It stilled night birds, deer, bobcat, coyote, and wild hogs all froze in place or quietly and cautiously slinked from the area. Again, the Beast raised its nose to the air, trying to detect a scent. It didn't get a scent, but it detected a presence, the presence of an enemy. The Beast began walking west, climbing a small hill. Upon reaching the top of the hill, it stopped and looked across a small ravine at the lair of its enemy. The draw toward its foe was strong, and the Beast stepped quickly and quietly into the ravine, crossing another small creek before once again climbing a slight rise. There it stopped again and watched. A form moved across the transparent opening in the dwelling, causing the Beast's breathing and blood flow to increase.

The Beast didn't possess the abstract brain function of humans. It couldn't understand how these beings built their lairs of wood, stone, and the frail transparent material which shattered so easily. It didn't understand the weapons they could bring to bear against him and his kind. It understood that its feud with the being inside this specific lair was a blood feud. He remembered fighting this being, along with others he would never forget, in the recent past. He knew this one was responsible for the deaths of two of his kind. Not death in a biological sense because the two could regenerate in time and escape the graves in which the humans had buried them.

This human differed from most. It did not succumb to the fear that normally sent other humans into a panic when the Beast encountered them. He knew the name of this human, Redstone.

The name burned into his consciousness. He knew there were two Redstone's, the elder and his son. No matter how they had tried to outmaneuver and outfight this elder Redstone, he was always one step ahead of them. Even when he held the younger Redstone in his grasp, the elder had turned the tables at the last moment and caused the creature and his one remaining comrade to retreat from the area. The elder Redstone had got an advantageous position, from which he could have downed them both for a long time, long enough for their bodies to be studied and the truth of their existence to be discovered.

The beast had changed since it had last encountered this human. It was bigger, stronger, and smarter; there were other changes as well. It had grown an extra toe on each foot and an extra finger on each hand. It was different from the other beasts in this area which it had encountered. Though similar in appearance, the beasts in this area lacked the strength, speed, and intelligence of this one and his other three clan mates. They were also docile compared to his clan, ducking out of sight should humans enter their area. Their diet consisted mainly of vegetation and whatever meat they could find in the way of roadkill or fish from the shallow rivers and creeks in the area. Occasionally they had a successful hunt for killing deer or wild hogs; they were not cold, calculating killers like this one. The local beasts avoided these four, usually by simply leaving the area when they sensed them. Those unfortunate enough not to detect them were usually beaten to death. If they happened upon a female, she was allowed to live and was released only after mating with one or all four of his clan. They had instructions to spread their seed at every opportunity; more of their kind would be needed in the future.

The human believed he had achieved a truce with the creature. There would never be a truce between the man and this creature or any of its kind. The creature was only one of many horrors that lurked in the shadows of the human's tidy, safe little world. There were more like him, and other creatures allied with him were more powerful and terrifying. The human, in his ignorance, had done nothing more than buy time from the devil. The human's time was nearly up, and his complete destruction was near. The man stepped out of his lair, into open ground, and moved toward his metallic vehicle.

Man was the word used by his kind to describe these beings. The Beast's blood boiled with the need for revenge. Its brain quickly calculated the complex geometry for three different attack routes to destroy this hated human, this man. Its hot breath was quick and heavy, leaving an enormous cloud of steam in front of it as it watched the man. Yet, it did not attack. Despite its lust to kill this man, it stood perfectly still, watching. It watched in anticipation and with great discipline, a discipline which was as much a part of its makeup as the large muscles which ached to tear this man into pieces.

As the man neared his vehicle, the Beast continued calculating ways to attack and destroy the man. It remained motionless due to a firm, unspoken set of instinctive instructions to not destroy this man - not yet. Although the Beast could only use the simplest of tools and had little to no understanding of the ways and thoughts of man, it had an ancient intelligence that differed entirely from that of men. This intelligence was not only a biological function for survival but also spiritually connected intelligence to others. This connection worked in a way similar to what man would call a 'network.' The others to whom it was connected were not only its own kind but other types of beings as well. Though diluted by the mixing of seed from advanced life forms from another realm with earthbound creatures, the intelligence came from a time before man was created.

The Beast would follow its instincts. It knew it was here for the complete destruction of this man. It would terrorize and kill this man's loved ones. It would also aid other beings under the control of his Master to torment this man. However, this man was not the priority; there was another who must die first. The Beast would use Redstone to lure the more dangerous man. The other man had become an enemy and a danger to all with whom the Beast was connected. The Beast would find him and destroy him, and then he would be free to slowly kill this man. With an ancient hatred, he continued to

11

watch as the man reached his vehicle. The Beast let a loud, long "WHOOP," which filled the chilly night air. The man stopped abruptly and reached for something inside his vehicle. Every muscle in the Beast tightened, ready to spring into the shadows if the man pulled one of his weapons from the metallic machine.

Instead, the man had one of the small, torch-like tools they used to project light in his hand. The man pointed the light in the Beast's general direction; the beam swayed back and forth until the light rested upon him. The Beast looked back at the man, unflinching and unblinking, into the bright light. The man went as still as a boulder on a mountaintop. A strong suggestion entered the brain of the Beast. Enough for now. Move away. The Beast turned and slowly faded into the tree line. As it left, it heard the man shout an oath or curse toward him in the night.

## Saturday, 19 November 2016, 10:00 PM CST, Redstone Ranch, two miles North of Talihina, OK

Addison Redstone was restless as he moved through his house trying to focus his thoughts. It had been a little over two years since he and his son Sam, along with their friends Daniel Greenwood and Nathan Parks, had fought to remove a threat to the citizens of Talihina, Oklahoma. They had barely won that fight; Nathan Parks and Daniel Greenwood had both been seriously injured but survived. It was a small price to pay for the removal of the threat, which very few of the community's residents even knew existed at the time.

In a little over four weeks, thirteen people had died as a result of this threat, and another three had died indirectly in a shootout with Addison's son, Sam, and other police officers. These three men were responsible for the death of Mike Sanders, whose murder could also be traced back to the presence of the creatures who haunted Addison's every waking moment. Though most citizens in the community were never aware of the danger, seventeen deaths in a short span of time, in and around the small community, were enough to bring his son's career as chief of police to an end. The fact that there seemed to be a cover-up of some kind caused even more suspicion to be leveled at the Redstone's.

Addison's son, Sam, had accepted the professional setback as the price paid for doing his duty. One thing the Redstone family was known for was doing their duty. Addison's father had done his duty in WWII, Addison himself in Vietnam, and Samuel had followed suit in Iraq. Neither Addison nor his son would have ever dreamed they would be forced into a life and death struggle for their lives and the lives of the citizens of Talihina. Yet their hand had been forced by circumstance, and both had struggled emotionally for the past two years with the fallout from what one news reporter called the "Unseen War of Talihina."

Addison and his son had always been respected, if not beloved, local community members. Though his true friends, mainly other Choctaw tribal members, knew exactly what he and his son had battled, most of the other citizens were confused and had no idea about the truth of what had occurred. Those who did know, dared not mention it for fear of being laughed out of town. Most of the citizens referred to the autumn of 2014 as the 'Dark Autumn.'

Addison attempted to take it all in stride; he loved people, and he loved his community. He had to admit sometimes it hurt when he saw old friends on the sidewalks in Talihina cross to the other side of the street to avoid contact with him. *Yes, they must stay away from the crazy, old Indian*, he thought to himself with some bitterness. He knew, as hard as it had been for him at times, it had been tougher on his son, Samuel. Sam had lost friends and local support over his involvement in the violence. He had also lost a budding romance because of it. So far, Sam had not completely healed from the loss of Monica Johnston and Vince Crawford. Both had died on the same day, fighting the very enemy Addison and Sam were eventually able to defeat. Sam blamed himself for the death of both his friends.

At the time, he'd been trying to navigate his way through the emotional roller coaster of a failed relationship with the love of his youth, Christa Fletcher-Sanders; he'd fallen for Monica hard and fast. Her death and the death of his good friend, Vince Crawford, plus the loss of his job as Police Chief, had darkened Sam. Those who knew him well knew that no matter how much he smiled and displayed a cheerful disposition, sadness lurked just beneath the surface. In the last year, Sam had finally married his old flame, Christa. The fact that she was the widow of Howard Fletcher, who had died in a shootout involving Sam and his officers, was another local hot topic of conversation which involved the Redstone's. Even juicer was the fact that a large tract of land owned by the late Howard Fletcher and inherited by his widow, the now Christa Redstone, was bordered on the west by Addison Redstone's large tract of land. This meant that the Redstone family owned just short of a thousand acres of some of the best land north of town. The area was known for its excellent hunting and fishing. The locals gave the area the unofficial name of the Redstone Ranch.

The Redstone's didn't mind if people hunted or fished on the land if they were respectful of its God-given gifts. These days however, people rarely, if ever, ventured onto the property. Addison knew why people stayed away. As much as the citizens of Talihina tried to deny it, many suspected something unknown and dangerous lurked on the property during the Dark Autumn of 2014 and most believed something sinister lurked there still. As time passed and the local gossip mongers added fuel to the flame to keep their stories from going stale, the tales grew bigger and more outrageous. The tales can't top the truth, Addison always thought to himself.

Shortly after the 'Dark Autumn,' Addison had married Marsha Johnston, the mother of Sam's deceased flame, Monica. It didn't matter that the two had quietly dated for nearly two years before the trouble started; again, it was more fuel for the fire. If Addison and Marsha were in town shopping or simply going out for a meal at one of the local restaurants, it was not uncommon to see local women stop and whisper to each other while looking in the couple's direction. Marsha ignored it; Addison tried to do so, but deep down inside, it bothered him. Marsha had lost enough when her daughter was killed. Having people, some of whom were old friends of hers, talk about her behind her back was more than Addison could bear at times.

Addison couldn't deny he was happy in his new life with Marsha; she was a wonderful wife and companion. Their personalities were finely tuned to each other, and they had a knack for instinctively reacting to each other's thoughts and needs. Addison's only disappointment was that they had to reside in town at Marsha's house. Knowing how her daughter had died, Marsha did not like going to the country where Addison's house and property were located north of town. "Those things may return," Marsha would say to Addison as she declined his every effort to entice her to enjoy the beautiful house and property where he had lived for years. The house in town was comfortable, and Marsha did everything she could to make it a home for Addison. Still, he missed his house in the woods overlooking the small reservoir named Lake Talihina, after the local community. Addison had also started referring to his place as 'The Ranch;' home was now in town with Marsha. As time passed, Addison began using the ranch as a base to do research on the Relics, as he now reluctantly called the creatures he and his son had battled back in the autumn of 2014.

He tried to include Sam in his research, but the younger Redstone was not as active in the endeavor as Addison had hoped he would be. His son was still convinced the creatures were some sort of ape, and if he did go out to investigate the phenomenon, it was usually in the company of a group of researchers from Texas who had an area staked out in Southeastern Oklahoma, which they identified as a habitation site. Sam quickly grew tired of this as well. He had already seen and experienced things those researchers couldn't even imagine. "You'll never find them unless they want to kill you," he told one of the researchers before leaving the group for good.

Addison's own opinion of the creatures had changed over the past two years. He had once referred to them as Okla Chito, which translates to Big People in his native Choctaw language. He now thought of them as Shampe, another name used by his tribe describing ogres or monsters that were a bi-product of an unholy union of evil spirits and Okla Chito females. His personal belief that the creatures were of natural origin had been shattered. The fact that they were a legend under different names in almost every first nation's tribe in North America no longer mattered to Addison. He could no longer cling to his long-held belief that they were an ancient tribe that had lived alongside the more modern human tribes for the past thousand years. *They're ancient alright, but more ancient than anything I could have imagined,* Addison thought to himself. His first hint of something more came at his last encounter with the creatures at Crusher Hollow on a cold November night in 2014.

A UFO which appeared then flew across the sky immediately before the Relic activity kicked off. Then to top it off, there was the fact that he had communicated with one of them in ancient Hebrew on the morning of that last battle in 2014. As a result of that conflict, two Relics had escaped, and two had been buried. US Army General Malcom Henderson had directed an engineer Task Force to dig up the two graves originally made by the surviving Relics and bury them in even deeper holes dug by a backhoe. Addison had slipped into the area periodically over the next few days to ensure that curious locals had not found the graves and dug them up.

The fourth day he visited the graves, he was shocked to find two large holes in the ground. The graves didn't appear to be dug up; instead, it appeared as if the Relics had dug themselves out of their graves. He immediately notified General Henderson, who met him at the site the next day. General Henderson didn't seem unduly surprised by the state of the graves or the fact that the remains of the Relics were missing. He repeated a couple of terms he first told Addison about immediately after the final fight with the creatures. Biological Relic Entity (BREN) and Relic Entity Unknown (RENU). Henderson said he couldn't elaborate, but creatures similar to those

15

he had just fought here were beginning to appear all over the world. Many were man-like, and General Henderson described them as Homo-Superius. All of this just confused Addison more. The General had another engineer team come to the area, where they filled in the holes and cleaned up any possible evidence.

Addison was both confused and angry about the situation. The buried remains would have served as a comfort to Addison, proving that he and his family were safe from these things. The fact that they seemed to have come back to life and dug their way out of their graves was too unsettling, even for the calm and even-keeled Addison. General Henderson was aware of Addison's anger and unease. Laying his hand on Addison's shoulder, he'd said, "Look, Sergeant Major, this subject is weirder and more complicated than you can believe. There is much more going on here than overgrown, monkey people. Not even I have full access to all the information. Just don't drink the Kool-Aid offered to you by the Forest Service people and that jerk, Eastman. This whole thing is part of an ultra-dark operation. It goes all the way to the top, and I don't mean only the White House. It's a global operation and darker than a black bat's ass in a cave at midnight. The answer to all this isn't in the forest and it isn't in the government."

"Then where is it?" Addison asked.

"The answer is in the last place most people would look in today's society," the General replied. Addison looked at the General in mounting confusion.

"Sergeant Major, you're going to figure out what we're up against, and I think you already have some idea. You're just not ready to admit it to yourself yet. You will, and once you do all of this will make perfect sense. You want to know how to keep your knife sharp and your powder dry to deal with this problem? If you open your Bible, you're going to the right place to find your answers. I'll be in touch if you need my help." General Henderson gave him a tired smile; then, clasping Addison on the shoulder, he shook hands and left.

After a few weeks, Addison assumed he'd never hear from the General again. Then in late 2015, Addison started getting short messages from General Henderson. It would usually be an email with a link to some website or YouTube video about various paranormal events. The topics varied; there were Sasquatch sightings and encounters. There were also humanlike giants spotted worldwide and even photographs of giant humanlike skeletons. Many of the articles were about UFOs, poltergeists, werewolf-like creatures, flying cryptids, and even little people. None of these made sense to Addison at first. What does any of this have to do with Oklahoma? he would think to himself. One day, there was a link concerning a ranch in Utah that was having a full-blown roll call of paranormal activity. The family who owned the ranch was having every kind of paranormal activity conceivable, including UFOs, cryptids like Sasquatch, and werewolf-type, animals. There was poltergeist activity in the house, as well as disembodied voices heard from overhead when working outside. The high strangeness even included cattle mutilations.

For Addison, the last straw came when he received an article about the Vatican Observatory on Mt. Graham in Arizona, followed shortly thereafter by a link to an article on CERN, the European Organization for Nuclear Research, which operates the world's largest particle physics laboratory in Switzerland. Addison was frustrated and fed up with the General's paranormal fascination; he finally sent an email back asking. "What does all of this have to do with me and the Relics? The General sent a short reply.

**Luke 17:26:** "Just as it was in the days of Noah, so also will it be in the days of the Son of Man."

Addison pondered the General's cryptic message. He wasn't sure how he would find the answers he was looking for in the Bible. He'd always considered himself a Christian. But only in the last year had he started attending church with his wife Marsha, who was a member of a local non-denominational church in Talihina. Addison had taken a liking to the church and its pastor immediately. This was a new experience for Addison, who had always looked upon religion with a large amount of skepticism and distrust. However, neither Addison's newly found faith nor the Bible seemed the proper place for him to seek answers to his Sasquatch problems. He once mentioned to Marsha that he and his deceased wife Julie had an encounter with one of the Relics years ago when their son Sam was young. He mentioned that Julie had told him the creatures were Nephilim, products of fallen angels breeding with human women. The offspring were of great stature; in fact, they were giants and fierce warriors. He simply could not connect them to the creatures he had battled two years ago. Surprisingly, Marsha reacted positively to his questions and encouraged him to seek their pastor's knowledge and input on the subject. Addison wasn't fond of the idea.

His biggest concern was reaching his son. The incidents of 2014 still haunted Sam. Addison knew that on the surface, it looked as if Sam had a wonderful life. He had time, money, and the love of a good woman. Still, Sam was dark and brooding, lacking his old zest for life. Looking at the clock, Addison sighed; it was getting late, and Marsha worried about him if he stayed at the ranch past sundown. He quickly shut everything down and made his way to the front door; just before reaching the door, he saw a bright flash of light through the house's windows, which illuminated the outside for a moment as if it was broad daylight. Addison stepped onto the porch and noticed a clear starlit night with no clouds or storms in sight. Hmm, that was strange, he thought as he walked to his truck. Just as he opened the door, he heard a thundering "WHOOP" and was hit with an overwhelming stench. His blood ran cold; it was as if he were back in 2014. The two years of peace were suddenly shattered.

Grabbing the spotlight he kept in the front seat of his truck, he shone it east toward the direction from which the sound had come; a pair of eyes shone in the beam. The eyes looked right into Addison, never wavering, never blinking; they reflected a gold-orange color in the light. There was no mistaking it; he'd seen these eyes before. Then the head turned away, and Addison could see the dark bulk of the creature disappearing into the darkness. Addison was shocked; even more than that, he was infuriated. "You should not have come back!" Addison yelled grimly into the night. He reached for his Marlin 45-70 caliber rifle, which was lying in the backseat of his truck. The weapon was the same heavy-caliber rifle with which he had killed one of these creatures back in 2014, or thought he had. *If I shoot it, how long will it be down? Will it just pop up and kill me? Or worse, rise and run amok in town killing others?* Addison let the rifle lay where it was but kept his hand on it. "Leave, or I will find a way to kill you," he yelled loudly.

Finally, his promise to Marsha not to get himself killed got the better of him. Making a mental note of exactly where the eyes had appeared, Addison climbed into his truck. As he began driving toward town, a thought entered his mind. *The smell*: Two years ago, he rarely encountered the oft-reported, overpowering stench which many people associated with a Sasquatch encounter. However, this time it was almost debilitating. *"Why am I now getting the stench so strong? What has changed?"* he asked himself.

## Sunday, 20 November 2016, 9:00 AM CST, Redstone Ranch, two miles North of Talihina, OK

Addison returned as early as he possibly could to the woods outside his house, searching the area where he had seen the eyes the previous evening. He went armed this morning, once again carrying the Marlin 45-70 carbine. Because of the size and power of the Relics, he trusted this weapon more than any other due to its "knock down" power. The rifle was scarred and scratched

18

from his last battle with them on that cold night at Crusher Hollow two years earlier. He also carried a Smith and Wesson Model 629 .44 Magnum pistol on his hip as a backup. Although he had always been a fan of the Colt Model 1911 .45 caliber automatic as a sidearm, there was always the chance of it jamming. With the .44 caliber magnum revolver, there were no such worries.

The stench from the night before still hung in the air, Addison was aware that the sulfur-like smell was a common occurrence in many Sasquatch sightings, but this was his first encounter with the stench of this magnitude with these creatures. It took only a minute to find the first track. It was huge, measuring twenty-four inches in length and nine inches across at the widest point. There was still a trace of the odor he had encountered the night before when he had seen the eye shine from the creature. It was limited to the immediate area around the creek bed. There was the second track, and there the third. Then, nothing. There was an odd difference to these tracks; they had six toes each. Thinking maybe it was a birth defect at first, he kept moving.

In the morning sun, Addison should have felt perfectly safe in this familiar creek bed, as safe as he would have felt sitting in his lounge chair at home. He wasn't though; something wasn't right. Addison could feel the hair on the back of his neck rising. He controlled his breathing and then steadied his nerves by trying to logically address the mystery. *Okay, so now we have disappearing prints. You guys are more resourceful than I gave you credit for. Just how did you pull this off, and what's up with the odor out here?*

Addison stood in the creek bed for some time, pondering the lack of prints leading out of the area. He looked all around the creek bed but could find no more evidence of prints. He looked high in the trees to see if maybe the creature had left the area by swinging or jumping from tree to tree. The trees showed no signs of damage or strain. Suddenly, Addison had the overpowering feeling he was being watched. He chambered a round into the Marlin and scanned the area, expecting to see one of the creatures silently watching him. He was shocked when his eyes rested upon a man standing on the slope of a small hill on the other side of the creek. The man stood motionless, staring in Addison's direction. At first, Addison had to stifle a laugh because the man appeared so out-of-place in the rocky, wooded hills of Addison's property. He was dressed in a black suit and tie and wore a white shirt. A black fedora and sunglasses added to his strange appearance. *This guy looks like one of the Blues Brothers.*

"Are you lost?" Addison yelled in the man's direction. The figure didn't respond, so he tried again to communicate with the man. "Do you need help?"

Again, the figure stood as still as a statue, looking in Addison's direction. The man removed his hat for a moment, revealing an oddly cone-shaped head, and then, just as quickly, returned his hat to his head. Addison also noticed the man's complexion was pale, almost blue like a drowning victim. His facial features were strange, almost alien. Addison lowered his rifle, thinking the man might be too frightened to answer. He also lowered the hammer on the rifle, making it safe.

When he looked up, the man had vanished. *Fella, you're not making this any easier on either of us*, he thought to himself as he walked to the area where he had last seen the strange-looking man. Addison reached the top of the slope where the peculiar man had been standing. There was no sign of him. He scanned the familiar terrain, dumbfounded. *No way you could have gotten out of sight so quickly.* Looking down at the ground, he saw fifteen rocks the size of his fist arranged in the shape of an arrow. The shaft of the arrow consisted of five rocks in a line, the tip of the arrow consisted of four rocks, two on either side of the tip of the arrow coming backward at 45 degrees, the remaining six arrows made up the feathers at the back of the shaft three on either side. Addison had seen this type of arrow symbology before; it was commonly used Choctaw symbol. The arrow pointed to the southeast; Addison gazed in the direction of the arrow, confused by its meaning. Nothing of interest caught his eye; it was just a ten-mile stretch of flat land, mainly grass with the occasional group of trees surrounding a pond or creek bed. Perfect for raising cattle until you got to the base of the Kiamichi Mountains. Where you could take a faster route to Hochatown and Broken Bow by traveling through the winding mountain road known as Indian Trail Highway as it curved its way through the small communities of Honobia and Bethel.

*I wonder what this is all about? he thought to himself. Addison started to walk in the direction of the arrow then something caught his eye. Ten feet beyond the top of this arrow was an identical one facing the northeast, the opposite direction. Addison realized what he was looking at, and his blood began to run cold. Two opposing arrows were the Choctaw symbol of war. Not to mention this second arrow pointed directly in line with his house. So this weird little man has declared war on me? Who is this guy, and where does he come from? This is starting to sound like some of the stuff General Henderson has been having me read, he thought to himself. If this stuff is what I'm beginning to think it is, I'm going to have to warn Sam. It's his problem as much as mine. Besides, I'm getting too old to fight this alone; my time is waning. Something needs to be done now, or Sam could be dealing with this for decades.* Uppermost in Addison's mind was how vital it was that Sam accept his father's theory of what these things really were, both for the sake of his own soul and the souls of his budding family.

Addison sighed deeply, trying to reason through his inner turmoil. He wondered how he should approach his son over his latest discovery. As he looked down at his phone, he saw it was nearly 9:45. He and Marsha were due at church at 11:00. During the walk to his truck, Addison conducted an internal debate on whether he should tell Sam of the events which had occurred since the previous night. Once he reached the vehicle, his decision was made. He climbed into his truck and, as he headed toward town, he phoned his son.

## Sunday, 20 November 2016, 10:15 AM CST, Pam's Hateful Hussy Diner, Talihina, OK

Sam and Christa had finished their breakfast; they sat patiently as six-year-old Erin played with and ate her breakfast. In her eighth month of pregnancy, Christa was getting uncomfortable and urged her child to finish her French toast and berries. "Mom if I eat too fast, I'll get fat!" the small girl said, looking to Sam for support.

Sam smiled at Erin and patted her hand, "That rule only applies when you eat too much, baby. The small amount of food you have is not going to make you fat. Plus, Mommy is uncomfortable sitting in this booth with your little brother kicking inside her. So, do Mommy a favor and eat a little bit faster, okay, sweetheart?"

"Okay," Erin said sweetly to her stepfather. Sam and Erin had bonded as close as any father/daughter combination could since he and Christa had married. Although thankful for their relationship, Christa sometimes felt outnumbered and outflanked by the close bond between her husband and daughter. Yet, she was thankful for the blending of her small family, and she knew the new addition would supply the much-needed link to complete the family circle. She worried about Sam this morning, as he seemed lost in thought. She had noticed him staring at the newspaper article, which hung on the diner wall, between two plaster casts of alleged Sasquatch footprints. They were constant reminders of a bad time in all their lives two years ago. She had lost her father and her husband in those long, frightful days and nights during the strange and unnatural war which was fought in and around Talihina. She had little sympathy for her late husband, Howard Fletcher. He was the reason her beloved father was dead, and her whole family still felt the sting of his loss.

21

Sam had suffered losses too. Christa was also aware that the losses they both suffered had helped bring them to the life they now enjoyed. She didn't understand how or why things happened the way they did. She only knew, for once, she was happy and secure. She also knew Sam was troubled, and she had no idea how to help him. She noticed Sam was watching a young boy who was looking at the plaster, footprint casts from the table where he sat with his father. They were in deep conversation, and then the father looked in Sam's direction and nodded to his son. They both looked nervously down at their plates when they noticed Sam was also watching them. Look, Son, there's the gun-slinging jerk who is responsible for the deaths of over a dozen people, Sam imagined the father saying to his son when they looked in his direction. Sam was still guilt-ridden over the events of 2014. He had yet to develop a way of coping with what had happened and was still second-guessing his actions.

As much as he loved Christa and Erin, he felt he didn't deserve the happiness he experienced with them. Sam turned his gaze from the man and his son toward the restaurant window. He was happy to see a familiar couple walking through the door; Jimmy and Jeri Chula entered the diner. Jimmy's Talihina police uniform now sported Sergeant stripes as he had taken over Dale Thompkins' position since Dale had replaced Sam as Chief of Police. Jeri no longer wore the Talihina police uniform; instead, she wore the brown and tan Oklahoma Highway Patrol uniform with its campaign-style hat, which made her look like a miniature Drill Sergeant. Both Jimmy Chula and his wife, the former Jeri Cruz, were held in high esteem by Sam.

"You guys still getting away with dating on duty?" Sam asked with a grin as they entered the diner. Jimmy and Jeri laughed and made their way to the Redstone's table. Sam stood shaking hands with Jimmy and hugging Jeri. "You look great in that uniform Jeri. I'm so proud of you for making the grade with OHP."

"Well, I couldn't very well stay on with Talihina since Jimmy made Sergeant. He might get confused about who is actually in charge when we get home."

"How could I ever forget that?" said Jimmy, acting like a henpecked husband. His response earned him an elbow in the ribs from his petite wife. After a few moments of chit-chat, Jimmy and Jeri moved away to find their own table. Sam noticed Erin was almost done with her breakfast when Christa said, "Your happiness returns when you see your police friends."

"What?" Sam asked, not knowing where this was going.

"Your happiness returns when you're with your police friends. Maybe you should return to law enforcement. You need a mission; you're the kind of man who needs to serve."

Laughing under his breath, Sam said, "A mission is the last thing I need, baby. What I really need is a way to clear my conscious. In case you've forgotten … I'm the guy who tortured a federal agent with a defibrillator and ran up a huge body count to boot! Nobody's going to touch me with a ten-foot pole."

"They would if they knew the agent and the truth," Christa said.

"Yeah, well the truth about what happened will never surface, and for all I know that agent is a poster boy for how to conduct federal operations. I dug myself a very deep hole, my dear." Sam's phone vibrated, indicating he had an incoming call. Seeing it was his father, he sighed. "It's Dad. He probably wants me to get baptized or run off chasing Bigfoot with him." Christa watched Sam's expression as he listened to his father on the phone. Sam never said a word during the call. Hanging up, he said, "I need to go to his house later. He's on to something."

"Well, Erin and I will be joining them for church this morning, you should go with us?" Christa asked hopefully.

"No thanks, I'm sure I'll get a sermon when I see him later," Sam replied.

"You know better than that, Samuel Redstone. Besides, I want both of our children to have a good foundation. As their father, you should want the same," Christa said with rising frustration.

Knowing he had hit a nerve, Sam tried to ease the stress. "I know baby, I'm just not ready to take the plunge yet."

"It's not a plunge Sam; it's being a good father and a good leader. These children will always look to you to set the course for our family, and so will I. Quit making this all about you and start making it about all of us. It's not like we don't know what you've been through. Erin and I were both there the day Jeri was taken. I know what you've been going through emotionally, and to be honest, you're ignoring what you're going through spiritually. I'm with your father, they're more than cavemen or overgrown monkeys. There's something else to this Sam, and if they're not going to go away, you're going to have to make a stand. You'd better make that stand in God's corner, not the corner of his enemies."

"Christa, you're starting to sound like my father. Did he indoctrinate you too?"

"There's your problem Sam. I sound like your father. You should be the one who sounds like your father. I'll see you at home later." Christa took Erin and headed toward her car. Sam sat alone at the table, watching her leave. After a moment, he picked up the check and rose from the table, watching Christa's white Escalade pull onto the road and head to the church to meet up with Addison and Marsha. Great! We're becoming Branch Davidians, Sam thought to himself as he headed for the cashier.

## Sunday, 20 November 2016 1:30 PM CST, Redstone Ranch, two miles North of Talihina, OK

When Sam arrived at his father's house, it was a warm, bright afternoon. Seeing Addison was waiting for him on the porch, a knot in his stomach started to develop. *Why can't he just leave this crap alone? Okay, ole man, let's get this over with*, he thought to himself as he exited the truck. "Missed you at church," Addison said, cheerfully.

"You should be used to it by now," Sam said with sarcasm before wishing he'd kept his mouth shut.

Addison didn't take the bait. Still smiling, he said, "Well, we sure enjoyed having Christa and Erin with us. When we received communion, Erin was so excited because she was getting juice and crackers too," Addison said with a laugh. "It was a beautiful moment, Sam. I hate you decided to miss it."

"Yeah, okay Dad, just remember, you missed a few communions yourself when I was Erin's age," Sam said, frustrated at the thought of another church recruiting drive by his father. Addison looked at his son for a moment before speaking.

"Yes, you're right, Sam, I made a lot of mistakes when I was younger. I'm just trying to keep you from making the same ones. You need to love, lead and protect your family, Son. If you're not going to see to their spiritual growth, then I will." Sam was surprised by his father's response and stood silently pondering his words.

"So, if I make a mistake with my family, you think it's your place to step in and interfere?" Son, we all make mistakes, I do, and so do you. Mistakes and failing your family are two different things. I understand where you are with a lack of faith. I've been there myself, and I wasn't the best role model for you in that regard. So, with that in mind, I can deal with your skepticism patiently. Your sarcasm and disrespect, however, I cannot. Sam, we don't have the luxury of time for you to cope with your faith issues. The fight is coming, and it's time to choose a side, and I'm not allowing you to choose the wrong side.

So, if you insist on disrespecting me and making light of all this, then I'm going to knock you on your butt, and you're going to stay there for however long it takes you to get educated!"

Sam felt anger rising in his stomach. He looked at his father for a moment, pondering his next move. His father held his gaze, not blinking. Then, as if out of the blue, a thought entered Sam's mind. He loved this man, and he knew his father loved him back and would give up his life to keep him safe. If he were dying of thirst, he would still give Sam his last ounce of water. He also knew if he were disrespecting this man, his father would still show him love and dedication by literally knocking him on his butt. It occurred to Sam that his own son was growing in Christa's womb, and he would soon be trying to teach him to be a man. A smile came across Sam's face as if a cloud was lifted.

"Fair enough, Pop. Show me what you have going on here." Addison headed east from the house and motioned for his son to follow him. Sam followed. They stopped where Addison had first spotted the creature in the beam of his flashlight the evening before. "You sure of what you saw, Dad?" Sam asked, hoping to debunk his father's sighting as some form of normal wildlife.

"I'm sure, Sam," Addison replied as he turned, walking further toward the creek bed. In a few moments until they came upon the first footprint. The sight made Sam's blood ran cold. As they moved further along, Sam saw how the prints mysteriously disappeared. The soft ground around the creek bed was the perfect medium for footprints, yet they just stopped, as if the creature that made them simply disappeared. Sam was confused by this. At the same time, he was also angry and fearful. A strong unpleasant smell also added to his discomfort.

"I'm not sure I'm ready for this again, Pop." Sam said, looking grimly at the spot where the prints stopped. Shaking his head, he said, "The last time we went through this, I lost so much. I'm not sure I want to chance what I have left in another fight with these things."

Addison could see Sam's complexion turn pale. Concerned by his son's reaction, he said, "Sam, I know you've seen prints while out with the researchers from Texas. Why do these shake you up so badly?"

"This is different, Pop! When I'm out with the guys, the prints don't seem as menacing as these do, and they damn sure don't just disappear into thin air as these do. There's something unearthly, or sinister about these. Plus, what's up with the six toes? Are we dealing with a retard one now? It isn't fair that we're dealing with this again. Let's leave it alone; just leave it alone. Maybe they'll go away." Addison didn't only see fear in his son, he also saw anger. It was the kind of anger that could ruin a man if not controlled. He also knew that if his son was experiencing fear, it wasn't for his own safety. He knew Sam was worried about the safety of his budding family, and he also knew the deaths from two years ago weighed heavily on Sam's heart. "We can't ignore this, Son. This isn't going to go away, and deep down inside you know it."

"How do you know that? Maybe we just happen to live next to a migration path for these things, and this one will move on if we ignore it."

"Sam, the one I saw last night was the same one we fought two years ago."

"You don't know that, Dad, besides this one has six toes on each foot."

"I do know it Sam, regardless of the extra toes and I think you know, it too. That's why you're having this reaction. This thing and its brothers killed your friends. This one also had you in its grasp. You not only shot it and peppered it with shrapnel, but you also stabbed it with a knife. That's personal. Its beef with us is personal. It's back, Son, and that means only one thing. It intends to kill us; both of us. So, you'd better get your mind wrapped around the idea that we may be in for the fight of our lives."

"I thought the fight of my life was two years ago, Dad. I expended so much love, fear, hate and remorse on that night. I'm just not sure I have what it takes for a rematch," Sam said, looking East toward Crusher Hollow, the site of what he thought was the most epic battle of his life. He felt his father's hand on his shoulder.

"There's more, Sam, I had a strange visitor this morning."

"What do you mean by a strange visitor? One of the Relics?"

"No, it may have been worse."

"Worse? What could be worse?" Sam asked, confused.

"Sam, what I saw was something I've read about, but never encountered."

"So, tell me!" Sam demanded.

"I can't tell you now, Son. It's not time. I will take you to the place where I saw it." Sam followed Addison to the spot where he had his mysterious sighting, then to the two arrows made with rocks on the ground. "You see, Sam, the lower one points off to the Southeast, the upper one right at my house. I have no idea who would be declaring war on me, Son." Addison's voice trailed off as something caught his eye. "What in the world?" he said, as much to himself as to Sam as he took off in a jog toward some high grass. Sam followed, not yet sure of what his father had seen. Addison stopped short and knelt. As Sam caught up to his father, he saw two bodies lying in the high grass. Both appeared to be teenage boys, wearing jeans and black and gold letter jackets. They weren't from Talihina High School. They were from another school, unfamiliar to the men. Sam's heart sank at the sight of the young boys. Then Addison turned to his son and said, "Call for help! They're alive, but they're comatose."

## Sunday, 20 November 2016, 4:30 PM CST, Redstone Ranch, two miles North of Talihina, OK

Sam stood at the spot where the arrows had been placed on the ground by his father's strange visitor earlier that morning. Both he and his father were in a state of shock over the events of the afternoon. An investigation revealed the two teenage boys were from De Queen, Arkansas, and had been reported missing from the site of a one-vehicle accident the previous Thursday evening. The boys were flown by helicopter to a hospital in Fort Smith, Arkansas. There was no explanation for their appearance on the Redstone property. Addison approached his son, and together they looked at the gathering of law enforcement officers from two states, which either busily talked amongst themselves or searched every inch of the property, including Addison's house. "Have you noticed, we've got an army of law enforcement out here, and nobody has come across one of the Relic prints, yet?" Sam asked his father.

"If they've seen any of them, they're playing dumb, or maybe they've quietly contacted somebody further up the food chain," Addison replied. As if on cue, a helicopter buzzed low over the two men before whipping around in a dramatic landing a hundred yards away. Two men wearing suits climbed out and began marching toward the scene, flashing identification and displaying poses of authority. "Well, looks like the FBI has finally arrived," Addison said with no surprise.

"Wonder what took them so long? With our history, I figured they'd have their X-File team giving us rectal exams by now," Sam said, sarcastically.

"That's right, Son, always look for that ray of sunshine," Addison said as both men snickered under their breath. "I have a feeling this is going to be a long night," Addison said when he saw the men in suits turn their attention to them after a Le Flore County Deputy pointed to the Redstone's.

"Do you think they know what happened here two years ago?" Sam asked his father.

"I'm thinking they got a full report once the name Redstone and Talihina came up. I'm going to play dumb. I'm not letting the government screw this up from the word 'go' this time."

"Sure, Pop. I got nothing better to do than fight paranormal events on my own time."

"Sam, if you recall, that was the only way we were able to win last time."

"Win? Excuse me, Pop, but we had two teens, who vanished into thin air three nights ago in another state, suddenly appear on your property. I might also add, this is the day after you said you had another encounter with a Relic. Plus, let's not forget the mysterious visitor you had this morning, whom you're not yet willing to share information about with me. Does that sound like we won?"

"Yes, it does, Sam. Had we lost, we wouldn't be standing here right now."

He's got a point, Sam reluctantly thought as the two agents walked up.

"Mister Redstone, I'm Special Agent Self with the FBI, this is my partner Special Agent Hayes. May we ask you a few questions?"

"Absolutely, Agent Self," Addison replied.

Looking at Sam, the agent asked, "And you are Samuel Redstone?"

Sam nodded, "That's correct."

"I have a few questions for you as well, Sir." The agent said. The four men walked to the helicopter, where the pilot seemed to be taking a nap in the cockpit. To both Addison's and Sam's surprise, the questioning took a little less than twenty minutes, and there were no questions or remarks about the events of two years earlier on their property and the surrounding community. Both men were very polite and professional. The questions centered mainly on whether either Redstone had seen any strange cars or trucks on or near their property in the past few days. After they finished, Addison decided to test them a little bit with a couple of questions of his own.

"Agent Self, how do you explain these kids appearing on my property out of nowhere?"

"We think somebody dumped them here."

"Dumped them here? Why?"

"We're thinking they may have overdosed on some kind of drug with other friends, and their friends dumped them here instead of facing the music."

"Doesn't sound like something a friend would do," Sam replied.

"They were probably scared and high, probably not thinking straight."

"How are the boys?" Addison asked.

"We received the last report as we were landing. They're both in stable condition and healthy, but neither has regained consciousness. Thank you for your time gentlemen. We'll have somebody notify you when there's a change in their condition." The two men climbed back into the helicopter. Sam and Addison moved to a safe distance as the engine started, watching the machine warm-up and lift away.

"Maybe all that happened here is forgotten about, Pop," Sam said, hopefully. Just then, a man walked up wearing an Arkansas State Trooper uniform and said, "Excuse me, gentlemen. I'm Brad Jennings with the Arkansas State Police; would you two be Sam and Addison Redstone?"

Addison looked at Sam and said, "You were saying?" "Yes, Trooper. I'm Addison and this is my son, Sam," Addison said, offering his hand.

The Trooper shook hands with both men and then said, "I was at the accident scene last Thursday evening. I have a couple of questions, and something I'd like to show you, if that's okay?"

"Go ahead," Sam responded.

"You know, I followed what happened here two years ago fairly closely. I read as many newspaper accounts and internet articles as I could find. You were the Chief of Police here in those days, weren't you Sam?"

"That's right," Sam replied.

"As far as the press was concerned, the problems you guys had here was from a Grizzly Bear which somehow escaped from a truck accident?" the Trooper asked, with some skepticism.

"That was all the news they saw fit to print. Not to mention we had a little dustup with some biker gang members, as well as a local man who went bad," Sam replied quickly.

"Yes, Sir, I remember reading about that, too. You were involved in a shootout with three of those men. Is that correct, Sir?"

"Two of them, Trooper Jennings, the third was a local man." Sam said, starting to get annoyed.

"Sir, didn't you marry the widow of the man in question?"

"Yes, I did indeed Trooper, and since you're from Arkansas, I assume you're married to your sister, or at least your cousin," Sam said, moving ominously closer to the Trooper. Addison quickly stepped between the two men.

"Trooper Jennings, if you have something to say, spit it out. If you just want to make accusations, I'm going to step away and let nature take its course with you two."

Jennings face blushed, "My apologies, Sir. I didn't mean to offend you. I went the wrong direction in my questioning. Please forgive me. I haven't had much sleep since Thursday."

Sam relaxed a bit and took a step back. Looking at Addison, he asked, "Sir, it was you the press said shot the bear? Is that correct?"

"Yes, it is."

"Is it safe to assume that what happened with the animal you shot, and what happened with the bikers was somehow connected?"

"Safer than your last line of questioning," Sam interrupted, not hiding the venom.

"Fair enough," Jennings said as his face reddened. Producing his cell phone, he said, "I want to show you a picture I took at the scene of the accident last Thursday night." Handing the phone to Sam, he let both men take a good, long look. Then he swiped the phone to another photo of an identical footprint. "This photo I took an hour ago down there at the creek bed." He motioned to the area where Addison had shown the print to Sam earlier. Looking at Addison, he said, "Does that look like a bear print to you?"

Addison said, "Trooper, what if I told you, I shot a bear that made a print exactly like that?"

"I'd say you have some mighty strange bears here, Sir. I'd also tell you, I'm no stranger to the problems this certain type of bear can cause."

Addison's expression softened. "I kind of had that feeling, Trooper Jennings. Tell you what; I'll keep you in the loop on what happens down here, if you'll do the same with us, if anything else happens in your neck of the woods. Something tells me, we're dealing with the same bears, and we may need to work together at some point. I happen to know from experience that some of the Federal boys are operating with a completely different objective than those of us who live amongst these things."

"I couldn't agree more," Brad Jennings said, handing Addison his card. "Call me if you have any more problems, and I'll be glad to help you in any way possible. Also, if I start having problems in my area, I would appreciate getting your input on the situation. Deal?"

"Deal!" Addison replied as he took the card.

# CHAPTER TWO

# Team Titan

*"Show me a hero, and I'll write you a tragedy."*
*~F. Scott Fitzgerald*

## Monday, 21 November 2016, 08:10 AM AFT, Kandahar Province, Afghanistan

Lieutenant Mitchell Walker leaned against a large boulder, allowing its sun-warmed mass to heat his left shoulder and arm. The night had been cold as he led his twenty-man patrol through the mountainous terrain. The patrol took a few moments for a quick break and some much-needed food and water. The term 'food' was probably a bit of a stretch, as most of the men were quickly downing energy bars; there was no time to consume an MRE. They had been inserted immediately after dark the previous night by Blackhawk helicopters and had slowly and quietly worked their way through the mountains. They were now some forty miles east of the airbase at Kandahar and roughly eighteen miles from the Afghan village of Mulla Wali Waleh on the Afghan-Pakistan border. They were not a lone patrol; other patrols from their unit, the 10th Mountain Division, were also busy patrolling these same mountains on this cold morning.

Presently, it was considered a search and rescue mission. A Royal Netherlands Army Special Forces unit had been missing for three days. The six-man Korps Commandotroepen were operating in the black. What they were searching for was a mystery to everyone but the highest-ranking General Officers in the theater. The fact that the Netherlands was no longer officially sending troops to the war in Afghanistan added to the mystery of the unit's mission. Radio contact with the Dutch Soldiers had been lost in the early morning hours of Saturday.

At first, there wasn't much concern. Special Forces units have a history of going quiet during their missions. Sometimes all you can do is duck, hide, and go quiet when you're in the bad guys' backyard. By Saturday afternoon, air searches were conducted over the area with no results. By late Sunday night, patrols from the 10th Mountain Division were dropped into the area to conduct ground searches. The Lieutenant's thoughts were interrupted by the familiar turbo fan screaming of two Air Force A-10 Warthogs which passed overhead. *Good to know the Zoomies have our back today*, he thought. Standing erect and stretching, Lieutenant Walker looked over his patrol Task Force. His gaze halted on one soldier. *Ah, our mystery guest*, he thought, with guarded humor. The black soldier, a Master Sergeant, had been assigned to his patrol at the last minute. The guy wasn't even 10th Mountain Division. He was part of some dark operations unit operating from the airbase at Kandahar. Much like the Dutch Korps Command, the Special Forces operators in Task Force Titan were running their own private patrols while saying very little to any of the other soldiers in the area. When it became apparent that patrols would need to be sent to look for the missing Dutchmen, each search patrol had a soldier from Task Force Titan assigned to them. It didn't sit well with some soldiers, while others simply shrugged off their mysterious guests as some kind of political move by higher headquarters.

In his mid to late thirties, the man was as fit as any special operator the Lieutenant had ever seen. The man looked much older from a distance because his hair was pure white. In fact, his troops had been referring to the man as "Q-Tip" during the patrol, but never to his face. The man reeked of violence, even though he kept quiet and to himself most of the time. If he did speak, it was quietly, politely, and always to the point. The man was always on guard as if watching for something. A something' that he was going to keep completely to himself.

*What's your story, Sergeant?* Lieutenant Walker thought to himself as he studied the soldier. Most of his gear was the same as the troops he accompanied on this patrol. One difference was he carried a Remington Model 870 Modular Combat Shotgun. *Probably not going to get too many shots off with that thing*, Sarge, he thought, with some humor, knowing most of the firefights here took place well out of shotgun range. *And what's with the damn broadsword?* The Lieutenant was referring to what appeared to be an oversized machete which the Sergeant carried on his backpack. One of the Lieutenant's own sergeants said he'd seen the guy loading the shotgun with slugs and TAC8 buckshot. The Sergeant also mentioned the slugs seemed to be made of copper or have a copper jacket at the very least. Last but not least, the Sergeant's units' patch on his left shoulder was the biggest mystery of all. Even the "Old Timers" in the 10th Mountain Division had never seen or heard of these guys.

The unit patch contained the image of an old Crusader Shield with a Winged Sword in the middle. The words TASK FORCE TITAN was arched

over the top of the shield, and a motto was arched under the bottom reading…
"WE THUMP THE BUMP IN THE NIGHT." Walker thought, *I wonder what that means? They must have been desperate for a motto.* "Okay, time to get the men back on the clock," Lieutenant Walker softly told Staff Sergeant Tollis, his second-in-command for the patrol. The Sergeant had the word passed silently through the patrol before making his way to position himself, where he could support the point man, as the patrol began working its way deeper into the mountain range. As he watched his men moving stealthily forward, doing what they do best, Walker prayed they would find the missing Dutchmen soon. *This damn place gives me the creeps; it just doesn't feel right.* He shuddered internally, not allowing his feelings to betray him physically.

The patrol had been moving steadily up a slope and deeper into the range of mountains for 40 minutes when the point man knelt to one knee, motioning for the patrol to freeze. Lieutenant Walker crawled his way to where the point man and Sergeant Tollis were waiting. "What have we got?" he whispered.

The point man whispered back, "It looks like bodies, or parts of bodies, Sir." The Lieutenant sighed deeply as he gazed ahead at what appeared to be a pile of broken and twisted bodies, thirty to forty meters ahead of them. The area was in the crevasse of a large canyon, the roof of which was some eighty to a hundred feet over their heads.

"That explains why the air units never spotted them," he told the point man and Staff Sergeant Tollis. "Okay, let's move up quietly. Everyone be on your toes." As the patrol moved into the area, they witnessed a scene of unbelievable carnage. Bodies and parts of bodies were strewn all over the ground.

"I guess we found our missing Dutchmen," Staff Sergeant Tollis replied between gasps for air. "Who are these other guys…Taliban?" one of the Privates asked.

"It looks as if the Dutchmen found who they were looking for, and they cancelled each other out," Lieutenant Walker replied.

"They've all been ripped apart, Sir," Sergeant Tollis told the Lieutenant.

"For crying out loud, something has been eating them. Look!" a Private said, pointing down at remains which were nothing more than bone with large, flat, tooth mark-like scratches in the bone.

Quickly, the Special Forces Sergeant was at Walker's side. "Lieutenant, we've got to get your people out of here now, and whatever you do, don't let anyone go near that cave!" He nodded to a large hole in the rock face which went upward at least twenty feet.

33

"Nonsense, Sergeant, we've found what we're looking for. We need to get an extraction team flown in here and remove their remains. Sergeant Tollis, get the men to set a security perimeter, and everyone, keep your guard up. Sergeant, I want grenades lobbed into that cave in case there are any more Taliban hiding in there." Turning to his communications troop, he ordered, "Specialist Warner, get me a line to the Colonel. Let him know we found our missing friends and the guys they came looking for."

"Lieutenant, I'm telling you we need to leave and leave now, or the extraction Task Force will be picking your troops up in the same condition," the Special Forces Sergeant said as two muffled explosions erupted from grenades lobbed into the cave.

"Your fears are duly noted, Sergeant. Now get the hell out of my face. I've got work to do and..." The Lieutenant's sentence was cut short as a loud booming scream came from the mouth of the cave. The dumbfounded men all froze, as a being, which appeared as if it belonged in an old Hercules movie, stepped from the cave. It was a giant, man-like creature which stood at least fifteen feet tall. The thing appeared human, but its size was immense. It wore a simple loincloth and had fiery red, long hair and beard and ice-blue eyes which seemed to glow with a horrific fury. It carried a huge club the size of a small tree in its left hand.

Everyone was frozen in place as the fantastic being screamed at the top of its lungs. The scream alone caused a couple of the soldiers to lose control of their bowels. In a flash, it attacked. The giant moved with supernatural speed and agility, despite its size. In the blink of an eye, the two soldiers who had lobbed grenades into the cave were struck with the club. Both soldiers flew twenty to thirty feet through the air, impacting the hard, rocky ground with sickening thuds. It then kicked a third soldier across the canyon as if he were a soccer ball. This finally snapped the soldiers from their stupor. They all began firing and retreating, searching for any rock which they could hide behind. The Special Forces Sergeant was the exception. He threw a grenade under the Beast, and as soon as it exploded, he had his weapon up and walked calmly toward the giant. "Aim for the head!" he yelled back at the other soldiers.

Yet, he did not aim for the head. As he closed on the giant, who was dazed by the grenade blast, he fired two quick blasts from his shotgun into its genital area. This caused the giant to have the universal male response to such an assault. It dropped its club and doubled over, attempting to protect its crotch from further damage. The Special Forces Sergeant started firing 12-gauge slugs into its head when this happened. The copper slugs knocked huge pieces of flesh and bone from the head of the giant, which was now on its knees. The giant bellowed in pain and fury. Even on its knees, it towered over the soldiers.

The Special Forces Sergeant calmly walked behind the giant and put two more slugs into the back of its head, destroying most of the top of its head, with one of the slugs exiting through its face. The giant pitched forward onto the ground. What happened next took all the 10th Mountain Division soldiers by surprise. The Special Forces Sergeant slung his 12 gauge over his shoulder and removed the large machete from his backpack. The blade gleamed reddish gold in the light as he began hacking at the back of the giant's neck. Looking up from his gruesome labor, he screamed, "Sergeant Tollis! Get your ass over here and help me!"

Tollis ran up to the grim, bloody scene. The Special Forces Sergeant stopped his hacking for a moment and unslung his 12 gauge, handing it to Tollis. "We've got to remove the head, shoot into its neck bone. Hurry! We don't have much time!" The other soldiers watched in disbelief as Sergeant Tollis and the Special Forces Sergeant beheaded the giant using the 12 gauge and the machete. Once the head was completely severed, the Special Forces Sergeant, with the help of Tollis, drug it a hundred feet away from the corpse of the giant. After moving the head away from the rest of the body, the Special Ops Sergeant did a peculiar thing. He pried the mouth of the Beast open with a knife, then inserted a large round copper slug the size of a coffee can lid inside it and forced the jaws closed. Walking over to the giant's corpse, he produced a telescoping pole with an M-49 flare at the end of it. Extending the pole its full six-foot length, he ignited the flare and began burning the neck wound of the headless giant. He repeated this process two more times until he was satisfied the wound was completely cauterized.

Task completed, the Special Forces Sergeant inspected the giant's corpse, noting wounds that appeared to be a couple of days old. Thank God those Dutchmen got some licks in and weakened this bruiser before he killed them. Lighting a cigarette, he took a long drag before looking toward Lieutenant Walker, who was standing near him, mouth agape, staring in confusion. "You'd better check on your downed soldiers, Sir. I'll call for that extraction force," he calmly said. Sergeant Tollis couldn't believe what had just transpired.

Offering his hand to the Special Forces Sergeant, he said, "That's the craziest thing I've ever seen Sarge! Mike Tollis is my name."

Still breathing heavily, the Special Operator grasped his hand, shaking it, and replied, "Nice to meet you, Mike. I'm Nathan Parks."

"What was the deal with cutting off the head? Is that thing a vampire or something?" Tollis asked.

"Worse. I think I'd rather take my chances with a vampire," Nathan answered, still gasping for breath.

Lieutenant Walker was still at Nathan's side. It was obvious the young officer was shaken and unsure of what to do next. "I've got three dead soldiers, Sergeant. I'm calling for the extraction," he said in a quivering voice.

"No, Lieutenant; I'll call for the extraction, Sir."

"You're not calling in anything, Sergeant. I need to talk to my boss. I'm going to have a hard time explaining these casualties."

"You won't be explaining anything, Sir. In fact, it's best that you stay off the air and let me handle this."

"Bullshit, Sergeant! I'm in command here and I'll be making the calls."

"Lieutenant, as soon as that redheaded bastard stepped out of the cave, I've been in charge and will remain in charge until we get your men out of here."

Another one of Lieutenant Walker's Sergeants yelled to him, "Lieutenant, all three are still alive! Beat to hell, but still alive, Sir!"

"Do us all a favor Sir and see to your men," Nathan Parks said, nodding toward some of the other soldiers, who were suffering from mild shock due to what they had just witnessed. Walker tried to regain control.

"Sergeant, I want to know what the hell that thing is and where it came from." "Sir, it's really too much for me to try and explain right now." Parks turned away and began talking into an AN/PRC-148 MBITR handheld radio favored by Special Operations units.

## Monday, 21 November 2016, 11:40 AM AFT, Kandahar Air Base, Kandahar Province, Afghanistan

Lieutenant Walker and the remainder of his men were sitting alone in a hot hanger. All were trying to come to grips with what had transpired during the operation. Many had heard rumors about past encounters between soldiers and giants in the surrounding area. It was always brushed off as myths or base legends told to make their tour in Afghanistan more terrifying as if it needed to be more terrifying. If the encounter with the giant wasn't enough to ponder, the wide range of resources available to Master Sergeant Parks was another mystery they had a hard time grasping. Within minutes of his first radio transmission, an Air Force Pararescue UH-60 Blackhawk helicopter arrived on the scene. As the Airmen jumped from the helicopter, Nathan Parks made his way over to the senior member of the team, who was an Air Force Master Sergeant. Parks intended to brief him on the situation and how he needed to keep quiet about what he and his fellow Airmen had witnessed. Two of the Airmen noticed the remains of the dead giant and stopped short.

Seeing this, the Air Force Master Sergeant barked loudly, "Move your asses! There are wounded who need attention. You guys act like you've never seen a giant before."

Amused and bewildered, Nathan approached the Air Force Sergeant. When the Sergeant saw Nathan, a smile came over his face. "I know you, don't I?" Nathan asked. "That's right, Sarge, we were both at that little party in Oklahoma a couple of years ago. I helped the Police Chief disarm the kid with the Mini-14 who was in shock after two of those hair balls were about to eat him. My name is Trent Simmons," he said, extending his hand. As Nathan shook his hand, it all came back to him.

"That's right, you went charging after the things, and ended up riding back into headquarters on the kid's horse. And a few days later, you treated me on the chopper, after I got my ass handed to me by one of them and had to be airlifted out."

"That's right, Sarge, like you, I'm one of General Henderson's sled dogs." He turned, exposing the left shoulder of his uniform, which had an Archangel patch. "We'll catch up another time. I've got to help my men get the wounded out of here. Something tells me we'll be at the same briefing later." He quickly joined the other Pararescue members, already in the process of loading the three injured Soldiers. "They're beat up all to hell, but it looks like they'll make it," Simmons yelled to Parks before jumping into the chopper, which quickly took off and flew away in the direction of Kandahar Air Base.

Moments following that, two Army UH-60s landed, Special Operators, also members of Team Archangel, spilled out and began ordering Lieutenant Walker and his men onto the choppers. As the aircraft began lifting, Lieutenant Walker and his 10th Mountain Division soldiers watched as the Special Ops soldiers set a perimeter, while others began dragging heavy ropes and other equipment to the corpse of the dead giant. One of the last sights they witnessed as their aircraft left the area was the arrival of a CH-47 heavy-lift helicopter landing on the scene.

Once the UH-60s arrived at Kandahar Air Base, both choppers containing the 10th Mountain Division soldiers landed at a secluded part of the base near the isolated hanger where the soldiers now sat. They were not alone. The Air Force helicopter aircrew and Pararescue-Men were sitting in the hanger when they arrived. For the past hour, the men had sat, each deep in their own thoughts. There was food, bottled water, and cold drinks available for the troops. Other than the water, everything else lay untouched. Those who spoke whispered amongst themselves about their fate. "They're going to put us in Leavenworth to keep us quiet," one soldiered muttered under his breath.

"That, or they'll just keep sending us out, until we're all dead," offered another.

"Look, they even brought in those Air Force guys who landed there. I'll bet they just take us all out and shoot us," a third soldier offered with glee, obviously trying to scare the first two.

"Knock it off," Staff Sergeant Tollis said loudly. "Be glad you're alive. The worst thing that can happen is a trip home and orders to keep your mouths shut." As if on cue, Master Sergeant Parks entered the hanger, and in a loud booming voice, called the men to attention. The men snapped to attention as a Major General, followed by Colonel Houston, their Regimental Commander, and a First Sergeant entered the hanger.

"At ease men. I'm Major General Malcolm Henderson. I'm the commander of Task Force Titan. I've come here along with your commander, Colonel Houston, to debrief you. First Sergeant Briggs is my right-hand man. By now, I'm sure you're all familiar with Master Sergeant Parks. I realize you men have had one hell of a morning. First, I want to inform you that your three buddies are all going to make it. They're a bit beat up, but they're 10th Mountain and tough. The fact that this Pararescue team got to them so quickly had a lot to do with it," the General said, nodding to the Airmen sitting alone in a small group. "Sergeant Parks has briefed me on what transpired, and all I can say is 'well done'. You men have performed in the highest tradition of the 10th Mountain Division. I realize you all have questions, and I promise I'll get to your questions as we go through debrief. Right now, I'm sure you've concluded that everything which transpired this morning is highly classified, and nothing we talk about during this meeting leaves this hanger."

"Now I intend to speak with each one of you personally and let me put you at ease; none of you are considered a security threat. You are all US Army, you're combat veterans, and you will be trusted to keep what happened this morning to yourself without the use of threats. Besides, who the hell would believe you anyway?" the General said, smiling. This broke the tension, and there were audible sighs of relief along with laughter. "Now that the ice is broken, I want you guys to relax and start attacking the food and liquids. It will speed up the process of bringing you back to normal. For most of you, this event will mean an early ticket home; you've earned it. For those of you who wish to stay, we will be offering you a position with Task Force Titan. That is the only way you are going to stay in theater. Join us or go home. Your choice. For those going home, it will be an honorable homecoming, along with a promotion and a citation of combat action against a very lethal, enemy force. For those of you who decide to join the Archangels, all I can say is... Welcome to the real war."

## Monday, 21 November 2016, 10:00 PM AFT, Kandahar Air Base, Kandahar Province, Afghanistan

Nathan Parks leaned against the concrete wall used as blast protection for the small tent city his unit used as their home while on the airbase. The night air was a cool forty-seven degrees. This was Nathan's favorite weather; not too hot, yet cool enough to make his heavy, military clothing and gear comfortable. Putting his hands against the concrete wall, he leaned in hard and pushed his legs out behind him, arching his sore back. After a few minutes of stretching his aching muscles, he stood and rolled his shoulders before pulling a pack of cigarettes from his breast pocket and lighting one. "Don't you know those things will kill you?" a familiar voice asked from the shadows. Nathan quickly swapped the cigarette to his left hand and coming to attention, crisply saluted with his right hand. This move had been perfected over the years he had spent in uniform.

"Lately, I've been under the impression they'll never get the chance, Sir," Nathan said, with just the right amount of humor.

General Henderson returned the salute, "At ease, Sergeant Parks. Any chance you could spare one of those?" Nathan dug in his breast pocket and pulled out the pack of Camels, offering it to the General. Smiling, General Henderson took the pack, pulling out a cigarette and putting it in his mouth, he asked, "Got a light?"

"Yes, Sir, I sure do. Would you like me to punch you in the chest to help get it started?" Both men laughed at the age-old joke. A serious look came across General Henderson's face,

"You know, Sergeant, those cigarettes have a better chance of killing you than anything you've encountered while operating with Task Force Titan."

"I find that a little hard to believe, Sir."

"That's because you don't know what I know, Sergeant."

"Sir, in that case, would you enlighten me with some of your knowledge? Going out with Task Force Titan members is one thing but going out as I did today with line troops who are not told of the true nature of the threat, is something entirely different. They had no idea a threat was imminent and even less of an idea what to do when it appeared and started using them for batting practice. We only survived because those Dutch guys weakened it before they were massacred. Sir, I'm not complaining, I'm just saying this is a pretty sketchy business we're in, and I'll take my chances with the smoking."

The General studied Nathan's face for a moment. He remembered meeting him in Oklahoma two years earlier when the Sergeant had stumbled upon a small community being terrorized by four Sasquatch creatures. Sergeant Parks had lent his time, talent, and blood to the community to help rid them of the danger. Of course, he had appeared a lot younger then; the things Sergeant Parks had seen and done in the past year had aged him. He was in his mid-thirties, but his dark hair had turned completely white. The same stress which caused his hair to turn white had also given him deep crow's feet wrinkles around his eyes. Other than smoking, he was fit; he kept himself in the best shape possible. He knew the nature of his enemy demanded this of him if he wanted to survive. General Henderson put his hand on the Sergeant's shoulder.

"Yes Nathan, I'll enlighten you. You're going home."

"Sir?" Nathan asked, confused.

"You're going home, Sergeant."

"Sir, we are nowhere near finished here."

"You're finished Sergeant, for a while anyway. You're going home and getting some rest before you're completely burned out. Besides, I'm going to need you in the future, so don't even attempt to argue with me. Start packing your gear; I'm getting you out of here on the first available bird in the morning. You've done a great job here, Nate. Now go home. Spend Thanksgiving with your family. Get some rest." General Henderson turned and walked back into the shadows, his mission complete, heading to the command tent. For the first time in a year, a feeling of relief swept over Nathan because he felt he was actually going to survive his tour with Task Force Titan in Afghanistan. He reached into his breast pocket for another cigarette and then realized the General had never given them back.

"Sir, my smokes," he shouted toward the General, who was now only a shadow moving into the darkness. "You're leaving, I'm staying. I need them more than you do, Sergeant."

Yes, Sir, I believe you do, Nathan thought, smiling. With a lightness in his step, he hadn't felt in a long time, he headed to his tent to start packing. Halfway to the tent, he stopped abruptly. Falling to his knees, he thanked God for allowing him to survive his tour in Afghanistan. After he finished, the thought crossed his mind; I think I'll spend my leave with my friends in Talihina. Surely Addison wouldn't mind if I did some camping and hunting on his property, Nathan thought. A little solitude would serve him better than partying and hell-raising with his old friends in the Little Rock area. What Nathan didn't realize was, even with his experience in Afghanistan, he had no idea how deep the hole was.

## Tuesday, 22 November 2016, 08:00 PM AFT, Kandahar Air Base, Kandahar Province, Afghanistan

Nathan was getting bored as he waited for his flight home. A C-17 transport plane was due to arrive in about an hour. Once it had landed and refueled, Nathan would board it for a ride back to the real world, or at least as far as Germany, where he would have to find another aircraft heading stateside. "Henderson run you out of town, too?" a voice said from his right. Turning, Nathan saw that the voice belonged to Air Force Master Sergeant Trent Simmons.

"How'd you know?" Nathan said, smiling, as he squinted into the intense morning light.

Trent Simmons replied, "I've seen him do it a dozen times to others. Especially when it's close to the holidays and he's worked somebody's tail off." Nathan noticed Simmons was built like most special ops troops. Thin but muscled, built more like a runner than a weightlifter. At six feet, even Simmons wasn't the most imposing man at first glance. Plus, he had a friendly, even playful personality. However, if you looked closely, there was a quiet edginess to the man. Simmons removed his cap, and Nathan could see his hair, for the most part, was sandy blonde, a few strands of grey hinting that this man had been fighting the beast as well. His steel-blue eyes were never still for long. He was constantly scanning his surroundings and the people near him. Situational awareness was his religion; he seemed never to relax fully.

"So, the General sent you home because you were getting ugly, and he thought turkey and dressing would improve your looks?" Nathan said, teasing.

"Something like that," Trent replied, smiling. "Where are you heading, Parks?"

"You can call me Nathan; after all we're on leave."

Laughing, Trent replied, "Fair enough, so where are you heading, Nathan?"

"Believe it or not, I'm going to Oklahoma, back to Talihina. I'm feeling hunting and camping in the quiet of the local mountains might do me some good. How about you? Are you going home to spend Thanksgiving with the wife?"

"Nah, she left me three deployments ago. I was thinking of going to the Bahamas and laying on the beach, drunk, for a month or two; or at least until Henderson sends somebody to get me." "Now that sounds like a lot of fun, except I've seen enough sand for a while, even if it is next to a beautiful ocean. I think I'm ready to roll around in the grass for a few weeks."

Trent nodded, pondering Nathan's words as his blue eyes narrowed from the glare caused by the combination of sun, concrete, and sand, surrounding the Kandahar flight line. The more he thought about it, the more he liked Nathan's idea. "I got no place special I need to be for the next five weeks or so. Do you think it would be possible for me to tag along with you? I remember I liked that area a lot. Saw a lot of game the short time I was there. I wouldn't mind playing mountain man until Henderson orders us back to this sand box."

Nathan didn't need to think twice. Without hesitation, he said, "I think having you along would be a hoot. You think you can keep up Air Force? We're not going to be sitting on our asses riding around in helicopters." A sly smile came across Nathan's face; he knew that Air Force Pararescue training was every bit as difficult as any other Special Forces training, but interservice rivalries had to be acknowledged.

"I should be okay, as long as I can bring my jammies and have a place to plug in my night light," Trent countered, smiling, "You got a place to stay there? Or are we going to stay in the hills?"

"I'm certain Addison Redstone will be more than glad to put us both up if we get tired of camping. Besides, he's got my weapons stored at his place."

"Speaking of weapons, I have no access to any weapons or gear there. I've got plenty of money saved though. What's the situation like for purchasing a decent deer rifle and shotgun in Oklahoma?" Trent asked.

Grinning, Nathan replied, "It's Oklahoma. You can get anything you need, and if for some reason we can't find what you want there... It's a short drive to Arkansas or Texas. Your biggest problem will be deciding which gun you want to buy."

"Awesome, let's ride cowboy," Trent said, hearing the distant sound of jet engines becoming louder as an Air Force C-17 was seconds away from landing. Looking at Nathan, he asked, "You know what that sound is?"

"What's that?" Nathan asked, playing along.

"That is the song of my people!" Trent said with a large grin.

## Tuesday, 22 November 2016 10::00 PM CST Indian Highway, two miles South of Honobia, OK.

Jim and Melinda Vaughn were returning home from a late dinner in Hochatown. The couple were new residents to the small town of Honobia, nestled in a narrow valley between two ranges of the Kiamichi Mountains. They loved their new home and their new life in what Melinda liked to call 'the sleepy Hamlet, Honobia.' Having moved to the area the previous summer, they were overwhelmed by the beauty of the area. The kindness of the residents also overjoyed them. Both were surprised they had made friends so quickly in the small community. They had moved to Honobia from a much larger Northeast Texas community that was friendly enough on the exterior. However, in that town, they were known as 'move-ins.' Jim was from the Dallas area, and Melinda was from West Texas; therefore, they had no family ties to the locals in the community. Although there was no hostility, there was always a sense of "you're not one of us," when working or attending social functions. This was not the case in Honobia; the couple was pleasantly surprised by how quickly they were accepted as part of the local community.

They had happily accepted a dinner invitation with some friends from the local church they attended. They planned to meet for dinner in Hochatown, a larger community about 30 miles south of Honobia. Honobia boasted one small store, which also doubled as the local restaurant and meeting place. The couple loved to eat there, but the grill and store closed by 3:00 PM on Sundays. A trip to Hochatown was a welcome event. Hochatown straddled Highway 259, and due to its location next to Beaver's Bend State Park and Broken Bow Lake, the small town was full of trendy restaurants which appealed to both locals and tourists alike. "I really like them," Melinda said, referring to the couple with whom they'd had dinner.

"Yeah, me too; ole Walt must have a lead foot though. I haven't seen his taillights since about two miles after we got on 259."

"Well, you are driving a bit slow. You haven't learned to keep up with the locals yet," Melinda said, teasingly.

"Yeah, well, I'm not interested in totaling the car when a deer or bear decides to step onto the dark road either," Jim replied. He started to slow as they came down the last hill and curve before reaching the Highway 144 intersection outside Honobia. Looking both ways and not seeing any traffic, as usual, he crossed the highway and started entering Honobia. As they passed Christ's 40 Acres, a Christian Mission on their left, Jim started slowing once again as the road going downhill had a few potholes before the bridge into Honobia. The bridge held its own charm. It was a metal truss bridge built in the 1950s which crossed the headwaters of the Little River. To the right of the bridge, Honobia Creek entered the Little River from the north, and Rock Creek entered the river from the south. Jim always enjoyed driving over its 100-foot span and searching the shallow waters to see if any wildlife happened to be in the creek bed.

"Is that a guy standing on the bridge rail?" Melinda asked.

"Looks like it," Jim said, slowing the car even more.

"Do you think he's a jumper?" Melinda asked with concern.

"I doubt it; the fall probably wouldn't kill him, but it would sure wreck his day," Jim replied. As the car slowed, Jim swung the front toward the right side of the bridge, where the man was standing on the top truss. "It's probably a local kid just out..." Jim's voice trailed off as the light of the car illuminated the figure in front of them. "You got to be kidding!" he exclaimed.

"Jim, backup! Backup! Backup!" Melinda screamed. The figure in the lights looked man-like but much larger. It was covered in hair and towered above the roadbed on the bridge as it stood on the trusses eight feet above the road. The figure was at least another seven to eight feet tall. "Backup, get us out of here!" Melinda screamed again.

"Wait, where are we going to go? This is the only way to our house," Jim replied. Both the vehicle and the creature remained motionless for a few seconds as if the occupants of the car and the occupant of the bridge rail waited to see what the other would do. So, they are real? Jim thought to himself.

"I don't like this, Jim." Melinda said, the fear slightly subsiding in her voice since there was no sign of aggression on the part of the creature.

"Well, this is the reason there's all this Bigfoot stuff everywhere we go up here," Jim said, referring to the numerous references to Bigfoot by retailers in the surrounding communities.

"You think that's what it is?" Melinda nervously asked.

"That's all it could be," Jim said matter-of-factly as he continued to watch the creature, fascinated by its size and apparent power. He heard a whimper from Melinda. "Easy baby, its way up on the truss in the middle of the bridge. We'll be fine. It will probably climb down in a minute and head off down the creek." The creature seemed to be passive as it studied the vehicle. The headlights of the Toyota Camry reflected a reddish-amber eye shine from the creature. "You're one big, scary guy," Jim said in a nervous whisper.

"I hope it doesn't head up the creek toward our home," Melinda said quietly.

"Nah, they're harmless from what I've heard. In fact, they avoid human contact. It's probably more scared than we are." Jim said as he honked the car horn to encourage the thing to move off the bridge. The reaction was of the creature was not the one Jim was looking for. The expression on its face became angry. It bared its teeth, which appeared to be humanlike but much larger. Then it roared loudly and began running along the bridge's truss with uncanny agility, effortlessly jumping across the 26-foot-wide bridge, landing lightly on the opposite truss. "Wow!" was all Jim could say. The creature started running along the truss, heading toward the Vaughn's and their vehicle.

"Jim! Do something!"

"Oh crap!" Jim barked; all he could think to do was stomp on the gas pedal, hoping to speed past the quickly approaching creature. As his car drove onto the bridge, Jim decided if the creature jumped onto the roadbed of the bridge, he would try and run it over. He didn't like his chances though. With the car accelerating and the creature in full stride, only about 40 feet separated the two. Once again, the creature used its unearthly physical agility and vaulted off the truss, planting one foot on the hood of the Vaughn's speeding Toyota, using it as a springboard to soar up and over the car into the darkness past the other side of the bridge. Jim crossed the bridge and slammed on his brakes, stopping the car on the other side.

"Jim, for crying out loud. Don't stop," Melinda pleaded.

"Hang on, honey. It's either gone or dead, after that collision." Jim stepped out of the car and went to the front of the vehicle. "Look at my hood!" he said, angrily. Melinda could see the middle of the hood was deeply indented, and the edges were protruding up as if a huge fist had punched it.

"Jim, if the car horn angered it, don't take any more chances. Let's go home now!"

45

Ignoring his wife, Jim looked back at the bridge, which was clearly illuminated by the moonlight. There were two small shapes moving along the truss. Raccoons? Jim thought to himself. He took a couple of steps nearer. Peering intensely, Jim noticed that the moonlight had suddenly vanished, and his vision was fighting to adjust to the sudden darkness. He glanced up, thinking a cloud had covered the moon and hoping it would move away so his vision would return. He was astonished at what he saw in the night sky. A huge triangle-shaped aircraft of some sort hovered silently in the sky, blocking the moonlight. The sight was unnerving, and for a moment, he forgot about the bridge and its strange occupant. Jim stood frozen, staring at the object as it hung silently over the area. The world around him instantly became an overpowering white light, as powerful as a welder's arc, as a beam from the object illuminated the bridge. Jim involuntarily shielded himself from the light with his arms and squinted back toward the bridge railing. What he'd thought may have been raccoons were actually two large, hair-covered hands. The hands seemed to tighten their grip on the truss as the creature swung itself up and over, landing lightly on its feet atop the bridge's truss.

The ease with which the creature moved nearly unhinged Jim. He started moving slowly back to his car. The creature emitted another roar and leaped from the truss onto the bridge's roadbed. The creature released a furious roar at Jim with its expression full of malice. The light that had been so overpowering seconds before now vanished, leaving Jim with no low light vision. He glanced skyward to see that the triangle-shaped craft now appeared to be a glowing ring in the sky. Regretting wasting the moment it had taken to look up, he now dove into the car and hit the accelerator, leaving it to the power of the acceleration to close his door. The tires loudly screeched as they tried to gain purchase on the loose asphalt of the road. The vehicle seemed to accelerate painfully slow. As the car got to 30 miles an hour, there was a tremendous bang on the back of the vehicle. The creature was right behind the car, repeatedly pounding a massive fist on the trunk lid. Jim pushed harder on the accelerator, but it was already to the floor. The car sped past the Honobia Creek Store, and there was one last loud bang against the vehicle as it finally began to pull away from the creature.

"Jim, slow down, you're going to miss our turn," Melinda warned.

"That thing is only a hundred yards behind us, Melinda. No way am I going to allow it to follow us home," Jim snapped as the Toyota began to roar up Indian Trail Highway, taking them up the North ridge of mountains above

Honobia. A light moving around a bend in front of them caused Jim to slow slightly, thinking it was an oncoming vehicle, possibly a motorcycle coming down the mountain into Honobia from the north. *Good! You can take the heat from this thing, buddy,* Jim thought with selfish relief for any escape from the hulking terror pursuing them. As the light and the Vaughn's Toyota began to come abreast of each other on the road, Jim realized there was no vehicle. There was no motorcycle. There was only one light. To make matters worse, the light was the size of a small bus. It had instantaneously reversed its course from heading down the mountain and was now pacing their car and lurking right outside the driver's door window. Jim could only take a quick glance; his mind was racing. *How in the hell did this thing reverse course instantly?* he thought as he stole one more glance, noting the vehicle or whatever it was took up the whole left lane of the highway. His heart sank as he imagined the outcome if another car came down one of the blind curves on the small two-lane mountain highway. Melinda screamed in escalating terror. "Quiet baby, we can't lose our heads."

"What is that thing? Why is it hanging outside the window?" Melinda cried.

"I don't know, but it's doing 55 miles per hour. Just be glad, we outran the hairy thing," Jim said, trying to concentrate on the dangerous mountain road and decide exactly where he and his wife could find the 'normal' world again.

"Jim, it's weird, it's not normal. Look at it!"

"You want me to have a staring contest with it or concentrate on this road?" Jim snapped. Then without any noise or warning, the strange glowing vehicle accelerated past the Vaughn's car, making another impossible reversing maneuver, carrying it high over the guard rail through some large trees at a turnout that provided a scenic overlook of Honobia. Jim slowed to a full stop, staring in disbelief over his left shoulder as the large, blue-white, glowing object continued climbing into the night sky. Finally, there was no trace of the strange object.

"Let's go home," Melinda begged.

"We're not going home tonight, darlin," Jim told his wife softly. *That Bigfoot, or whatever it is, is probably waiting to ambush the next car coming down the hill. Well, it won't be me, and this is the last time I drive around here unarmed,* Jim told himself.

The Vaughn's nervously continued the climb up the mountain road. As they made a sharp, right turn around one of the switchbacks, yet another figure appeared in the headlights. Standing next to the road was an elderly man who appeared to be in his 90's. He had distinct Native American features and was dressed in worn jeans and a long-sleeved shirt. Jim slowed as he got closer to the figure. "Jim, don't you dare stop," Melinda said, sternly.

"I'm not," Jim replied. As they passed the ancient-looking man, both Jim and Melinda got a good look at him. He raised a hand as they passed. The gesture didn't seem like a greeting; it seemed more like a benediction of peace. A calm feeling of security came over Jim as he said, "We're okay now, Melinda."

"We're okay? Did you just say that we're okay?" Melinda asked with growing anger. "Are you out of your mind? We were attacked by something out of a horror movie, and had a UFO try to melt our car, followed by another one chasing us up the mountain. On top of all that, we drive past a guy who looks like he's twenty years late to his own funeral, and you think we're okay? I feel like you moved us to, Transylvania? I want to move back to Texas."

"We're not going back to Texas; this was just some kind of weird hallucination we suffered."

"Look at the hood of the car. Is that a hallucination, Jim? I'm not going to live up here with hairy monsters, flying saucers, ghost lights and zombies chasing us all over the mountains. We're going to Texas for Thanksgiving anyway. I say we stay there and not come back," she fumed.

"Whatever happened wasn't normal; just give me time to think. That man we saw was only a man, he meant us no harm."

"You don't know that, Jim. For all we know, he could have been the angel of death."

"I know he meant us no harm, baby. Besides, we're not going back to Honobia tonight. That much I do know!"

"Where are we going to go then?" Melinda asked.

"I don't know yet," Jim said quietly, pondering what he should do next. The rest of the trip through the mountain pass was uneventful. They never passed another vehicle. When they arrived at the intersection of Hwy 271, Jim paused for a couple of minutes as both he and his wife sat in silence. Jim had an overwhelming urge to go into Talihina. It was as if he were being drawn there.

With a sigh, Jim made a right turn onto Hwy 271 and headed toward Talihina. They drove for another five minutes before spotting a lighted, yellow Dollar General Store sign. In the store's parking lot, Jim could make out a white police cruiser. He slowed the vehicle, preparing to turn into the parking lot. "You're not going to tell the police what happened are you?" Melinda asked. "They'll think we're nuts."

"Something is telling me this is the thing to do, Melinda. It's going to be okay," Jim said as he made a left turn into the parking lot. Jim purposely parked in front of the police vehicle with his headlights pointed away. He turned the engine off and turned on his interior lights, enabling the police officer to see him clearly. The last thing he wanted to do was appear as a threat and get himself shot. Jim slowly exited his vehicle and had his hands in full view of the officer, who had also begun exiting his cruiser.

"Officer, we need assistance," Jim said, standing next to his car as the police officer approached. Jim watched as the officer walked slowly toward him. Though not appearing concerned, the officer approached Jim with caution and shone a light on Jim, Melinda, and the damaged car before approaching carefully. He noticed the officer was young and fit. He also wore the three chevrons of a Sergeant. Good, I need a veteran tonight, not a rookie, Jim thought with relief.

"I'm Sergeant Chula of the Talihina Police Department. Are either of you two injured?" the officer asked.

"No, officer, but we are a bit shaken up." Jim noticed the officer's flashlight was inspecting the hood of their Toyota as it traveled down to the grill and came to rest on the Texas plates. "Did you folks hit a deer?" he asked. "Actually, an animal of some type hit us, Officer," Jim replied. He noticed the officer's eyebrows rose quizzically for a moment.

"Okay, Sir, if you would let me see your driver's license and proof of insurance."

Jim produced his driver's license as the officer requested, then said, "The insurance card is in the glove box. Do you want me or my wife to get it?"

"Tell you what, just stand here in front of the car." Then leaning down, he said, "Ma'am, would you mind stepping out of the vehicle? And bring the proof of insurance with you, please?" Melinda followed the officer's instructions. Sergeant Chula studied the Oklahoma driver's license and then looked back at the couple. He had been checking for signs of intoxication or influence from another substance, but all he could detect was fear. "You have Texas plates and an Oklahoma driver's license; you folks new here?"

"Yes, Officer, that's correct," Jim replied.

"This address in Honobia, is current, Sir?"

"Yes."

"You say an animal hit you? Your vehicle is beat up but appears to still be able to operate safely. Neither of you appear injured, but I can tell you're shaken up. Can you folks tell me what happened? That way I'll have a better idea of how I can help you."

"Well, Officer, you've probably never heard anything like this before. I don't know how to tell you, except to just tell you exactly what happened."

"The complete story is usually the quickest way to a solution, Sir," Sergeant Chula said in a soothing tone. Jim looked at Melinda, who gave him a nod as if to say, 'Go ahead and get it out.' Jim began to explain to the young officer what had happened to them a half-hour earlier. To his surprise, the officer didn't show disbelief or sarcasm. In fact, his manner and questions showed deep concern as if he'd witnessed the event himself. When Jim finished his story, he also related how they didn't feel safe returning to Honobia tonight.

The officer nodded knowingly and replied, "We'll fix you up with a place to stay here in town tonight. Tomorrow, you'll feel better and be yourselves again. In the meantime, I need to let my Chief know what's going on, and he'll want to talk to you as well. He may even need you to repeat the events to a couple of other gentlemen."

"I half expected you to treat us as if we were crazy. You act as if you've had experience with this kind of thing," Jim said, confused.

The Sergeant smiled and replied, "It's going to be okay, folks. You're not the first people to have a night like this. Sometimes things happen that can't be explained." Then speaking into the radio mike on his shoulder, he said, "Dispatch, you'd better give the Chief a call to come in. He'll want to personally talk to these folks. They're going to follow me to the station. If you don't mind, put on some fresh coffee. They look like they need it." "Okay folks, follow me, and we'll get you a place to stay this evening."

Melinda looked at Jimmy Chula with some skepticism. "You don't mean in jail, do you?"

She was relieved when he smiled and said, "Of course not. We're here to help, Ma'am. We'll take good care of you tonight, and tomorrow everything will be much better. Trust me; you came to the right place."

### Wednesday, 23 November 2016, 03::00 AM CST, Mena, Arkansas.

Paul Eastman awoke from his sleep in a cold sweat. What sleep he had been getting lately was sparse and constantly interrupted by nightmares. It had all started two weeks earlier as he was working his job at Queen Wilhelmina State Park, not far from his home in Mena. The job was new and a far cry from his previous position as a Special Agent with the U.S. Forest Service in charge of the local district. In those days, he had clout, control, and most of all, power. All of it was gone as of two years ago when he'd been caught up in a scandal that rocked the USFS all the way to its highest levels. It all started with the crash of a USAF F-16, which went down in a ravine near the grounds of the lodge at Queen Wilhelmina State Park. The pilot had ejected safely, but he was never seen again. However, amid the crash debris, Arkansas National Guard troops had discovered three charred corpses, each over seven feet tall. Only Eastman and a few select people in the U.S. Forest Service had knowledge of the true existence of these creatures, officially named "Relics" by the government. The rest of the country knew these creatures by their more popular names: Bigfoot or Sasquatch.

The crash had caused a large, forest fire which took four days to get under control. It was believed the fire had forced four more Relics to flee west from the flames until they eventually stopped in the hills and forest outside Talihina, Oklahoma. Once there, the creatures began their usual hunting and feeding. The real problems started when they came in contact with humans. Unfortunately, their first contact was with five members of an outlaw motorcycle club from Texas. Hardened club members and Relics ended up being a volatile mix, and the five bikers were mauled to death, their body parts strewn all around a scenic overlook outside of Talihina. The incident made national headlines, which made it difficult for Eastman to keep the existence of these creatures a secret, as his superiors expected. More incidents occurred, including the deaths of two hunters, a Game Warden, and a female Oklahoma State Trooper, who happened to be dating the Chief of Police in Talihina. Once this happened, Eastman started losing control of the situation, especially once the Talihina Chief of Police and his father started looking into the mayhem that was occurring near their community. Eastman had brought in the military to hunt down and kill the Relics, but it was too late by then. His earlier mistakes had started a domino effect, causing Washington to get involved. His biggest mistake was calling in a MIB team. Most conspiracy theorists assumed the term MIB to mean Men in Black. In truth, they are men, and they do wear black; but any similarity to the MIB portrayed by Will Smith and Tommy Lee Jones ends there.

MIB stands for Mission Integrity Branch. When a classified situation is about to get out of control, a MIB unit is the best way to keep it under wraps. The teams excel at terrorizing witnesses and quieting tongues. Although he'd never used a MIB team, Eastman had never heard of one failing its mission.

51

Of course, no MIB team had ever run across people like Addison and Samuel Redstone or the other citizens of Talihina. The team leader, a man named Mason, made the fatal mistake of taking these people too lightly. Mason was a terrifying individual who, when initially assigned to the case, quickly frightened a television crew into complete silence. But he became an absolute failure when he tried to take out the Redstone's, their family, and friends. In fact, other than the Redstone's, nobody knew what had happened to Mason and his team. In the end, Eastman was humiliated and cast out of the USFS. He had hoped for a lateral move to the National Park Service, but after the disaster for the government around Talihina, the NPS wanted nothing to do with him.

One of the few friends he had left in high places arranged his current job with the Arkansas Department of Parks and Tourism. It was a far cry from his days as a special agent. Nowadays, he took orders, not give them. He emptied trash cans, cleaned public restrooms, and checked to see if people had paid their camping fees. It was a thankless, mindless job, in his opinion. He had even thought of taking his own life instead of living without the power he'd once had. Two days earlier, he had been doing repairs on a public restroom inside the park grounds. A door had been torn off the ladies' room, probably by teenaged vandals. The hinges had been completely ripped out of the heavy steel frame, and it had taken him hours to repair the door. As he was walking to his truck to put his tools away, a drill fell out of his tool bag. He leaned over to pick up the drill, and he saw it - a footprint. The impression, made in a piece of soft earth, was almost perfect. He knew he was looking at the footprint of a Relic. Quickly he grabbed a measuring tape. The print was twenty-four inches long and eleven inches wide at its broadest point. The odd thing was… the print had six toes.

Looking around nervously, Eastman grabbed his tools and fled to his truck. The incident had so terrified him, he'd called in sick the last two days. He had thought he'd return to work in the morning, but again he couldn't sleep. He had come to the decision he would not go back to his current job. He lay in a cold sweat in the dark, feeling scared, weak, and impotent. "I swear I will do anything to get my power back!" he screamed into the darkness. Cursing his cowardice, he rose out of bed and made his way to the kitchen. Opening the refrigerator door, he grabbed a bottle of beer. He snapped the cap off and guzzled the entire beer in a single gulp. Then he closed the refrigerator door, and the kitchen fell back into darkness. He walked over to the sink and turned on the cold water. He put his head down into the sink and let the water run over the back of his neck. He stood up straight, not caring that water dripped from him onto the kitchen floor. It was then he noticed the kitchen was no longer dark. There was a dull whitish glow that filled the room. Looking for the light source, he saw that it was coming from the back of his house, which was on the wood line of the forest. Pulling back the curtains, he was nearly blinded by a brilliant, blue-white glow from a light source that seemed to be hovering above the house. "What the hell?" he mumbled.

"Now that's what I like to hear," a voice said from behind him, causing Eastman to jump and defecate in terror. "Shit!" He exclaimed, looking at the tall, strange-looking man in front of him.

"Yes, exactly. Shit! Your job is shit; your life is shit. And now you've gone and shit yourself, too."

"Who are you?" Eastman asked, no longer caring about his fouled underwear.

"I have to say, Paul, as you stand there covered in fearful sweat and your own shit, you possess courage enough to ask my name? My last Lieutenant didn't have the nerve to ask."

"Well, he must have been a total wretch if he was a bigger coward than me right now," Eastman said, shaking.

"Oh, on the contrary, he wasn't a coward; he was more cautious. He knew there were things best left unknown."

"Well, good for him, sounds like a great guy. Now you want to tell me who you are and what you want? And what the hell are you doing in my house?" Eastman said, seeing the tall, lean figure more clearly.

The man was extremely odd-looking; his build was tall and thin, except for his head which had a bulbous yet cone shape to it. His features were almost feminine but very formidable, the wide top of the forehead and face thinned as you followed the face due to a slender pointed chin. "As I recall, you didn't find him to be a great guy. In fact, you were terrified of him. Do you remember John Mason?"

John Mason? Eastman came close to defecating again. "What about him?"

"I was his superior before he went missing, so to speak."

"Yeah, he was a peach of a guy; but I had nothing to do with his disappearance. But I can say, I'm glad he's gone. By the way, you're haunting the wrong guy. Everybody knows the Redstone's killed him and his men."

"The Redstone's didn't kill him and his men; I did."

"Who are you again?" Eastman asked as he began to shiver uncontrollably.

53

"Again, you're frightened to the point of not being able to control your body. And yet, you have the courage to ask my name again. My name is Nergal, you will never speak my name unless you find yourself in the direst of emergencies. When you speak to me you will call me Master, and when speaking to others about me, you will only refer to me as your Superior."

"Why would you kill Mason and his men, because he failed you?" Eastman asked

"Mason was sadistic and efficient; he was the perfect man for the job. Unfortunately, he had one weakness. When he didn't have the upper hand, he became an even bigger coward than you. Once the Redstone's captured him and his men, they dropped them in the forest with the creatures you were trying so hard to cover up. When the creatures found Mason, he cried out for the Jewish Carpenter. I merely ordered the creatures to send Mason on his way to meet his so-called savior."

"By Jewish Carpenter, you mean…" Eastman never got the name out, as he was cut off in mid-sentence by the man in front of him.

"Never speak his name, or you will die like Mason! When you are in trouble, it is then you will speak my name."

"What if I don't take the job?" Eastman asked.

"You want one of two things: your old power back, or you want to quit living. I am here to give you either. The choice is yours, more power than you ever dreamed of, or ending your miserable existence right now."

"How long will it take for me to get back to where I was?"

"Kneel before me, take my hand, and this very day, you will have more power than you ever imagined." Eastman nervously knelt before the strange man. Holding out his right hand, he gave no opposition to the figure as it turned his hand and forearm face up. With a quick flick of the wrist, the strange man cut an inch long gash, six inches above his wrist on the inside of his forearm. Eastman felt no pain from the cut and felt no pain as the man inserted a small pellet or chip into the wound. "With this I can always be with you," the figure said. "This will also enhance your thinking, and powers of control and dominance. No longer will lesser men rule you; you will be their master now."

Then the figure swept his index finger along the wound, and it was healed, leaving behind only a slight scar. "You will prepare a location in the Kiamichi Mountains for my minions to enter this place. Your work will begin this day." The room was dark again, and Eastman found himself kneeling on the floor. He was beginning to think he'd only had a vivid dream when his phone rang.

As he went to his bedroom to answer his cell phone, the clock on the nightstand read 6:00. He realized the event he'd just experienced had lasted three hours even though it had seemed like no more than ten minutes had elapsed.

**Eastman:** Hello.

**Mitchell:** Hello, Paul Eastman?

**Eastman:** That's right, who the hell is calling this time of the morning?

**Mitchell:** Yeah, sorry to call so early, Paul. This is Dave Mitchell. I'm one of the directors with the Oklahoma Office of the Bureau of Land Management in Norman. Look, we've had a Special Agent slot we need to quickly fill for Southeastern Oklahoma. Would you be interested in interviewing for the job?

**Eastman:** Look, Mitchell, if you were really doing interviews, you wouldn't be calling at six in the damn morning. Somewhere, somehow, your ass is in a sling, and you need me to get you out of it. So quit screwing around, I'm not going to do an interview, but I will come to Norman and let you know what and who I'll need and what my pay grade will be." *Where in the hell did that come from?* Eastman thought, shocked at his own words.

**Mitchell:** Well, uh… I want you, Paul. We have a potential mess brewing down in the Choctaw Nation. From what we've been told, the problem we have is your specialty. So, how long until you can get down to Norman where we can talk?

**Eastman:** What the hell you asking me that for? You want me, send a damn airplane down here to get me. Mena, Arkansas. The airport here is well known to the government. They've run plenty of scams through it. I'll be waiting for your return call to let me know when to meet the plane."

**Mitchell:** Okay Paul, I'll get rig…(Click)

Eastman hung up the phone and hurriedly called his boss at Queen Wilhelmina State Park. A sleepy voice on the other end said, "Hello?"

"Hey, Frank, this is Eastman, wake your fat ass up and listen. I quit! You need to send somebody over to pick up the truck. The keys will be in it, so I wouldn't wait too long as this area of town has gone to shit, and it could get stolen. I'm not playing, send somebody to get it, and I hope you choke on one of those chicken wings you wolf down every day, you fat bastard."

Once again, Eastman hung up the phone. He looked down at the small white scar on the inside of his forearm. Curiosity began to eat at him; he went over to his computer and Googled the name Nergal. All the links he came across for the name described a Mesopotamian god of death, war, and destruction. I'm now the Lieutenant of a god, and I will have my revenge!

# CHAPTER THREE

〜〜〜〜〜

# The First Warrior

*"Every man should lose a battle in his youth, so he does not lose a war when he is old." ~ George R.R. Martin*

## Wednesday, 29 January 1947 10:00 AM Local, USS Philippine Sea, 660 miles off Antarctica

Lieutenant Junior Grade Joshua Nashoba leaned over the rail of Vulture's Row on the island superstructure of the USS Philippine Sea. This aircraft carrier's superstructure area earned its title because it provided a perfect vantage point for critics to witness the faults or failures of a Naval Aviator's takeoffs and landings. Aviators would usually hear about their shortcomings during a formal debrief from their Squadron Commander. Then there were the informal debriefs given by squadron mates in the Ready Room or Officers' Mess. These were usually well-meaning, and comical prods given by guys who had gone through their own formal debriefs with the Squadron Commander.

The 23-year-old Lieutenant was not interested in critiquing anyone's aviation skills on this cold morning. He, along with other members of his squadron, had squeezed into the area to witness what one of his friends called "Byrd's Flying Circus." Looking down, Josh took what would probably be his last look at the circus's main attraction, at least as far he and his squadron mates were concerned. Six Douglas R4DY transport aircraft filled the flight deck of the US Philippine Sea. The aircraft was the Navy version of the Army Air Force's venerated C-47's, made famous during many airborne operations in Europe and the Pacific during WWII.

The aircraft was rugged and had earned its reputation as the backbone of airborne operations. They had also performed as an aerial bridge, supplying Allied units and bases no matter where they were in the global battlefield that was World War II. Four of the six aircraft rested peacefully below him on the flight deck. Two, however, had awakened, starting their twin engines and warming up in preparation for their launch. At the controls of the lead aircraft was none other than Rear Admiral Richard E. Byrd, who had led three other

57

expeditions to the Antarctic in the late 20's and 30's. His third expedition took place from 1939 into 1941. Then his expeditions had to take a backseat to the war. Joshua didn't care about adventures to the South Pole. Now that the war was over, Admiral Byrd headed up Operation High Jump. This was an expedition to find and secure natural resources in Antarctica for the United States and its Allies before the Russians got to them.

He sighed deeply, looking at the transport aircraft cluttering the deck of this proud warship. The addition of skis attached to the landing gear to assist their landings in the snow made the aircraft appear even more ridiculous in his mind. This wasn't exactly the kind of operation the Lieutenant had in mind when he'd struggled, fought and scratched his way into Naval Aviation from a small town in the Kiamichi Mountains of Southeastern Oklahoma. We're not meant for this, Josh thought with disappointment. This is a warship. We are a fighting squadron, and our warbirds are stuck below in the hanger deck. They're useless there, while the flight deck is populated with these man-made gooney birds. As he continued to watch the actions on deck, he heard the engines rev to a higher RPM as Admiral Byrd followed the hand signals of the young sailor wearing a yellow jersey beside his aircraft. The handler gave Admiral Byrd the signal to apply brakes. The R4YD was now spotted perfectly for its takeoff. Something just isn't right about this whole operation. I don't know why, but I have this uneasy feeling, he thought, keeping his eyes glued on the flight deck operations below him.

The transport plane was too large and heavy, and the deck too short for it to attempt a normal launch. Admiral Byrd and his other aviators had an answer for this. The handler saluted the Admiral, then dramatically went to one knee with his left arm pointing toward the ship's bow. Both engines of the R4YD belched a puff of blue smoke and growled loudly as they were brought to full power. The aircraft shuddered and fought against its wheel brakes at full power, threatening to roll down the flight deck. For the merest of moments, there was a break in the clouds and sunlight danced along the silver fuselage of the R4YD and gave life to its bright yellow identification band along with its blue star and bar insignia of the United States.

Lieutenant Joshua Nashoba's heart raced. Inevitably, aircraft always managed to achieve an overwhelming beauty in his eye. Even a struggling plow horse like this Douglas transport had achieved beauty, if only for a moment. The sunburst was quickly over, and everything returned to the somber tones of grays and blue grays. The R4DY was shaking even harder now, like a wild animal struggling to break free. As the brakes were released and the aircraft began to lumber down the deck, there was a crashing roar. The Admiral had fired the four (JATO), or jet-assisted takeoff bottles, two of which were mounted under each engine. Though the system was called jet-assisted, they were solid-fuel rocket motors. The roar of the rockets was accompanied by a large cloud of white smoke from each separate rocket.

Taking a quick look aft, Joshua could no longer see any of the other five aircraft due to the smoke. Turning back to his right, he witnessed the big R4YD liftoff the carrier's deck with the grace of his own F8F Bearcat fighter. *Not bad for an old guy in an old bird,* Joshua thought to himself, somewhat impressed. Looking down through the quickly clearing smoke, he saw the second R4YD gingerly moving into position for takeoff. He observed the slowly diminishing shape of Byrd's aircraft and, as it turned south, he thought, *Admiral, I'll be even more impressed when the rest of your herd is out of my way so that I can get my thoroughbred released from its corral.*

Lieutenant Joshua Nashoba ignored the hoots and excitement of his squadron mates as they waited in anticipation of the next R4YD launch. He quietly made his way into the superstructure of the carrier's island and went down to the hanger deck to visit his aircraft. The hanger deck was well illuminated, and there was a lot of activity. No doubt, the long month of traveling with the flight deck clogged with transport aircraft had everyone, including the mechanics, itching for flight operations to return to normal. Nashoba had to cut through a squadron of Marine F7F-2N Tigercat's. These large, twin-engine night fighters were designed by the same Grumman aviation company that made its own F8F Bearcat. As with the rest of the aircraft in the hanger deck, the Marine aircraft had their wings folded and were parked mere inches from each other.

"Where you off to Okie?" a familiar voice boomed from his left. Easing up from his crouch and looking around carefully to ensure he didn't bang his head into a protruding piece of an airplane, Joshua turned and saw the face of 1st Lieutenant Jack Fossier. The Marine F7F pilot and Joshua had befriended each other over two years ago in one of the many aviation classes young Navy and Marine officers went through on their quest to become aviators. The class they attended together at the Naval Air Station in Pensacola, Florida, had somehow been assigned an overabundance of young men from the Northeast part of the country. Fossier, a Texan, immediately latched onto Nashoba and referred to him as his pet "Okie." The two had developed a close yet competitive friendship. Fossier often remarked to Nashoba about how he could understand the misfortune of being from Oklahoma, as that was an accident of birth. However, Fossier would never cut Joshua any slack about joining the Navy instead of the Marine Corps.

"You off to pick rust somewhere?" Fossier continued sarcastically, referring to his favorite term for sailors: rust pickers. Nashoba was ready; in fact, he'd been saving this remark for days as he'd pondered the wasted flight deck full of twin-engine Douglas transports.

"Jack, what the hell are you doing down here? I could have sworn I saw you and your airplane launch not five minutes ago," he said, referring to Admiral Byrd's ungainly Douglas transport, which had just taken off. "Nice trick with those rocket bottles. You'll be able to fly to the scene of your crash much quicker with those babies."

Fossier faked a hurt look. "You know this baby is one hundred percent pure war bird," he said, patting the fuselage of his assigned F7F Tigercat.

"All bombers are war birds," Joshua smirked.

"Bomber, you say. You'll think bomber if I cut loose on you with my four, 20mm cannons and four, 50 Cal machine guns," Fossier countered, giving his plane another loving pat.

"You'll never get the chance, Jack. My three-legged dog back in Oklahoma could outmaneuver that behemoth you fly. Did I mention, he's 14 years old?"

"Ah, yes. If I fight your fight, you might have a chance, rust picker. Just imagine a dark night, a night so inky black you squids would never venture off the deck. However, on the off chance you were to stumble into my dark sky, you'd never see me coming."

"Well, there's the real kicker, Jack. We're operating in the Antarctic Ocean. The sun never sets this time of year. You might catch one of the Admiral's transport planes with their pants down. Or maybe one of those mechanical dragonflies over there," Josh said, motioning with his head toward the four H03S-1 helicopters in the far corner of the hangar bay. "But you'll never catch one of our Bearcats in that dump truck, without us seeing you first."

Jack looked over at the four helicopters as his mind struggled for a comeback. "You know, they say those whirlybirds are the future. Just like our aerial radar, sailor. We'll be able to pinpoint your location long before we're in visual range. Plus, with radar this baby can see through the clouds. My radar operator here," Jack said, patting a young Marine sergeant on the shoulder, "would pick you up on his magic box and guide me right to a gun solution. You'd never know we were coming," Fossier said, crossing his arms over his chest victoriously and smiling from ear-to-ear.

Joshua pointed at the young NCO, "Is this correct, Sergeant? You guide him to his target and put him into position to fire his guns?"

"Yes, Sir, I do," the Marine replied.

"Could you fire the guns if needed?"

"Yes, Sir; I could," the Marine replied again. Joshua then looked at his friend's smiling face with a huge grin of his own.

"You know what you got here in this fine Sergeant, don't you Jack?"

"What's that?" Jack asked curiously.

"A gunner and a navigator. Fighters don't have gunners and navigators; bombers do. You fly a bomber, Jack. If that's too hard to handle, you could always put some pontoons on it and fly from one of those seaplane tenders tagging along with us." With that, a smiling Joshua crouched and began making his way to his own squadron's aircraft.

"This is a fighter, you rust-picking smartass," Jack yelled at the fleeing figure of his friend.

Josh stopped again and turned toward his friend. "For crying out loud Jack, your aircraft has been designed to carry a torpedo." Joshua then turned back to the business of getting to his own aircraft. "Bomber!" he yelled loudly as he moved down the line. There was no reply from Jack Fossier.

Josh made his way along the hangar deck until he was amid the aircraft of his squadron. The object of his quest was in sight. There sat his Grumman F8F-1B Bearcat, appearing every bit as lethal sitting on the hangar deck as it did in the air. He walked up to the plane, running his hands along the leading edge of the left wing until he was at the outboard muzzle of one of the aircraft's AN/M3 20mm cannons. Two of the weapons were mounted in each wing. The original version of the Bearcat had been armed with four 50 caliber M2 machine guns. Josh's squadron VF-10A was one of the first units to receive the cannon-armed Bearcat. As his hands continued along the aircraft, his mind couldn't help but picture himself flying this bird into battle.

Josh had grown up in the Kiamichi Mountains of Southern Oklahoma, near the tiny hamlet of Honobia. His father, Ronald, supported the family by doing any work he could find. Ronald Nashoba would work every day for weeks or even months at a time. He cut timber, helped build roads, or worked with cattle. Josh's father ensured his wife, son and three daughters had every chance he could possibly give them. This included their salvation. If Josh's father was working, his mother would take their four children to the small church down the mountain from their cabin in Honobia every Sunday. Josh's father would join them when he could. He demanded his children learn to read. The Bible, schoolbooks, and chores occupied the days of the Nashoba children.

Ronald Nashoba's grandparents had met on the Choctaw Trail of Tears in the early 1830s when they were small children. Though Ronald insisted on his family knowing their Savior was Jesus, he also insisted they maintain the history of their people. Josh's mother dutifully trained her daughters in the ways of Choctaw womanhood. Ronald Nashoba spent every free moment with his son teaching him the ways of the Choctaw hunter and warrior. Josh was mesmerized by the old teachings and legends of his people. Sometimes, he was confused because the Christian and Choctaw ways seemed at odds. When he would approach his father with his confusion, the elder Nashoba would smile and say, "The two ways are closer than you realize. One day you may face the exact same enemy in these mountains which your namesake, Joshua, fought in the Old Testament." At the time, Josh couldn't understand what his father meant. Little did he know it would become all too clear later in his life.

Josh enjoyed his childhood, for the most part. He and a couple of friends spent hours hunting, fishing, and exploring the local mountains and forests. Josh especially loved spending time with his Uncle James, who was only five years older than Josh and a bit spoiled. Josh was captivated by the fact that his Uncle James held views and opinions which were worldlier than those of his father. "There's more to this world than these mountains," he told his nephew. "Don't let Ronald tie you down here. Get out as soon as you can, however you can, and see what this world has to offer," he constantly advised Josh.

James stayed true to the advice he gave Josh, and in 1939 he left Honobia and joined the Army Air Corps as an aerial gunner. He was stationed at Hickam Field in Hawaii. His postcards and letters to Josh painted a picture of a tropical paradise and more adventure than seemed possible in one lifetime. Josh was hooked on the idea of leaving Honobia. Then came December 7th, 1941. During the Pearl Harbor attack, James Nashoba was killed when a Japanese A6M2 Zero fighter machine-gunned the aircraft James, and others were trying to push away from a burning hanger. Like the rest of the country, young Josh wanted his revenge on the Japanese. He determined that he too, would join the Army Air Corps as soon as possible and avenge his uncle.

Then one Saturday afternoon in late October 1942, Josh Nashoba's life changed forever. He was sitting in the Ritz Theater in Talihina, Oklahoma. To celebrate his recent 18th birthday, he was waiting to watch the motion picture

"Flying Tigers." Josh was lucky to see one motion picture a year. He figured that watching John Wayne flying P-40s and clearing the skies of Japanese fighters would be his birthday present to himself. Then, to finish the birthday celebration, he'd walk down to the local recruiter and enlist in the Army. He wanted to become an aerial gunner like his uncle. Before the main feature played, there was a short eighteen-minute documentary about the Battle of Midway, directed by John Ford. Five minutes into the film, his heart began to race as Army B-17 bombers roared into the sky to attack the Japanese fleet.

Toward the end of the film, Josh found his true calling. Navy fighter pilots in their pugnacious Grumman F4F Wildcat fighters were shown landing on one of the carriers and climbing from the cockpits of their mounts following the battle. The film was shot in 16mm color. Color films were still a rare treat. The combination of khaki flight suits, blue-grey fighter planes, and the color of the sea overwhelmed young Josh's senses. Then he saw them; the red and white, rising sun flags decorating the sides of the aviators' aircraft; a small Japanese flag representing every Japanese plane shot down. *That's it, that's what I want, Josh thought to himself. I want to be a Navy fighter pilot. I want to fly those Wildcat fighters and cover my plane in those flags.*

The fire to avenge his uncle had more fuel now than ever before. Young Josh forgot about the Army. Immediately after the movie, he made his way to a Navy recruiting office and inquired as to how to become a naval fighter pilot. The recruiter was more interested in getting Josh to sign on the dotted line and enter straight into the Navy. "We need more sailors than pilots, kid," the crusty Chief told him. "Look here bub, sign up now, and I can get you trained as an aerial gunner. In a few months, you'll be in the Pacific with more Japs to shoot than you can shake a stick at."

But Josh was having none of it. The recruiter continued, telling Josh he'd need two years of college first, and even with that, he'd probably "wash out." At the mention of college, Josh's mind raced. After that, he ignored most of what the Navy Chief said. He looked at the recruiter and said, "I'm going to college. I'll be back in two years."

The recruiter smirked, "Yeah, right, kid. You probably can't even spell "airplane." If you don't let me get you signed up as a sailor right now, you'll be scooped up by the draft and land in the Army as an infantryman."

Josh looked at the recruiter with fire in his eyes. "I'll be back in two years," he said before turning and walking into the chilly afternoon air. Having saved every penny possible in his youth, Josh had enough money to get himself enrolled in basic science classes at Southeastern State College in Durant,

Oklahoma. Money was tight, so he rented a small room from a local Choctaw family and did odd jobs wherever he could, enabling him to stay in school and maintain his meager lifestyle. His luck was about to change for the better.

In early July of 1943, the US Navy instituted its V-12 program, which was designed to supplement the officer corps of both the Navy and Marine Corps to support the war. Josh took a qualifying exam and scored high enough to secure for himself a V-12 spot at the University of Oklahoma in Norman.

Many of his classmates grumbled at the workload, but the program was a dream come true for Josh. Along with attending classes, he was required to wear a uniform and report for drill and physical conditioning. To Josh, this was an exceedingly small price to pay for free education and $50 a month, plus the uniform. The military drill made him feel like he was already part of the Navy. He had found his path. He devoured his studies and kept a close eye on the war's progress. He specifically monitored the progress of the US Navy and Marine Corps in their campaign to liberate the Pacific. By July of 1944, he was reading article after article about the Battle of the Philippine Sea, where the US Navy and Japanese Navy carrier fleets squared off in a large battle. This was the first major aircraft carrier battle since 1942.

Gone were the old F4F Wildcats, which held the line for the Navy and Marine Corps during 1942. American carriers now operated the Grumman F6F Hellcat, the successor to their older Wildcat fighter. As for the Japanese Navy, their carrier units were still flying the A6M5 Zero fighter. Although improvements had been made over the old A6M2 models, they were no match for the Hellcat in speed, climb, armament, or toughness. The American fighters decimated the Japanese carrier-based fighters, dive bombers, and torpedo planes. This left the Japanese fleet wide open to attack from American dive bombers and torpedo planes which were also of a newer design. The battle was no contest.

The Americans enjoyed better equipment and better-trained aircrew. The Japanese could not keep pace with American industry. Additionally, Japan had lost most of her world-class naval combat pilots during the four big carrier battles of 1942. Their skill and experience had been second-to-none. Now, only a handful of those elite Imperial Japanese Navy pilots remained. Even if they could replace the equipment, they could never replace the men. Their training programs could not keep pace with that of their enemies. During the Battle of The Philippine Sea, the Japanese Navy lost three aircraft carriers and some 600 aircraft. The Americans had one battleship damaged and lost 123 aircraft. The battle was so one-sided that the American pilots nicknamed it "The Great Marianas Turkey Shoot."

In his last semester of the V-12 program, Josh read about the exploits of naval pilots. The Wildcat fighters of his fantasy were gone. The Japanese aircraft were no match for the new Grumman Hellcat fighters. If that wasn't bad enough, the Chance-Vought Corsair fighter, which had been in Marine Corps service for over a year, was starting to make its way onto Navy carriers. It promised more speed and capabilities than the Hellcat. Once finished with his current program, he'd still need to get through the additional ninety days of the V-7 program to get his commission before he could get to flight school. The war could be over by then, he worried. He decided to drop that thought and press on as if the war would last forever.

However, Josh did miss the war. He graduated from advanced flying school in August of 1945, mere days before two atom bombs convinced the cooler heads in the Japanese leadership that further pursuit of the war would be nothing more than national suicide. Now, as he looked at his Grumman Bearcat, he marveled at what this plane could have done during the war. Not only did it outclass the old Wildcats and Hellcats in a fight, it was more than a match for even the mighty Corsair. Like Josh, the Bearcat had barely missed the war. In fact, the carrier which was home to both him and his aircraft barely missed the war. The USS Philippine Sea launched in September 1945, a mere few days after the Japanese surrender. Me, my plane, and my ship were all a day late and a dollar short, he thought to himself.

He walked around the wing toward the fuselage of the dark sea blue Bearcat. He noticed the young, enlisted man who maintained his aircraft was busy applying tape to the white bars on either side of the star, which served as the national emblem on American military aircraft. The men who maintained the aircraft were called Plane Captains. They took as much pride in their aircraft as the pilots did. Greeting the young sailor, Josh barked playfully, "What the hell you doing to my baby, Sailor?"

The young sailor jumped in surprise and looked up at Josh, "You scared the hell outta' me, Sir!"

"Sorry, James, the boredom is killing me. Seriously though, what are you doing?"

"The order came down from Fleet. We're to paint a red stripe down the middle of the chevrons on the national insignia," the Plane Captain said, nodding toward the aircraft next to theirs, which already had the painted stripes completed.

"That looks pretty sharp, now we're showing red, white and blue, as it should be."

"If you say so, Sir," the young sailor replied, not enjoying the task of applying paint to what he considered a pristine aircraft.

"Other than the paint, is she ready to go?"

"Yes, Sir, I've pampered her for days, and as soon as they launch those airliners off the flight deck, we'll start running engines and get everything loosened up and ready to go."

"Good, James, good. Something is telling me, they'll be needed."

Looking up with curiosity, the young sailor said. "Really Sir? I mean I've heard there are Russian ships shadowing our task group. You think we'll have problems with the Russians?"

"I doubt it. From what I hear, they only have a couple of fishing boats tagging along. I don't know James; something feels off to me. I don't feel like we're getting the whole story on why we're down here poking around Antarctica."

Looking around the hangar deck, James said, "Well, all we have is the sixteen Bearcats of our squadron and six of those Marine night fighters, plus the four helicopters. We're not exactly manned and ready for a full-scale battle; so, I hope you are wrong Sir."

"I do too, James," Josh said as he walked away in the direction of his squadron's Ready Room.

## Wednesday, 23 November 2016, 7:00 AM CST, Talihina, OK

Addison Redstone was trying to be as quiet as possible as he moved through the kitchen, attempting to make himself a cup of coffee without waking his wife, Marsha. Addison, a notorious early riser, had slept past his usual 5:00 AM wakeup. Normally, he would rise early and drive to his ranch house. He enjoyed walking the property or doing needed repairs. He'd often target shoot or service one of his many rifles. Most of the time he spent there, he researched the Relics, as Sam called them. He'd review any and all sightings, reports, and information he could find on the internet. He'd often receive and exchange information with General Malcolm Henderson, whom he'd befriended two years ago during the Dark Autumn. The General had been quiet lately; Addison assumed it was because he'd been deployed. Addison managed to get himself a cup of coffee from the single cup coffee maker Marsha had in the kitchen. As much as he hated to admit it to himself, he liked the single-serve coffee maker much better than the usual full-pot maker he kept at the ranch. He'd scoffed at the coffee maker when he'd first moved into town with his new wife, *just another one of those girly things he'd have to get used to*, he thought to himself.

Addison was anxious to get to the ranch since his sighting of one of the creatures Saturday evening and the discovery of the two missing Arkansas boys on his property Sunday afternoon. He knew the relative peace of the past two years was coming to an end, and something was about to happen involving the Relics again. He also knew the 'something' would probably not be good. Addison was grateful the two boys had regained consciousness and were unharmed. Neither could recall how they came to be on Addison's property after disappearing from the scene of an accident in Gillham, Arkansas. As he looked at a map of the surrounding area, Addison thought to himself, *something is about to pop around here.* The return of the creatures, the strange man on his property, and the two missing teenagers ending up in the same spot had Addison on edge. Now, he wasn't sure what his next step should be. He had plotted the recent events on a map of the surrounding area. He was tempted to setup a kill zone on his property, as he had done two years ago near Crusher Hollow, when he, his son, Nathan Parks, and Daniel Greenwood had fought the creatures. *Evidently, your kill zone wasn't effective if they've returned,* Addison thought to himself as he quietly moved over to the kitchen table and logged into his email account on the laptop.

As his email loaded, he was excited to see he had a message from Nathan Parks, the young man who had assisted him and his son during the troubles they'd had back in 2014. Nathan had left the Arkansas National Guard and joined the regular Army, working under General Henderson's command. He was even more excited to see Nathan was on leave and headed to Talihina to visit. *Well, this is convenient timing.* Although thrilled to hear Nathan was on his way and bringing a guest, Addison wondered if it was too much of a coincidence. *Why is all this happening now?* Addison quickly typed a reply to Nathan's email, expressing his excitement about the upcoming visit. He desperately wanted to head to his ranch and see if there had been any other strange occurrences since Sunday, but he thought he'd stay close to home today. Marsha was worried about the recent activity, and tomorrow was Thanksgiving. Better to stay close and help Marsha prepare some of the food for tomorrow's planned celebration with Sam, Christa, and Christa's family. He'd been looking forward to the holiday and spending time with family and friends, but the recent events were beginning to worry him. His thoughts were interrupted by a quiet tapping at his front door. Looking out the dining room window, he could see a Talihina Police Department SUV parked in the driveway. Opening the door, Addison saw the face of Dale Thompkins, the Chief of Police.

"Good morning, Addison. I hope I didn't wake you. I need a minute of your time."

Addison stepped onto the porch, quietly closing the door behind him. "Sure, Dale. Marsha is still sleeping, so if you don't mind, we'll talk here on the porch."

"That's fine, Sir. I was going to talk to Sam about this, but I know he's been a bit edgy about the subject, and who can blame him?"

"What's going on Dale?" Addison asked.

"I'm just going to get to the point. Last night, at roughly 10:25, Jimmy Chula was sitting in the Dollar General parking lot, monitoring traffic. A couple from Honobia pulled in with their vehicle all beat to hell. They said they'd been attacked by a Sasquatch while crossing the Honobia bridge."

"The old iron truss bridge on Indian Highway that goes across the point where Honobia Creek runs into the Little River?" Addison asked.

"Yes, Sir, that's the one. They claim the thing jumped on the hood of their car and as they tried to escape, it ran behind them banging on the trunk. The car is drivable but pretty beat up; they were scared to death and stayed at the police station last night. We let them sleep on the foldout bed in the break room. I wanted to get Sam to talk to them, but the more I thought about it, I realized you'd probably be the best one to speak with them."

"Dale, you've been as up close and personal with them as anybody. Why do you need me?"

"Addison, the wife was so frightened by what they'd been through, the last thing I wanted to do was make things worse by telling them how one tried to drag me out of my truck a couple of years ago. You and Sam are pretty much the experts, and I figured if anybody could help them, it would be one of the Redstone's."

Addison nodded his head and said, "Okay, where are they now, and what do you want me to tell them?"

"They went home as soon as it got light this morning. The man's name is Jim Vaughn; I think you'll want to talk to him. Especially, since we're starting to have strange occurrences around here again. Here's the thing though, his wife does not want you to come to their house. She's afraid that even talking about the subject in their home will cause more trouble. The man was wondering if you'd be willing to meet and talk with him at the Honobia Creek Store."

Addison sighed deeply, I don't need other people's problems on top of what I already have, he thought. "I suppose I could go talk to the man. I have no idea what I can do for him though. Do you have his number?"

"Yes, I do," Dale said, handing Addison a card with a cell phone number on it. "Oh, and Addison, there's something else... They claim a UFO was involved when they were in contact with the creature. After they fled the scene, they were followed by a smaller type of UFO as they were going up the mountain. After a bit it sped away... Then they claimed to have seen some sort of apparition on the side of the road." Addison took the card from Dale and promised he would contact the man and try to meet him at some point that morning. Dale thanked Addison and climbed back into the SUV. As Addison went back into the house, he felt as though he was being summoned or challenged. *Honobia, why Honobia?*

The small community was known for its annual Bigfoot Festival, which took place every October, but there had not been any significant reports of activity around there for years. In fact, most people, including the locals, looked at the festival as harmless fun and a nice moneymaker for the small community. *Oh well, it won't take long. It's only a short drive over the mountains Southeast of here*, Addison thought. Southeast? Suddenly a light came on in Addison's mind, *The arrow is pointing Southeast!* Recalling the arrow made up of fifteen stones he had found on his property, Addison took out a map he had of the local area, which he'd used to keep track of sightings and the events from two years ago. He'd also plotted his recent sighting, as well as the spot where the two boys were found and the location of the arrow. He'd assumed the arrow had something to do with his enemy's location, but he had not actually run a plot of the direction. The arrow was pointing Southeast at a compass heading of 150 degrees. Addison grabbed a protractor he kept in a desk drawer in the small office at the house. Quickly, he drew a straight line from the location of his house at 150 degrees. The line intersected perfectly with the Honobia Bridge.

Addison couldn't believe it, he replotted the course twice more, and both times 150 degrees from the spot of the rock arrow on his property intersected perfectly with the bridge in Honobia. His mind was racing, trying to think of anything else he may have failed to put together. *Fifteen rocks, why fifteen? Could each rock represent a mile*, he wondered as he measured the distance between the arrow on his land and the bridge's location in Honobia. The measurement was roughly seventeen and a quarter miles. A little disappointed, Addison again plotted his map to discover exactly where the fifteen-mile mark was. The spot on the map rested on a flat area at the bank of Honobia Creek named "Dead Man's Hollow." So much for good news, Addison thought grimly, remembering the ordeal at Crusher Hollow two years earlier. *Bad places have bad names for a reason*, he thought as he picked up his cell phone to call Jim Vaughn in Honobia.

# CHAPTER FOUR

# Convergence

*"There are no coincidences in the universe, only convergences of Will, Intent, and Experience."*
*~Neale Donald Walsh*

**Wednesday, 30 January 1947, 4:00 PM Local, USS Philippine Sea, 320 miles off Antarctica**

Josh Nashoba was once again lurking on Vulture's Row aboard the Philippine Sea. Earlier in the afternoon, the carrier had launched the remaining aircraft of Admiral Byrd's mission to Antarctica. The weather had been beautiful most of the day. The temperature had been a balmy 45 degrees, with an unusual sea temperature of 49 degrees. As the last of the Douglas transports had lifted off, two of the HO3S-1 helicopters had been spotted on the flight deck and launched. As the strange-looking aircraft had buzzed around other ships in the fleet, Josh watched as one landed on the USS Pine Island as deftly as a fly landing on a sandwich. Then it was up again and making its way back toward the carrier.

Looking down at the flight deck, Josh's pulse quickened. There sat his aircraft number 202 along with seven other Bearcats. The Air Boss had decided his aviators had been idle long enough. The plan was to put up two of the Marine Tigercat's and eight Bearcats from Josh's squadron. They were to do some proper Combat Air Patrol practice and stretch their wings a bit. Four figures caught Josh's attention. It was the Marine Corps aircrew walking to their aircraft. They will be launching first this afternoon. He couldn't help but smile as he watched his friend, Jack Fossier strut toward his F7F. The young Marine looked up at Vulture's Row and spotted Josh. Yelling loudly, he said, "Well, look who the boss wants in the air first, Rust Picker!"

Smiling, Josh yelled back, "Ladies first!"

"You know better than that, Rust Picker. The cream always rises to the top," Jack countered.

"So do turds!" Josh yelled back, receiving guffaws of approval from his Navy squadron mates. At a loss for a comeback, Jack smiled, made the universal finger gesture of disapproval, and moved to his aircraft. Josh watched his friend perform his preflight checks and climb into the cockpit. Within minutes, Jack started the first of his two engines. The Pratt and Whitney R-2800 Double Wasp engine on the aircraft's left wing made its high-pitched whirring sound as the starter began bringing the big, radial engine to life. The prop spun slowly, making six complete rotations. When the engine came to life, there was a puff of blue smoke and a bang.

The noise changed from the high-pitched whirr to a loud, clunking noise, which made one think the aircraft was coming apart. Josh knew better since his own aircraft used the same engine. *Wake that big cat up,* Josh willed his friend silently. For all the kidding between the two friends, both their aircraft were made by Grumman, and both had a proud heritage. Like their predecessors, the F4F Wildcat and F6F Hellcat, they were bestowed with predatory cat names. The other Marine Tigercat also had its left engine running, and both pilots began starting their right engines. As this was happening, the carrier began a left turn, bringing the bow around to the east. Once settled on course, the captain of the big ship ordered her speed to 28 knots. This, along with the wind coming across the ship's bow, would assist the Marine Tigercat's on their takeoff runs.

Josh could feel the big ship's speed increasing and watched as his friend went through his final checks. He could tell Jack and the young, Marine radar operator in the rear cockpit was completing equipment checks of some type. *It probably has something to do with their radar. Man, am I glad I don't have to carry a passenger;* Josh thanked his lucky stars. The deckhands were making final checks of both aircraft. Josh watched as Jack tightened his harness straps and waited patiently to launch. Jack looked up at Vulture's Row to Josh. Seeing this, Josh stood at attention and saluted his friend. Jack smiled, returned the salute, and gave Josh a thumbs up. Jack was second to takeoff. The big F7F Tigercat rolled down the flight deck and for a moment disappeared under the bow of the ship before clawing its way for altitude and making a right turn to the south. Thirty seconds later, Jack's plane rolled down the deck, and unlike the first Tigercat, his aircraft lifted from the deck and climbed smoothly away with at least thirty feet of deck to spare before banking left and heading north.

*You got the touch, ole buddy,* Josh thought, admiring his friend's takeoff. Both aircraft continued to climb, heading in opposite directions. *Probably going to play tag with their radars.* Josh was making a mental note of which direction his friend went. He knew he and his squadron mates would probably make practice intercepts on the Marines, as their flight was scheduled to be airborne in a little over an hour. The last thing he wanted was for Jack to get a jump on him. If that happened, he knew he'd never hear the end of it. Looking at his watch, Josh noted he was due for his mission briefing in about ten minutes and started making his way down to his squadron's Ready Room. It took Josh about eight minutes to navigate his way through the big ship to the VF-10A Squadron Ready Room. He entered and saw the "Skipper" or Squadron Commander. Lieutenant Commander Richard Brandt was standing casually behind the podium, chatting with some of the other pilots. The front of the podium was decorated with the VF-10A Squadron Crest; a large, red gun site with a blue devil face behind it, taking aim through the crosshairs; the words BE-DEVILERS underneath.

"Ah, Nashoba, I was about to get worried about you," he said, looking at his wristwatch.

"He's got a girlfriend in the Marine F7 squadron he had to see off," teased one of the other junior pilots sitting a few feet away. This brought laughter from the other pilots in the Ready Room.

"Hey, when you've got it, you've got it," Josh said, bringing more hoots and laughter.

"Okay, let's get down to business, you guys have been sitting on your sorry asses long enough." Lt Cmdr. Brandt said, quieting the room. Brandt was one of three seasoned combat pilots in the squadron. He was also the squadron's only Ace, having achieved twelve aerial victories during the war. Brandt had participated in the Marianas Turkey Shoot in 1944, where he was credited with four kills, three Japanese Navy A6M5 Zero fighters as well as a Japanese Navy D4Y dive bomber. A year later, off the coast of Okinawa, he added seven more kills while defending the fleet from Kamikaze attacks. His twelfth and final victory came in late July 1945 while escorting dive bombers off the coast of Japan. He and his flight of four were jumped by six Japanese Army Ki-84 fighters. In a protracted and exhausting fight, Brandt lost two of his flight before he was able to down one of the Japanese Army fighters. He and his wingman were still facing five of the Ki-84s when they abruptly broke off the fight and headed inland.

Brandt learned an important lesson that day. Never underestimate your enemy. He and his other squadron mates had gotten comfortable shooting down novice, kamikaze pilots who usually flew older planes with no offensive armament. The skill and finesse of the Japanese Army fighter pilots flying the excellent KI-84 fighter came as a rude awakening. Brandt never knew why they broke off and left the fight. He had always assumed it was a lack of fuel or ammo. Whatever the reason, he'd always felt lucky he made it home from that mission. It was the last time he saw enemy aircraft during the war, which ended the following month. The fight made a lasting impression on him.

Brandt brought up a map of Antarctica and the surrounding ocean. "Here is our location approximately three hundred miles North of Admiral Byrd's camp, Little America IV. As you can see, it's South of the Bay of Whales. There should be no reason for us to be flying anywhere near the coast. However, if something happens and you cannot locate the fleet, you should have enough fuel to make it to the airstrip adjacent to Little America IV. The purpose of this mission is basically to stretch our wings after being grounded for so long, and to sharpen our Combat Air Patrol tactics. The two Marine aircraft will be acting as the enemy, attempting to penetrate the fleet defenses and make a mock attack on our carrier. Our ship's radar and Combat Information Center, (CIC) will be giving us intercept vectors to the F7s. Remember, those F7s have their own radar, and they will probably see us with their gear long before we see them with our eyes. They'll be able to counter our moves as soon as we make them. Okay, listen up for your flight assignments. I'll be leading Blue Flight. Nashoba, you'll be flying number two on my wing. Fowler and Henson will be numbers three and four. Lieutenant Austin will be leading Gold Flight…"

Brandt was interrupted by the buzz of the Ready Room phone, which was connected straight to the ship's (CIC). Picking up the phone, he answered, "Lt Cmdr. Brandt." Nashoba watched as a puzzled look came over the Skipper's face. "Be right up." Hanging up the phone, Brandt looked at the Gold Flight Leader, saying, "Austin, finish up the briefing, I'll be right back." Then, looking at the other pilots, "There may be a change in our mission profile boys. Be ready for anything. In the meantime, listen to Lt Austin and make sure you're ready to go."

## Wednesday, 30 January 1947, 4:50, PM USS Philippine Sea CIC, 295 miles off Antarctica

Lt Cmdr. Brandt entered the darkened room. Blinking and trying to force his eyes to adjust to the darkness, he could see sailors busily plotting on various illuminated Plexiglas maps. One plot showed the positions of ships in the task force relative to the USS Philippine Sea, which was the center of the plot. Another showed the positions of aircraft. This map also portrayed the carrier in the center and the air contacts respective to their position from the carrier. There was a third and larger plot at one end of the room, which displayed the coastline of Antarctica as well as positions of all known ships and aircraft. Everything on this plot was centered on Admiral Byrd's base, Camp America IV.

"Over here, Dick," came the familiar voice of Commander Mitchell Saunders, the man in charge of all the aerial operations. His title of Commander Air Group was commonly referred to as CAG. Nothing flew off the deck of the USS Philippine Sea without his approval. For this cruise, his job should have been easy, as they only had a token force of aircraft onboard to facilitate the needs of Admiral Byrd's Antarctic mission. Brandt could see some concern in Saunders' face as he approached his boss. "Dick, we've got something strange happening to our South. Earlier this morning, around eleven hundred, Admiral Byrd flew out from Camp America, heading South. This wasn't a planned flight to the South Pole; it was only the ole man taking in the sights and doing a little recon. The folks at Little America said they started getting some strange radio transmissions from the Admiral."

"Strange as in what, Sir?"

"The Admiral started reporting green trees and grass as they moved south. At one point, they reported their aircraft wasn't responding to their control input. They stated they had visitors and were being escorted. Immediately after that, everything went quiet. Admiral Cruzen is ordering the Task Force to move toward the coastline. He's trying to give our radar operators more room to work. He even dispatched the destroyer, Brownson, closer to the coast to determine what she can get on her radar. She was roughly 30 miles to our South and steaming at flank speed toward the Antarctic coast. Eighteen minutes ago, they reported faint, aerial radar contacts moving their direction. Ten minutes ago, they reported their vessel had been buzzed by unknown aircraft types traveling at tremendous speeds. The seaplane tender Currituck is about halfway between us and the Brownson. She had deployed one of her PBM-5 seaplanes, which is airborne now, heading toward the Brownson. Both vessels have been ordered to reverse course and rejoin the fleet."

"Dick, I don't have the assets to fight a battle. We've got your sixteen fighters, the six Marine night fighters and that's it. We have no offensive forces. I need somebody out there with some damn combat experience and a cool head to tell me what's happening. Is there really a threat, or do we just have some nervous, new sailors looking at seagulls and seeing aircraft? I've ordered both Marine F7s to stop what they're doing and head south. I need you to get yourself and your flight airborne and get your butts down there as well."

75

"Yes, Sir," Brandt replied.

"What about the pilots assigned for this flight?" Saunders asked.

"I've got Austin flying lead in Gold flight, both of us are dragging youngsters but they're all tigers, Sir."

"They'd better be, it looks like they may have to grow up quickly today."

"Sir, I should bring Torrez, my executive officer, up to speed in case we need another flight ready."

"I sent a runner to him just before you came in, Dick. I told him to make sure the rest of your guys were geared up and ready to go. Maintenance is ready to spot your other eight birds as soon as you clear the deck."

Just then, a sailor operating the surface-to-air radio interrupted. "Sir, I've got Major Vaughn, the Marine Flight Lead, on the radio wanting to speak with you."

"Put it on the speaker, Son," Saunders said.

Saunders picked up a microphone and said, "Nighthawk, this is Panhandle, go ahead Major."

"Roger that. Sir, my radar operator picked up multiple bogies two minutes ago. They just blew past us giving me a visual."

"Okay Major, what are we dealing with?"

"Foo Fighters, Sir." The words of the Marine pilot caught Saunders off guard. Foo Fighter was a term used to describe mysterious aircraft or aerial phenomena during the war. They were often described as nothing more than balls of light; occasionally, they were reported to be solid craft of strange shape and unusual performance. Often, they were reported to easily outperform the most advanced Allied aircraft. The phenomena were witnessed by both Allied and Axis pilots over the Pacific and the European continent. Allied pilots assumed they were Japanese or German secret weapons. When the war ended, it came as a surprise that German and Japanese aircrew reported the same type of craft, assuming them to be of Allied origin.

"Foo Fighters? I got no time for games, Major. What did you see?"

"Sir, it was a flight of four aircraft, in a finger four formation, traveling at incredible speed. I've never seen aircraft move so fast. They were shaped like boomerangs for lack of a better description, Sir."

"Are you still in contact, Major?"

"Not visual, Sir; but my radar operator still has a fix on them. They are moving South now, Sir."

"Roger Major; maintain your position. We are ordering the other F-7 to head your way and we're launching you more help. Keep me posted on any further contact."

"Roger, Panhandle. Nighthawk out."

Turning to Brandt, Saunders said, "Dick, get your guys up, and see if you can figure out what the hell is going on." Then he picked up the public address microphone and, in a booming voice which blasted throughout the ship, said, "ATTENTION THIS IS CAG. ALL PILOTS MAN YOUR PLANES. REPEAT, ALL PILOTS MAN YOUR PLANES." Josh had been sitting nervously, awaiting the return of the Skipper, when the Man Your Planes order came over the loudspeaker. There was a second of hesitation as the pilots all looked around at each other, a bit confused.

Lieutenant Austin had heard this message during the war, and even though it had been a couple of years, he instinctively leaped into action. "Move it, Greenhorns. You heard the man," he shouted as the pilots bolted from their seats, heading toward the Ready Room door.

"Nashoba!" Austin shouted. Turning, Josh barely had time to raise his hands up before the Skipper's flight helmet, and Mae West life jacket landed in his arms. "The Skipper will meet us on deck, and he'll be needing these," Austin said, matter-of-factly. The men quickly made their way up to the hatchway, which led out onto the flight deck. Lt Cmdr. Brandt was waiting there. Josh handed him his gear.

"Thanks. Okay, listen up guys. I don't have time to give you details. Things have changed. We may very well have company up there. I don't know who, and I don't know what they may be flying. Be ready for anything. I want both flight and radio discipline. If you see something, anything, tell me, then shut up and listen for my instructions. Understood?"

The other seven aviators shouted, "Aye, Aye, Sir!" in almost perfect unison.

Brandt couldn't help but let the slightest of smiles cross his face. "We're going minimal warm-up on the engines, boys. I want to launch eight minutes after startup. Okay, guys, let's go see who's messing around in our sky today."

As Josh ran out onto the flight deck, his mind was racing. *Eight-minute warm-up, in this weather? Something big must be going on*, he thought to himself. In this climate, he knew they should be doing a twelve-minute warm-up at a minimum, and fifteen would make him feel better. Suddenly, the air felt much colder, and the sea looked more frigid to him. He spotted his aircraft, with its white block 202 on the fuselage side standing in stark contrast to its overall dark sea blue paint. His bird was spotted immediately aft and off the left wing of the Skipper's aircraft number 210. All the squadron's aircraft were numbered 200 through 216, and all had a large white PS painted on the tail. Josh was quick to get strapped in and go through his engine start procedures. He checked both his watch and engine temperature gauges intently while waiting for the Pratt and Whitney to reach the minimum cylinder head temperature of 130 degrees C and the minimum oil temperature of 40 degrees C. *Come on, baby, wake up*, he urged his aircraft. He looked up and saw one of the Marine F7F Tigercat's, which had launched earlier, fly high over the carrier heading south. *Probably Jack. If he beats me to the action, I'll never live it down.*

Josh still wasn't sure if there would be any action. In fact, he had no clue as to what was happening. He knew that he was capable of following orders and had complete confidence in his ability to fly and fight in his F8F Bearcat. *I know all I need to know*, he reassured himself as he reviewed the Deck Launch Checklist, Canopy Open, Shoulder Harness Tight, Flaps Down, Control Tabs Set. He reminded himself to use the full 60 inches of engine manifold pressure for takeoff from the deck. As he looked over at the Skipper's Bearcat, he noticed the twelve miniature Japanese Rising Sun Flags below the cockpit. They represented the twelve aerial victories Brandt had achieved against the Japanese during the war. The Navy still allowed Squadron Commanders to decorate their aircraft with the victory symbols from the war. Brandt called them his "scalps." Not being sure if the current level of excitement was real or perhaps a drill, his mind drifted for a moment, and he wondered whether or not he'd get any scalps today. Then just as quickly, he thought, *Better make sure I don't end up as a scalp on some other guy's plane.* His thought process came back to the task at hand, and he watched as the Skipper's aircraft began to move forward slowly. Brandt followed the hand signals of the deck handler, who was positioning him for takeoff.

*Okay, I'm next, time to shine*, Josh thought in anticipation of his own launch. One of the deckhands ran to Josh's plane, holding up a chalkboard with the ship's magnetic heading provided by the air boss. Josh quickly began jotting the heading down on the kneeboard attached to his right leg. There was a loud roar as the Skipper brought his engine up to takeoff power. As quickly as he had the ship's heading written on his kneeboard, the Skipper's Bearcat roared down the deck and lifted lightly into the sky. It was now Josh's turn. The yellow-clad sailor began giving Josh exaggerated hand signals to position his aircraft correctly for his takeoff run. As he slowly taxied forward following the sailor's signals, Josh was also attempting to secure his pencil and kneeboard. *If they give me one more thing to do, I'm going to need a secretary; maybe Jack has the right idea flying that Tigercat.*

## Wednesday, 23 November 2016, 10:20 AM CST, Indian Highway, 2 miles North of Honobia, OK

Though only a short distance, the drive from Talihina to Honobia was a bit stressful if you were not accustomed to making the trip. The second half of the trip was twelve miles of twisting mountain roads. The fall colors were still present for the most part, and much to Addison's surprise, the normally subdued Sam remarked about their beauty a couple of times. "I'm glad you made the trip Sam. I really wasn't expecting you to."

"I guess I'm getting to the point where I've realized the only way we're going to getting rid of this curse is to face it head on," Sam replied.

"I'm not sure it's a curse, Son, but it is a problem that we're being forced to deal with," Addison said as he negotiated a sharp, left curve in the road. Then looking to his right, he noticed a small overlook that gave him a quick view revealing the small community of Honobia below. "I've always liked this area, probably should have bought some land up here years ago."

"Yeah, this seems like a place where you can get lost from the all the madness and enjoy a simple life. Well at least until a Sasquatch decides to chase you all the way to Talihina. I haven't heard of much going on up here, but they do have the Bigfoot Festival every year. Do you think with all we've got going on, it's wise of us to stick our noses into whatever is happening up here?" Sam asked.

"Well, we're about to find out," Addison replied as the road leveled into a straight line through the tiny community. One of the first things they noticed was a blue road sign which read, 'INDIAN HIGHWAY HOME OF BIGFOOT.' "Looks like they're cutting into our business Sam," Addison said, laughing.

"They can have my share; I'll give it to them for free," Sam replied.

After passing an area of thick trees, the Honobia Creek Store came into view on their left. "Not much to it," Sam said, as his father slowed and turned into the nearly empty, gravel parking lot. There was a late model Toyota Camry parked in the lot. As Addison pulled up next to it, a middle-aged man exited the vehicle and stood next to it. "Are you Mr. Redstone?" he asked as Addison and Sam exited Addison's truck.

"Yes, Sir, I am. Please, call me Addison; and this is my son, Sam," Addison said, offering his hand.

"Jim Vaughn, it's nice of you to come up here." After shaking hands, Addison and Sam walked around the Camry. The hood was caved in as well as the trunk lid on the back of the car. Other than that, the car appeared normal and well-maintained.

"I take it, you didn't hit a deer?" Addison said with a grin.

"No, Sir, that would have been much easier on both me and my wife."

Addison pointed to the storefront. A large, sheet metal Sasquatch adorned one of the poles, which served as a support for the porch. Looking at Jim, Addison half chuckled, "A little more intimidating in real life, aren't they?" Jim nodded. "I know it's still early, but we're a bit hungry and could use a bite to eat. I hear the food's good here. Maybe you could go over what happened while we eat?" Addison asked.

"Good idea, Addison. Come to think of it, I haven't eaten anything all day myself. I've been going on coffee all night and morning and have a bad case of the jitters," Jim agreed. As the men entered the store, both Addison and Sam noticed it was similar to a lot of small-town stores in Southeast Oklahoma; there were a couple of aisles with basic needs; bread, canned meat, pastries, cake and pancake mixes, chips, candies, jerky, soft drinks along with hygiene and toiletries. There were also basic hardware items, duct, and electrical tape, fuses, glue, tire sealant, and a few basic tools. On the other side of the aisles were six long folding tables that were used for dining. Addison noticed an elderly man at the far corner table, who had his back to them. The man was quietly eating alone. Two ladies behind the counter greeted them cheerfully, both mentioning Jim by name. Both Redstone's took in all the Bigfoot merchandise for sale in the small store as they sat down. The place was full of Bigfoot stuffed animals, coffee cups, tee-shirts, caps, and even books.

"I guess you can't help but see Bigfoot when you come here," Sam said, jokingly.

"Yeah, I guess we should not have been surprised," Jim said, somewhat embarrassed.

Addison was mildly shocked but proud of his son's response. "It's okay, Sir. We've seen them up close and personal, too. We know how you feel. When it happens to you, all of this harmless fun goes out the window. You're scared for your life, and you wonder how anybody thinks this is a joke. We understand, Jim; all too well." After that, the three men quietly looked at their menus. After a few moments, one of the ladies came around from behind the counter to take their order, "You guys ready to order?" she asked cheerfully.

Sam had noticed the Bigfoot Burger on the menu, "Is your Bigfoot Burger shaped like a foot?" The woman laughed, "No it's not shaped like a foot, but we do make it out of real Bigfoot meat," she said with a wink.

Addison spoke up, "Well you better give me one of those! Better to eat Bigfoot than to have Bigfoot eat you." The group got a laugh at Addison's joke. After getting their order, the lady went back behind the counter to the grill and began preparing the food. "So, Jim, go ahead and tell us what happened to you last night."

Jim quietly related the events of the previous evening. As he told his story, beginning with the initial sighting and progressing through his story, both Addison and Sam could see the fear in him. "Well, what do you think? Are my wife and I crazy?" Jim asked.

"No, you're fortunate you got out of the situation with only a beat-up car. I know your wife doesn't want us coming to your home and that is understandable, but where do you live exactly?" Addison asked.

"As you came into town, you probably passed within a hundred yards of my house. We live on Cline Road, about a half-mile from here. The damn thing chased us past this very store and almost all the way to where you start climbing up the mountain. That's why we drove all the way to Talihina," Jim said, visibly upset from having to relive the encounter. As I told you before, we've had some similar encounters, even UFO activity, when we were near these things once. What did the big UFOs look like exactly? Was it a sphere, a triangle, or a group of lights clustered together?" Sam asked Jim. As Jim related the UFO portion of his story again, Addison noticed the elderly man in the corner had finished his meal and was slowly making his way to the counter to pay for his food. As the man neared the table where the three men sat talking, he stopped.

"The first one was a huge triangle, it completely blocked out the moon and some of the stars. The one that paced us on the road was smaller but still bigger than my car. It was shaped cylindrical, like a propane tank you see around people's houses out here. Another weird thing, before I jumped back in the car I glanced up and the triangle had changed to a glowing ring of light…"

"Triangle?" Sam asked, remembering his sighting of such a craft on the night he and his father, along with Nathan Parks, had their own battle with the Relics at Crusher Hollow back in 2014. Jim began to elaborate on the UFO when suddenly he cut off in mid-sentence, and a look of fear came over his face as he looked behind Sam. Addison turned to see the elderly man standing behind his son. Looking the man in the face, Addison could tell he was Choctaw. He didn't look old - he looked ancient. The man stared at Jim for a moment, then turned his attention to Addison.

"I knew your father." Then turning his attention back to Jim, he said, "You're in no danger. They got what they wanted out of you. So, you can relax and get on with your life."

Addison could see Jim was terrified as the man turned and walked toward the door, stopping for a moment to lay some money at the cash register. "Excuse me, what do you mean they got what they wanted out of me? What did they want, and who is they?" Jim asked. The man opened the door halfway and turned, looking back at the three men,

"They don't want you," he said to Jim, then nodding in the direction of Addison and Sam, he said, "They want those two."

"You say you knew my father? How did you know him?" Addison asked. The man looked at Addison for a moment; the slightest hint of a smile came across his face.

"You Redstone's need to be careful. I know all about what happened in Talihina. Things are a bit different up here, these people were terrorized for one purpose," he said, nodding toward Jim Vaughn.

"What purpose is that?" Addison asked. "

To draw you two and one other here?" Becoming slightly irritated by the man's vagueness, Addison continued,

"Well so far the plan seems to be working because here we sit, so who is the other?"

"Your other comrade is already on his way; he will join you soon enough."

Then the man eased quietly out the door and was gone." He's referring to Nathan, Addison thought. How could he know? A cold chill came over Addison as he considered his own question.

Curious, Sam rose from the table and rushed to the door ·to see what direction the man went. When he got to the door, the man was nowhere to be seen. Almost as if he'd vanished into thin air. Returning to the table, he looked at his father and said, "He knows the same trick you do, in fact he may be a little better at it."

Addison was confused; he looked at his son and then turned to Jim. "Do you know him? Why did you look so scared when you saw him?"

Jim still appeared pale from the encounter. "He's the man we saw on the mountain last night as we were running from the Sasquatch and the light. He looked like a ghost or a phantom, or something... He still looks like one if you ask me." Jim replied, shuddering. The two ladies appeared at the table with the food the men had ordered. After everyone had their plate in front of them, Jim asked one of the ladies, "Kim, do you know that man who just left?"

"Yeah, that was Josh Nashoba. He lives alone up in the mountains. He's pretty much a hermit and keeps to himself. I've heard he has some strange ideas, and some people are scared of him. In fact, a few of the people around here refer to him as 'The Mad Footer', because of his wild, Bigfoot tales. I think he's harmless though. He comes down once or twice a month for a burger, and that's the only time I ever see him. He's always quiet and polite and even though his order is less than ten dollars, he always leaves a twenty and doesn't ask for change."

"He said he knew my father, I'm wondering how. My father was a veteran, and I'm wondering if that is where he knew him from?" Addison ventured.

Kim looked over behind the counter to where the other lady had returned to chopping vegetables, "Sarah, is Josh a veteran?"

"Yes, he was a pilot in the Navy. He got into trouble of some kind late in his career and was forced to retire. My son Levi is an airplane nut. He says Josh shot down a couple of Migs during Korea and Vietnam. Levi had read about him in a couple of aviation magazines but had never met him. I remember a few years ago Josh came in while Levi was here, and he was very excited to finally meet him. He sat and talked to him for a while. After Josh had left, I asked him if he got to hear the story about shooting down Migs. My son told me that Josh said the Migs were easy. He said he had shot down a couple of scarier things than Migs."

## Wednesday, 30 January 1947, 6:10 PM, 15,000 feet above the Antarctic Ocean

Josh checked his position off the Skipper's right wing for a moment, then went back to scanning the surrounding sky. His fighter's big Pratt and Whitney engine was purring like a cat. The quick warm-up and launch earlier had paid off. The Skipper had gotten them on station just South and 15,000 feet above the USS Currituck in good time. The second flight of Bearcats, led by Lieutenant Austin, was operating out-of-sight some fifteen miles to their West. The two Marine F7F Tigercat's were operating ten miles to his flight's South with a five-mile spread between them. The Marines were hoping to use their airborne radar to detect any of the strange aircraft which they had encountered earlier. There was also the large Martin PBM-5 seaplane with a crew of seven operating directly south of his flight, hoping to get a visual on any aerial intruders.

"Panhandle, this is Nighthawk Two." Josh recognized his friend Jack's voice over the radio as his friend alerted the carrier to the potential threat. "We've got bogies to our South; they look to have an altitude of Angels Ten. They're moving north. We show them five miles out and closing fast." *Well, we've got an altitude advantage on them at least,* Josh thought. The voice of the CAG responded to Jack's warning.

"Roger that, Nighthawk Two, maintain contact, advise on any changes. Blue Flight, this is Panhandle, adjust your heading to one six zero degrees, maintain current altitude and be alert."

*Okay, here we go, they're putting us on an intercept,* Josh thought, his heart racing. "Copy, Panhandle, Blue Flight, changing course," Lt Cmdr. Brandt replied. "Okay, boys, let's bring it right to one six zero...NOW!" Brandt instructed his flight. The four dark blue Bearcats maintained perfect formation as they made the course correction. Josh knew the other two aviators in formation were probably as nervous as he was. Yet nobody bungled the flawless course correction. "Good job, boys, keep your eyes peeled," Brandt said, maintaining a calm, soothing voice.

"Gooney, this is Panhandle, correct your course to three five degrees and expedite." Josh surmised that the boss wanted the lumbering seaplane out of the way now that there were confirmed strangers in the area.

"Nighthawk, this is Panhandle. We have radar contact on your bogies now. Turn north to zero zero five degrees. Contact Blue Flight and assist if necessary."

"Roger, Panhandle."

"Gooney, this is Panhandle, make your angels minus one and expedite."

"Roger, Panhandle," replied the big seaplane.

"Nighthawk Two, this is Panhandle. We lost our radar contact. Suspect they dropped in altitude. Keep your eyes peeled."

"Roger, Panhandle."

Josh checked his position once again off the Skipper's wing, thinking, Man, I need more room, so I can look around. As if reading his mind, the Skipper's voice came over the radio. "Blue Flight, spread...NOW!" The flight was ordered into a Combat Spread formation. Josh instinctively broke right, giving himself a half-mile distance from the Skipper. Blue Three and Four broke high, climbing to an altitude of fifteen hundred feet over Brandt and Nashoba. Blue

Three positioned himself at the high six o'clock position over Brandt. Blue Four identically positioned himself above Josh.

The formation freed each pilot to scan the surrounding area more efficiently while still keeping an eye on their wingman. Josh began looking in earnest for other aircraft. Suddenly, he spotted movement low on the water. Pushing the microphone button, he excitedly said, "Tally Ho! Bogey at two o'clock low." Josh made the radio call he had wanted to make for years and regretted it as soon as it left his mouth. His sighting was nothing more than the lumbering Martin seaplane.

"Copy, Two. I see it. Confirm, Gooney is moving through your low two o'clock. Good eyes, keep it up." What Josh thought might be a mistake that annoyed the Skipper was actually a positive. It showed that he was focused and on alert. Josh continued to scan low to the gray-blue water, looking for any sign of the intruders.

A moment later, he heard Jack's voice over the radio, "TALLY HO! Blue Lead, you've got four on the deck, closing fast on Gooney."

"Copy, Nighthawk. I've got a visual on Gooney. Blue Flight, come left to 100 degrees…GO GUNS HOT but fingers off the triggers. Let's be ready, but don't get carried away. Okay, Tally Ho, Blue Flight, I've got four at one o'clock, low about three miles, closing fast. Bringing it down to Angels Eight, Blue Flight."

Josh followed orders and eased the nose of his Bearcat down to drop his altitude to eight thousand feet. At the same time, he banked slightly to the left, cutting the distance between himself and the Skipper. As he descended, Josh double-checked that his guns were set to "ARMED," and his Auxiliary Fuel Pump was selected to "ON" in anticipation of maneuvering against the mysterious craft. He also glanced at the fuel quantity gauge to confirm there was sufficient fuel remaining in his centerline drop tank, making a mental note to monitor his fuel and switch over to the main internal fuselage tank fairly soon. He didn't want to allow the excitement and adrenaline flow to result in his making a fatal mistake. Within seconds, he was positioned where he felt he could clear any threats off the Skipper's tail. Looking back toward the direction the threats were reported, his heart jumped. *There they are!* He saw four bluish-silver, crescent-shaped aircraft closing on the PBM-5. They were in a standard Finger Four formation which had been adopted by air forces of almost every nation. Keying his microphone, he let his leader know he had a visual on the intruders and was in position to cover him. "TWO, TALLY 4, SADDLED UP!" His heart was pounding in his chest.

"Roger, Two, stay with me. We're about to ask these ladies to dance. Let's take it down a bit more Two. Blue Three and Four hold at Angel's Eight. Cover us and keep your fingers off the triggers unless I tell you different."

Josh replied to the Skipper with a "Roger," as did Blue Three and Four. Josh's initial excitement had passed abruptly. A strange calm came over him as he realized the four odd aircraft had made a tactical error. They had given the Navy Bearcats the advantage of the high ground and Lt Cmdr. Brandt had positioned his four fighters perfectly to make the most of the intruder's error. Josh had a second to admire the leadership and combat experience of the Skipper. That's why he's the boss, he thought. Then one of the oldest rules of warfare reared its ugly head.

The best-laid plans go to crap as soon as contact is made with the enemy. Josh was astonished as the lead intruder and what he assumed was his wingman accelerated at an astonishing speed toward the Gooney. He had never seen anything move so fast. The two aircraft covered the mile within seconds, which separated them from the PBM-5. One aircraft passed a few feet from the left wing, and the other passed a few feet from the right wing. There was an apparent disturbance in the air as what looked like a cone-shaped cloud appeared for a fleeting moment around the two aircraft. They continued their course to the North, rapidly becoming mere dots.

"TWO, BREAK RIGHT, BREAK! BREAK! BREAK!" Exploded in Josh's ears as the Skipper called for Josh to follow him through a combat break. Josh saw that the other two crescent-shaped aircraft had climbed up to him at a tremendous speed. He felt the heaviness and stress induced by the tight-high G, climbing turn. Watching, to be sure he wouldn't collide with the Skipper's Bearcat, Josh took a quick glance to his left, knowing their opponents were closing fast. He was shocked when first one and then two of the metallic-blue, crescent-shaped aircraft zipped past the left side of his plane.

Even though the event lasted less than three seconds, time seemed to stand still during the near-miss of the two aircraft. The first steel crescent flashed by, and to Josh, it looked as if the craft were nothing but solid metal. He could see no window or clear canopy. He noticed the strange aircraft were not a pure crescent. They had a fairing where the tail would be, which gave the rear of the aircraft a bat-like appearance. In the microsecond of the aircraft merging, Josh also noted markings on the wing. It looked like a black sunburst inside a black circle. Josh shook his head in disgust. *You're in a damn fight. Worry about markings later,* he mentally scolded himself. Two long pillars of flame shot from the back of the aircraft. Josh's brain was trying to comprehend the phenomenal performance he was witnessing. A loud roar accompanied the aircraft as it passed. Rockets, he thought as the second craft merged with him. This time Josh could see a canopy and a pilot in the vehicle. *You can barely tell the top from the bottom,* he thought, realizing there was no vertical tail or stabilizers; the aircraft appeared to be all wing.

The occupant appeared to be wearing a helmet, with a dark visor of some kind, which gave Josh the impression he had eyes like an insect. Josh could feel the other pilot's stare as the planes passed. In that instant, the strange cone-shaped cloud erupted around the aircraft, and there was a thundering boom. His Bearcat rocked and shuddered as if a large hand had swatted the fighter. Nearly losing control of his aircraft, Josh realized he was about to stall. He dropped the nose slightly and pushed the throttle forward to increase his airspeed. Radio discipline was gone. The crew of the Gooney felt as though they had been fired on and were calling for assistance. Panhandle was ordering Gold Flight to intercept and assist Blue Flight. The two Marine Tigercat's were trying vainly to join up for mutual support and were clogging up the transmissions. Josh nearly missed the Skipper's voice telling Blue Flight to reform and go to their secondary frequency. He quickly changed channels on his radio just in time to hear the Skipper's voice.

"Blue, Check." Josh replied, "Two." The simple answer of "Two" told the Skipper that Blue Two was on channel and ready. The other two pilots in Blue Flight quickly followed. "Three" "Four."

"Roger, Blue Flight, stay on this frequency, I'll monitor the other channel. Okay boys, looks like we've got our hands full. Keep your wits and maintain your flight discipline. Two do you have damage? I heard a boom and thought maybe you collided."

"Negative Lead, I don't have any idea what the boom was. I'm with you and ready."

"Skipper, who are we tangling with…Buck Rogers?" asked Blue 4.

"Lead, I saw markings on those things, never seen any like them." Josh replied.

"Quiet!" Brandt ordered his pilots. "Keep your head in the fight. We'll worry about who they are later. Okay, bring it back North a bit and keep a steady climb. Let's find the Gooney. Those guys are saying they were fired on." Human nature caused Brandt's pilots to close with their leader, forming into a tight, Finger Four formation. It was okay for flying straight and level but virtually useless in combat as everyone was too fixed on their position in the formation to look for the enemy. Brandt knew it was inexperience and the shock of what they'd seen that caused his pilots to naturally close ranks like a pack of wolves when threatened. "Okay, boys, Combat Spread, and let's get our eyes and heads back into the fight here. Shout out when you spot them, and don't shoot unless you're fired upon, or I give the order. We still don't know what the hell is going on out here."

Brandt's pilots slipped out and away, giving themselves plenty of maneuvering room. Brandt couldn't help but feel proud of his men; although they were rattled at first, they didn't lose their effectiveness. After all that had just occurred, he could see they were itching to engage with the strange aircraft they had encountered. As his flight climbed back through ten thousand feet, he saw two objects moving from his nine o'clock to three o'clock a few thousand feet below and to his North. Dropping the nose of his Bearcat slightly, he identified the dots as the two Marine Corps F7F Tigercat's that were flying flat out and dropping slightly in altitude. "Nighthawk, Blue Lead has visual on you at my low three o' clock."

"Roger that Blue Leader, we have visual on the Gooney at our twelve, about three miles out and on the deck heading north. We also have radar contact on the four Foo Fighters. They're about Angels Three, six miles out and closing fast on the Gooney. No visual yet."

*Foo Fighters. He actually said Foo Fighters again.* Although Brandt had heard of Foo Fighters, he had never seen any. *Well, Marine's love to be first; this guy can be first to tell the Admiral we're fighting Moon Men or Martians. I don't want any part of it.* "Bring it right, Blue Flight." Josh made a slow correction to an easterly heading as his leader had instructed. Now, he could see the two Marine Corps Tigercat's as well as the Martin PBM-5 Gooney Bird.

"Here they come." Josh heard the lead Marine pilot say matter-of-factly over the radio. Two of the strange, crescent-like aircraft zipped past the PBM-5 at an incredible speed. They were there and gone in a flash. Again, the pilot of the Martin seaplane exclaimed, "They're firing on us!"

"Nighthawk, did you witness any kind of weapon discharge from the bogies?" Brandt inquired of the lead Marine aircraft.

"Negative Blue, nothing visual. There was a hell of a bang when they went by. I can't explain it. No sign of a weapon firing though."

"Roger that, Nighthawk. Gooney, this is Blue Lead. Stay calm and keep working your way toward the fleet."

Brandt could see the ships of Task Force 68 in the distance as the aerial maneuvering by all aircraft had brought them closer to the fleet. He also noticed that the Destroyer and Seaplane Tender dispatched earlier from the main Task Force was now moving back toward the other ships at flank speed. *Don't blame you boys; it's downright spooky out here today*, he thought grimly.

"Blue Lead, this is Gooney, my tail and dorsal gunners report the other two bogies are closing in on us now."

"Roger, Gooney. Again, stay calm; nobody has thrown a punch, yet."

Josh Nashoba could see the second set of the crescent-shaped aircraft closing on the PBM-5 again, and at a speed he didn't think possible for even the most modern jet aircraft. An instant before the aircraft merged with the Martin seaplane, the lead aircraft went up and over the top of the big Martin and zipped through the narrow space between the two Marine F7F Tigercat's. Both Marine pilots maneuvered their aircraft violently to avoid a midair collision. The second strange aircraft did something more amazing. It decelerated from its high-speed pass with its leader and, in an instant, was going the same slow 180 miles an hour as the Martin seaplane. It appeared to be in echelon formation, directly off the right rear of the aircraft. The two Marine Tigercat's had been scattered and were trying to reform. Josh watched as the strange aircraft continued to fly formation with the flying boat. He could see both the tail gunner and the dorsal gunner of the seaplane had their weapons trained on their unwanted visitor. The strange craft rolled to its right until it was inverted, never leaving its position in the unusual formation. *These guys like to showoff,* Josh thought, his anger starting to rise. The crescent stayed inverted for about five seconds and then rolled back to its normal level attitude. Josh was beginning to wonder how this situation was going to play out when all hell broke loose.

The crescent-shaped aircraft made a hard left turn, and an explosion of fire came from behind the aircraft. In a few years, this technology would be commonly known as "afterburner." However, in early 1947, very few people in aviation had ever heard of such a thing. Josh assumed it was a rocket engine of some type like Admiral Byrd's R4DYs had used to takeoff from the carrier the previous day. What Josh and the rest of the pilots in blue flight did not experience was the thunderous boom caused by the ignition of fuel. Unfortunately, the nervous gunners on the PBM-5 not only heard it but also felt the shock wave and believed they were under attack. The gunner, positioned in the tail, fired his twin, 50 caliber, machine guns as the crescent-shaped craft broke across his field of fire. Sparks ignited on the bottom of the aircraft as several rounds found their mark in the rear of the aircraft. Showing no ill effects from the gunfire, the strange aircraft pointed its nose upward and accelerated in a ninety-degree, vertical climb. *Crap! That is going to change things.*

"Okay, Blue Flight, let's get in there, clear to fire," Brandt ordered, knowing the situation had gone bad. He also radioed the carrier to let it be known to the fleet that playtime was over. "Panhandle, this is Blue Lead, we are FANGS OUT, engaging Bandits." The interloping aircraft had just had their status changed from "unknown" to "enemy" by the simple use of the word "Bandits."

The fight was on; Josh quickly switched his fuel feed from the centerline, drop tank to his main internal fuel tank. Then he pushed the "JETTISON" switch on the armament panel, which blew the external fuel tank away from the belly of his aircraft. He didn't want to drag the extra weight around while he was doing battle. Dropping his nose, he kept his spacing with Brandt. As they dove to intercept the Martin PBM and its tormentor, the Bandit had shot up to five thousand feet above the Martin, then flipped over and dove back toward the sea. A greenish stream of light emitted from the left wing root and shot into the Martin seaplane, blowing the right vertical stabilizer off the tail of the seaplane, causing the large aircraft to skid to its left and slam into the surface of the sea. Josh noted splashes in the water, which appeared to be bullet or cannon rounds fired from the Bandit. The shocking thing was the number of rounds hitting the water. Josh knew of no weapon that could fire that many rounds in that short amount of time.

"The Gooney is down. They shot it down!" somebody screamed into the radio. Josh recognized the voice of his friend, Jack Fossier. The crescent-shaped aircraft passed low over its victim but did not fire on it again. Time seemed to slow as Josh watched the two Marine F7Fs engage the bandit. The two Marines were in a typical Two Ship combat formation. The lead aircraft was maneuvering for a firing solution on the crescent-winged enemy. Jack's aircraft was covering him about 150 feet behind and to the right of his leader. The enemy aircraft easily maneuvered away from the lead, Marine Corps aircraft, and popped above it with an amazing climb rate. Its path above and to the right of the lead F7F gave Jack Fossier a fleeting shot at the bandit. A large puff of smoke emitted from Jack's F7F from the wings and forward fuselage. He fired all eight of his guns; four 50 caliber machine guns and four 20-millimeter cannons all sent a deadly wall of lead toward the metallic crescent. He failed to account for its incredible speed, and the rounds flew harmlessly below and behind his intended target. Josh watched the tracer rounds from Jack's tracer rounds begin to slow and arc harmlessly back into the cold ocean below. The crescent was continuing its climb and would give both him and Lt Cmdr. Brandt a shot at it in a matter of seconds.

Once again, fire emitted from the tail of the aircraft, and it rocketed ten thousand feet above the four Navy F8F Bearcats before Brandt, Josh, or either of the other, two aviators could blink. Then it leveled off and began heading north toward the fleet at a high rate of speed. "What in the hell are these things?" He heard Brandt say in disgust. Followed by "Blue Flight level and reform left turn to a heading of 360 degrees." As they turned to the left, Josh saw the Martin seaplane was down in the water but seemingly floating safely with no obvious sign of sinking. Hatches were open, and men were moving around as if getting ready to abandon the aircraft if necessary. Jack could also see the two Marine Tigercat's reforming as they circled the flying boat. In an instant, another one of the crescent-shaped aircraft came out of nowhere and discharged its weapon, and Josh watched in horror as the greenish stream of fire slammed into Jack Fossier's Tigercat, causing it to explode into a ball of fire, smoke, and airplane parts. Both Jack and his radar operator never knew what hit them. The two Marines, like their aircraft, were gone in a flash.

The crescent that killed Jack, like the one above them, sped north, heading to the fleet staying low on the water. "We can't fight these things if we don't see them coming. Keep your eyes peeled boys, call out anything you see," said Brandt over the radio. Josh was overcome with a strange anger. It wasn't a hot anger as one would expect. He was no longer excited, scared, or even concerned about his own survival. He had a cold determination to avenge the death of his friend.

More excited voices came across the radio, "This is Panhandle. The fleet is under attack. All aircraft reform and defend fleet." Looking to the North, Josh could see ugly, black smudges caused by five-inch antiaircraft shells exploding in the air. He could see the ships of the fleet were maneuvering wildly in the distance as if each vessel was taking evasive action. The whole fleet seemed to be in chaos.

As they closed on the fleet, Josh observed the Bearcats from Gold Flight were engaged with the higher of the two-enemy craft. Like their own engagement, Josh's squadron mates were being outflown as if the Navy aircraft were mere toys for the aggressor's amusement. A flash went through Josh's cockpit and was gone. That was a reflection of something behind me. A sudden sense of impending doom came over Josh. Instinctively, he screamed into the radio, "Blue Flight, Break Now!" as he rolled his aircraft to right and dove. Josh watched the other; three aircraft in his flight take immediate evasive action, breaking into diving turns. An instant later, the two missing, crescent aircraft blew right through the empty airspace they had once occupied. They continued flying at high speed toward the fleet. The reflection in Josh's cockpit had been the sun bouncing off the highly reflective surface of the two intruders.

"Good job, Blue Two!" Brandt said over the radio, confirming Josh had saved Blue Flight from disaster. Josh didn't have the time or desire to tell his squadron commander he had acted on a hunch instead of seeing the aircraft coming behind their formation. Josh had learned a costly lesson through the death of his friend; these things were way too fast to not constantly be taking evasive action of some sort. For the moment, all four of the bandits were in front of them and in their field of vision. The two aircraft which had come behind his flight began zigzagging among the ships of the fleet. He also saw one of his squadron mate's aircraft from Gold Flight dropping in flames and crashing into the sea. "Get in the fight guys. Do whatever you can!" Brandt ordered his pilots. Josh had a hunter's as well as a warrior's instinct passed down from his Choctaw heritage. He had the green light to fight and kill. He also had a burning desire to avenge his friend. He chose his target. The enemy aircraft was making a hard, right turn a few feet above the ocean. He watched helplessly as it fired into one of the destroyers outside the fleet. The fire from its weapon detonated torpedoes in the aft torpedo tubes of the destroyer. There was a blinding flash as the weapons detonated.

Luckily, the location of the tubes above the main deck meant the structural damage was not nearly as destructive as an explosion in the ship's ammunition magazines would have been. Still, there was a large fire and a huge cloud of black smoke billowing above the ship. The explosion had knocked out the two 40mm, antiaircraft gun turrets amidships and damaged the aft, 5-inch gun turret. Josh had dropped to 500 hundred feet above the waves as he approached the ship. His Bearcat had accelerated past 400 miles per hour in the dive. He was downwind and concealed from the Bandit by the smoke cloud of the ship, which was now a half-mile from him. As he raced toward the ship, once again, the Bandit performed a pure 90-degree, vertical climb.

He watched as the enemy aircraft used the same vertical maneuver he'd seen twice before as it reversed its course heading down toward the destroyer. *You're getting predictable, and I'm going to make you pay,* he thought grimly of the pilot operating the crescent. Completely obscured from above by the smoke from the burning ship, Josh calculated the enemy aircraft's path from its current course, pointing the nose of his aircraft into empty space immediately off the destroyer's starboard stern. He held down the trigger. As he heard the staccato bark of his four wing-mounted cannons, the smell of the gun powder filled his cockpit. He watched the silver-blue crescent fly into the stream of cannon shells. The aircraft had been in a sharp bank with its right wing pointed at the water when the stream of 20mm rounds impacted the left-wing root, ripping it away from the rest of the aircraft. Josh watched as the left wing fluttered loose from the aircraft flying high into the air as the rest of the crescent-shaped plane smacked the surface of the water, then skipped back into the sky as if trying to escape its inevitable doom before falling flat like a pancake into the water.

Josh let out a loud "Hoyopa Tash," or war hoop as known by his people. Keying the microphone, he screamed into the radio, "Splash One!" Also, he instinctively broke into a hard left turn and then instantly rolled back right to clear any pursuers off his tail. Looking back toward the fleet, he was surprised to see the three remaining enemy planes form up and speed away from the fleet to the South.

"They're leaving!" somebody screamed excitedly over the radio.

This was followed by the voice of Lt Cmdr. Brandt, "Who called the Splash One?"

"Blue Two," Josh responded over the radio, followed by, "What's left of him is floating just off the destroyer Brownson."

"Roger, Blue Two, good job. Okay, boys, let's climb to fifteen thousand and set a Combat Air Patrol above the fleet until we can get some help," Brandt ordered. Josh formed on his leader's right wing as the flight began their slow climb. Brandt ordered the three remaining Bearcats from Gold Flight to join them over the fleet. "Who did we lose?" Josh heard Brandt ask the Gold Flight leader.

"We lost Gibson, he never got out," was the response from Lieutenant Austin, Gold Flight's leader.

"Roger that, Gold." Brandt responded. "Okay, guys, keep your eyes open high and low. We don't know if those things are coming back. Everybody check your fuel and ammo, no telling how long we'll be up here."

Josh began taking stock of his aircraft. His fuel was good as he had well over half his fuel load. He was good for at least another 500 miles if there was no more combat. If the bad guys showed up again, it could go fast. His ammunition load was cause for concern because he was running with 40 rounds left in each of his four 20mm cannons. He had fired off more than a hundred rounds from each gun when he sprayed the air in front of the enemy aircraft. Enemy aircraft. What enemy and what exactly were those things? he thought to himself. He had seen an article about a German-designed aircraft, one of Hitler's wonder weapons that never got off the ground that was remarkably similar.

He stopped pondering the strange aircraft and got back to the business at hand. He scanned both sky and sea for any sign of more hostile aircraft. As they passed over the fleet, he could see the seaplane tender, USS Pine Island, had moved alongside the destroyer Brownson and was helping fight her fires which seemed to be diminishing. He could also see his squadron's carrier, the USS Philippine Sea, was readying more aircraft for launch. Three of the strange, new helicopters brought along for the mission were darting to and from ships of the task force busily going about whatever tasks assigned them by the Admiral. Josh's flight would spend another hour over the fleet before being relieved by eight more of his squadron's Bearcats and two more Marine Tigercat's.

Josh made a successful landing on the USS Philippine Sea at 2020 hours. He was surprised he had been airborne for over two hours. He was more surprised when he had to be helped from his cockpit. The rush of adrenalin from the combat and the stress of watching for the enemy to return during the post-combat patrol had physically worn him down. Also, there was the loss of his friend, Jack Fossier, which he hadn't yet begun to process. Once his Plane Captain and another sailor helped him from the aircraft, he stood leaning against the Bearcat for a moment. After a few minutes, barely able to stand and support his own weight and looking up at the cockpit of his aircraft, he thought about everything that had just transpired. "Looking for a place to put a kill mark?" Lt Cmdr. Brandt asked, slapping Josh on the shoulder. Startled, Josh looked at his squadron commander, then lurched forward and vomited on the flight deck.

"Sorry, Sir," Josh said, confused and embarrassed. Brandt's facial expression softened, and his voice became gentle, almost fatherly.

"Josh, it's okay. I puked all over the cockpit of my Hellcat during the Turkey Shoot back in forty-four. You got a kill today, Tiger. Two years ago, you'd be posing for pictures in front of a small, Japanese flag painted on your bird."

"Oh, yes, Sir, I certainly would. I don't think those were Japanese, Sir."

"I don't think so either, Lieutenant. I have no idea who those bastards were," Brandt said, looking up at the carrier's island and vulture's row. Two figures were looking down at the flight deck. "Go get debriefed and get yourself some coffee and something to eat. There are other people who will want to talk with you later," Brandt said.

"Sir?" Josh replied, confused.

Nodding toward vulture's row on the superstructure of the carrier, Brandt said, "Those guys for instance." Josh looked up to see Captain Cornwell, the ship's Captain, and Admiral Cruzen, the Taskforce Commander, staring down at him.

*Oh great*, he thought to himself.

As if reading his mind, Brandt gave him another slap on the shoulder. "Don't worry, kid, you did good out there. We were totally outclassed by whatever those were. They shot down a PBM-5, a Marine Tigercat and one of our Bearcats. Not to mention, they also damaged a destroyer. When it was looking hopeless, you gave those turds a bloody nose and they left. You did great, Josh. Now, go get yourself together. I'm sure the ole' man up there will want to speak with you at some point."

Feeling his strength beginning to return, Josh saluted his Squadron Commander and headed to the Squadron Ready Room. His flight suit was sweat-drenched in spite of the intense, Antarctic cold, his heart still pounding in his chest.

# CHAPTER FIVE

# High Strangeness

*"Something unknown is doing we don't know what*
*~ Arthur Eddington*

## Wednesday, 23 November 2016, 11:40 AM CST, Honobia Bridge, Honobia, OK

After their meal, Addison, Sam, and Jim Vaughn walked from the store to the Little River Bridge, which was a couple of hundred yards south of the store. As usual, there was little to no traffic going through town. The three men had to move aside only twice for traffic, once for a logging truck and once as a local woman drove across the bridge on her way out of town. She hardly gave the men a glance. Honobia, long known for its Sasquatch legends, was no stranger to visiting curiosity seekers from all over the world. The bridge happened to be a central point of focus for Bigfoot investigators when coming to the area. The Little River at this location is more of a creek flowing from east to west. The river is joined by Honobia Creek flowing from the north and Rock Creek flowing in from the south only a few yards east of the bridge. The river is roughly 217 miles long, with most of it in Southeastern Oklahoma for 130 miles, with the remaining 87 miles running through Southwestern Arkansas before emptying into the larger Red River, near Fulton, Arkansas. The Honobia area basically serves as the headwaters for the river.

Jim Vaughn explained where he and his wife first spotted the creature and where he had stopped his vehicle both before and after crossing the bridge. There were some large, mud-smeared footprints as well as what appeared to be handprints on the bridge railing, but nothing that provided proof that a large creature had been climbing around on the bridge structure.

"I noticed there were traces of mud on the hood of your car, Jim, and it looked to be the same mud we're seeing on the bridge rail," Addison said.

"Yeah, well a little mud won't convince my family we're not crazy," Jim said, sarcastically.

"So, how many people have you told? "Addison asked.

"Nobody around here, that's for sure. You know we've made some good friends up here, and I don't want them to think we're crazy or lying."

"What makes you think that would be their reaction?" Addison asked.

"Honestly, even with all the Bigfoot trappings here, people rarely talk about it. Most of the locals I've met scoff at the idea when it comes up, and we'd really like to keep this thing under the radar."

"Hmm, so the locals are skeptics?" Sam seemed surprised.

"Well, not all of them, but I made the conclusion early on to avoid the topic, unless its festival time in October. I have heard a few locals say they have seen and heard things here. Plus, you've got that whole Siege at Honobia story, but I've heard some locals scoff at that, too."

"That's interesting but understandable, unless you've seen one up close and personal the whole idea is absurd. I can vouch for that from my own experience," Sam replied. Looking down into the creek, he commented, "Pop it's pretty rocky down there on the riverbed, but if there are smeared prints on the railings up here, there may be muddy areas down there with prints clear enough to make a cast."

"You guys are going to make casts of footprints if you find them?" Jim asked, sounding a little concerned.

"We'd like to if we find any, Jim. We'll match them with prints from our own property. Does that worry you?" Addison queried.

"I don't want to be publicly connected to anything you guys find if that's okay. I don't want to be known as a 'Bigfoot Nut.' I mean we've got friends. Plus, I wouldn't want any publicity getting to the company I work for. I'm too old to go job hunting and too young to retire."

Addison reassured him, "Jim, we're not here for publicity. In fact, we're going to keep this thing as quiet as possible. After what we went through a couple of years ago, it's the last thing we want as well."

Sam climbed down the north side of the riverbank and worked his way to the water. As the two other men continued their conversation on the bridge, he could hear Jim Vaughn explaining to his father, "We're leaving in a couple of hours for Texas. We'll be spending the Thanksgiving weekend with our children. When we return, I'm hoping everything will be back to normal."

Sam was walking as carefully as possible along the riverbed; the water level had dropped over the past few days, and there was still moss on some of the rocks. Sam decided to walk the twenty yards or so to where Honobia Creek emptied into the river. There was an area with soft soil, and as Sam had guessed, it contained footprints. There were at least eight footprints, and like the ones on his father's property, these also had six toes. Looking toward the creek and not watching his step properly, Sam slipped on a moss-covered stone and ended up on all fours. As he started to stand up, his eyes locked upon the gaping eye sockets and the grin-like display of upper teeth from a human skull. His initial reaction was to recoil from the sight. Catching his breath, he calmed himself and took a closer look. The skull was resting upon a large, sandstone rock roughly three times the size of the skull. Moving some grass aside, Sam noticed some kind of runes or symbols scratched into the rock. It was writing, and it seemed to be Arabic.

Sam stood up and took a closer look at the immediate area in case the rest of the skeleton was nearby. He didn't see any other bones, but he did notice large impressions in the riverbank where the water was only about a foot deep. From his position, he could clearly see that the area of soft soil did indeed contain massive footprints. Sam looked back at the skull and the rock it rested upon with the strange writing before looking back to the prints. He could clearly hear his father and Jim Vaughn speaking on top of the bridge. Sam yelled to the men on the bridge, "Pop, you better come down and see this. Mister Vaughn. your trip to Texas may be delayed a few hours. This is now a crime scene."

### Thursday, 31 January 1947, 5:30 AM, USS Philippine Sea, 250 miles off Antarctica.

The post-flight debriefs had been brutal. Each question he answered brought on more questions. Commander Saunders, the CAG attended the debriefing, occasionally asking questions. His eyes never strayed from Josh, making him feel as if he were being "sized up" as the main course for a feast. At one point, the Commander interrupted the debriefing, asking Josh, "What kind of college courses did you take, Lieutenant?"

"The usual courses needed to become an aviator, Sir - science, physics, and math. I also took a lot of engineering classes, Sir. I found the subject appealed to me." The Commander's eyes seemed to be boring holes into Josh's skull as if looking for his diploma.

"That's good, Lieutenant, it seems you were in the right place at the right time." Looking to Lt Cmdr. Brandt, he said, "Dick, I'm heading up to the bridge. I'll need you to come with me. The Admiral has a few questions for you."

"Aye, Aye, Sir!" responded Brandt, slapping Josh on the shoulder. "Great job out there, Josh. I could have used you back in 1944. Now get some food and some sleep - that's an order." He followed Commander Saunders from the Ready Room. Josh tried his best to follow the Skipper's orders. After the debriefing, he made his way to the Officer's Mess where he struggled to force down scrambled eggs and toast. His body wasn't ready for food. All he could do was nervously drink coffee while smoking one cigarette after another. A few of his fellow VF-10A pilots would stop by and congratulate him on bringing down the mystery plane, but Josh could only nod and force a smile.

The adrenalin rush from the flight the previous afternoon had long passed. He felt completely drained but could not sleep more than a few minutes at a time. Each time he drifted off, his body would go still, but his mind would come alive with vivid nightmares of large, flying insects. He would wake, jolted from his sleep. He awoke to his own screams at one point, and he didn't dare try and sleep in his bunk. He knew the other pilots would notice his nightmares. After the squadron was told to stand down and get some sleep, he spent the night alone in the Ready Room. The large, cushioned chairs provided enough comfort for Josh to continue his fitful catnaps. Adjusting his body and attempting to wiggle as far into the chair as possible, Josh was just beginning to relax when the Ready Room door opened, and Lt Cmdr. Brandt entered.

Looking at Josh, Brandt said, "I thought I'd find you here. You're supposed to be in your bunk."

Josh noticed Brandt appeared every bit as tired and haggard as he felt. "I tried, Sir. I just can't sleep soundly, so I came down here. Besides, I don't want to keep the other fellas awake."

Brandt smiled and nodded knowingly, "Well, you're still in your flight suit and jacket. That's probably going to come in handy. Follow me; you're wanted on the Flag Bridge." Josh came to his feet, confused and a bit intimidated. He followed the Skipper from the Ready Room, making the long climb to the Flag Bridge of the USS Philippine Sea. *The Flag Bridge, why does the Admiral want to see me?* Josh's mind raced, *I must have really screwed the pooch,* he thought to himself. It took almost ten minutes to navigate the passageways and climb the numerous sets of stairs through the ship's bowels before going upwards to the Command Bridge.

As they entered the Flag Bridge, Josh noticed Admiral Cruzen also appeared as worn out as Lt Cmdr. Brandt and himself. Looking across the room, the Admiral said, "I want all of you to step outside and catch some fresh air." The sailors quickly followed his instructions and moved to the catwalks outside the Flag Bridge. A young, Lieutenant Junior Grade wearing the same Navy, winter uniform of green trousers and a long-sleeved, khaki shirt with a black tie as the Admiral remained behind, holding a manila folder and standing at the position of attention. The Admiral extended his hand, and the Lieutenant handed him the folder and returned to the position of attention. Looking at the Lieutenant, the Admiral said, "I want you outside as well." Motioning Josh near, the Admiral said,

"Nashoba, you pulled off an interesting piece of work yesterday. You were able to bring down something we've been thinking were only myths, reported by exhausted pilots. Luckily for us, you brought this Foo Fighter down close enough that the sea plane tender, Pine Island was able to pluck it from the water with one of its cranes. Between your flying ability and the quick thinking of the Captain of the Pine Island, we've come into possession of some remarkably interesting technology. I have here some photos taken of the wreckage once they got it aboard the Pine Island." Handing Josh a photo, he continued, "Here is the craft, or what's left of it, after you sawed off one of the wings with your cannon rounds." Josh looked at the photo, which clearly showed the craft sitting on the deck of the Pine Island, missing its left wing but otherwise intact.

"Here's your pilot," he said, handing Josh another photo. This photo showed the remains of a male Caucasian, obviously deceased. Instead of feeling guilty, Josh felt anger over his dead friend, Jack Fossier. "Does seeing your dead foe disturb you, Lieutenant?" Admiral Cruzen asked.

Looking up from the photo, Josh replied, "Sir, if I could bring this bastard back to life, I'd gladly kill him again. As far as I'm concerned, the books aren't balanced, yet."

Nodding, the Admiral handed him another photo. "He was wearing this contraption for a flying helmet. It has a hard shell, probably some sort of plastic, with an adjustable visor which can be positioned over the eyes or slid back into the helmet. Wearing this along with the oxygen mask is probably why you said the pilot appeared insect-like in your debrief." This made sense to Josh, who was impressed with the obviously advanced flying gear.

The Admiral continued, handing him another photo, "Your debrief along with the debriefs of others who witnessed the attacks on our aircraft and ships mentioned their weapons seemed to be almost like a ray or beam. We found, what we believe to be, the gun on this aircraft; it is positioned in the left-wing root. It fires shells which appear to be your run-of-the-mill, 20mm aircraft, cannon shells used by Germany during the war. The catch is, the gun is not single-barreled; it is a six-barreled, Gatling like cannon. We haven't determined if it's electrically or hydraulically driven, but at first glance, it looks capable of firing an extremely large number of rounds per second."

"That makes sense, Sir," Josh replied. "I saw rounds hitting the water. What I had a hard time believing was the number of rounds hitting the water. The gun must have been loaded with tracer rounds firing at incredible speeds, it gave the appearance of a ray or beam weapon." Admiral Cruzen nodded, impressed with how the young Lieutenant thought.

"You also reported wing markings." The photo he handed Josh showed a close-up of the right-wing area, and there was the black sunburst-like marking he'd noticed during the millisecond his Bearcat had merged with one of the crescent-shaped aggressors. As he remembered the markings were in simple and stark black. An outer circle with a black bullseye in the center, from the center twelve lines, came out to a point roughly two-thirds of the way to the outer ring. From there, each line made an abrupt right turn for a short distance before once again abruptly turning back to the left then ending at the outer ring. Where each line touched the ring was the exact position on a clock—the top line at twelve and the rest following in the one through eleven positions.

"It looks like some kind of half assed clock Admiral." Josh said.

"That emblem, young Lieutenant, was checked out by my intelligence chief and, believe it or not, the ship's Chaplin. It is what is known as a Black Sun. It dates back to Babylonian and Assyrian places of worship, Lieutenant.

"I don't think those were ancient Babylonians flying those things Sir. It looks almost German, Sir."

The Admiral shook his head in amazement, "You're very astute Lieutenant, the Nazi's adopted the emblem for many of their occult practices. However, I wouldn't be so sure about your Babylonian statement."

"I'm confused Admiral."

"We all are Lieutenant. These next few photos may confuse you even more," he replied, handing Josh another photograph.

This photo was of a nondescript piece of metal, with what appeared to be German writing on it. "That, Lieutenant, is your basic Luftwaffe (German Air Force) Dog Tag. It appears our enemy pilot was a member of the German Luftwaffe. His name was Rudolph Moritz. He was a successful fighter pilot during the war. In fact, according to my intelligence officer, he was so successful that late in the war he was assigned to one of the Luftwaffe's jet fighter squadrons. Then early in 1945, he simply disappeared from all records. It was believed he had been shot down and killed at some point."

"Where did all this information on him come from, Sir?" Josh asked.

"Our Intel division has been running coded inquiries to Pacific Headquarters and Washington since all hell broke loose with those bastards yesterday afternoon. In fact, Lieutenant, you have been mentioned by the President of the United States."

"All I did was my job, Sir. Just like everybody else in the fleet yesterday," Josh replied, feeling a bit intimidated at the thought of being mentioned in the White House. "What does this mean, Sir? Are we still at war with Germany or some rogue Babylonian god worshiping Luftwaffe squadron? There is one thing that does make sense to me Admiral."

Cruzen was intrigued that the young Lieutenant could find something which made sense in this whole mess. "What is that Lieutenant?" he asked hopefully.

"Well, Sir, I was hot to get into the war. If I wasn't studying or flying, I was reading everything I could get my hands on concerning the air war. I was especially interested when the first reports of German rocket planes and jets were made public. After the war ended in Europe and our people started investigating the German technology, they found the remains of an aircraft which appears to be very similar to the things we fought yesterday. It was made by the Horten Brothers and was called the Ho229. I believe, if you have your Intel people get some info on that aircraft, it might shed some light on what we encountered here. If it's not one of these things, it's damn close, Sir." Josh waited and watched as the Admiral considered what he had said.

The Admiral was especially interested in what Josh had to say about the final photograph he held in his hand. "Lieutenant, what we haven't told you, is that this aircraft carried a crew of two." Josh was not surprised to hear this, thinking the plane was big enough to carry two people. "These are the remains of the second crewman. As far as we know, this individual was not burned, nor did he seem to come in contact with fuel or other flesh-eating material. This is his actual appearance. You seemed to make a possible connection with the pilot and aircraft. What do you make of his co-pilot?" Cruzen said, handing Josh the final photograph.

The photo was a shock to Josh, who was expecting to see more human remains. Instead, he saw something completely different. The remains had been laid out next to the remains of the dead German for the purpose of showing scale. The creature appeared to be roughly four feet tall and very slight of build. The head was unusually large compared to the rest of the body. There was no protruding nose or ears, only slits for nostrils, ears, and mouth. The eyes were huge and almond-shaped. The creature appeared not to be wearing any suit or clothing and showed no signs of sexual organs. "Well, what do you think? Maybe a Babylonian Lieutenant?"

"Sir, my father brought us up in a Christian home, and he taught us that our tribal religion and the Christian religion of the white man are both tied to the Torah. Our angels and devils are the same ones as the white man's. Only they have different names and different ways of helping or tormenting humans based on the people's geographic location and needs."

"Based on the Torah, you say?" The Admiral asked, bemused.

"Yes, Sir, the Torah, or Old Testament as you probably call it. Sir, I have no idea what this being is, but I'm willing to bet it's an evil entity of some kind, a demon or devil perhaps. I just don't buy the things written by H.G. Wells about men from mars."

The Admiral stepped closer to Josh, "Lieutenant Junior Grade Nashoba, congratulations, you've just been promoted to full Lieutenant. I wish I could tell you where your final destination will be, but all I know is right now, you're on your way to the USS Pine Island which is going to take you and your mysterious Foo Fighter and its occupants to New Zealand. After that, it's anybody's guess. Who knows, before it's all said and done, you may be briefing President Truman on angels and devils." Josh was thunderstruck. *It took so much effort to become a naval fighter pilot, and now they were sending me to a Seaplane Tender?*

"Don't look so blue, Lieutenant, this isn't the end of your flying career. Something tells me you're going to punch your own ticket because of this thing. You did an outstanding job! You'll be back in fighters before you know it." The Admiral shook Josh's hand and said, "Anchors aweigh, Lieutenant. There are pointy-headed professors everywhere waiting to see your trophies." As Josh and Lt Cmdr. Brandt walked out onto the flight deck, the engine started, and the rotor blades on one of the H03S-1 helicopters began to rotate.

Lt Cmdr. Brandt stopped Josh before they approached the helicopter. "Josh, I have a sailor down in your quarters packing all your gear. We'll send it over to the Pine Island once this eggbeater returns from delivering you. First of all, I want to give you these." Brandt opened a small box containing a set of Lieutenant Insignia. Brandt reached up and removed the single, silver bar Lieutenant Junior Grade insignias from Josh's collar and replaced them with the double, silver bar Lieutenant Emblems.

"There, you look better already. I'll have a couple more sets of these thrown into your sea bag before we fly it over to the Pine Island. Hang in there, Josh, and see this assignment through; once it's over, contact the squadron, and we'll get you back home to us. In the meantime, find out what the hell these things are and how to fight them. Good luck, Josh," Brandt said as they shook hands.

Josh came to attention and saluted his Squadron Commander. "Thank you, Sir. I'll do my best." Then he approached the helicopter, ducking under the spinning rotor blades, he climbed into the rear seat of the aircraft.

The pilot, a Chief Petty Officer, looked back at him, motioning to a headset hanging on a hook near the side door. Putting on the headset, Josh heard the thick, southern accent of the Petty Officer. "Y'all strap dat seat belt down good n' tight now, Lootinat. I aint lost me a passenger, yet. Tain't no need in you being the first 'un." As the pilot increased throttle on the helicopter, the machine began to vibrate wildly. "Hang on, Sir, this aint no Burrcat, but it's still a hell of a ride." With that, the machine lifted vertically off the deck of the Philippine Sea. Hovering fifty feet over the deck for a few moments, the aircraft then rotated to the left, and as the nose dropped slightly, the machine moved out and away from the carrier.

The vibrations seemed to increase, and for the first time he could recall, Josh was nervous while flying. Looking out from the helicopter, Josh took in the ships of the task force. The wakes of the mighty ships left billowing, white trails in the blue-grey, Antarctic water. Josh marveled at the beauty. Usually, he was too busy piloting his aircraft to enjoy the views from the air. "You the guy that shot down that Martian, aint ya?" the pilot asked as he guided the helicopter to the USS Pine Island, which was sailing in the Southeast corner of the task force.

"Martian?" Josh asked, confused. "Damn straight Martian, dem had to be Martians or Moon Men or sumptin' from out there in outer space," the pilot remarked matter-of-factly, starting to slow the machine a bit as they neared the Pine Island. "Hell, I was in the air when dem sumbitches attacked yesterday. The ships was a shootin', you fighter boys was a shootin', and dem space fellers was a shootin. I never in all my years seen nuthin like them things they was a flyin'. All I could do was hover real low over da water, playin' possum, till everything simmered down. I seen you shoot dat one down. The fellers on the ship said you was an Injun... What tribe?"

"Choctaw," Josh responded.

"Choctaw, huh? Well, you sure put the tommyhawk to that Martian feller, Sir. Hang on now, I'm gonna' to be a mite busy landin' us."

"You got enough room down there?" Josh asked nervously, looking at the small space on the USS Pine Island where the pilot was attempting to land.

"Hell, Lootinat, if they'll open a porthole, I'll land this thang in the Officers' Wardroom for ya," the pilot said happily as he guided the aircraft down onto the deck of the Pine Island. The helicopter drifted slightly off course for a moment, but the pilot skillfully brought it back over the small, deck space and the machine touched down, much to Josh's relief. "Here ya' go, Sir. If ya' play cards, there's a feller onboard here by the name of Hughes. He's a Yankee bastard and he cheats... Steer clear of him."

"Will do Chief, thanks," Josh said, unbuckling the straps of his lap belt and climbing out of the aircraft.

"Okay, Lootinat, you best run on over 'der by the bulkhead when I takeoff. I don't wanna' blow you overboard. The brass might get a bit ill with me for that. Y'all take care now." The helicopter engine began to rev at higher RPMs, and Josh jogged over to the nearest bulkhead and grabbed onto a ladder rung. The helicopter lifted lightly off the deck, and the pilot guided it clear of the cranes and mast of the Pine Island before setting a return course to the USS Philippine Sea.

As Josh watched the helicopter fly away, a voice from behind him said, "Lieutenant Nashoba."

Josh turned, seeing a Navy Commander; quickly, Josh saluted the man and said, "Permission to come aboard, Sir."

Smiling, the Commander returned the salute and extended his hand. "Welcome aboard, Lieutenant. I'm Commander Birdsall, Admiral Cruzan's Chief of Intel. It looks like you bought us both a free cruise to New Zealand."

"Well, Sir, I'm not real keen on going to New Zealand. I'd rather stay with my squadron."

"Things could be worse, Lieutenant, a lot worse. Besides, we won't be in New Zealand for long. Air Transport Command is sending one of their new C-97s to the air base in Auckland. There we will load your Foo Fighter into it. Then you and I and the machine will be heading to Ohio."

"Ohio? There's no Naval Air Station in Ohio, Sir."

"We're handing this baby over to the Army Air Force at Wright Field. They've got scientists standing by to dissect this baby and see what it's made of."

"We're giving it to the Army? What the hell, Sir?"

"Washington wants this thing buried in Middle America, Lieutenant. Don't worry; you are going to accompany the machine and its occupants the whole way. You'll be working with the scientists and engineers as they investigate exactly what this contraption is. You'll be briefing them on what you witnessed in its performance and how you brought this thing down."

"I brought it down by flying through the smoke of a burning ship to conceal my approach. Basically...I cheated."

"Well, Lieutenant, that is one of the biggest rules in combat."

"What's that, Sir?"

"There is no cheating in combat. If you're not cheating, you're not trying. Now, do you want to get a good look at this thing you brought down?"

"Yes, Sir, I sure do."

## Wednesday, 23 November 2016, 1:50 AM CST, Honobia Bridge, Honobia, OK

Addison was somewhat surprised by the rapid response of law enforcement to the call they made about finding human remains. Le Flore County Deputies were the first to arrive, followed by none other than Jeri Chula and another Oklahoma Highway Patrol Trooper and two Special Agents with the Oklahoma State Bureau of Investigation (OSBI), as well as a State Crime Scene Investigator. Addison and Sam decided to leave the suspected Relic tracks undisturbed and didn't search the area any further. Jim Vaughn was none too happy about the discovery. "I should have kept my mouth shut. Now, everyone in the area is going to hear about this," he complained.

"Don't worry, none of this has anything to do with you, or your wife. We'll just tell them the truth; we were here investigating a Sasquatch sighting and blundered onto the skull. If anybody is going to be scrutinized, it will be Sam and myself," Addison said, attempting to reassure him.

"You guys must have really stirred up some trouble somewhere. The Talihina Police told me you'd be helpful... this isn't helping. My wife is going to be pissed! We should have been on the road already."

"I'm sure this won't take much longer," Addison replied as he watched the activity below the bridge around the riverbed. One of the OSBI agents was squatted down, looking at the prints in the sandy riverbank where Honobia Creek entered the river. He waved for his partner to join him. Jeri Chula joined the two agents as well as the State Crime Scene Investigator. There seemed to be an intense discussion in the area of the footprints. Both agents and Jeri Chula were pointing at tracks and a grassy area along the creek. The Crime Scene Investigator was busily snapping photos.

After a few minutes, Jeri Chula started making her way to the bridge. "She's awfully small to be a State Trooper," Jim Vaughn remarked.

Sam chuckled under his breath, then replied, "She's all fight, Jim. She had an experience that makes what happened to you on this bridge look like child's play. She's the best friend we have here, right now. In fact, the Police officer who helped you in Talihina last night is her husband."

Jeri walked up to the three men; looking at Jim Vaughn, she said, "Sir, you're free to go. If we need any other information from you, you'll be contacted."

"Really, I can go? Nobody is going to tell me what's going on? We're going to Texas for a few days. Is that okay?" Jim seemed shocked and confused by the lack of closure.

"Yes, Sir, those remains appear to be over a year old. You've only lived here a few months. Right now, there's no reason to hold you. If questions come up later, you'll be contacted."

"Okay, thank you." Then turning to Addison, he said, "I've got to get going. May I contact you when we get back? I'm still not sure what I should do about all this. My wife is freaked out as it is. If all these police cars are here when we leave, she's really going to worry."

"Sure, Jim, Sam and I will look into this. The biggest thing is don't worry too much. You'll probably go the rest of your life and never see anything like this again. In case you do though, remain calm and go the other direction."

"We live here now, Mister Redstone, not even three hundred yards from that creek. What's to keep one of those things from coming to our house?"

"That's not likely to happen, Jim, but if you have any problems or strange occurrences, call me. I would stay out of the hills and away from the creeks for a few weeks though, until it or they move along. Don't go looking for them, they usually move on after a little while."

"If you say so, this is all so weird. I would never have thought anything like this would happen to us." He stood there a few more seconds as if there was something he was forgetting, and then it occurred to him. "One more thing Mister Redstone, on your way back home, stop at the overlook just a mile up the road," he said, nodding in the direction of Talihina.

"Okay, Jim, I'll do that. What am I looking for?"

"Look at the trees, you'll know why when you see them." With that, Jim shook hands with Addison, Sam, and Jeri, before making his way back to the store and his vehicle.

"Addison, they found more remains at the mouth of the creek, lots of human bones. It looks as if it's the rest of the skeleton belonging to the skull Sam found. Look, these OSBI guys know all about what happened two years ago, and they know about the boys found on your property the other day. They're asking a lot of questions about both of you. Their opinion seems to be that you are finding too many missing people along with these footprints. I'm thinking they're getting the idea you guys are kidnapping people and possibly killing them to perpetuate some kind of Bigfoot hoax."

"Well, you can't blame them. We have a bad habit of being right in the center of the turd every time one of these Relics takes a crap," Sam said, as an OSBI van pulled up and two men exited the vehicle.

"Hopefully, whomever the remains belong to has nothing to do with either of you. They seem to be itching to tie the corpse to you guys."

"So, their big hunch is we're abducting and killing people, then blaming it on Bigfoot?" Addison asked, almost laughing.

"Don't laugh too much, Addison; you're not exactly the golden boy of certain federal agencies. You scared the hell out of the Forest Service Brass a couple of years ago. Plus, you know as well as I do that in their opinion, you have too much knowledge of their cover-up of these things. All it takes is for a Fed "big shot" to have a buddy that's a State "big shot… Don't let yourself get outflanked, Addison. Plus, if you know of any friends or acquaintances who haven't been seen for a couple of years, you might as well let me know so that we can head this off."

"Paul Eastman!" Sam said, "The US Forest Service Agent, whatever happened to him after the meeting with you and all the brass back in 2014?"

"Hell, if I know, Sam. I never saw him again after we came out of the VA Hospital where we met with the USFS brass and General Henderson."

"Addison don't forget either Eastman or the Feds had a team of black ops here. We also know a few of them have never been heard from again. There are people saying that you two, some locals and even my husband made sure they'd never show up again. I know for a fact one was taken out of my hospital room, never to be seen again," Jeri said, looking at Addison intently.

"Jeri, those were not Black Ops guys. They were hired goons and killers who the government doesn't want to claim as theirs anyway. Besides, if I, Sam, or Jimmy were involved in something like that, we wouldn't be this sloppy," Addison said, pointing down at the activity along the riverbank.

"The fact is, Addison, some operators are missing, and the government seems to be looking at you about it." "Well, they can't prove anything unless those boys show up somewhere, Jeri," Addison said, looking at her intently. "And they're not going to show up anywhere."

"I hope for everyone's sake, this doesn't turn out to be one of those operators," Jeri replied, watching the two crime scene techs begin loading skeletal remains into a body bag. "Oh! The OSBI guys seem to think the markings carved into the rock may be Arabic. Perhaps this has something to do with terrorism and nothing to do with you guys at all."

"That's not Arabic, it's Hebrew," Addison said matter-of-factly.

"Do these Bureau guys want to talk to us?" Sam asked as the two agents began climbing the slope up to the bridge.

"Of course, they do. You two guys have been mentioned all over the state the last few days."

Surprisingly the two agents asked the Redstone's very few questions and gave the impression that they already knew everything they needed to know. They milled around for another half hour, waiting on the crime scene techs to load the remains as well as the large stone upon which the skull had been discovered. After they left, Sam made his way back down to the creek bed. Jeri continued to talk to Addison for a few more minutes, "I would like to know what the engraving on that stone means."

"Well, Sam took photos of it and sent copies to my phone. I'll get the writing translated, or do it myself if I have to," Addison replied.

"Any idea what it means?" Jeri asked. "Not at all," Addison replied.

Then looking around, Jeri noticed her vehicle was the last one on the scene. "Guess I better head out, Addison. I need to spend some time on Highway 259 to keep the holiday traffic safe." Looking down to the creek, she yelled to Sam, who was working his way back to the bridge. "See you tomorrow; don't hurt yourself on those rocks." Sam gave a wave. "Addison, you two be careful," Jeri warned. "Things are getting strange again; I was hoping this was all over."

"I was too, my dear, you be careful this evening. Marsha and I will be at Sam's tomorrow when you and Jimmy stop by. Maybe we'll know a little more by then."

"I'd be just as happy if we never heard anything about any of this ever again," Jeri said as she got in her patrol car. Once in the car, she headed South on Indian Highway, toward highway 259 to monitor the traffic in and out of Broken Bow.

Sam returned to the bridge, and as the two men started walking back to the Honobia Creek Store, a white SUV approached them from the North with

Texas plates. As the vehicle slowly drove past them, they recognized the driver as Jim Vaughn. His wife was seated in the passenger seat, and the vehicle seemed full of luggage. Jim barely waved as he passed the Redstone's. *Lucky for Jim, all the police vehicles are gone,* Addison mused. "Maybe he and his wife will be able to enjoy their holiday. You know, Pop, they destroyed the tracks like we knew they would, but they missed one. I have some casting material in my backpack, do you want me to mix some and make a cast?"

Addison thought about it for a moment; he was torn between collecting evidence and going home to his wife. He noticed that the further he moved into his sixties, the more he noticed peaceful time at home with his wife was far more attractive than adventure. After thinking for a moment, he sighed and said, "Yeah, let's get a cast of it, then we're going to go home to our family and enjoy the holiday. I've had enough mysteries for one week."

"That sounds good, I would love a peaceful holiday tomorrow. I have a feeling we may not get to enjoy the next few weeks. It feels an awful lot like 2014 right now," Sam said as he walked toward the truck.

*I hate to say it, Son, but this feels worse to me,* Addison thought to himself. As they made their way back up the mountain heading to Talihina, Addison asked Sam to pull over onto the asphalt pad that acted as an overlook down on Honobia. Sam turned off the engine, and both men exited the vehicle; Sam was busy looking at the tree trunks and foliage, not sure of what he was looking for.

"What are you hoping to find, Pop?" Sam asked.

Seeing nothing near the ground, Addison shifted his gaze higher into the trees, "I'm looking for that," he said, pointing two-thirds of the way up to the top of two large pine trees. Glancing up, Sam also took in the sight of Addison's discovery. The two large pine trees appeared to be roughly the same age and both around 75 feet tall. Being only thirty feet across, their large branches had long ago mingled and interlocked with each other. What caught Sam's attention was a hole in the tangle of branches and limbs, a perfect circle, not near perfect, but perfect. It looked to be twenty to twenty-five feet in diameter. There were no broken branches or burn marks; Sam searched for fifty feet all around the trees, there were no broken or burned branches on the ground. From either side, the hole in the tree formed a perfect circle; no branches, pinecones, or even a stray pine needle interfered with the circumference of the hole through the branches. That is where the second UFO left the road and went back into the sky. "I'd say with all this physical evidence, Mister Vaughn is telling the truth. Wouldn't you say, Sam?"

Addison asked. Sam didn't say a word, he just stared at the perfect hole in the trees.

### Thursday, 24 November 2016, 3:30 PM CST, Sam and Christa Redstone residence, Talihina, OK

Sam and Christa were a bit nervous about hosting the family get-together in their home located North of town on Highway 82. The house was less than two years old and sat back from the site of the original house Christa had shared with her late husband, Howard Fletcher. Howard had died at the hands of an outlaw biker he had hired to kill Christa's father, Mike Sanders. Moments later, her current husband, Sam, who was the Chief of Police for Talihina at the time, shot and killed the biker. The house was confiscated days later by US Government agencies to use as a headquarters to coordinate operations led by Paul Eastman, a US Forest Service Special Agent, in an attempt to put an end to the Sasquatch, or "Relic" activity in the local area.

In January 2015, Christa had the original house demolished and all evidence of it, including the original plumbing removed. The house had never been a home to her. In fact, it was more of a prison. In the early spring of that same year, she started construction on the current house, which sat back further in the woods by some two hundred feet. Christa put all her energy into designing a home that would be a positive and peaceful home for her and her daughter. Her late husband was a scoundrel, but he had not squandered the fortune left to him by his parents. Even though money was no problem, Christa worked hard to ensure she got the most she could out of every dollar she spent on the house. She gave headaches to a lot of local contractors due to her attention to detail and insistence on knowing where every dollar was spent in the construction. She paid the contractors well, but if she found any wasted material or shortcuts taken, there was hell to pay. Although Christa was extremely beautiful and kind, she was also the daughter of Mike Sanders, and like her father, she had the heart of a lion and could make even the toughest construction worker sorry he tried to pull a fast one on her.

Christa also realized that all the sorrow and loss of 2014 in both her life and that of Sam Redstone's had given them a second chance. She wasn't about to squander it, so her design was a large, log cabin-style home she knew would appeal to Sam. The home sat on a base of native stone carved from a small hill. Below was a large garage and workshop. The main house sat on top of this and contained four bedrooms and three bathrooms. Vaulted ceilings with an airy loft and cathedral windows gave the home a well-lit and comfortable feel. A covered porch wrapped its way around the whole house, and a large, upper deck that faced Addison Redstone's property was accessible from the loft. The home was topped with a copper metal roof, complementing the rich, reddish cedar finish to the exterior.

Sam and Christa had worked late into the night preparing the feast. Christa was stuffing two large turkeys in her huge kitchen, and Sam had gotten up twice during the night to check on a large brisket and three racks of ribs in the smoker behind the house. Christa couldn't help but notice both times Sam left the bed to add wood to the smoker; he took with him a .45 caliber pistol which he kept in a nightstand. She didn't ask him why he went outside armed, but she knew it wasn't his normal behavior. This can wait until after the Thanksgiving party, she told herself.

The meal turned out to be a true feast. Along with the food prepared by Christa and Sam, Christa's mother, Diane, brought sides including mashed potatoes, green bean casserole, and a fruit salad. Christa's brother, Derek, also came with his young son, Little Mike, and surprisingly his ex-wife April, who brought a cheesecake. Seeing Wendy, Sam was confused at first, then looking to his wife, he saw her give him a quick wink. Christa had worked hard to get her brother's drinking under control and apparently help him reunite with his son and ex-wife. When Addison and Marsha arrived, they brought food to add to the event. Marsha had made six pies, two pumpkins, two pecan, and two chocolates with whipped cream. Even Addison got in on the act, bringing a couple of native, Choctaw dishes, Banana bread and a Tanchi Lanona, a hominy and pork dish. Although Jimmy Chula and his wife Jeri were on duty that day, they dropped by with a fruit basket and joined the feast before returning to duty.

By 3:00 in the afternoon, everyone's stomach was filled, and the women were flirting with the idea of getting up early the following morning for Black Friday sales in Ft. Smith or Texarkana, while the men were sitting on the balcony drinking coffee and enjoying the cool, autumn air. After a few minutes, April and Derek's son, Little Mike, appeared on the balcony. "Derek, we still have my folks we need to visit and it's getting about that time,"

April reminded Derek, who stood up glancing at his phone, "Sorry hon, you're right, we'd better get going to Poteau." Well, guys, we better say our goodbyes. We really enjoyed the celebration."

Rising, Sam said, "You guys should take some food with you, we'll never eat all this by ourselves."

"The food was wonderful, Sam, but I'm certain my mother will send us home with at least half as much as you have down there in the kitchen. She loves to overcook during the holidays."

"Well, little man, the next holiday is the big one, huh?" Sam said, playfully rubbing Little Mike's hair. The young boy smiled, but Sam could tell he wasn't thrilled about having his hair tousled. There was a fire in the young boy, and Sam smiled; he'd seen that same fire in the boy's deceased Grandfather and in his own wife. After Derek and his family had gone, Sam and Addison went back to their vigil of sitting on the balcony, enjoying the afternoon." The weather is starting to turn colder," Sam commented, leaving the balcony.

He returned moments later with a bottle of Maker's Mark Bourbon. "Here, Pop, let me spike that coffee up a bit." Addison offered his mug as Sam poured the amber liquid from the bottle with red wax around its neck.

"They say if you drink this stuff enough years, you can actually determine the individual styles of the workers by looking at the wax, because they hand dip the bottles."

"Yeah, well, a little touch now and then is fine, but if you think you're an expert on the wax patterns, you're probably drinking way too much of the stuff. The story does make a good marketing ploy though." Addison replied with a wink.

"True enough Pop, I wanted to bring it out earlier, but didn't want to tempt Derek, he's done great the last two years. He's dried up, and grown up, in fact he's been a pillar for Diane and Christa both to lean on since Mike was killed. I'm glad to see that he's getting his little family back together too. His son has Mike's eyes; the little toot almost intimidated me there for a second." Sam said, chuckling.

Addison leaned back in the rocking chair on the balcony, recalling his friend Mike Sanders. "Yes, Mike was a good man. And, yeah, he was big and scary; but he really had a heart of gold. I miss fishing with him. You know he could scare the hell out of you one second, then have you in tears of laughter the next." Addison said, thinking of his friend and the day he saw him murdered just two years earlier. "You know, Son, that's how life is, sometimes, the strong have to fall so their offspring can grow into their own strength. If Mike were still alive, Derek might not be the man he is today. Mike's strength had to be taken away, so Derek could grow into his own."

"Getting a bit philosophical aren't you Pop?" Sam said, taking a seat in another rocking chair beside him.

"I wouldn't say philosophical, Son. I do think God has a plan for each of us. I also think we're all here to serve a purpose. Some of us don't find the purpose; the purpose finds us. God put a lot of strength in Mike Sanders, Mike passed it on to his offspring, but the strength could not be realized by his children, until Mike's own strength was not there for them to lean on anymore. Mike wasn't going to break his children's chains, they had to do it themselves. While he was alive, Mike would protect them and guide them both to a point. If Mike were still alive, who knows what things would be like? Derek might still be on the bottle and Christa might still be with Howard."

"But Howard was killed by the same guy that he hired to kill Mike, so your theory has holes in it, Pop." Sam countered.

"True enough Sam, but my point is, Mike's physical strength was like a laser. It had a narrow focus. Instead of trying to guide Howard over his interference with Derek, he scared him. Howard was too weak both mentally and physically to handle that fear. Howard was strong financially and he used that strength to counter Mike, but he was too feeble minded to see he was signing his own death warrant. Once Mike was gone, both his children rose to the occasion. Howard never saw it coming from Christa and would never have dreamed that Derek was capable of overcoming his own personal demons. Derek and Christa have their father's strength and spirit, but they also have the blessing of their mother's peace and wisdom. God blessed Christa with the intelligence and guts to remove herself from that house before all hell broke loose."

Sam contemplated his father's words for a few minutes as he thought back to the night two years ago when he and members of his Police Department were involved in a shootout with two bikers holding Howard Fletcher hostage just a few hundred feet from where he was now sitting. "Well since we're on the subject, it looks like we've underestimated our own struggle with the Relics. They're back and I'm not the Chief of Police anymore. I don't have the ability to wage war on them like we did last time. How are we going to keep our families safe from them? We need help Pop, and I don't know where it's going to come from. Do you have any ideas, other than praying?"

Addison sighed, not so much at his lack of faith but more at his sarcasm concerning faith. "Worry and fear are bigger enemies to you than these creatures, Son. There's a verse I like in Mark, Sam. Whatever you ask for in prayer, believe that you have received it, and it will be yours."

Now it was Sam's turn to sigh, "You know, Pop..." He was cut off by the ringing of Addison's cell phone. He watched his father as he answered the phone. He could see joy and surprise in his eyes. *Probably an old Vietnam buddy calling to wish him Happy Thanksgiving*, he thought, getting up to freshen his coffee and bourbon. When he returned, his father said goodbye and told the caller that he would see him tomorrow. "Who was that?" Sam asked curiously.

"That was Nathan Parks. General Henderson ordered him to take some extended leave. Trent Simmons, the Air Force Sergeant that helped you with the Locke kid is with him too. They're at Dover Air Force Base in Delaware and they have a hop on a C-130 to Fort Smith Arkansas at Zero Dark Thirty in the morning. They're going to rent a car and come to Talihina once they land. I told them they could stay at the ranch. They're looking for some excitement to keep them sharp. Looks like ole Mark was right, doesn't it, Son?"

Sam looked shocked, he stood there with his mouth opened, but nothing came out. "I can't believe the good luck!" he said.

"It's not called luck, Son, it's called blessing. Get yourself together, you look so shocked you could be knocked over by a popcorn fart," Addison said, laughing.

## Friday, 25 November 2016 2:30 AM CST Highway 144 between Octavia and Honobia, Oklahoma

Forty-nine-year-old William Blakeslee was fighting sleep. The only thing keeping him awake was the pain of a full bladder. The only thing keeping him from relieving the pain in his bladder was the dread of pulling over on this dark stretch of road in Southeastern Oklahoma. William was spooked. He was returning from a hunting trip in Southwest Arkansas. He and an old friend who lived in Little Rock had planned on a full four days of hunting just North of Russellville, Arkansas, at a place known as Long Pool Recreation Area in the vast Ozark National Forest. Their trip had been cut short. What happened at the deer camp some three hours ago, and what happened to him the last time he was in this part of Oklahoma in the middle of the night two years earlier, spooked him even more.

At the time, William had been returning to Texas from Missouri with a load of fiber optic cable over a route he had become awfully familiar with during his twenty years as a trucker. One beautiful night in October 2014, William decided he had earned a rest and parked his rig on a pullout just North of Talihina, Oklahoma. The area was in some of the bigger peaks of what is known as the Kiamichi Mountains. William had been asleep for a few hours when the sound of motorcycles woke him. A group of Harley riders pulled in next to his rig. At first, William was concerned, but the bikers didn't stop; they turned and sped off back into the night in the direction they had come from. Awake, William had stepped outside the truck to relieve himself. He noticed the bikers had pulled onto Highway 1, which ran parallel to Hwy 271, where he was parked.

Though less than a quarter-mile away, the bikers were on a hill some 200 feet above William. He could hear them turn off their motors and would occasionally hear voices but couldn't understand what they were saying. He assumed they had found another pullout or scenic overlook to take care of business just as he was doing. It was a beautiful night, and William decided to have a cigarette and look at the stars before returning to the sleeper cab in his truck. He was about to extinguish his cigarette when all hell broke loose on the hill above him. It started with curses, then the curses led to gunfire and wild animalistic screams and whoops. The last noises he heard were the sound of men screaming in terror, or worse, extreme pain. William jumped into his truck and was instantly grateful he had left the truck idling. He took frantic glances up the hill as he eased his rig onto the highway. The downhill grade toward Talihina allowed him to build up speed more quickly than he'd hoped. He'd begun to breathe a sigh of relief; then he saw them. Four figures crossed the road in front of him. At first, he thought they were men. The extreme size was the first indicator that whatever the figures were, they weren't human. The beams of his headlights illuminated the creatures with their massive muscle tone and hair-covered bodies.

The figures never looked his way as they quickly crossed the two-lane highway in front of him in what seemed like two or three steps. Their movement was graceful and effortless. When they reached the opposite side of the highway, they melted into the dark trees and down the side of the mountain; at least, that's what he hoped. After a mile, he was breathing easier. Although tempted to drive on through the night, he knew he had to report what had happened. He thought to himself, there are people hurt and possibly dead up there. William stopped in Talihina to report what had happened. He gave his statement and was released to go on about his business. Later the next day, listening to the news on his radio, he wasn't surprised to find out that five people were dead on a scenic overlook above where he had been parked.

The media was playing it off as some type of gang war. William knew better. Although he never said Bigfoot, or Sasquatch, during his statement to the police, he knew what he had seen. Even worse, for months, strange men in black suits would come to his door and question him about that night outside Talihina. They had government credentials, but there was something off about them; he got a feeling of being in the prescience of evil when these men came to his door. William never strayed from his story, he never mentioned that what he saw was anything other than four large men, but he knew better. He also knew he never wanted anything to do with the incident or any other government agency again.

Now, a little over two years later, he found himself in the same area of Oklahoma and once again in the middle of the night on a dark, lonely rural highway. Once again, he was scared. The same fear he'd had two years ago had come upon him at the hunting camp in Arkansas near Long Pool Recreational Area. He and his friend had met there the afternoon before Thanksgiving. The first night had been peaceful enough. Thursday gave them good weather, and both men saw a lot of deer, but neither saw the trophy buck they were seeking. However, the number of deer made both men hopeful about the remaining three days of hunting. The trouble started around 9:00 that evening when both men heard heavy footsteps as if somebody was crossing the creek they were camped next to.

They shined their spotlights up and down the creek bank but could not find the source of the footsteps. William knew that whoever or whatever was walking in the creek was doing it on two legs, and he began to get nervous. He told his friend of his concern, only to have him laugh it off. "Heck it was probably that big buck we're wanting; there's nobody else out here. You can't see a light or campfire any direction you look. Everybody's home sleeping off their turkey dinner. We have the entire forest to ourselves." He tried to reassure William, not knowing the lack of people made the footsteps seem that much more menacing to him.

Around 11:15, there was a strange growl, followed by an almost ape-like whoop just outside of their camp. The whoop was answered across the creek by a similar whoop. The growls became louder and closer, but try as they might, the two men could not see the source when they shone their lights in the direction it came from. There was quiet for about five minutes, then the sound of muffled grunting, which almost resembled talking, started coming from the forest to their front. It, too, was answered from across the creek as if the two were conversing.

Then there was splashing in the middle of the creek as if whatever was there decided to join its friend on the same side of the creek as the two hunters.

The sound of the running was bipedal. This was the final straw for William. "That's it for me," he said, grabbing his cooler and flashlight.

"You're leaving?" His friend asked, confused.

"You're damned right I am, and if you've got any brains in your head you will too." William said as he threw his gear and gun into his pickup before starting the engine. William wasted no time. He immediately put the truck in gear and began to roll out of the camping area. Rolling down his window, he said to his friend, "I'm not kidding; I wouldn't stay out here alone if I were you."

Bewildered, his friend asked, "What the hell is wrong with you, what about your tent?"

"I don't need it anymore," William replied. "I'm begging you, pack your crap and get out of here while you can. I'll cover you until you get in your truck, but if you're not rolling in thirty seconds you're going to be standing here alone."

"I'm not going anywhere, this is my vacation, and I'm not going to run away like a kid scared of the booger-man."

"If you were smart, you would," William replied. "You're probably hearing foxes or raccoons Will. For crying out loud, do yourself a favor and calm down."

"I am doing myself a favor, believe me." William said as he proceeded to drive out of the campgrounds.

Three hours later, William's bladder was screaming for relief. He'd hoped he could make it to Antlers, Oklahoma, before making another pit stop. Back in Arkansas, he had stopped as soon as he got onto Interstate 40 and purchased a large coffee to help him stay alert for his drive all the way to Paris, Texas. This was now proving to be a mistake, and the dark, heavy forest on either side of the small winding highway he was on did not look inviting. *Maybe I should have gone through Talihina on 271; at least they have an all-night gas station,* he thought to himself. But after thinking about the experience he'd had two years ago, he vowed never to take that route again. His current route on Hwy 259 to Hwy 144 only added about 14 extra miles, but it also added another thirty minutes as the roads were very steep with a lot of switchbacks and curves because it was on one of the steepest areas of the Kiamichi Mountains. William knew he was going to have to stop. With no shoulder on the small highway, he began peering ahead, hoping to see a pullout or any area where he could get off the road long enough to relieve himself.

A small wooden sign with the words "Rose Cabins" appeared ahead, and just ahead of it was a promising area to pull over. The sign promoting the cabins was under a pole containing a mercury vapor light. *Well, at least I won't be in pitch dark*, William thought hopefully. As he slowed his vehicle near the entrance to the cabin area, he noticed a yellow wooden sign with the telltale shape of a Bigfoot on it and the words, "Bigfoot Crossing." He knew the sign was a joke and an advertising ploy to entice adventurous people to stay at the cabins. *If you people ever see what I've seen, you won't think it's so inviting.* He thought to himself, pulling off the road into a small area of gravel. Leaving his pickup running and the lights on, William made his way to the vehicle's passenger side and began relieving himself.

As the pressure on his bladder began to go away, so did his nervousness. He finished and zipped. Looking up at the stars, he took in their beauty along with the gentle breeze out of the North. The temperature in his truck showed 44 degrees which were comfortable to William. In fact, he was at ease for the first time since he'd left the campground back in Arkansas. He began to stretch his muscles before getting back into the truck. As he leaned over, stretching out his back, his truck's motor stopped, and the lights went out. The sudden and complete darkness startled William, and he stood straight up groping for his truck's hood. *What the hell?* he thought to himself nervously as he started moving back to the other side of his truck, he noticed the mercury vapor light mounted on the pole at the entrance to the cabins was also out. In fact, there was no man-made light to be seen in any direction he looked. Climbing into the cab of his pickup, he attempted to start the engine. As he turned the key in the ignition, nothing happened. The truck was completely dead.

He reached into the glove box and pulled out a .357 Magnum pistol and a flashlight; his nervousness and fear had returned. He attempted to turn on the flashlight, it too was useless. William broke into a cold sweat and considered walking over to a house that was located on the cabin rental property. *Hope I don't get my ass shot off beating on their door in the middle of the night.* The prospect of dealing with a possibly belligerent and armed property owner was far more agreeable in his mind than sitting by himself on this dark, lonely road. He opened the door and exited his truck once again when a light caught his attention. His pickup was facing West, behind him to the East, he could see a bright bluish-white light above the highway. The light was so bright it illuminated the road underneath it. The light was about a mile away but moving in his direction. Thank goodness! A helicopter! His spirits began to rise. *Probably police, or possibly the military. Maybe the power outage has something to do with a terrorist attack,* he thought hopefully, not yet recognizing how ludicrous it was to prefer a terrorist attack over sitting alone in the dark for a while.

William stood in the middle of the road, waving both of his hands above his head as the light approached, hoping they would at least send help. The area around him began to be basked in the glow from the light, which was nearly on top of him. To William's surprise, the light was no helicopter. It was shaped like a large triangle; it passed noiselessly over his position, leisurely heading West above the highway. There was no wind, no sound, and no reaction from the light. There had been no red and green running lights as you would see on normal aircraft either. Just light and silence. What the hell? Must be military, one of those stealth planes, or drones, or something, he thought. About a quarter of a mile past William's position, the light came to a stop and hovered above the highway quietly.

Now more curious than fearful, William took a couple of steps in the direction of the light. *Maybe they saw me and just couldn't stop in time,* he thought as he began waving his hands over his head again. The light didn't waver, it just floated a couple of hundred feet above the highway. The glow underneath the vehicle began to get brighter to the point that it hurt William's eyes. Putting his right arm in front of his face to shield himself from the glare, he thought he could make out movement on the ground below the aircraft, the intensity of the light began to recede, and William could, in fact, see four figures moving around on the ground. *They must have dropped off troops; it's probably a new military toy like they used in the Bin Laden raid,* William thought, beginning to relax.

The light on the aircraft had now dimmed to its previous glow as William watched the troops milling about on the ground below it. There was something odd about their movement and shape; *I'll bet they're soldiers, something big must have happened, maybe an EMP strike that knocked out the grid.* However, William's theory was short-lived, as the light shot away soundlessly to the West following the highway. As the object disappeared, the mercury vapor light across the road from him made a popping noise and began to illuminate. William turned and noticed the lights on his truck were now on, as well as his flashlight. Breathing a huge sigh of relief, his senses were overcome with a foul smell that caused more than unease; a sense of panic began to overtake him. He quickly started to climb back into his truck and took a glance in the direction of the troops ahead of him on the highway.

He could see their shapes as they walked in his direction, *All three of them.* He began to shake uncontrollably as they moved closer. As they neared his truck, William suddenly quit breathing.

Now he knew why they looked familiar; he'd seen them before. It was the same shape he'd seen two years earlier, twenty miles north of here. William turned the key in the ignition again, praying it would start. His vehicle rocked violently as huge, hairy muscled bodies swarmed over it. He knew without looking the creatures were in the bed of his truck. One of the creatures leaped over the cab and onto the hood of his truck, crushing it. William was now frozen in fear. He knew his death was imminent; both his bladder and his bowels now emptied as he lost complete control of his muscles. The creature stepped off his truck looked back into the cab at William. In its eyes, William saw nothing but pure menace. It looked as if it were smiling at him with its large square teeth, but William knew better. The stench of the creatures was almost as overpowering as their appearance. It was as if the gates of hell had opened, and all of its putridness was emptied into the night. William just sat in the truck motionless as the creatures continued past his vehicle before suddenly darting into the tree line to the right and disappearing in the dark forest. William couldn't believe his good fortune; the creatures ignored him and moved off into the dark. It was as if they had a greater quarry than him on their minds. His body began to shake, his teeth to chatter, and the stench of the creatures were now replaced with the smell of his own bodily waste.

Try as he might, he couldn't move - his shock was too great. He was still sitting there motionless two hours later when a Le Flore County Deputy spotted him sitting on the side of the road. Noting the damaged hood of the truck, he stopped to see if he needed assistance. William was unresponsive. Thinking he'd had a stroke or was under the influence of drugs, the deputy called for an ambulance. When the EMS techs arrived, they took his vitals and determined he was suffering from some form of shock. Initially, they were going to take him to the Choctaw Nation Center in Talihina. Hearing this, the man began screaming hysterically, "Not Oklahoma, get me out of Oklahoma." Confused, the EMS techs transported him to Saint Edwards Mercy Medical Center in Fort Smith, Arkansas.

# CHAPTER SIX

~~~~~~~~~

# Summer of the Saucers

*"I wouldn't fool you, but I've seen the saucers"*
*- Elton John*

**Thursday, 26 June 1947 9:30 AM Eastern. Pentagon Office of Naval Intelligence, Washington DC.**

Lieutenant Josh Nashoba sat at his desk going over photos and schematics sent to him by aircraft engineers at Wright Field, Ohio. The photographs and schematics were taken from the crescent-shaped aircraft he'd shot down over Antarctic waters six months earlier. Since the engagement between the strange craft and ships and aircraft of Task Force 68, the young Lieutenant's life had been a blur. His odyssey had begun the day after he had been involved in an aerial engagement with this very craft and three others. The aircraft had, at first, appeared impervious to anything ships and aircraft from the task force could muster. Be it luck or fate, Nashoba had managed to hit one of the craft with 20mm cannon fire from his F-8F Bearcat and bring it down.

The quick thinking and reactions by the commander and crew of one of the seaplane tenders were the reason Josh now sat at a desk in Washington instead of with his squadron aboard the USS Philippine Sea. Following a short briefing with Admiral Cruzen, the young Lieutenant Junior Grade was promoted to Lieutenant and transferred to the USS Pine Island, the seaplane tender that held the remains of his aerial victory. He recalled seeing the aircraft up close shortly after he had arrived on Pine Island, where he was met by Commander Henry Birdsall, an Intelligence officer, and his current boss. He had been shocked by the technology of the aircraft; it was basically all wing and carried a crew of two. One of the crew was human and sat in what would be called the pilot's position. The other occupant was yet to be identified by scientists, but Josh referred to him as Okwa Naholo, a name given by the Choctaw people in the Kiamichi Mountains of Southern Oklahoma.

The aircraft was propelled by a form of jet engine that was way more advanced than any engine known to American technology. It was far more advanced than anything found in Germany after the war. It had several curiosities; among them, its armament, an electrically driven, multi-barrel 20mm cannon mounted in the wing root, much like the Gatling guns from the American Civil War, but far more advanced. The gunsight appeared to be similar to the new reflector sites that had come into use by most air forces during the war, but when engineers were able to apply power to it, to their surprise, it was more than a mere gun sight. It also seemed to display altitude, speed, and other in-flight information, allowing the pilot to monitor his aircraft's performance, altitude, and systems without having to look down into the cockpit.

The second position in the craft was the most bewildering. The occupant sat in a station that was too small for a normal man; it looked as if it had been designed to be manned by one of the strange beings. There was no window or canopy as the pilot had. The occupant of this position had no way of seeing outside the aircraft, but he had several displays or screens that resembled the radar screens currently used by the military but were much more advanced. It also contained a small joystick on the right console that had nothing to do with the aircraft itself. Engineers were speculating that it was for the deployment of some type of weapon. Perhaps a remote control for rockets or guided missiles; nobody was certain yet. Even bigger mysteries were found in the electronics. There were no vacuum or thermionic tubes. Everything was what the engineers were calling solid-state and far more advanced than the crude transistor devices just now being made available by the best scientists in America.

Josh and Commander Birdsall had stayed at Wright Field in Dayton, Ohio, gathering as much info as they could on the aircraft. Their presence was starting to draw unwanted attention among the Army Air Force personal stationed there. Being the only two Naval Officers on the base day after day was one thing. They were also going in and out of what the Army Air Force guys referred to as "Hangar 18". The building had an ominous quality, with a separate fence and four Military Police guards manning the entrance twenty-four hours a day. The average soldier or airman couldn't help but wonder what secrets were held inside, especially when the only ones allowed in were lab rats in their white coats or intelligence officers or two certain mysterious naval officers. The investigation needed to be low-key and not draw any undue attention. It became obvious that the course of best discretion would be for Nashoba and Birdsall to take the information they currently had and relocate to an office in the Pentagon. Once buried inside the Office of

Naval Intelligence section, they would be safe from curious eyes and vivid imaginations. Both men were summoned to Washington.

On their first day, while organizing their offices, they were interrupted and sent to the White House to meet with the President. Josh remembered how impressed he was with Harry Truman's down-to-earth nature and blunt honesty. It never occurred to Josh that the President of the United States had been just as impressed with him. Being a thorough man, Truman had read the records of both men prior to meeting them. He was very impressed by the young Lieutenant Nashoba, who had toiled, educated, and fought his way into the cockpit of one of the US Navy's hottest fighter planes. To Harry Truman, Josh Nashoba's life story was the story of America.

Josh remembered how President Truman seemed to hang on his every word as he re-told the story of the air battle that broke out around Task Force 68 back in January. He was just as attentive when they shared the technical info as well as the identities of the occupants. As they were leaving, the President grabbed Josh by the arm and told him, "Son, God didn't have you go through all the challenges you had to face to become a fighter pilot for nothing. Of all the pilots in the sky that day, you were the one that brought this thing down and delivered it to us, so we could study their secrets. We're not sure yet if those occupants are some escaped Nazis, or men from the moon, or God only knows where. I do know this; God has you in place for a reason and I'm going to tell you right now, you're my go to guy on these strange aircraft. Don't let me down, Son."

Shocked that the President held him in such high regard, Josh replied, solemnly, "I'll give you my very best, Sir." With that, Truman's eyes flashed the inner fire he was famous for. He patted Josh on the shoulder and returned to his desk.

Josh picked up a photograph of the deceased human occupant of the craft. Both Naval Intelligence and the Army's OSS, identified him as Oberst (Colonel) Rudolph Moritz. The Oberst (Colonel) had enjoyed a successful career as a Luftwaffe fighter pilot during the war. He had fought on both fronts and achieved over 150 victories against British, French, Russian, and American foes. He was instrumental in creating Luftwaffe tactics against the large formations of American B-17 and B-24 bombers during the war. His last known assignment was with Jagdeverband 44, which was commanded by the famous Adolph Galland and assigned Germany's most advanced aircraft. The Messerschmidt 262 jet fighter. His trail went cold after that. Being a disciple of military aviation, Josh knew that the flamboyant Galland, having survived the war, had recently been released from a British Prisoner of War camp and returned to Germany. I may need to talk to this guy, Josh was thinking to himself as there was a knock on his office door just as it opened. Josh popped out of his chair at the position of attention as his boss Commander Henry Birdsall entered.

"For crying out loud Josh, keep your seat," Birdsall said, throwing a group of photos on his desk.

"What is this, Sir?" Josh said, picking them up.

"They're something you haven't seen yet. Those are stills from the gun camera footage from your aircraft and others during the fight last January." Josh looked at the photos and was shocked that he'd never thought of them before. After his hasty departure from his squadron and the USS Philippine Sea, it never crossed his mind to see the gun camera footage from the engagement.

"These are nice. I guess we can find a use for them, but it's a little late since we already have all these other photos and documents."

"There's a private pilot who claims he saw nine of these over Washington yesterday." Birdsall replied.

"Here? Washington DC?" Josh asked, confused.

"No, Washington State. A Mr. Kenneth Arnold. An ordinary everyday American businessman, claims to have spotted these things while flying his private airplane near Mount Rainier yesterday afternoon."

"Where is this Mr. Arnold at now?" Josh asked.

"As luck would have it, he's at Pendleton Army Airfield in Oregon. He flew there yesterday evening to attend an air show this weekend. Now, I need you to pack your gear and get your butt over to Andrews Field. The brass has a special aircraft ready to take to you to Pendleton Field as soon as possible. There you will find and interview this Kenneth Arnold before this story starts hitting every radio station and newspaper."

"Are you sure you want me to go all the way out there to talk to this guy? He's already at an Army Airfield. Why can't the boys in green interview him?"

"Because there's a certain President, who was so impressed by a certain Naval Aviator, that he won't accept anybody else interviewing this guy. He wants you to do it." Birdsall countered.

"Well, there's an old saying that exceptional people, get exceptional treatment." Josh said, smiling.

"Exceptional treatment is right. You'd better wear your flight suit but pack a couple of uniforms and some civvies."

"Why a flight suit if I'm a passenger on a transport?" Josh asked in mild confusion. "President Truman ordered the brass to deliver you to Pendleton Field using the fastest means possible; and you're going to love this particular means possible. Now get moving Josh, the Army is waiting on you."

## Thursday, 26 June 1947 11:35 AM Eastern, Andrews Army Airfield, Washington DC.

The Army Private had maneuvered the olive drab Plymouth G522 sedan through Washington traffic like an experienced racer. He even used the siren to clear a path through groups of slow-moving cars a couple of times. At the Andrews Airfield gate, he didn't even come to a full stop, he merely held some type of pass out the window, and the Sergeant guarding the entrance to the airfield waved him through and saluted. He used the same maneuver as he drove through the entrance to the flight line, once again barely slowing while holding the pass out of the window, although now, he did slow to 15 miles per hour, the max speed allowed by non-emergency traffic on the flight line.

As the sedan drove around to the front side of the Military Transport building, Josh saw the usual lineup of Army Air Force transports, a couple of C-47s and one C-54. There was also an Army A-26 medium bomber. Josh's heart was beginning to sink, *A bomber, I wore a flight suit for this?* The Private continued driving the Plymouth to the other side of the A-26, just when a disappointed Lieutenant Josh Nashoba was attempting to make peace with the fact that a bomber was going to be his ride to Oregon; then his eyes fell upon the P-82 Twin Mustang parked on the other side. "Is this my ride Private?"

"Yes, Sir, that's about the weirdest looking airplane I've ever seen. Never say we don't treat the Navy well sir." The Private said, looking at Josh in the mirror with an enormous grin as the sedan came to a stop. "Good luck, sir!"

"Thank you, Soldier." Josh said, exiting the sedan and grabbing his sea bag. He'd seen a P-82 before. The aircraft was basically two P-51 Mustang fighters joined together mid-wing to make one aircraft. This provided longer range and was first intended as an escort for Army B-29s bombing Japan. Like Josh's F-8 Bearcat, this aircraft also missed the war. Currently, the Army was using the aircraft as a long-range fighter, and like everything else with propellers, it was probably already on the chopping block as the jet and rocket technology in the United States military was getting all of the development dollars. As he

126

walked up to the aircraft, he noted the name Betty Jo painted on the nose. It occurred to him that this was the very same aircraft that had made the record-beating, non-stop flight from Hickam Field to La Guardia Field in New York. He'd read about the flight that took place earlier in February while he was at Wright Field in Ohio, which was, in fact, the home of both this aircraft and its pilot, Lt Col Robert Thacker.

A young, fresh-faced Army Air Force Captain came out from under the far wing of the aircraft. "Good morning, Lieutenant, I'm Captain John Archer, I'll be your pilot today. Since we're the same pay grade, I was thinking we'd just be informal and go by first names on this hop."

"Works for me, I'm Joshua Nashoba; you can call me Josh," he said, smiling as he shook hands with the Army Air Force Captain." I've seen this aircraft before at Wright Field. Never dreamed I'd get a chance to fly in her. This is the bird Colonel Thacker flew when he set the record non-stop flight from Hawaii to New York, correct?"

"That's right. I was his copilot on that hop, and I can tell you... Be glad we're only going to Oregon. From the east coast to Hawaii is hard on the ole tail feathers," Archer said as a look of recognition came over his face. "I've actually seen you at Wright Field. You're the mystery sailor that is seen going in and out of Hanger-18, aren't you? Now this all makes sense."

"Makes sense?" Josh asked, confused. "Yes. I was jolted out of bed early this morning and told to fly this bird to Andrews and that I'd be picking up an especially important officer who I was supposed to get to Oregon as soon as possible. For the life of me I couldn't figure out what was so important, until I recognized you."

"I'm nothing special Captain; I mean, John. Just a sailor doing his duty."

Archer chuckled, "Great we've got a little over six hours of flying time ahead, you can tell me all about how unimportant you are while we're flying. Let me finish my pre-flight and we'll get out of here. By the way, the right cockpit is all yours, and there's a standard AN6510 seat parachute. I hear it's similar to the Navy S-1 type, so you should be familiar with it. Also, there's a travel pod hanging on the wing on your side; you can stow your gear in there."

Josh looked over at the right side with its separate fuselage and cockpit. He stored his gear in what Captain Archer called a "travel pod." This was nothing more than a five-hundred-gallon drop tank with a small door on the side. An Army Sergeant assisted Josh with putting his gear inside the tank. Once this was done, the Sergeant closed the door and secured it with screw-type fasteners. Josh scrambled up on the wing and looked into the cockpit, which was fairly typical of any military fighter aircraft in the mid-1940s. Stepping back down onto the flight line, he could see Captain Archer was completing his pre-flight inspection.

"This is quite an aircraft, John. Did you fly Mustangs during the war?"

"Well, I did I train on P-51s and was on my way to the 35th Fighter Group at Okinawa when the first bomb was dropped on Hiroshima. By the time I got to my squadron, the war was over. I did get a chance to fly over Tokyo Bay the day the surrender was signed on the USS Missouri. Then, the next thing you know, I'm spitting and fighting just to stay in the Army and keep flying. I got assigned to Materials Command and just knew my flying days were over. Then one day Colonel Thacker walks into my office and tells me that he's my new boss. He orders me to pack my bags and get to Dayton Ohio and the North American plant there and get checked out on the Twin Mustang. I had no idea what a Twin Mustang was until I got there and saw this very aircraft. Next thing you know, I'm his copilot for that hop from Hawaii to New York. You never know what the military has in store for you. I was told this morning my passenger was a Navy Fighter Pilot. Corsairs, or Hellcats?"

"Bearcats, actually," Josh replied.

"Ahh the Bearcat. That's the one fighter I haven't had a chance to see yet, but I hear they're a hot little plane."

"Yes, they're an awesome fighter. But, like you, I missed the war too. I'm just another frustrated fighter pilot."

"From rumors I've heard around Wright Field, there's more to you than you let on. There's talk that you shot down a space craft, something out of a Buck Rogers or Flash Gordon story..." Josh was a little shocked by this; he was under the impression that he and Commander Birdsall were written off as a couple of naval engineers by the Army personnel at Wright Field.

"I'm just an engineer, John."

Looking up from the right fuselage rudder he had just inspected, Archer pointed at Josh's Gold Naval Aviator Wings on his flight suit. "Engineer my ass Josh. Everybody hears the talk about what they keep in that hanger. Not to mention the Army brass doesn't fly Navy Lieutenants from one coast to the other in an aircraft like this every day. You can downplay your position all you want, but there's something up with you. You've got clout, so I wouldn't be surprised if you did see some machine from the Moon, or Mars, or planet Mongo, for all I know."

Josh couldn't help it. He snickered for a moment before answering. "You fly one of the fastest, weirdest looking, aircraft in the United States Military and you're worried about strange craft from other planets? I've got news for you John. Your airplane looks like it came from the planet Mongo, which in my book makes you Flash Gordon. So, get me to Oregon, will you Flash?"

With a huge grin, John Archer replied, "Sure thing, Buck. Go ahead and get strapped in. I'll have you on the planet Mongo in a little over six hours."

### Thursday, 26 June 1947 1:15 PM Central, 9.500 ft over South Dakota.

The flight had been fairly exciting at first; the P-82's takeoff and climb out from Andrews Field was as thrilling as any that experienced in an F-8 Bearcat. At first, Josh enjoyed the fact that he was a passenger, and he took advantage of the visibility provided by the bubble canopy, taking in all the historic sites as the aircraft climbed out over Washington DC. While low enough over the city, Josh could see people stop and look up, undoubtedly intrigued by the strange-looking aircraft flying over them. Josh and Captain Archer had spent quite a bit of time with small talk about their flying experiences. However, they'd dropped the agreed-to-first-name basis. Instead, they had fallen into comical Flash Gordon-Buck Rogers identities for each other. Captain John Archer was Flash, and Lieutenant Josh Nashoba was now Buck. Both men even managed fairly decent imitations of movie star Buster Crabbe, who actually played both characters in Hollywood movies of the mid and late 1930s. Josh had been reading reports on the second occupant of the craft and was stunned by the medical examination of the remains.

There was a quote from the medical examiner. "We believe the body of the deceased is obviously organic. Although it appears the body is more like a suit or even a vehicle rather than an actual living entity, even though a strange form of living tissue makes up its entirety. Also, the hands and feet each have six fingers and six toes. The remains appear not to be carbon-based but something similar to, if not actually, a silicon-based life form. Silicon, I was taught all life was made up of carbon? Josh thought, confused, as John Archer's voice came over the intercom. "Hey there, Buck, you want to take the controls for a bit?"

Looking to his left at the opposing cockpit, Josh could see Archer's face grinning hugely through his own bubble canopy.

"Thought you'd never ask, Flash." Josh said in his best Buster Crabbe imitation.

"Flash needs to use the relief tube," Archer said, laughing.

"You mean this thing has a relief tube? Heck, I've just been pissing all over the cockpit floor the whole trip." Josh said, looking across the wing into the other cockpit. He could see Archer's shocked expression.

"You peed in the cockpit?" Archer asked in horror.

"We call it swabbing the decks in the Navy, Flash."

"That's the cockpit I normally sit in, and I don't think I want to smell squid piss, next time I'm in it!" Archer said worriedly.

Josh laughed loudly and eased the worry of his new friend. "Don't worry, Flash, I found the relief tube when we were over Ohio."

"Thank goodness, I was about to demote you from Buck Rogers to Popeye the Sailor. One more thing, Navy, this bird doesn't have a poop deck." Both men burst into laughter. "Let me finish my business here, and I'll let you wring this bird out a bit Josh," Archer said.

"Looking forward to it Flash!" Josh said in anticipation of performing some aerobatics with the aircraft.

Once Captain Archer had finished his personal business, he looked across to Josh and keyed the intercom saying. "Okay, Buck! Scare me!" Josh didn't hesitate. He immediately took the aircraft into a left aileron roll. Although the larger P-82 wasn't as nimble as the F-8 Bearcat he was used to flying; he was surprised how quickly and smoothly the plane rolled. Josh did a couple more rolls before performing a Split S and then an Immelman maneuver to bring himself back on course.

"This is a smooth flying bird you have here, Flash. I like that I'm not fighting the propeller torque. I still prefer my Bearcat, but if I was going to war in a twin-engine bird, I think this is the one I would choose. I lost a good friend a few months back, a Marine who flew the twin-engine F-7 Tigercat. I think he would have loved this bird too."

"Can't beat the counter rotating propellers for smoothness, although there are times the torque is useful. Sorry to hear about your friend Buck. I'm missing a couple myself. Sadly, friends are lost fairly frequently in our occupation. Okay, brother, better let me take over the controls again and get us back on schedule. I've got to get you to planet Mongo before the sun sets."

"Yes, you do. You wouldn't want me to blame the Army for my lack of punctuality." Josh said, laughing.

"So, can you tell me, what you're doing there?" Archer asked.

"I've got to find a Kenneth Arnold at this air show and interview him about an incident that he witnessed yesterday."

"So, can you tell me about this incident?"

130

"I don't know yet; but you're more than welcome to help me hunt down this Mr. Arnold at the air show."

"Chauffer and now personal servant, I'm sure not climbing the social ladder hanging out with you Navy types."

## Thursday, 26 June 1947 2:00 PM Pacific, 9.000 ft over Western Oregon.

Josh was anxious to get out of the aircraft. John Archer had started a slow descent toward Pendleton, Oregon, and informed him they should be landing in a little less than an hour.

Josh was pondering his gun camera photos on the craft he'd shot down months ago. His mind was clogged with questions about who made it, and even more, who was operating it. The more Josh thought about the mysterious German pilot and his even more mysterious otherworldly crewmate, who appeared to be exactly like the creatures his father had taught him about through Choctaw tribal legends as a boy, the more questions he had. *What are you, and how did you get here?*

His thoughts were interrupted by John Archer over the intercom. "Hey, Buck, you did say that guy's name was Kenneth Arnold, correct?"

"That's right, why?"

"I've been listening to a KWRC Radio in Pendleton, Oregon just to get a feel for the place. They're about to broadcast a taped interview with a Mr. Kenneth Arnold. I'm going to put it on the intercom. You might want to hear this." Josh reached down and turned up the volume slightly; he was hearing a commercial about a department store in Pendleton, followed by a plug for the upcoming air show.

Then the voice of a radio reporter named Ted Smith came on excitedly describing the guest he was about to interview named Kenneth Arnold. *Oh man, I'm thirty minutes too late.* Josh thought as the interview started.

**Ted Smith:** "The nation, every newscaster, and every newspaper across the nation has made headlines out of it, and this afternoon we are honored, indeed, to have here in our studio this man, Kenneth Arnold, who, we believe, may be able to give us a first-hand account and give you the same on what happened." "Kenneth, first of all, if you'll move up here to the microphone just a little closer, we'll ask you to just tell in your own fashion, as you told us last night in your hotel room, and again this morning, what you were doing there and how this entire thing started. Go ahead, Kenneth."

**Kenneth Arnold:** "Well, about 2:15 I took off from Chehalis, Washington, en route to Yakima, and, of course, every time that any of us fly over the country near Mt. Rainier, we spend an hour or two in search of the Marine plane that's never been found that they believe is in the snow someplace southwest of that particular area." "That area is located at about, uh... [cough] its elevation is about 10,000 foot, and I had made one sweep in close to Mt. Rainier and down one of the canyons and was dragging it for any types of objects that might prove to be the Marine ship, uh... and as I come out, uh... of the canyon there, was about 15 minutes, I was approximately 25 to 28 miles from Mt. Rainier, I climbed back up to 9200 feet and I noticed, to the left of me, a chain which looked to me like the tail of a Chinese kite, kind of weaving and going at a terrific speed across the face of Mt. Rainier." "I, uh... at first, uh... I thought they were geese because it flew like geese, but it was going so fast that, that I immediately changed my mind and decided it was a bunch of new jet planes in formation."

"Well, as the... as the plane come to the edge of Mt. Rainier, flying at about 160 degrees south, uh... I thought I would clock them, because it was such a clear day, and I didn't know where their destination was, but due to the fact that I had Mt. Saint Helens and Mt. Adams to clock them by, I just thought I'd see just how fast they were going, since among pilots we argue about speed so much."

"And, they seemed to flip and flash in the sun, just like a mirror, and uh, in fact, I happened to be in an angle from the sun that seemed to hit the tops of these, uh... peculiar looking things, in such a way that it almost blinded you when you, when you looked at them through your Plexiglas windshield."

"Well, uh... I, uh... it was about one minute to three, when uh... I started clocking them on my, my sweep secondhand clock, and uh, as I kept looking at them, I kept looking for their tails, and they didn't have any tail! I thought, well, maybe something's wrong with my eyes and I turned the plane around and opened the window, and looked out the window, and sure enough, I couldn't find any tails on 'em." "And, uh... the whole, our observation of these particular ships, didn't last more than about two and a half minutes and I could see them only plainly when uh, they seemed to tip their wing, or whatever it was, and the sun flashed on them."

"They looked something like uh, a pie plate that was cut in half, with a sort of a convex triangle in the rear. Now, I thought, well, uh, that maybe they're jet planes with just the tail, the tails painted green or brown or something, and I didn't think too much of it, but kept on watching them. They didn't fly in a conventional formation that's taught in our army, they seemed to kind of weave in and out, right above the mountaintops, and I would say that they even went down into the canyons in several instances, oh, probably a hundred feet, but I could see them against the snow, of course, on Mt. Rainier and against the snow on Mt. Adams as they were flashing, and against a high ridge that happens to lay in between Mt. Rainier and Mt. Adams." "But when I observed the tail end of the last one passing Mt. Adams, and I was at an angle, uh, near Mt. Rainier from it, but I looked at my watch and it showed one minute and 42 seconds. Well, I felt that was pretty fast and I didn't stop to think what the distance was between the two mountains."

"Well, I landed at Yakima, Washington, and Al Baxter was there to greet me and ha, he told me I guess I better change my brand [of clock], ha ha, ... but he kind, he gave me a mysterious sort of a look that maybe I had seen something, he didn't know, and well, I just kind of forgot it then, until I got down to Pendleton and I began looking at my map and taking measurements on it and the best calculation I could figure out, now even in spite of error, would be around 1200 miles an hour, because making the distance from Mt. Rainier to Mt. Adams, in we'll say approximately two minutes, it's almost, uh, well, it'd be around 25 miles per minute. Now allowing for air, we can give them three minutes or four minutes to make it, and they're still going more than 800 miles an hour, and to my knowledge, there isn't anything that I've read about, outside of some of the German rockets, that would go that fast. These were flying in more or less a level, uh... constant altitude. They weren't going up and they weren't going down. They were just simply flying straight and level and I, ha ha, I laughed, and I told the Pendleton [unintelligible], they sure must have had a tailwind. But it didn't seem to help me much. But to the best of my knowledge, and the best of my description, that is what I actually saw, and, uh... like I told the Associated Press, I'll, I'd be glad to confirm it with my hands on a Bible because I did see it, and whether it has anything to do with our army or our intelligence or whether it has to do with some foreign country, I don't know. But I did see it and I did clock it and I just happened to be in a beautiful position to do it and uh, it's just as much a mystery to me as it is to everyone else who's been calling me the last 24 hours, wondering what it was."

**Ted Smith:** "Well, Kenneth, thank you very much. I know that you've certainly been busy these last 24 hours, 'cause I've spent some of the time with you myself, and I know that the press associations, both Associated Press and our press, the United Press, has been right after you every minute. The

Associated and the United Press, all over the nation, have been after this story. It's been on every newscast, over the air, and in every newspaper I know of. The uh, United Press in Portland has made several telephone calls here at Pendleton to me, and to you this morning, and from New York I understand, they are after this story, and that we may have an answer before the fortnight... because, if it is some new type of army or Navy secret missile, there would probably a story come out on it from the army or Navy asking, uh, saying that it is a new secret plane and that will be all there is to it, and they will hush up the story, or perhaps that we will finally get a definite answer to it."

"I understand the United Press is checking on it out of New York now with the Army, and also with the Navy, and we hope to have some concrete answer before nightfall. We certainly want to thank you, Kenneth, for coming into our studio. We feel very pleased that this news, which is making nationwide news across the country, we are able to give our listeners over KWRC a first-hand report direct from you, of what you saw. And we urge our listeners to keep tuned to this station, because anytime this afternoon or this evening, when we get something on it on our United Press teletype, which is in direct communications with New York, Chicago, Portland, in fact, every United Press bureau across the nation, why, we'll have it on the air."

Josh's heart sank; *man, this cat is out of the bag*. He thought to himself as he felt the P-82's engines advance and the aircraft pick up speed. "Buck, I'm picking up the pace a bit brother. I think we'd better get there and find this guy before he does anymore interviews," Archer said over the intercom.

"Good idea, and now I guess you know why the brass rushed me out here," Josh replied.

"Oh yeah, now a lot of things make much more sense. You can tell me all about it over the drinks you're going to buy me at the O club tonight."

"I don't drink, Flash."

"That's even better, you'll have more money to spend on me then, Buck," Josh knew Archer was grinning ear to ear; he didn't even have to look.

### Thursday, 26 June 1947 2:50 PM Pacific, Pendleton Army Airfield, Pendleton, Oregon

John Archer made good on his attempt to get Josh to Pendleton a bit quicker. They arrived over the base at 2:45 Pacific Time. Captain Archer buzzed the runway with a high-speed pass before moving into the landing pattern. "That might make this Arnold guy easier to find Buck. There's never been a P-82 flown into this base, after a scorcher of a pass like that, any pilot civilian, or military, will come over and check this bird out once we're parked." Josh had to agree - it was a good idea. He looked the base over as they taxied toward the main military terminal. Josh saw a couple of Army T-6 Texans, what the Navy called SNJ trainers. There was a small gathering of aircraft obviously in for the upcoming air show over the weekend. Two P-51s, a P-47 Thunderbolt, and a P-38 Lightning made up the Army's contribution to the air show. Josh's heart leaped when he saw an F-8 Bearcat and an F-4U4 Corsair parked together.

"Looks like they invited the Navy and Marines to this shindig. When we get time later, I'll show you around the Bearcat."

"That's a deal, Buck," Archer replied. Dozens of people were approaching the area near the main terminal where the P-82 would park. Archer was right, the high-speed pass he had performed as well as the strange-looking aircraft was drawing everyone who had an interest in aviation to them, like moths to a flame.

"Flash, your high-speed pass was a great idea, if Arnold is anywhere near this flight line, he'll show up to check out this airplane." Josh said.

"I didn't get this far in life on looks alone, Buck," Archer replied.

The P-82 came to a stop as Archer followed the instructions of an Army Sergeant who marshaled him into his parking spot. In another two minutes, both engines were shut down, and both men were standing up in their respective cockpits, attempting to stretch their cramped muscles back into functioning well enough to allow them to climb out of the aircraft without spilling onto the tarmac. A fairly large crowd had gathered around the aircraft. Curious onlookers began to question the two men.

"What the heck kind of plane is this?"

"Which one flies it, and which one navigates?"

"How come you're a Navy guy in an Army plane?"

"Where did you guys come here from?"

"You gonna give rides during the air show?"

A tired Josh Nashoba smiled down at the crowd on his side of the aircraft. "I was just a passenger; any questions you have should be addressed to Captain Archer," he said, pointing to the opposite fuselage. The whole crowd moved toward Archer, who was now standing on the aircraft's left wing.

He gave Josh a sarcastic look, "Gee Thanks!"

Then once again, Archer did something brilliant. "Ladies and gentlemen, I'll be more than glad to answer your questions about the P-82 Twin Mustang, but if I can have your attention for one moment, please." The crowd grew quiet and attentive. "Is Mr. Kenneth Arnold among this group and if not, do any of you know him and where we may be able to find him? We've flown all the way from Washington DC today so Lieutenant Nashoba here could talk to him."

"I'm Arnold," a man said, stepping from the crowd; Josh saw a broad-shouldered man with strong facial features, who appeared to be in his early thirties, move toward him.

"Mr. Kenneth Arnold of Yakima Washington?" Josh asked.

"Yes, Lieutenant, that's me. Am I in some kind of trouble?" the man asked, worried.

"No, Sir, not at all, but I will be if I don't get a chance to sit down and interview you." Josh replied.

Looking back at the P-82 and then again to Josh, the man said. "I'll be glad to tell you anything you want to know, if you'll tell me about flying in this airplane."

"I'm sure we can work that out, Sir. I'd like a chance to stretch these cramped muscles and get a shower. Is there a decent place to eat around here? We could talk about your incident over dinner. The Navy will pay for it."

"Can't beat a deal like that!" Arnold replied.

## Friday, 27 June 1947 12:05 AM Pacific, Pendleton Army Airfield, Pendleton, Oregon

Josh sat at the metal desk inside the (BOQ) Bachelor Officer Quarters at Pendleton Field. The desk was the typical grey government model found in any military, federal, or state building anywhere in the world. The room was small and dark, with one bedside lamp and another small lamp on the desk. The base was due to close completely within the next year and would probably end up as a civilian airport. With the conclusion of the war, the Army no longer needed training bases from one end of the country to the other. Not to mention that just a little over a month ago, John Gurney, a senator from South Dakota, had introduced a bill to Congress that would make the Army Air Force a separate branch from the Army. The bill had legs and looked like it would pass through Congress with no problems, so the Army was going to get rid of as many airbases as possible before they ended up giving them to a new branch of the military. Still, Pendleton Field was functioning with slightly more than a skeleton crew, the BOQ was clean and comfortable, and the Officer's Club still served up a good steak. Josh had treated Kenneth Arnold to dinner there along with Captain Archer.

The interview and dinner went as well as could be expected. Mr. Arnold had been very forthcoming about his sighting, even to the point of plotting the positions of the unknown aircraft on maps Josh provided. Then Josh produced a couple of still photos taken from the gun camera footage of his F-8 Bearcat back on January 30th over the Antarctic Ocean. Kenneth Arnold got very excited when he saw the photos. "That's what I saw!" he exclaimed loudly. "Where did you get these?" he asked Josh.

"I really can't tell you that, Sir, but you are sure this is what you saw?"

"It's exactly what I saw, only I wasn't able to get as close to them as these photos show." He continued to study the photo taking in as much detail as possible. Then, looking at Josh, his eyes narrowed a bit. "Lieutenant, I'm not a military pilot, but I know gun camera footage when I see it. Look at the splashes in the water, those are made by machine guns, and that black puff in the distance… That looks to me like anti-aircraft fire. There is also a heavy smoke cloud in the background as if something large is burning, something like a ship. Did these come from some kind of air-sea battle? Are we fighting these things?"

I'm not allowed to tell you anything information, Sir. I'm here to take your witness statement, nothing more."

"Let me see those," John Archer said, grabbing the photos from Kenneth Arnold. After looking at the photos for a few minutes, Archer said nothing more as he handed them back to Josh. After a few minutes, Kenneth Arnold gave up on any attempts to get more info about the photos from Josh. The three men spent the rest of the evening doing what pilots do. They talked about flying; Mr. Arnold was very interested in hearing about Archer's P-51 Mustang flying and especially interested in the P-82 Twin Mustang. He was just as excited to ask Josh about flying the F-8 Bearcat and what it was like to fly from a carrier.

At the end of the evening, Mr. Arnold thanked Josh for the meal; Josh, in turn, thanked Mr. Arnold for answering his questions. "You know Lieutenant, it I ever see those things again, I'm going to fly in the other direction. They just didn't seem normal, something just wasn't right about them, and now that I've seen your photos, that feeling is stronger. Whatever you're investigating, I hope you find the answers."

Now with the late hour and Spartan accommodations, Josh was beginning to wish he'd never seen, much less fired on the strange aircraft over the

Antarctic. *You should have missed,* he thought to himself. At least that way, he'd be with his ship and squadron mates right now. The last word he'd gotten was his carrier, the USS Philippine Sea, was doing a cruise through the Caribbean. What an improvement that had to be over the Antarctic Ocean. Now he was stuck with an Army Air Force Captain at a dying base on the wrong coast from his beloved ship. *I'm not even sure what they want of me,* he thought to himself. *The president wants a full report... A full report on what? It appears that Kenneth Arnold saw the same type of aircraft that attacked our fleet off the coast of Antarctica. I don't know where they're coming from or why. It's going to take more than one Naval Lieutenant sitting on his butt in an Army BOQ to figure this out. What can I contribute to this other than words?*

A knock at the door broke the puzzled trance Josh was in. "Come in," he said. The door opened to reveal a tipsy-looking Captain John Archer, holding a bottle of Scotch and what looked to be a yellow telegram.

"Hey, Sailor, it's time to celebrate," he said sluggishly.

"Hope you can handle that by yourself; like I said earlier, I don't drink," Josh replied with a curious grin. Archer looked at the bottle quizzically,

"Oh this, well, I did warm up the ole engine to prepare for take-off. The real reason for celebration is this," he said, holding the yellow paper high in the air. "It looks as if your boss, got with my boss, or our bosses, bosses, got together..." He paused for a moment, trying to collect his thoughts, then shaking his head, he continued. "Anyway, I'm to stay here with you for another ten days or so. We're supposed to fly Arnold's route near Mount Rainier daily, starting Monday. We're also ordered to fly the route he says the objects took and precisely record the distance and time to complete it."

"Why do we have to wait until Monday?" Josh asked, disappointed at the prospect of spending more time in Oregon.

"They don't want us getting in the way of the local air show this weekend. We're supposed to lay low and blend in until Monday, then we start doing the test runs. We are also under orders to keep an eye out for any strange aerial craft and report on them. My guess is they probably don't want us dragging any Moon people back over the base where all the civilians can see them. So Buck Rogers, we wait until Monday to get started."

Josh wasn't happy with the news, but he was an Officer, and he would do his duty. "Well, Flash, I have to tell you, that does not sound like a reason to celebrate, so you can keep the bottle for yourself."

"Whoa, hold your horses, Buck," Archer said, squinting at the telegram. There's also this little tidbit of news... The National Services Act has passed through Congress. The President will be signing it into law sometime in September. It means the Army Air Force will become a separate branch from the Army." Looking around the room, Archer spotted two glasses near a small sink. Grabbing both, he filled them halfway. Handing one to Josh and lifting his own, he said, "To the United States Air Force, live in fame or die in flame!" Then he emptied the glass.

"Okay John, this is big news and I'll make an exception to toast your new branch. To the United States Air Force, long may they fly," Josh said, emptying his own glass and wincing as the amber liquid burned a path down his throat. *I'll never understand how people enjoy this.*

Looking down at the stack of files on Josh's desk, Archer was especially intrigued by the photos. "Do you mind?" He asked, pointing at the photographs.

"It would seem to me that you are as involved in this investigation as I am. Go ahead," Josh replied. Picking up the stack of photos, Archer began studying each at some length before going to the next one.

"You know, I've seen something like this before in a report on the German Luftwaffe, and their secret weapons found after the war. They were developing a jet-propelled fighter plane that looked very similar to this," Archer said as he thumbed through the photos. Then, suddenly, he started organizing the photos in the correct sequence from a pilot's perspective. "Okay, here's the first photo, you can see tracers, and the craft is just coming into the frame of the photo," he said, dropping the photo on the desk, followed by three more in succession. Archer held the last three in his hands. "Did you show Mr. Arnold these three?"

"No, he identified the craft on the first four, so there was no reason to show him the rest."

"Is that the only reason you didn't show him these photos? Or is the real reason you didn't show him was because you didn't want him to see the destruction of the thing?" Archer said with a sly grin before continuing. "See that bright spot on the upper wing that looks like a flash? That is a round impacting, there's a smaller flash just behind it, which means a second round is also just making contact. In the next frame there are two puffs of smoke where the rounds hit, in the final frame you can see that there is a large amount of structural damage because the wing is beginning to separate from the rest of the aircraft. That amount of damage from two rounds along with the size of the flashes and the puff of smoke tells me... Those are 20mm cannon rounds striking the thing. The only fighter aircraft in the Army Air

Force using the 20mm cannon is the P-38, and there are very few squadrons still flying P-38s. The 20mm cannon is primarily used by Navy and Marine Corps fighters, like Corsairs and Bearcats... So, don't bullshit me, this gun camera footage is from your Bearcat, isn't it?"

Grabbing the bottle, Josh poured himself another drink. "Like I said, it seems you're as involved in this investigation as I am, so yes, that's my gun camera footage and that's my kill."

Archer grabbed the bottle of scotch off the desk, not bothering to pour another drink. He took a long pull straight from the bottle itself, looking at Josh with newfound admiration, "Wow, you really are Buck Rogers!"

## Monday, 7 July 1947 8:00 AM Pacific, Pendleton Army Air Field, Pendleton, Oregon

Josh Nashoba and John Archer were doing a quick walk-around inspection of the P-82 Twin-Mustang. They had scheduled another set of tests to run early this afternoon near Mount Rainer in Washington State. So far, every test they had tried failed to debunk the reported speed of the nine-mystery aircraft reported by Kenneth Arnold. They had tried every possible angle of Arnold's reported flight path and the flight path of the objects he had reported. They'd managed to get a couple of Army Air Force P-51s to fly the reported route as they timed the passes. On each occasion, John Archer has reproduced Arnold's reported path 25 to 28 Miles south of Mt. Rainier, heading east at an altitude of 9,200 ft. The biggest problem they had was keeping the P-82 as close as possible to Arnold's. His small Call-Air A-2 aircraft had a top speed of 110 miles per hour. He reported his speed was about 105 miles per hour at the time of the sighting.

The P-82 Josh was riding in needed more than 102 miles per hour to stay airborne, so while Archer fought to keep the P-82 in the air as it struggled sloppily at such slow speeds, Josh would spot and time the P-51s as they flew the reported route at a heading of 160 degrees and roughly 10,000 feet in altitude. Four times the P-51s flew the reported route as Josh timed them as they passed the small, jagged outcrop on the southeast slope of Mt Rainier until they passed the summit of Mt. Adams, a distance of 48 miles. Each run, the calculated speed that Josh plotted was close to if not the same exact speed reported by the pilots flying the P-51s, approximately 425 miles per hour. On Saturday, Nashoba and Archer had an opportunity to clock a jet fighter making the route. A P-80 Shooting Star out of Muroc Army Airfield in California had been flown to Pendleton on the previous Friday to assist with their test. Once again, four passes were made with the aircraft along the reported flight path, and once again, Josh's calculations matched with the reported speed of the P-80 pilot of 560 miles per hour.

After the P-80s last pass, Josh was out of ideas and patience. "We don't have anything that can fly as fast as what Arnold reported, the P-51s and now this P-80 were at top speed and we're not even close," Josh said to Archer.

"Well, I got news for you we don't have anything that can fly as slow as Arnold's Call-Air either." Archer said tiredly as he fought to keep the P-82 airborne. So, with a few days left to burn and no test aircraft available to clock, the two men decided they would patrol the area between Mt. Rainier and Mt. Adams, hoping to spot some kind of aerial anomaly that might explain Arnold's sighting and have something of substance for the report Josh was supposed to write for the brass in Washington. The walk around complete, both men were tiredly climbing up into their respective cockpits when a young Corporal came sprinting toward Archer's them from the direction of the Field Operations shack waving a yellow telegram. "Lieutenant Nashoba!" he yelled excitedly as he approached the aircraft.

"Over here, Soldier." Josh replied, sliding off the wing back onto the flight line.

"This just came from Washington for you sir; it's marked Urgent."

"Thank you," Josh said, taking the telegram and returning the salute of the young Soldier.

"Tell me they're ordering us home. I'm sick of the O' Club food," Archer said. Josh read the message twice before responding.

"Hope the food is any better in New Mexico, because that is where we're heading next. We've been ordered to Roswell Field in New Mexico, but first we're supposed to fly over a ranch about 75 miles Northwest of Roswell and report whatever we see."

"What are we supposed to see?" Archer asked. "It says to be looking for a crash site. John, can you run by the BOQ and grab our stuff? I'll go back into the operations shack and plot a course to this area they want us to search."

"I've been pretty patient being your chauffer, now I have to be your butler too. My, but you sailors are spoiled. Okay, Buck. I'm on it, just make sure your navigation is correct. I can't believe I'm saying this, but you just about have me sick of flying." Josh moved off hurriedly to the operations shack, hardly acknowledging Archer's comments. "Sheesh serving with Navy guys is a pain in the butt, no wonder Marines are always in such a bad mood," Archer mumbled, climbing out of the cockpit of the P-82.

141

## Monday, 7 July 1947 1:50 PM Mountain, 5000 feet over Lincoln County, New Mexico

Josh yawned and looked down at the stark landscape; the small mountains and craggy boulders gave the impression of a moonscape. The hues varied from a sandy yellow to a reddish-brown, with small bits of green vegetation and, at times, what appeared to be lakes of brown dried grass. Rubbing his eyes, he continued his vigil as John Archer did a lazy S pattern over the rugged terrain, both men looking for anything unusual. The aircraft's base heading was south, interrupted by the slow turns left and right to visually cover as much territory as possible. In the distance, Josh detected what at first looked like snow or frost on the ground. Turn to two o'clock, he told John Archer, who obligingly banked the aircraft slightly right before leveling out. "You see that in the distance?"

"Roger, Buck, I see it. Looks like debris of some kind, maybe it's a dump," Archer replied. "There's a lot of dust to the southeast of it, maybe its vehicles, let's take a look." Archer dropped the nose of the P-82 slightly, picking up speed as the aircraft headed in the direction of the activity. The area was indeed a debris field as Archer had suspected. The ground was littered for hundreds of yards with what looked to be pieces of metal and other materials. "Looks like nothing but junk," Archer replied. "Head toward the dust cloud, would ya Flash?" Josh asked. "You got it," Archer said, leveling out at 1,500 feet above the desert floor. "Keep a sharp eye out for hills, Buck. All this sand and rock kind of blends in and I don't want to cut this flight short."

"Roger that," Josh replied, looking at the line of dust they were fast approaching. It's two jeeps and six trucks, John. It's probably Army vehicles out of Roswell."

"Well, let's make their afternoon more exciting," Archer said, dropping the nose even more as he brought the aircraft down on the deck, speeding toward the convoy of Army vehicles. "I love doing this to ground pounders," he said as the P-82 flashed over the trucks at two hundred feet and four hundred miles an hour before pulling up into an aileron roll and turning back toward the convoy.

Laughing, Josh said, "Well if any of them were napping, they're wide awake now."

Letting the airspeed on the P-82 bleed off, Archer did a slow pass on the right side of the convoy, rocking his wings. Both he and Josh could see soldiers looking up from the convoy, some waving, some displaying slightly less than friendly gestures. "I'll circle the debris field to help them find it." Archer said, moving northeast away from the convoy. After circling the debris three times, Archer could see that the soldiers in the vehicles had caught on to what he was doing and were heading in the direction of the debris below.

Josh had been looking intently at the material spread out across the desert floor. "John, I think some of that debris is fluttering in the breeze, I think it's paper of some kind. Do me a favor and buzz that large group of it on the south side, get as low as you can. I want to see what happens." Archer brought the P-82 around as requested, dropping to just a few feet off the ground and doing 250 miles an hour. Josh watched as the area rapidly filled his windscreen. "Give me a sharp pull up and high angle climb when you're in the middle of it Flash. Make it something I want to write home to mom about." Looking to his left at the other cockpit, Josh could make out a mixture of concentration and pure glee on John Archer's face as the P-82 began speeding even faster just above the floor of the desert. Just as they flashed over the outer edge of the concentration of debris, Archer expertly brought the nose of the P-82 up at a 50-degree angle, climbing like a rocket above the desert. Fighting the heavy G loads of the maneuver, Josh forced his head around and watched the debris on the ground flying in all directions, some of it even climbing up as if pursuing the aircraft. "It's foil; either tin or aluminum. You blew it all over the state," Josh said, laughing. "I don't know what they're worried about at Roswell Field, but this is nothing more than junk. I guess we'd better keep circling for a bit and make sure the guys on the ground have everything under control. Maybe we can head home tomorrow, Flash."

"The whole time we were up in Washington, you had me struggling to keep this thing in the air at a snail's pace, now that I get to do some real flying you want to go home. I ought to land and turn you loose with those soldiers picking up trash," Archer said, only half-joking.

Josh hardly heard a word Archer had said; to their northeast, he had caught another metallic flash at the base of a small hill. He also caught a glimpse of a shape with the flash. "John, see that hill to the northeast? There's something resting at the base of it. Take us over there and let's check it out." "Aye Aye Captain Bligh," Archer said before mumbling profanity under his breath and making a couple of comments about being shanghaied by the Navy. Then, as he got his first glimpse of what Josh had spotted at the foot of the small mountain, he became silent.

Slowing the aircraft, John Archer banked it forty-five degrees on his left wing and slowly circled an unworldly looking craft that had obviously impacted the ground a good half-mile away from the base of the rocky peak.

Several skid marks cut deep into the hard-packed ground gave evidence of its speed before it hit the base of the mountain with enough force to heavily damage what must be the front of the craft. It wasn't shaped the way Kenneth Arnold described the aircraft in his sighting, nor was it shaped like the photos Josh had shared with him. The best way to describe this vehicle was a boot heel. Along the centerline of the craft was a raised area that could possibly serve as a cockpit or control area. On the outer edges of each side was a small airfoil. Then he saw the bodies. It appeared that one of the occupants was sitting in the shade of the craft, two tiny legs just barely visible, but what really got his attention was the small, man-like-looking body, obviously deceased, laying about fifty yards behind the vehicle. The body was small; the head appeared bulbous. "Does that look like somebody or something you've seen before?" Archer asked Josh.

"Yeah, I'm afraid it does," Josh replied. "Change your bank over to the right wing; I want to get some photos of this. We'd better get the attention of those soldiers over there; I think this is what they're supposed to be looking for." Josh snapped ten photos of the scene lying before them before Archer flew the P-82 back over the troops milling about in the debris field. He made two passes, buzzing them, before wagging his wings, then flying the two miles north of them and circling the area of the crashed aircraft several times. One of the jeeps finally began moving in their direction. When the jeep arrived, the three men jumped out and began walking around the craft. Josh noticed one of them had a Walkie-Talkie and was obviously talking to somebody back at the debris field.

All the vehicles in that area were now converging on the strange object that had skidded into the small mountain. "Well Flash, you've seen what the guys from planet Mongo look like as well as what they fly. We might as well go on to Roswell and call it a day."

"Are you going to show them the photos?" Archer asked.

"Not a chance in hell, we're not developing these until we get back to Washington. Besides, I'm sure they'll have their own."

## Friday, 26 September 1947 9:30 AM EST. The Pentagon Office of Naval Intelligence, Washington DC.

Josh Nashoba sat at his desk studying the results of his investigative efforts since his first experience with the mystery of flying saucers in combat over the Antarctic Ocean some nine months before. *For all I've been through, I have yet to see a flying saucer*, he thought to himself. The aircraft he had been engaged with in January was by no means saucers. Crescents would be a better description. Even the disabled vehicle he and John Archer had seen on the desert floor near Roswell, New Mexico, back in July wasn't saucer-shaped. The object looked more like the detached heel from a pair of boots or shoes. Yet, he had spent the entire summer investigating reports of mysterious saucer-shaped aircraft witnessed by people in all walks of life, civilian as well as military. Cops, housewives, pilots, truckers, ranchers, businessmen, the phenomenon was not limited to a certain category of witnesses.

He was looking through the report he had submitted to his boss, Commander Birdsall, who had taken the report. He remembered that hot July afternoon in New Mexico, when he and Captain John Archer had located a debris field, and then, what appeared to be a spacecraft and its occupants. After alerting a convoy of Army vehicles that had obviously been dispatched to the area, the two men landed at Roswell Army Airfield. Josh had managed to get a phone call through to his boss at the Pentagon. Upon hearing the news, Commander Birdsall ordered Josh to find out as much as he could on the recovery activity surrounding the craft and report his findings back to him.

The following day, on July 8th, Josh and Captain Archer hung around the flight line witnessing trucks and soldiers coming and going from the base. Boxes and crates were loaded onto several C-46 aircraft, which would then hurriedly takeoff from the base. Try as they might, neither man could get any information on the aircraft's destination. Early in the afternoon, Archer, who was suffering from a sinus headache brought on by sand or some type of desert fauna, had made a quick trip to the base hospital to try and get some medication. Not being familiar with the hospital, John Archer had entered the first door he found near the rear of the building by the Emergency Room. To his surprise, there were two gurneys with what looked to be small, child-like forms covered in sheets, parked casually just inside the hospital back entrance. There was a small hand hanging out of one of the sheets. The color was fishlike silver or grey. Even more disturbing than the color was the realization that the hand had six digits - five fingers and an opposing thumb.

By the afternoon, an even larger truck pulled onto the flight line with a large object loaded on its trailer. The object was covered with an even larger canvas tarp to keep its identity secret. Both Josh and John witnessed the truck and its cargo. They also witnessed an Air Transport Command C-97 arrive at the base and taxi over next to the truck. The object on the truck was then loaded on the transport plane. While the loading was taking place, the aircraft was refueled and immediately took off again with its mysterious cargo.

"I've seen this show before," Josh told John Archer. "Want to take a guess where that thing ends up?"

"That damn thing is going to be home before I am," Archer said with some disappointment before they were suddenly interrupted by an Army M.P.

"Excuse me, gentleman," he said, saluting the two men. "May I see some identification?" Both men handed their Military ID Cards to the young Private. "Captain John Archer, US Army and Lieutenant Joshua Nashoba US Navy, are you two men together?" he asked with some confusion.

Josh let Archer take the lead on this question as this was his branch of the service. "Yes Private, we're the aircrew for that P-82 sitting on the ramp over there," John said, pointing to the Twin Mustang, some three hundred yards away.

"I see, Sir; I've never encountered a combined Army/Navy aircrew before. If I may ask gentlemen, what is your business here on the flight line?"

"Like I said, Private, we're the aircrew for the P-82 over there," John Archer said once again.

"I understand that part sir. Why are you over here, when your aircraft is way over there? We've been ordered to keep all non-essential personnel away from this part of the ramp, Sir. Will you be leaving today, Sir?"

"No, Private. We're here from the Pentagon. We've been ordered to stay here until told to return," Josh replied, entering the conversation.

"So, you have orders then sir, may I see them?"

"Well, no Private. They were telegrammed to us while we were in Oregon yesterday. Once we landed here, my Commander instructed me to stay put until I was ordered back to Washington. I have no written orders to show to you."

"Just so I have this straight Sir, you're here from the Pentagon, by way of Oregon. You're here for an undisclosed amount of time, am I understanding this correctly Sir?"

"That's correct Private," Josh said, suddenly comprehending how out of place all of this must seem to a young Private just trying to do his job.

"Are you gentleman staying in the BOQ?"

"Yes, we are." Josh responded again.

The Private had written their names on a piece of paper mounted on a clipboard he was carrying. "Very good gentlemen, I do have to ask you to vacate this area. If you're going to be on the flight line Sir, please make sure you're at your aircraft. Like I said, this area is off limits to all non-essential personnel."

The Private handed both men back their identification, saluted and left. The two men made their way back to the BOQ to freshen up and then grab a bite to eat. As they entered the lobby of the building, the lobby had a coffee pot and a soda machine to one side, along with a rack containing newspapers. Josh picked up a copy of the local paper, the Roswell Daily Record. The front-page headline read in bold letters; **RAAF Captures Flying Saucer on Ranch in Roswell Region.** The article went on to say how an unidentified rancher had come across the wreckage and reported it to the local sheriff, who, in turn, reported it to officials at Roswell Army Airfield. A detail had been sent out to the area where the wreckage was located and recovered it. The story also went on to say how a couple who lived on Penn Street in Roswell reported seeing a large glowing object zooming across the sky just the previous week.

The report had been released to the newspaper by Major Jesse Marcel, who worked as an Intelligence Officer on the base. Josh handed the paper to John and went to the desk to see if there were any messages for him or Archer. A Corporal working the desk informed him there were no messages before asking, "Are you two officers here for the flying saucer sir?" Josh replied with a "No," although he did wonder how long it would be before someone of higher rank began to question their presence at Roswell. He found out just before noon the following day when they were approached by two more M.P.s, one a Major and one a Sergeant. Josh was informed that he and captain Archer had been summoned to the office of Colonel William Blanchard, the Commander of the 509th Bomb Wing. When the two men reported to the Colonel, he was in a foul mood. He demanded to know why they were on the installation and by whose authority.

Josh politely told the Colonel that he was here on verbal orders from the Office of Naval Intelligence at the Pentagon. The Colonel then angrily pointed a half-chewed cigar at Captain Archer and asked who had ordered him to fly this rust-picking swabbie to his base. When Archer replied that he was acting on orders from his Commander at Wright Field, Blanchard stuck the cigar back in his mouth and chewed on it for what seemed an eternity, while he gave both young officers a look that could freeze fire.

"Let me tell you two clowns something." He began jabbing the soggy cigar toward their faces as if it were a spear. "This is the 509th Bomb Group; we're the only atomic strike group on the entire planet. We put an end to the war. If it wasn't for us, you two clowns would be flying over Japan getting your asses shot off. Nobody, and I mean nobody, snoops around my base. You two guys have exactly one hour to get your crap and get off my airplane patch. If you're here sixty-one minutes from now, I will have you arrested, and I will have your asses dropped off in the desert somewhere miles away where you will disappear. When your people come looking for you, we'll say we never heard of you and never saw you. Now get the hell out of here," he screamed as his face turned red. Then he turned his attention toward the M.P.'s; "Follow them, if they aren't out of here in one hour put their ass in the brig."

Josh and John saluted the Colonel and quickly filed out the door into the outer office. There they noticed a slender Major with an overly concerned look on his face. There was a large amount of foil-like material and wooden sticks piled in a heap on the floor next to him. The Colonel's voice boomed from the inner office, "Get in here, Major!" As it turned out, the nervous Major was Major Jesse Marcel, whose photo Josh saw in a newspaper a few days later. He was posing with material from a crashed weather balloon, which ended up being the official story given to the press. The Major had a sheepish grin on his face in the photo, and anyone who had ever been in the military could tell he was posing against his will in the photo. Josh knew what he and Captain John Archer had seen on the desert floor was no crashed weather balloon.

Josh had returned to the Pentagon, and Captain John Archer had returned to Wright Field. The two men's paths would never cross again, but their nearly two-week adventure in the Western United States would be an experience neither would ever forget. Josh closed the folder and dropped it in a box containing other folders from other investigations over the summer of 1947. After the Arnold sighting, people all over the United States and the world were reporting sightings of what was popularly known as flying saucers. Josh was busy investigating many of them; most were hoaxes or misidentified conventional aircraft. However, there were some, like the case in Roswell, that couldn't be explained.

He was also becoming aware of something more sinister; there was a cover-up. Josh didn't know where it was coming from, but it seemed to be a government agency. As hard as the government had Josh investigating sightings, some other agency worked just as hard to suppress any valid sightings or information. More than once, Josh had interviewed witnesses who claimed to have already been questioned by 'men from the government.' These witnesses always seemed fearful of talking about their encounters. They would explain they had been warned to keep quiet. Some claimed they had even been threatened. When Josh asked by whom, the answer was universally, 'a couple of strange-looking guys in black suits.'

Josh himself had seen one of the dark-suited men back in August as he left the home of a witness in Idaho. He noticed a strange man in a dark suit had been waiting on the sidewalk outside the witnesses' home. When Josh approached the man, he became very uncomfortable. Something about the guy wasn't right. The man would not let Josh near him; he had an uncanny ability to walk away, quickly putting distance between himself and Josh. Josh couldn't explain the experience; it was almost as if the man was operating on a different law of physics. He had seen the man three times, and each time, the man had evaded Josh with this strange ability.

None of it mattered to Josh now, as he threw his last file into the box. Just the previous week, the United States Air Force had formed. They would now be the primary agency that dealt with the strange aerial phenomenon. For his efforts, Josh had been awarded a sweet assignment. He was heading to Bethpage, New York, where he had been assigned to the Grumman F9 Panther project. The long line of Grumman naval fighters named for ferocious cats was continuing into the 'Jet Age,' and Josh was getting in on the ground floor.

# CHAPTER SEVEN

~~~~~~~~

# The Bane Returns

*"It is by its promise of power that evil often attracts the weak."*
*- Eric Hoffer*

**Friday, 25 November 2016 6:30 AM CST, Kiamichi Mountains Honobia, Oklahoma**

Fifty-two-year-old Andrew "Boomer" Jefferson crawled slowly across the ground, stopping next to an oak tree on his one-hundred-acre property which took up the top of the first mountain just above the community of Honobia. Boomer, as he was known by all the locals, enjoyed his life on the top of the small mountain. He had moved on top of the mountain twenty years earlier from Texas after buying the property from a cousin, who also lived a few miles away along the banks of the Little River. Boomer was a hardworking, hard-playing man. Having divorced years ago after raising his children, he spent most of his days enjoying his life and freedom in the Kiamichi Mountains. He had built his home himself, where it rested overlooking Honobia and the Little River Valley below. If Boomer wasn't working, he was hunting, fishing, or off on an adventure on his Harley Davidson motorcycle. Boomer had even been known to brew a little homemade whiskey now and then too. He enjoyed his sentinel lifestyle alone on his mountain.

Not to say Boomer didn't enjoy female companionship, he was extremely popular with women and had quite a few female friends in some of the nearby towns like Hochatown and Broken Bow to the south and McAlester, Poteau, and Pocola to the northwest and northeast of Honobia. Boomer was no stranger to the bars and clubs in these towns, nor to the local casinos for that matter. It wasn't rare to find Boomer in the company of a beautiful woman dancing until the clubs closed and then going to a casino where he and his female companion would spend the rest of the night gambling. Boomer got the most out of every minute he was living, be it working or playing.

This morning Boomer was hunting, and his entire focus was on a huge twelve-point buck that was well within range. He stopped and lay in a prone position next to a large oak tree watching the buck through his rifle scope. The crosshairs of his scope rested right behind the animal's right shoulder, *a perfect heart shot.* He thought to himself. The only problem was the buck was on the other side of the fence, a good one hundred and fifty yards on an adjacent property. The four hundred-thousand-acre piece of property was under government contract to a timber company based in Texas. Each year the timber company would make a killing off the property, leasing deer hunting rights on it to people down in Texas. It was no secret that there were more Texans than locals in the area during this time of year, most of them in the area to hunt deer on this piece of property the locals referred to as "The Lease." Boomer looked back over his right shoulder, looking to see if his younger cousin Levi Taylor was aware of the deer he was waiting on. The twenty-year-old young man was also prone on the forest floor, partially hidden by a tree. Boomer could see the smile on his face as he gave a slight nod. *Yeah, I know that smile, that's your, better not miss or I'll shoot him smile.* Boomer thought to himself with amusement. Levi was the son of his first cousin who had sold him this land, he was also a skilled hunter and an outstanding long-range shooter. Easing his head forward toward the deer, Boomer willed it to keep moving in his direction and jump the fence that separated the lease from his own property.

*Keep coming, big boy*, he silently willed the animal as it slowly moved closer to the fence. Boomer could tell the animal was nervous as if it sensed danger of some kind; it would stop every few steps and stick its nose into the air taking in giant breaths as of trying to locate something by scent. The wind was out of the north; Boomer's position was perfect as he was to the animal's South. That meant the animal was not smelling Boomer, and it was moving away from a scent to its north; as luck would have it, the animal was walking in Boomer's direction. The animal stepped under a pine tree that stood alone in the middle of a large clearing, sticking its nose into the air once again. Boomer lined the animal up in his rifle scope to get a good look at it. He was quickly disappointed as the tree next to the animal suddenly had a low hanging branch splinter and snap from a bullet, followed by the loud sound of a rifle shot from the North. The animal bolted, heading to a group of trees to its left; another rifle shot rang out, followed the tell-tale whistle of a ricochet going over Boomer's head. Damn Texans, he thought angrily, knowing the shooter who couldn't hit the animal standing still should never have taken a rushed shot as the animal fled.

Boomer rose to one knee, disgusted with the sudden turn of events. He heard Levi move up to his position, joining him under the tree. "Well, that sucks, whoever took that shot must have buck fever. The first shot was way too high, and the second shot wasn't in the same zip code." Levi said with some amusement.

"Damn, ricochet went right over my head," Boomer growled angrily. "I'm going to stay right here and see if whoever took those shots shows up, and then remind them that damn lease borders private property and they need to know the boundaries and avoid shooting into areas where their damn bullets have no reason landing."

"Probably some rich Dallas city boy." Levi replied.

"Well, if he's that careless with his shot placement, I hope he has an expensive lawyer, sooner or later he's going to need one." Boomer growled again, still upset with the lost opportunity to bag the buck he'd been stalking, as well as an errant rifle round flying through his property.

"Hell, he probably is an expensive lawyer." Levi said, amused at the older man's grumpiness.

The sound of a side-by-side All-Terrain-Vehicle engine starting in the distance broke the silence that had fallen on the forest since the rifle shots. "Maybe you're going to get your chance." Levi quipped.

"Let's wait here, and if he comes this way and stops, I'll let him waste his time looking for the deer and then tell him what a lousy shot he is," Boomer said.

The two men stayed partially concealed behind the tree listening to the sound of the ATV getting closer. After a few minutes, a brightly colored ATV came into view. Levi was following the ATV's approach through a pair of binoculars. "Wow, that's a TRAILMASTER 300E, yeah I'd say they got money." He said to boomer.

"What do those things cost, about ten grand?" Boomer asked.

"Try sixteen grand, there's two people in it, a man and young boy." Levi said, still watching the progress of the ATV.

"Well hell, I don't want to scare a kid, and I don't want to give a fella an ass chewing in front of his kid. Let's just stay put and be quiet unless they decide to cross the fence. Man, all the fun is running out on this morning more every minute." Boomer said in disappointment at the young boy's presence as the ATV came to a stop in the large clearing near the lone pine tree. A medium-sized man who appeared to be in his late thirties to early forties climbed out first, followed by a boy who looked to be twelve to thirteen years old. They walked over to the lone pine tree, obviously looking for blood or any other signs that the shot had hit the deer. The man looked up to the branch that was hanging limp, broken from the earlier rifle shot. Both Boomer and Levi could hear the man perfectly as he spoke.

"Here, Danny, your shot hit this branch, see the damage?"

"Yes, Sir," The boy's voice said with some disappointment, followed quickly by an enthusiastic, "Maybe my second shot hit him!"

"Danny, you should have never taken that second shot, the deer was running, and I doubt you had a clear view of it, or the area. See the fence?" The man pointed at Boomer's fence line and directly at the tree where Boomer and Levi squatted motionlessly. "That is somebody's property Danny, the guy who owns it probably wouldn't appreciate stray bullets coming into his land," the man said.

"Listen to your daddy, Danny," Levi whispered, which caused both he and Boomer to struggle to keep from laughing and giving their presence. The thumping sound of the rotor blades of an approaching helicopter could be heard suddenly. Boomer noticed the boy gave up looking for blood spots, and using his right hand, she shielded his eyes against the morning sun looking for the aircraft.

"He's got the same bug you do," Boomer said to Levi, knowing the young man's fascination with anything that flew, aircraft, or birds; young Levi loved anything that took to the air.

"I'm going to have my own airplane one day, you watch," Levi said to his cousin, as the sound of the helicopter grew louder, washing out any other noise in the area. The two cousins under the tree and the man and his son standing in the clearing on the lease were surprised to see the aircraft come in low and hover near the ATV before landing in the clearing. The man and his son had to shield their faces until the debris of small twigs, clumps of loose grass, and small stones washed into the air by the rotor blades of the large black aircraft abated. The aircraft pilot had cut the engine and released the drive train of the rotors, and they started to wind down silently. Once they had stopped, three men exited the helicopter.

"That is an H-60 Helicopter," Levi said with growing curiosity." I want to go check it out," he said, starting to rise.

Boomer reached out and pulled his younger cousin back behind the tree with his right hand. "Hang on a minute, I don't know about helicopters like you do, but I've never heard of a black helicopter bringing good news."

The three men who had exited the helicopter walked swiftly toward the man and his son. Both Boomer and Levi noticed the man in front seemed to be in charge; the two men with him followed behind a couple of steps, and both looked to be armed with AR-15s, or the military equivalent M-4 carbines." Can I help you?" the hunter asked in a confused voice. "I need to see identification." The leader of the three men barked aggressively toward the man. "Why?" The man asked. The two men behind the leader brought their rifles up, not pointing them at the man but undoubtedly displaying them to intimidate the hunter. "Your identification, now," The leader of the group barked again.

"Okay, take it easy. My license is in my wallet." The man said slowly as he nervously reached into his back pocket to retrieve his wallet. Paul Eastman was ecstatic as he watched the man fumble for his identification. A bully at heart, he liked nothing better than to intimidate people, causing fear in others was like a drug to him. Eastman might not have been so comfortable if he knew his two minions were both in the sights of Boomer and Levi, who were still undetected a mere thirty-five yards away, ready to drop the two men with rifles, then quickly turn them on Eastman and his pilot if they perceived the situation warranted their involvement.

"Who are these asshats, ever seen anything like this?" Levi asked his older cousin.

"No, but I'd say they're government and you know how much I hate them interfering with people. Be careful now, don't shoot unless this goes bad for the guy with the kid," Boomer whispered.

The man handed Eastman his identification; Eastman jerked it out of his hands with as much aggression as possible. He looked at the photo on the Texas driver's license, then back at the face of the man. "Gerald Mann, from Plano Texas… What are you doing here, Gerald?"

"We're hunting, what else would we be doing, and just who are you?"

Eastman flipped the license back to the owner than reaching inside his jacket, he took out his identification. "I'm Paul Eastman, Special Agent with the US Forestry Service, and you're on Federal Property without permission." He said, flashing his credentials in front of the man's nose before putting it back in his jacket.

"The hell I am, I paid good money to hunt here." Gerald Mann replied.

"Do you have a receipt from the Federal Government, Gerald." Eastman asked.

"Of course not, I paid the lumber company to hunt here."

"Then you're trespassing Gerald, you need to leave this area at once, the lumber company's lease with the Federal Government has been revoked. I can take you into custody right now if I choose."

"The hell you can, I've done nothing wrong."

"Gerald, do you think I'd waste my time having this bird land here and coming out with two armed men for the hell of it. Are you camped here, Gerald?"

"No, we have an RV at the park next to the store."

"Then I suggest, you jump in your little buggy," then suddenly with a scream, "AND GET THE HELL OFF THIS MOUNTAIN!" Then softer, "If you don't, I'm going to arrest you for trespassing, poaching, and obstruction of justice. I'll throw your ass in the dirtiest jail I can find in Southeast Oklahoma; it's Friday and that means it will be Monday at the earliest before you see a judge. I'll be forced to put your young son in a juvenile detention center for safe keeping until his mother can be found to retrieve him. That could take days, he could receive quite an education from some of the older boys... If you know what I mean, Gerald."

"I'm not liking this crap at all," Boomer whispered to Levi.

"This guy has my vote for jerk of the decade," Levi replied softly.

Boomer kept the scope of his 30-06 rifle trained on the chest of the man in charge. "If this guy harms this man or his kid, I'm going to drop him and his goons, then you know what's going to happen?" Boomer whispered, turning his gaze toward Levi.

"No, what's going to happen?"

"You're going to have yourself a helicopter." Levi smiled and nodded as Boomer turned his attention back to the scope. Boomer could tell the man and his son were both in shock; sheepishly, the man turned to his son and led him to the ATV. They strapped in, and the man started the engine and began driving down the trail that would take them off the deer lease and away from the three men as quickly as possible. Both Boomer and Levi watched curiously, expecting the three men to board the helicopter; instead, the pilot had now exited the aircraft as well and was busily unstrapping something in the cargo section. As Boomer and Levi watched, the four men removed what looked like a small tower shaped like a pyramid from the chopper and set it on the ground, in the center of the open area. The object seemed to be camouflaged to match the surrounding dry grass and stones. They could tell it was heavy by the amount of labor it took the four men to move it.

"What the hell is that thing for?" Levi asked. The two men continued to watch the activity; their curiosity and suspicion peaked. The pilot and two underlings proceeded quickly back to the helicopter, leaving the group leader alone with the object. To their surprise, the engines on the Blackhawk helicopter started; as the turbines came to full speed, the four blades began to turn slowly. Boomer turned his attention back to one man remaining at the strange object. He noticed the man turned the top of the pyramid-like you would a dial. Once he did this, the object seemed to blur, and Boomer felt an uncomfortable ringing in his ears, he assumed the uncomfortable noise was caused by the helicopter, and he willed the thing to take off. To his relief, he saw the man walk slowly to the helicopter and climb in. As soon as the man boarded, the machine lifted off the ground and sped off to the northeast, staying low over the trees.

It dawned on Boomer that even with the aircraft gone, the uncomfortable noise was still assaulting his ears; it seemed to be burrowing into his brain. He looked to Levi, who had now risen to his feet and was backing.

"Boomer the noise from that thing is brutal, lets back away." Boomer quickly rose and joined the younger man as they backed up deeper into his own property and away from the maddening sound emitted from the strange object. The sound was not a loud ear-splitting screech or thunderous roar. It was almost ethereal, as if you didn't hear it, you sensed it. After moving roughly two hundred back, the sound had lost most of its effect on the two men.

"That thing has to go!" Boomer said angrily, then looking at Levi, "What the hell is that thing for you think? Is it some sort of aircraft beacon?"

"Maybe, I've never seen or heard of something like that," Levi replied, moving to his right to get a better look at the object through the trees. Boomer watched as his younger cousin moved; he could tell the sound's painful effects increased as he moved to a point where he had a better view. *This thing has got to go*, he thought, deciding he would shoot the object to see if he could disable it.

"Boomer, come here, you're going to want to see this." The younger man told him. Boomer braved the irritating grating in his ears and mind and moved next to Levi. Looking toward the object, he saw four massive man-like hair-covered beings standing mesmerized around the object. They seemed to sway back and forth as in a trance.

No way, Boomer thought. He had never bought into the local Bigfoot stories; all the years he'd lived in these mountains and hunted these woods, he had never encountered one or found any traces. To him, it was all fairytales.

"You got to be shitting me." Levi said. Boomer wasn't quite sure what to think or say. His view of the world's reality was taking a sudden change. Even at this distance, the noise was once again taking a toll on the two men. Boomer began to raise his rifle; he could no longer take the noise, and if he had to shoot the object and the four hairy brutes standing around it, so be it. He was not going to have the peace of his property broken by some overgrown monkeys and their government caretaker. The largest of the four animals approached the object; as the two men watched, it grabbed the top point of the object and twisted it as the man had done earlier but in the opposite direction. Suddenly the noise stopped, the pain and irritation stopped with it. The view of the creature Boomer had through his scope gave him chills. The creature who had manipulated the device looked almost human in its facial expressions. Its fingers moved with the same certainty and purpose a human would. There was no clumsy fumbling or pawing.

The creature's finger and hand control gave Boomer the impression it could manipulate its fingers as delicately or precisely as any human surgeon. Then in an instant, the four creatures were dark grey-black blurs as they went to the ground on all fours and bolted away, heading west. The raw display of animal strength, and speed, combined with their ability to perform precise tasks with their hands, all while containing the intelligence to do so, unnerved Boomer. Confusion and disbelief swirled through his mind. He looked to Levi blankly, who smiled and said, "So easy a caveman can do it."

## Friday, 25 November 2016 9:30 AM CST Redstone Ranch Two miles North of Talihina, OK

Sam pulled up to his childhood home; his father's truck was there as well as a new jeep that looked to be a rental. Since his father had moved into town after marrying Marsha, Sam never came out to the ranch much. In the last week, he'd been out here more than he had in the past year; and that only because of the recent strange events. The place gave Sam a sense of dread as he climbed out of his truck. He could hear raucous laughter as he approached the front of the house. Evidently, his father and his guests were having quite a reunion.

Sam entered the front door just as the laughter was reaching its zenith. He saw his father sitting at the kitchen table with two other men; at first, Sam didn't recognize them. A black man was sitting at the table with his back to him, whose hair was completely white. So white it almost glowed with its own light. The man turned, and Sam was stunned to see the face of Nathan Parks.

157

"Nathan, I was expecting you, but not with that hair. I didn't recognize you at first." Nathan rose from the table and stepped toward Sam; the two men shook hands before pulling together to hug and slap each other on the back.

"Well, you haven't changed much Chief," Nathan said, laughing. "I brought a pet Airman along; you might remember this guy too," Nathan said, pointing toward Trent Simmons. "Howdy Chief, I don't know if you remember me, but I was on the chopper with you when we had to land and help that kid who was about to have a show down with those two booger men."

"Oh, yes, I remember you. Thank God, you were there to help me unarm him. Those things had him so scared I was afraid he was going to shoot me."

"So was I, Chief," Trent Simmons replied.

"I thought you were the craziest guy on earth when you ran off into the woods after those two things," Sam said. He remembered when Simmons had helped him rescue a local teenager named Henry Locke. That was during the height of the Government's attempt to 'solve the problem,' the last time the creatures were a threat to the local area. "It's good to see you, I'm glad you didn't get hurt going after those things alone."

"I'm glad I found the kid's horse," Simmons said, laughing. I ran my legs out chasing those things, never even got close. Then it started getting dark, and I knew I was going to be in a bad spot out there alone after dark. I knew General Henderson would end up sending guys out to look for me, and I started worrying about getting somebody else hurt. The horse was standing behind some cedar trees no more than fifty feet from me. I had no idea it was there. When it snorted, I nearly left a load in my skivvies. Didn't waste any time jumping on him and riding him back to the command area. So how is that kid doing, Chief?"

"Henry fooled us all. I figured he'd go to film school or something like that. The kid joined the Marines after he graduated from high school; I guess all the excitement struck a chord in him."

"The Marines, well I guess he hasn't gotten any smarter, has he Chief?" Simmons said with a wink.

"He does seem to love a challenge. By the way, just call me Sam. I haven't been the Chief of Police for some time now." Both Nathan and Trent Simmons nodded. "What's with your hair Nathan? Is that natural or did you do that on purpose?" Sam asked.

"Well, Sam . . . the best way to describe it, is earned. There's a lot scarier stuff than Sasquatch going on in the world."

"I'll take your word for it," Sam said just as Addison's cell phone rang.

"Excuse me a moment," Addison said as he walked out the door so he could hear better.

Addison: "Hello."

Brad Jennings: "Mister Redstone, this is Brad Jennings with the Arkansas State Police."

Addison: "Yes, Trooper Jennings. How are you?"

Brad Jennings: "I'm fine, Sir, please just call me Brad. I have some information you might find interesting; well, interesting is putting it lightly. Actually, it's downright bizarre."

Addison: "Well, tell me what you have, Brad."

Brad Jennings: "Well, Sir, I'm awakened by a very early morning phone call and brought in to be questioned by a couple of FBI agents and some jerk from the Bureau of Land Management this morning. They informed me that human remains were found in a creek bed in Honobia, Oklahoma, by a father and son with the last name Redstone. When the dental records were identified, they belonged to Captain Jacob Nesbit, United States Air Force. This is the pilot who has been missing over two years after crashing his plane in Queen Wilhelmina State Park back in July of 2014. They brought in anybody and everybody that had anything to do with the crash site. As I told you and your son, I witnessed some strange occurrences at the crash site.

Mister Redstone, what the hell is going on down there? First, the missing boys from Gillham are found on your property, and now the remains of another person who has been missing for over two years are discovered by you and your son next to a creek in Oklahoma. Sir, you might want to know that the government hack from the BLM was especially interested in the fact that I had been in contact with you."

**Addison:** "Did you get his name?"

**Brad Jennings:** "Yes sir, Special Agent Paul Eastman. Does that ring a bell?"

**Addison:** Yes, Brad, I'm afraid it does. The man is trouble. Both my son and I are not exactly his favorite people."

Brad Jennings: "Well, I would say keep your eyes open around this guy. There's something not right about him; plus, he seems to have a lot of clout.

He has a government helicopter at his disposal as well as two goons, who seem to be bodyguards. I've never seen anything like it."

**Addison:** "Have they figured out what the carving on the stone says yet?"

**Brad Jennings:** "Well, they mentioned there was a stone the remains were resting on and there was some kind of runes or symbols carved on it."

**Addison:** "Tell them it's not runes. It is ancient Hebrew. You can also tell them to stop reading it from left to right."

**Brad Jennings:** "So you know what it means?"

**Addison:** "Well I know what it says. What it means is something entirely different, I'm afraid. Now that I know who the remains belong to, the message is making sense. I'm afraid we're in for a lot of trouble here."

**Brad Jennings:** "How's that, Sir?"

**Addison:** "Brad, if I told you, you would either not believe me or it might frighten you to the point where you'd think twice before helping me again; and I may need your help again. Thank you for the call, Brad, if you hear anything else, let me know please."

**Brad Jennings:** "I certainly will, Sir."

As Addison entered the house again, the concerned expression on his face was evident to the three other men who fell silent. "What's wrong Pop?" Sam asked.

"Nathan, you were at the crash site of the F-16 at Queen Wilhelmina State Park back in 2014, weren't you?"

"Yes, I was, and I still think the pilot was carried off by a Sasquatch, because he's never been found." Nathan responded.

"Well, he's been found. The remains Sam came across along the creek in Honobia Wednesday belong to Captain Jacob Nesbit, who's been missing since he ejected from his aircraft over Queen Wilhelmina State Park back in 2014. Add that to the current activity and it is getting very strange around here," Addison said, walking over to a desk and computer he had set up in the adjoining den.

"There you have it Addison. You guys were shocked by my hair turning completely white. I'm telling you there is something much stranger to all of this. This isn't just giant, hairy, ape-looking creatures running through the forest. It goes deeper; much deeper," Nathan replied, looking at Trent Simmons, who just nodded in agreement.

"Nathan, the remains Sam found were resting on a large rock in the creek bed. The rock was basically sandstone and fairly soft. This was carved into the rock. Does it look familiar to you?" he asked, handing a piece of paper to Nathan which contained a printed photo of the rock Sam had taken on Wednesday afternoon.

Looking at the photo, Nathan saw a line of unfamiliar text characters; shaking his head, he said, "It isn't anything I'm familiar with; looks like some kind of symbols or maybe Arabic writing."

"Actually, what you're looking at is Hebrew writing. If you translate what is written here to English, it says, 'We were with you there Nathaniel.' When I first translated it, I had a hunch that it was intended for you, but I couldn't make the connection. This was before I knew you and Trent were on your way here, and I had no idea the remains were those of Captain Nesbit. With all that has been happened to us lately and your presence here, I can only assume this message is meant for you. They knew you would be here before I did."

Looking at Sam, Nathan said, "Well, now you know why my hair is so white. Hell, they probably knew I was coming before I did. Well, this gives me the worst case of the creeps I've ever had, and I've had some world class cases."

"That is the creepiest thing I've ever heard of in my whole life," Sam said with a visible shudder.

"It's going to get creepier my friend," Nathan said, solemnly.

Trent, who had been reading a copy of the local paper, The Talihina American, spoke up. "The Talihina paper has an article about UFO sightings by folks in the community lately. What do you guys know about that?" he asked.

"I haven't heard much about it," Addison replied. "Then again, I've been a bit busy with this other stuff. I do know that the Vaughn's reported a small glowing object that paced their car on the mountain road from Honobia after they put distance between them and the Relic that was chasing them."

"That's not a good sign," Trent replied.

Nodding in agreement, Nathan said, "No it isn't. Maybe we better hear everything you guys have been through lately in chronological order."

"That's a good idea," Addison said as his phone rang once again. "We'll, do just that after I talk to my wife." As he returned to the front porch.

**Addison:** "Mrs. Redstone, what a pleasure. How may I help you?"

**Marsha:** "I'm not sure you really want to know; the list is pretty lengthy, Mr. Redstone. There are lights that need to go on the house, and the Christmas tree needs to come out of the shed and be setup in the living room. And that's just for starters…"

**Addison:** "You're right. I don't want to know; so just tell me you love me, and we'll call it even."

**Marsha:** Laughing. "Okay; tell you what. I'll let you off the hook and go shopping instead."

**Addison:** "Thank you, I knew you loved me."

**Marsha:** "All the Redstone women will be going; Christa and Erin will be joining me. So, be sure Sam knows they're with me, would you?"

**Addison:** "I certainly will. Where are you ladies off to? Ft. Smith?"

**Marsha:** "No; actually, we're going to Hochatown to visit some of the gift shops for Christmas decorations."

**Addison:** "How are you going? I mean what route will you be taking?"

**Marsha:** "We're going over the mountains through Honobia and Bethel."

**Addison:** "I wish you'd take a different route, how about taking highway 63 across to Big Cedar then down to Hochatown?"

**Marsha:** "That takes too long darling, besides the drive through the mountains is much prettier."

**Addison:** "I really wish you wouldn't go through Honobia, Marsha."

**Marsha:** "Addison, I'll take it slow. It's a beautiful day, the weather is perfect. We'll be fine."

**Addison:** "Okay, Marsha, do me a favor. If you're running late and it starts getting dark, do not go through the mountains on the way home. Take the long route through Big Cedar. Promise me you'll do that."

**Marsha:** If it gets dark, I promise we'll come back through Big Cedar, darling. Quit worrying so much. Oh! And tell Sam, Christa said there's still a ton of food at their house, and you guys should take your friends over there to eat. Okay, I've got to run; I love you and will see you this evening. Bye, baby."

**Addison:** "Bye, sweetie," he said, just as he heard the click of her hanging up.

Addison went back into the house. Looking at Sam, he said, "The ladies are all out shopping, so there's plenty of time to go over what's been happening around here step by step and see if we can come up with a plan of action."

### Friday, 25 November 2016 11:20 AM CST, Indian Highway, four miles North of Honobia, Oklahoma

Christa was enjoying the view as Marsha navigated the winding mountain road between Talihina and Honobia. "It's really beautiful up here. Sometimes I think we should sell our place and buy some land to build a cabin up here somewhere," she said, almost to herself.

"Well, it is beautiful. But after 2014, and losing my daughter, you'll never get me to live anywhere but in town." Marsha regretted what she said had said as soon as the words were out of her mouth, recalling that her daughter Monica had been involved with Sam at the time of her death. "I'm sorry sweetie; I forget sometimes how all of this came about."

"No, it's okay Marsha, you shouldn't apologize. We all carry scars from 2014. Back then, I never would have pictured our lives as they are today. I'm sure you didn't either," Christa said.

"You know, when Sam was Chief of Police and I was working as a dispatcher, I sometimes wanted to 'mother' him. Sometimes Addison would come in to see Sam and one day we just kind of hit it off. He had a twinkle in his eye whenever he spoke to me. I tried not to allow myself to be attracted to Addison, but it just happened. Then I started entertaining the thought of being Sam's stepmother one day. Addison and I were talking on the phone and had met each other at Pam's Diner a couple of times, not an official date mind you. It was obvious to me he was extremely interested in me and I certainly was interested in him. Then Addison and I found out that Sam and Monica had started seeing each other."

"That must have caused some confusion on what to do?" Christa replied.

"Yes, it certainly did, for about half a day. The afternoon after we'd found out, Addison called and said that he'd thought about it long and hard. In his mind we had both enjoyed a happy marriage with our deceased spouses, and if the two 'kids,' as he called them, could find happiness together, maybe we should step out of the way and put our interest and desires aside; let them have their chance."

"That must have been a hard thing to do, Marsha."

"Oh, it was, believe me. So, we agreed that we would stop seeing each other until we knew what would transpire between the kids. If they got serious, we decided to remain just friends." Then laughing, she said, "Then Addison tells me, if they don't become a serious couple, he'd burn a path to my door. Then Monica was killed, and my world started spiraling out of control. Addison came to me and helped me in every way possible. He made no romantic advances or even mentioned his feelings for me; he was just there to help me get through those rough first months. He would make sure I had food and other things I needed in the house. If I needed things, he would insist I go with him to get them. He didn't allow me to turn into a hermit and check out of life. He did give me plenty of room to grieve, but he insisted that I remain on my feet and not give up on living. I'll always love him for that and be grateful. Then one day I went to the Post Office and noticed Leigh Sheppard, the Postmaster was doing her best to flirt with him."

"Oh no, what did you do?" Christa asked.

"I stormed right out onto Main Street where his truck was parked. When he got into his truck, I opened the passenger side door and I'll never forget the confused look he had on his face as I slid in. I grabbed him and planted a long kiss on him right there in front of the entire town. I told him it was time we quit dragging our feet and become a couple. We got married six weeks later."

"You kissed Gran Addy?" Little Erin asked, nestled comfortably in her child seat, using her pet-name for Addison."

"That's right sweetie, I kissed Gran Addy so good he got dizzy!" Marsha replied as the little Erin laughed with glee.

"My daughter is gone Christa, but I'll see her again. In the meantime, I have a new daughter, a new granddaughter, and a new grandson on the way." She reached over and lightly patted Christa's stomach. "Not to mention a new husband and son who are two of the most stubborn men I've ever met in my life; I wouldn't trade them for the world though. My new life is blessed Christa, and I wouldn't give it up for anything."

Christa was nearly brought to tears and was about to reply when Erin said excitedly from the backseat, "Look at the big monkey Mama!" Christa looked out toward the driver's side back window where Erin was pointing. To her horror, she saw a tremendously large animal on all fours running through the trees along the side of the mountain parallel to the road and pacing the vehicle. "Oh my, it's one of those things Marsha!" She stammered.

Marsha glanced over and got a glimpse of the creature; a sudden burning rage filled her heart. "Not today you bastard," she said as she pushed down on the accelerator of her six-month-old Jeep Cherokee. "There's a couple of more curves and then we'll be in Honobia, the thing won't follow us off the mountain," she said, watching the road ahead intently. "The road is pretty curvy here. Christa, you keep an eye on that thing; I have to watch the road."

"Okay," was all Christa could manage as she watched the impressive display of strength and speed the creature was capable of; it plowed through small trees as if it were a high-speed, runaway freight train. The creature was now ahead of them and still off to the left. "It's out running us Marsha," she said with disbelief as it began to disappear in the heavier trees ahead. "I lost sight of it in the trees Marsha, I think it's gone," she said with relief.

Marsha let off the accelerator slightly, saying, "Good! You know, Addison asked me not to take this route; next time I'll heed his advice. By the way, we're going home through Big Cedar; no more of this stuff. One more mile and we'll be where there are some people. I'm sick of hearing about these things. Maybe it's time we all moved to a beach community," she said, smiling toward Christa, trying to comfort her. Suddenly she saw a look of horror come over Christa's face. Turning her head back toward the road, her last glimpse in this world was of a large, hair-covered, man-like creature standing just on the left side of the road.

What she didn't see was the stone the size of a cantaloupe that the creature had already thrown with uncanny precision. The stone penetrated the windshield of the Jeep Cherokee, striking Marsha just at the base of her neck and shoulders. The force of the impact broke Marsha's neck, killing her instantly. Her body went limp and the Jeep Cherokee, still moving at forty-five miles per hour, continued in a straight line. The road turned sharply left, and there was a small scenic pullout in the vehicle's path. The vehicle smashed through the guard rail of the pullout as if it was nothing more than paper. Both Christa and Erin screamed in horror just before the vehicle left the pavement and became airborne. Both passengers fell silent as the impact with the guardrail deployed the airbags in the vehicle. Almost immediately after becoming airborne, the weight of the Jeep's motor and front end caused the vehicle to nose down, where it made contact with the ground covered in small, three-year-old pine trees.

## Friday, 25 November 2016 11:22 AM CST, Honobia, Oklahoma

Walt Myers was leaning against a fence rail just behind his house. He was looking up the slope of the mountain that was basically his backyard. He had seen a nice buck just a few minutes earlier from his kitchen window while sipping coffee. He and his wife Andrea had lived in Honobia for the past ten years after moving from Wisconsin. Moments like this were exactly why he moved to Honobia; mild winters and he could deer hunt from his kitchen. The buck had moved behind some of the small pines planted along the south slope of the mountain. The trees were no more than four to five feet in height and offered perfect hiding places for the animal, which was too close to the road on the mountain anyway. Walt waited patiently for it to move down the slope where the trees were less dense, and he could safely get a shot at it. After pulling his gun to his shoulder, he looked through the scope mounted on his Remington Model 700 bolt action rifle. He could see the animal clearly now. Ten points and good eating, he thought, smiling to himself.

Without warning, the deer bolted through the small pines, whitetail flagging the sign of danger. It was quickly gone from sight. Walt never got a shot at it through the few breaks in the trees. Lowering his rifle, the confused Walt was about to head back into his house when he saw an unbelievable sight. A white SUV was flying through the air after obviously departing the road behind it. The vehicle seemed to hang motionless for a moment before nosing over and crashing into the tree-covered slope. The vehicle did one and a half somersaults before finally coming to rest on its roof on the slope of the mountain. The sound of bending and breaking metal and crashing trees was tremendous. Quickly, Walt dug his cell phone from his jacket pocket and punched in the number to the Honobia Creek store where his wife was working.

**Andrea:** "Honobia Creek Store."

**Walt:** "Andrea, if there's anybody in the store get them over here to help, a car just crashed down the side of the mountain from the overlook!"

**Andrea:** "Is that what we heard? We were wondering what..."

**Walt:** "Now, Andrea! The people in the car are probably hurt bad; and call for an ambulance and the police."

Walt hung up on his wife and stuffed the phone back in his pocket as he began to climb the fence. His eyes caught movement near the vehicle. *What the hell?* At first, he thought he saw three large men in black or dark gray colored coveralls milling around the vehicle. They seemed to be trying to get inside it. *Must be some people trying to help,* he thought, until the primal screams assaulted his hearing. Looking again, he saw they were not men but three huge ape-like creatures beating and tearing at the vehicle. They had no intention of helping; they were furiously attacking the vehicle as if in an attempt to get to its occupants. Then the sound of a terrified child began coming from the vehicle. This caused the creatures to become even more violent in their attacks.

Quickly he reached down and grabbed his rifle; bringing it to his shoulder again, he peered intently through the scope at the figure he could see most clearly. The thing was standing on top of the overturned vehicle jumping up and down as hard as it could. Every time its weight came down on the vehicle, Walt could hear metal stressing and plastic braking. The face was almost human-like but very nightmarish as if the creature had been sent here to bring on the end of the world. A second creature was on the ground next to the wreck, busily pulling at something; whatever it was pulling on suddenly gave way as it flew backward from the release of its own force. When this happened, the screams of the child filled the air again, and Walt saw the creature stand to its feet and sling what was the door from the vehicle thirty yards across the slope. Even worse, it was heading toward the vehicle, no doubt about to reach in and claim the screaming child.

*Relax Walt, deep breath, make it count,* he thought as he squeezed the trigger on his Remington. There was the satisfying recoil as the weapon fired. The sight was even more satisfying as he saw a spray of blood and tissue eject from the head of the creature, and it dropped to the ground. Quickly Walt cycled the bolt putting a fresh round in the chamber, and sighted in on the chest of the one standing on the vehicle, which now had a confused expression on its face as it looked curiously at its comrade flopping around on the ground like a fish on dry land. The recoil of the rifle nudged his shoulder again, and the report of its firing echoed across the small valley. The round impacted the second creature's center mass right where he was aiming. Walt could see blood on the thing's chest, but instead of falling, the animal just looked curiously at its chest. Then toward Walt, by the time the creature made eye contact with Walt, a second round was on its way and impacted the creature in the left shoulder. Again, the creature took the round without falling, then it leaped off and away from the vehicle doing a rear somersault and landing on its feet. To Walt's amazement, it started running up the mountain away from the vehicle as if it was unharmed. Even more amazing was the first creature he'd shot was also on its feet and running up the mountain, blood, and gore pouring from the exit wound on its head. The third creature that Walt lost sight of suddenly in view as it bolted from its position near the vehicle and started running up the mountain in an effort to flee the scene with the other two.

Walt was in no mood to let this one get away unscathed. The thing had dropped to all fours as it ran up the mountain, leaving only one obvious target for Walt. *You want it up the ass? Then you get it up the ass, pal.* Walt thought, pulling the trigger for the fourth time. He almost laughed when the round impacted the right buttocks of the creature, and it leaped what looked to be ten feet in the air. *Serves you right.* Walt dashed into his house and grabbed his AR-15 and two extra magazines along with a 357 Magnum pistol. This took him less than twenty seconds, but it seemed like twenty minutes because he knew people were hurting in that vehicle, but after what he'd just seen, he didn't want to get into a close-quarter fight with these things armed with a bolt action rifle should they decide to come back. He half climbed, and half fell over the fence, rushing as fast as he could up the mountain; the vehicle rested no more than a hundred and fifty yards from him, but the climb seemed to take forever. As he got to the vehicle, he could now tell it was a Jeep Cherokee, or what was left of one. He could hear the whimpering of a small child coming from inside it. Before daring to look inside, he scanned the area above him to be sure none of the huge creatures he saw earlier were coming back to exact revenge on him.

Looking around quickly but still not sure if he was safe, he had to try and calm the frightened child. He went to his knees and peered inside the vehicle; in the driver's seat, he saw a female roughly his own age; she appeared to be deceased. Another adult female who was much younger was in the front passenger seat, she looked to be breathing, but Walt couldn't be sure at the moment. Looking in the back, he saw the tear-covered face of a young girl no more than five or six was strapped snuggly in a large child seat. *Thank God for the child seat.* He thought to himself. "Hi, sweetheart, my name is Walt, I'm going to help you, okay?"

"Okay," The small voice said from the child seat, full of fear and confusion.

"What's your name, sweetie?"

"Erin," was the reply, again fighting through sniffles and on the verge of crying. "I want my mommy," She spoke, fighting back her fear.

"Okay, Erin, honey, listen to me. I have to help you first then I'll help mommy, okay?"

"Okay."

"Is this mommy here in the front seat?"

"Yes, Mommy is there, and Mimi Marsha is driving."

"Okay, Erin, now listen to me closely, are you hurt?"

"No, but I'm scared."

"Do me a favor, Erin; wiggle your fingers for me." He watched as the little girl wiggled her fingers. "That's good, that's real good," he said, reaching in and putting his hands on one of the girl's feet. "Now, Erin, can you wiggle your toes for me?" He could feel the toes moving through the soft, cloth-like children's shoes. "Wow that is really good, you're a strong and brave little girl, now I'm going to try and get you out of the car seat." Walt felt a hand grab his ankle, and his first thought was one of the creatures had returned; pulling the 357 from his waistband, he quickly spun away from the window of the Jeep and shoved the gun into the face of his neighbor Brandi Sloan who lived a half-mile down the road from him.

"For crying out loud, Brandi, you scared the hell out of me. How'd you get here?"

"Your wife called me, I'm the only medical professional for miles, now get that gun out of my face so I can help these people?" Brandi Sloan said angrily. "What's wrong with you anyway? I can't believe you're waving a gun around here."

"Brandi, you don't understand."

"Obviously not, now get out of the way," she said, leaning into the opening left by the missing rear passenger door pulling a first aid bag along with her.

"The little girl's name is Erin her Mommy and Mimi are in the front seats. I've got to check something out, be right back."

"I could use your help Walt," Brandi said angrily.

"Brandi, you didn't witness what I witnessed, now when I tell you I have to check something out, you'd better believe it's just as important as what you're doing." Walt said angrily, picking up his AR-15 and advancing up the slope.

Brandi had given up on Walt, assuming he was in shock or had taken up drinking. Looking at the carnage inside the Jeep, she forgot all about Walt and concentrated on the task at hand. "Hi there, I'm Brandi," Walt heard her say to the little girl as he moved further up the mountain toward the road. He found blood trails for all three creatures, and they kept going from the looks of it. He saw some local men who worked on the grounds at the Kiamichi Christian Mission, which was located a mile away, as well as the Mission

Director, all below him climbing up the slope from his house. *Good, now we're getting somewhere,* he thought to himself.

As he made his way onto the road, he saw a couple of cars had stopped, both with Texas plates; the occupants were out of their vehicles standing near the demolished guard rail. "What happened? Is there anything we can do to help?" They asked.

"If any of you have medical training, they could use you down at the vehicle, if you don't have medical training then there's nothing you can do down there. However, you can do something here. Move your damn vehicles and get down the mountain, most of the help is going to come down the mountain using this very road and we don't need gawkers." Walt said, thinking, *Damn Texans, you can't have a holiday weekend and not be knee-deep in them.* The people got back in their vehicles and continued down the mountain, no doubt not willing to argue with what they assumed was a crazed Okie walking around with an AR-15.

Walt found three separate blood trails on the road pavement above where the car went off. The sound of a four-wheeler came to his attention; Boomer Jefferson came around the corner and slowed seeing Walt. "Hey, you okay, Walt? Was that you popping off rounds earlier?"

"Yeah, it was me, have you been down there yet?" Walt asked, nodding toward the wrecked Jeep down the slope. "Yeah, it's bad, the little girl is fine, the female passenger in front has come around, but she's pregnant and they're not sure about the baby. The woman who was driving didn't make it."

"What the hell went on here? Why were you shooting after calling in the wreck to your wife?"

Walt was about to answer Boomer's question when he looked up and saw the ancient-looking man standing next to the guard rail. "Who the hell is that?" He asked Boomer.

"Oh, that's just old Josh Nashoba."

"Is he the one they call the Mad Footer?"

"Yep, that's him, you mean after all the years you've lived here, and you've never seen him? So, tell me what you were shooting at."

"Never laid eyes on him before and I'd rather not say what I was shooting at," Walt replied, walking away from Boomer. Walt was usually a very talkative person and loved sharing his hunting exploits with whoever would listen. Boomer felt he knew what Walt was shooting at and why old Joshua Nashoba had come to the scene.

## Friday, 25 November 2016 12:30 PM CST Redstone Ranch Two miles North of Talihina, OK

Addison and Sam had gone over all the events that had transpired in the past week. Addison told of his encounter with the creature. The footprints and the arrow pointing to the southeast, the strange man near the creek, and the missing Arkansas boys found on the property. Then they were told of the couple in Honobia who had been chased from the bridge and all the way to up the North range. They told them of the strange light the couple had witnessed as well of the ghostly looking man they encountered on the side of the road. They finished with the discovery of the bones that turned out to be the remains of the Air Force pilot missing for over two years from a crash site in Arkansas being found by Sam on a creek bed in Honobia, Oklahoma, not to mention the rock that seemed to have a message carved into it intended for Nathan.

Both men assumed once Nathan and Trent heard their stories that they would be shocked or at least a bit uneasy by the strangeness of it all. Instead, the two men accepted the story calmly, not showing signs of doubt or fear. Their calm attitude about the situation concerned Addison slightly. He played a card he'd been holding out with Nathan. "Nathan, you remember that cold night back in 2014 when we fought and defeated these things in Crusher Hollow?"

"How could I forget? That was also the night General Henderson got his hooks into me." This caused Trent Simmons to chuckle.

"The man knows talent when he sees it."

"Nathan, we buried two of those creatures in Crusher Hollow, I returned a few days later and the graves were empty, it was as if they dug themselves out," Addison said, watching Nathan for his reaction.

"That's because we never killed them," Nathan replied.

"The hell we didn't, one laid dead in the basement of the VA hospital for days before it was buried. I should know, I shot and killed it, then scalped it." Addison said, not believing that there could have been any life left in the creature.

"I know Addison, but what you don't understand and what I didn't understand at the time is these are not natural creatures. In the past year and a half that I've been with General Henderson, I've learned things about them I didn't know before." Nathan said.

"So, you've been fighting these things since we last saw you?' Sam asked.

"I've been fighting worse things since then, Sam," Nathan replied.

The conversation was interrupted once again by Addison's cell phone. Sam noticed a confused look on his face when he checked to see who was calling. "Jeri, hello;" Addison said into the phone. Sam watched as his father's expression became one of shock, followed by sorrow. He sat silently listening to the caller; at one point, he winced visibly, then nodding his head, he said, "Okay I'll tell him, yes, he's right here, yes, okay."

He hung up the phone and looked at Sam. "There's been an accident, Sam, you've got to get to Saint Edwards Hospital in Fort Smith, they flew Christa there, she's going to be okay, but there's concern about the baby. Erin is unhurt and with her mother. I've got to go to Honobia."

Sam jumped out of his seat, "What do you mean, she's okay and they flew her there? Nobody that gets transported by care flight is okay," he said incuriously.

"Sam, that's all I know right now, that was Jeri Chula on the phone, if she says Christa is okay, that means Christa is okay, she doesn't sugar coat things."

"Where is Marsha, Pop?"

"Jeri is with Marsha at the accident site, Marsha didn't make it," Addison said with sorrow before looking at Nathan and asking. "Will you two go with him and make sure he gets there okay. He may need help once he's there. I'll be up there to relieve you as soon as I can."

"Certainly, Addison, what about you, don't you need somebody with you at Honobia?" Nathan asked. "Jeri is there waiting on me with Marsha. I'd rather handle this alone." "I'm going with you Addison, I'll stay in the background, but somebody needs to be with you. Trent is a medic by trade, he should go with Sam, so he can translate any medical information Sam might have questions about. I'm not going to argue, now let's get going, I'll drive Addison, Trent you drive Sam." Nobody questioned Nathan's instructions; the men all filed out and headed for their destinations.

## Friday, 25 November 2016 1:25 PM CST, Honobia Oklahoma

Nathan slowed the truck as they came upon what was obviously the accident scene; they had made the drive to the spot on the highway, which was just above the small community of Honobia in silence. The only words spoken have been by Addison as he informed a Le Flore County Deputy running the roadblock at the base of the mountain twelve miles back of his identity and his need to go to his wife at the accident. As Nathan brought the truck to a stop, several law enforcement officers and a few volunteers stood near a large break in the guardrail, looking down the slope. "You'd better find a place to park this thing; I'm going down to find Marsha." Addison told Nathan as he exited the vehicle.

A State Highway Patrol Trooper walked up to Addison to stop him. "I'm Addison Redstone, my wife was driving the vehicle that crashed through this guardrail."

"Sir, your wife is still in the vehicle, we're waiting on the folks from the medical examiner's office to transport her," the Trooper said.

"You left her down there alone?" Addison asked, heading toward the edge of the slope."

"No, Sir, she isn't alone. A friend of yours, Trooper Chula is down there with her as well as a member of Clergy, from the Kiamichi Mountain Christian Mission, Sir."

"Good, that's good. Marsha would want that," Addison said quietly as he started to make his way down the slope; he came to a sudden stop. The guardrail damage made by Marsha's vehicle showed her vehicle went between the two large pine trees, still showing the perfect circle where the UFO reported by Jim Vaughn had shot off into the night sky. Marsha's car had gone the same direction off the road, though much lower than the Vaughn's mystery tormentor. Unlike the perfect circular hole in the tree foliage above, there was plenty of damaged branches and vegetation to show the path of his own wife's vehicle. For a moment, Addison's strength and force of will wavered, and he felt he would lose his balance.

"Let me assist you, Sir." The young Trooper offered Addison his hand. Restoring his poise, Addison said.

"Thank you, Son, but I've been running up and down these mountains for sixty-five years. You'd just slow me down." Addison worked his way down to Marsha's Jeep, which rested some two hundred feet below the road. As he came upon the vehicle, he saw Jeri Chula with her head bowed and her hat in hand. A giant of a man, who towered over her, was leading the two in prayer. Sam paused and bowed his own head and prayed his wife would be at peace, joining her daughter in heaven. The large man finished his prayer, and Jeri donned her headgear and noticed Addison.

"Addison!" she said, moving to his side and hugging him. "I'm so sorry, we have her wrapped in a blanket and laying inside the vehicle until she can be transported to the medical examiner's office."

"I assumed this was an accident; why would her remains need to go to a medical examiner?" Addison asked in confusion. I was the second law enforcement officer on the scene; evidently, Christa and little Erin made some remarks about foul play," Jeri replied.

"How were Christa and Erin, Jeri, will they be, okay?" Addison asked worriedly. "I think they'll be fine Addison, little Erin came through without a scratch, and Christa luckily just had some bumps and bruises, although she did lose consciousness in the accident. The biggest concern is the baby she's carrying."

"What about the baby, Jeri? Is he going to be alright?"

"Fortunately, there is a registered nurse that lives just down the road below us, she was the second one to reach the vehicle, and she couldn't get vitals on the baby, or detect a heartbeat. She told us she didn't have the equipment here to properly check on the baby, which is the biggest reason they transported Christa by helicopter."

Addison shook his head and looked at the ground; his mind was racing. "You said foul play, what did you mean by foul play?"

"Christa said the vehicle was attacked and that caused the accident, and Erin said there were monsters trying to get into the car until a man shot them."

"Was she suffering from some kind of injury that could have caused her to hallucinate? "

"That is possible, but we have two victims both of which are claiming attacks of one form or another, that is why they are taking Marsha to the medical examiner's lab." The afternoon light was starting to cast long shadows; daylight faded fast in the little valley, especially in November. Addison looked down the slope and saw a hearse had arrived, and several men from the volunteer fire department were climbing up the slope carrying a stretcher; they were just a few yards from the wrecked vehicle. The scene was almost surreal to Addison, a quiet, beautiful afternoon in the Kiamichi Mountains draped in tragedy; he looked down at the blanket that covered the remains of the woman he had just laughed with and loved. The enormity of his loss was beginning to take hold as the faint beat of rotor blades in the distance became louder. A helicopter appeared suddenly from the west and flew low and at high speed right over the spot where the Jeep rested, blowing grass into the air and nearly blowing over Addison and the others that were near the vehicle. Small pine trees whipped and swayed wildly in the rotor wash as the aircraft sped low over the slope before flaring up at the road to the east and settling into a landing about a half-mile away.

"What kind of person does a thing like that?" The large man that had been praying said angrily, watching the helicopter land. Then he began directing the men with the stretcher to the side of the vehicle where it would be easiest to extract Marsha's remains. The man then looked at Addison, saying, "Sir, we're going to place your wife on this stretcher and carry her down to the hearse now. Is there anything you'd like to do or a prayer you wish to make before we mover her?"

"I would like to help carry her, as far as a prayer... I heard your prayer earlier when I approached; I don't think I could add anything or improve it and I thank you for that." Addison replied.

The big man gave Addison a slight nod, then said, "Okay sir with your permission, we're going to load her onto the stretcher now."

"Yes, let's do that, the sooner we get her to lab, the sooner I can take her home."

It took less than five minutes to get Marsha's remains down the slope. A small road at the bottom ran from east to west, providing access to a fair number of homes and cabins that sat along 'The Little River, which ran through Honobia along the valley floor. After Marsha was loaded into the hearse, it departed, heading north back up the mountain road she had been coming down just hours before. The giant of a man turned to Addison and shook his hand. "Sir, I'm Carter Anders, I'm the director of the Kiamichi Mountains Christian Mission, we're just on the opposite bank of the river there. I'm deeply sorry for your loss; I'm going to give you one of my cards; if you need anything, call me. We have a church in Talihina as well should you need our services. God bless you, Sir."

"Thank you, Carter for everything," Addison said to the man taking his card. The man turned and walked away as Addison began looking for Nathan in the small crowd that was milling around the edge of the road. Addison noticed three men in suits walking toward him; there was something familiar about the middle one. All three were wearing dark suits and sunglasses, almost as if trying to pass themselves off as celebrities. Addison stared intently at the middle one; just before he started speaking, Addison finally recognized him.

"How come every time there's a corpse, there's a Redstone nearby?" Paul Eastman asked sarcastically.

"Paul Eastman, let me guess that was your helicopter, wasn't it?" Addison said aggressively, closing the distance between himself and Eastman.

The two men accompanying Eastman both put themselves between Addison and him. The men were not overly large, but they had a powerful build, and both were armed. Their expressions never changed; Addison had years of experience when it came to dealing with violent men. There's was something about these two, something entirely different Addison couldn't put his finger on.

"Take it easy, Addison; we wouldn't want them to have to carry two Redstone's out of here today, now, would we?" Eastman said with an infuriating smirk on his face.

"You tried this game once before, Eastman, you're not very good at it. I let you go last time; I see that was a mistake on my part. It won't happen again." Addison said angrily; realizing he wasn't armed; his mind began to calculate the best way to defeat the two men and get to Eastman.

"Things are different this time, Redstone; I have a better boss and unlimited resources. In fact, I have an entire army of gentlemen like these two at my disposal. My new boss has big plans for this area, plans that you will not be interfering with this time. If I wanted, I could drop you right here," Eastman said as the two men with him moved closer to Addison.

Nathan Parks appeared out of nowhere, stepping between Addison and Eastman's men. "That's enough, back away from him right now." Parks warned the two men.

"Ah, the Crusader is here as well, how convenient for me." Eastman said, looking at Nathan, who stared back at Eastman and then looked into the eyes of the two men with him. He recognized the presence behind the eyes of all three men.

"Crusader, I like that. It fits me perfectly, now back away like I told you." Nathan warned the men a second time.

"You know we could take you two right now, don't you Crusader? All these people milling about will forget what they saw, they'll testify that you attacked us, and we had no choice but to protect ourselves from you and this old man you call a friend." Eastman said, testing Nathan.

"You might decide that turning around and walking away would be your best choice asshole. I've seen those eyes before; I know the juice you're on. I've killed bigger and scarier things than you three retards will ever be." Nathan replied with every bit of venom in his voice he could muster.

"Watch your mouth," one of Eastman's guards snarled under his breath as he pulled his jacket away from his waist, exposing a holstered pistol.

Nathan moved so quickly Addison nearly missed it. With the speed of a striking cobra, Nathan was on the man who had exposed his gun; his left hand shot down to the man's waistband and removed the weapon pointing into the face of the second guard. In Nathan's right hand was a switchblade that had released a six-inch razor-sharp copper blade which he held tightly against the man's neck. "Smell that tough guy?" He asked the man whose neck he held the knife to. "I'm not talking about the load your boss just left in his underwear either. You know the smell I'm talking about, don't you? It's the smell of the copper blade. Smells like blood, doesn't it? the knife that scares you because you know that smell is the smell of death, your death." Nathan never blinked, but neither did his adversaries.

The men stood motionless before Eastman finally broke the silence, "You're not scaring anyone, Crusader."

"What I'm doing right now is called recreation Eastman, if I wanted to scare you, these two geldings would be dead, and I'd be carving you up nice and slow." Then addressed the second guard who was staring into the barrel of the gun Nathan was holding, "Now pull your gun out nice and slow and hand it to Mister Redstone." The man did as Nathan had instructed, removing his own gun and handing it to Addison. Once Addison had the gun in his hand, Nathan stepped away from the other two men and ejected the magazine from the handle of the Glock-19 9mm pistol; examining the rounds and clearing the chamber, he said, "That figures, amateurs. Here don't let it go off in your pants," he said tossing the now empty gun back to its owner. "Addison, unload that and give it back to goon number two."

Addison removed the magazine and emptied it along with the round still in the gun, then returned the pistol to its owner. "It's never been a good idea to flash guns at people in Oklahoma boys." Addison said as he handed the gun back. *Why am I so slow today? I should have seen all this coming. Something isn't right here.* He was thinking. He noticed that nobody was aware of what had transpired between Nathan and Eastman's men; it was as if everyone was oblivious to the confrontation that had just taken place.

"You over played your hand, Eastman," Nathan said.

"I'm just beginning to show my cards, Crusader." Eastman said with a strange grin on his face. Addison suddenly felt a fear rising in his chest; it was faint at first but getting stronger by the second. *What is wrong with me? My wife was dead, my daughter-in-law and unborn grandson were in the hospital.* His world was spinning out of control; he was dizzy, he couldn't quite catch his balance, life was fast becoming more than he could handle. He thought as he looked to Nathan, who he could tell was struggling as well, but his gaze remained fixed on Eastman as if they were locked in some form of combat. Eastman was just about to say something when suddenly…

"SILENCE, LEAVE THIS PLACE NOW!" A booming voice spoke; its effect on Eastman and his two goons were immediate and powerful. They seemed to wilt before Addison's eyes. It was as if they were whipped dogs cowering in fear and moving away with their tails between their legs. Looking for the source of the voice, Addison noticed the old man he had seen in the Honobia Creek Store on Wednesday was the source of the voice.

Eastman and his goons kept moving backward, then just before turning toward his helicopter, Eastman said, "You'd better stay away from this old man."

"Your two girlfriends will need new magazines; I'm tossing these down the shitter," Nathan said in a parting remark to the men.

The air suddenly felt clear and fresh, free of the dark heaviness of just moments before. Addison looked at the elderly man; he seemed to be ancient, he had obvious Native American heritage, but Addison didn't know what tribe. The man looked at Addison sternly and spoke, "Be strong and courageous. Do not be afraid or terrified because of them, for the Lord your God goes with you." Addison's knees were close to shaking; never in his life had the pure might of the word of God been witnessed by him in such a powerful fashion. Eastman and his goons melted from the words of this small, frail man, and he himself suddenly felt he was covered in the armor of God by the words the man spoke.

"Who are you?" Addison asked. "I am Joshua Nashoba, and you and I must talk, but first you need to tend to your family. Go and help ease the pain of your family, then return and speak with me. There is work for you in these mountains," he said, then nodding toward Nathan, who was at Addison's side assisting him in regaining his balance. "Work for all of you."

"Nashoba, a Choctaw name, how is it you knew my father?" Addison asked.

"I will tell you all in time, just understand, an evil entity is trying to establish himself as the territorial god of this valley, we must hold the line against him. Now go, you have a lot to do for your family, and a lot more to do here. When you return, you can find me here." He handed Addison a wrinkled piece of paper with a map scrawled on it. Then the man turned and walked away, leaving Addison and Nathan behind.

*I'm ashamed to think it, but he's right; I forgot where my strength comes from and who gives it to me.* "Nathan, is Jeri Chula still here?"

"Yes, Sir, she's standing over there by your truck, talking to the man who was first on the scene."

178

"I need to talk to both of them," Addison said. The two men made their way over to Jeri, where she was talking to a man close to Addison's age. The man seemed upset and shaken; obviously by the experience he had gone through over the afternoon had been rough on him as well.

"Addison, this is Mr. Myers, he was witness to the accident."

"Sorry I couldn't do more sir, but after the Jeep came off the road and tumbled down the mountain, things got very strange for a few moments, and I couldn't get to the vehicle as quickly as I would have liked to." The man told Addison.

"Sir, maybe you should tell Mr. Redstone what happened this afternoon," Jeri said.

The man quietly told Addison and Nathan about how he had been looking for the opportunity to bag a buck that was on the side of the mountain; then he went on to tell of seeing the Jeep come crashing down the side of the slope and of the three creatures that assaulted it. He went on to tell of shooting the creatures but with little effect and finally making his way to the wreck and trying to calm Erin and do whatever he could until more help arrived.

"You sure you hit them with your shots, Sir?" Addison asked.

"Yes, I am, in fact there are three separate blood trails I found, one for each."

Looking at Jeri Chula, Addison asked, "Were you the only officer he's given a statement to?"

"Yes, Sir, I got his as well as the testimony of Erin and Christa. Erin saw the creatures, so did Christa just before the accident."

"I don't want Marsha's body butchered just so some government boy can make up a lie and say they hit a bear or some nonsense like that. Jeri, I need you to talk to whomever necessary. I don't want Marsha cut open, we all know how this is going to play out." Jeri looked at Walt Myers, "Sir, would you retract your statement and make it bears, that will save a lot of heartache. I'm afraid to say we've been down this road before." "If I say it was Bigfoot, people will say I'm crazy. If I say I shot at bears, I'll have fish and game all over me."

"You have a point, Sir," Jeri replied, "how about we forget the animals and the shooting. We'll call this an accident caused by a rockslide."

Then looking at Addison, "I'll talk to the other officers, and we'll get Christa to adjust her story as well, that will make this look like just an unfortunate accident."

"Please do, Jeri it would mean the world to me." Addison replied. "What kind of gun did you shoot these things with, Sir?" Addison said, looking at Walt Myers.

"I used a .308 caliber Remington 700."

"Did you see where your rounds made contact?"

"Yes, Sir, on the first one it was a head shot, he dropped quickly, then second I put one shot center mass of the chest and second in the left shoulder area. The third all I had for a target was his ass, but I put a round in his right buttocks. I was shocked that all three of them got over their wounds and ran off."

Looking at Nathan, Addison said, "Nathan a 308 to the head should have put one of those things down for good. Would you mind staying behind and looking at Mr. Myers' blood trails? As soon as I get to the hospital, I'll send Trent back with my truck to pick you up. I want us to get a fix on these bastards while we have a fresh track. I'll also give him the keys to my gun safe; you boys take anything you need out of there. Plus, my 45-70 is behind the seat of my truck, I'm going to leave that here with you just in case."

"I'll be glad to Addison, are you sure you're okay to drive?" Nathan asked.

"Yes, I'll be okay."

"Then I'll get the ball rolling here." Nathan said, then he turned to Walt Myers, "Sir, let me grab the rifle out of the truck, then if you don't mind showing me the blood trails, I want to get a fix on them before dark."

"Sure, I will, but I'm not going in those woods after dark."

"I don't blame you sir; it causes your hair to turn grey prematurely," Nathan said with a wink. Then turning to Addison in a more serious tone, he said," Addison, there really is more going on here than you realize. Maybe you ought to stay in Talihina and let Trent and I handle this. Eastman isn't the same guy you dealt with two years ago and the old man who spoke with us is all the proof I need that things have amped up in this area. Something is cooking and it isn't what you think, this may feel personal, but it's gone beyond that now. This is the same stuff Trent and I have been dealing with in the Middle East, and it gets ugly and spookier than you can imagine. Even after all I've seen, I'm not convinced I really understand what is going on, but I do know caution and faith is needed above all else."

"I understand Nathan, and I may not know the extent of what is happening, but it is obvious that it needs to be stopped once and for all here in Oklahoma. Eastman chose the wrong team, and he hasn't seen ugly yet.

First though I have to check on my family and bury my wife," Addison replied.

Nathan's heart was aching for his friend; he wanted to give Addison time to sort through his thoughts. Nathan also knew he needed to alert General Henderson about his suspicions concerning the area around Honobia. The smell of evil coming from Eastman was overwhelming, and Nathan had the same visceral reactions to Eastman and his henchmen as he did to some of the nastier entities he had run across in Afghanistan. He needed General Henderson's advice and the General's rank and influence to get the equipment that he and Trent Simmons required to fight and defeat the presence trying to take hold in this area. This isn't going to be a duel of rocks and rifles in the hills like two years ago. This is going to be very ugly, Nathan thought to himself. With his mind made up, he assisted Addison to the truck so he could drive himself to the hospital to support his son. Meanwhile, Nathan would get as much information as possible from the local man named Walt on exactly where the creatures retreated to. Then he, and Trent Simmons would contact General Malcolm Henderson to let him know that he had two members of Team Archangel engaged with the enemy in Southeastern Oklahoma.

## Friday, 25 November 2016 5:50 PM CST, Myers Residence Honobia, Oklahoma

Walt Myers was shivering uncontrollably; he knew it had to be nerves because the temperature in the house was 71 degrees. His experience earlier in the day had unnerved him. Since living in Honobia, he had always scoffed at the idea of Sasquatch and assumed it was just a bit of local color used to lure in tourist dollars every year during the annual Bigfoot Festival. What he had seen today had shaken his view of reality. He recalled many times how he had scoffed at the stories of one of the guys in charge of running the annual festival; the man claimed to have had multiple encounters with the creatures in the local area. *Maybe I should listen closer next time I run into him*, he thought.

Deer season was opening, and now, he had no intention of going into the woods ever again. In fact, he was considering warning everyone he knew about what was lurking in the mountains that surrounded the small community. Then he thought, *What if people think I'm crazy, maybe I should stay out of this*...Walt wondered if he had made a mistake giving information to the young black man who was with the husband of the lady deceased in the vehicle. He was also worried about his wife Andrea, making the short mile-

181

long drive home from where she worked at the Honobia Creek Store in the dark. He was about to pick up the phone and call her to say he would come get her when he noticed headlights in the gravel drive to his home. He opened his front door and saw three men exit a black Chevrolet SUV and approach his porch. *This is different*, he thought as he reached for a pistol he kept hanging just inside the door for such situations. Stuffing the 9mm in the back of his waistband, he stepped out on the porch and asked, "May I help you?"

All three men were dressed in matching black suits with white shirts and black ties, the one in the front was obviously the leader. Walt could tell from his posture and the fact the other two men stayed slightly behind him, one on either side. "Would you be Walter Myers?" The man in front asked.

"Yes, I'm Walt Myers, may I ask who you are?"

The man produced a wallet and opened it, displaying a badge and identification card, "I'm Special Agent Paul Eastman, with the US Forest Service. I'd like to talk to you about the accident you witnessed earlier today. Walt started getting nervous; he didn't like dealing with anything or anybody from the Federal Government.

"I already gave a statement to the Oklahoma Highway Patrol," Walt said, hoping it would be enough to stop any questioning by this guy.

"I realize that, Sir, but we need to know exactly what you saw happen and a statement of your actions immediately following the accident." The man said.

"Why does the Forest Service need to talk to me? It was a traffic accident, and it didn't happen in a National Park, or National Forest."

"Sir, this whole community is surrounded by federal land and the Government does have jurisdiction in most of this area. Just a few quick questions and we'll be on our way."

"Okay, so what's your question?" Walt asked nervously.

"I would like you to give me an account of what exactly happened and what your actions were. Just start from where you were and what you saw as the accident happened up until the time you returned to your home," The man said in a friendly manner.

"No harm in that, I guess," Walt said as he began sharing his experience from earlier in the day. After he finished, the man looked at his two assistants and turned back to Walt.

"This is an unfortunate event, Mister Myers; it always is when there is a loss of life. I believe the stress of the situation caused you to see things that never actually happened."

"Oh, they happened alright, and there's blood trails on that slope behind my house to prove it." Walt replied as he felt anger rising in his chest.

"I'm sure you think you saw things as you described, but I believe you were under stress and made a very deadly mistake."

"Deadly mistake, how?" Walt asked. "What if I told you, the woman who died in the accident had a .308 caliber rifle wound in her chest? Is it possible, you were poaching deer and your aim was off and struck the lady driving the vehicle which caused both the accident and her death? You're in a lot of trouble Walter, manslaughter and poaching, for starters."

"Hold on a minute. I never shot a human and every shot I made hit what I was aiming at." Walt stammered. "I didn't shoot the lady in the car, in fact I was the first one to the car, and there was no bullet wound, you can ask one of my neighbors…"

"I've already interviewed with Ms. Sloan, Walter. Funny thing she is willing to testify that the deceased woman had what appeared to be a gunshot wound to her chest," the man said, smiling.

"Now wait a minute, you can't just make things up and charge people with something that never happened." Walt said, trying to get some control back on the situation, but also aware his hands were shaking, and his voice was cracking."

"I work for the Federal Government of the United States Walt, I can make up anything I want, and what's more I can make it stick." The man paused for a moment, letting the threat sink in. "Fortunately, Walt, there is some good news for you."

"What's that?" Walt asked.

"I can make all this go away for you, in fact if you cooperate, I can make things much better for you."

"How?" Walt asked, defeated and terrified.

"Let me show you what I can do, you owe a little more than twenty-five thousand dollars on your home and property right now."

"How do you know that?" Walt asked, dumbfounded.

"Like I said, I work for the government Walt. You keep your mouth shut and I mean shut, never speak of what you claim you saw ever again, to anybody." Eastman could see Walt's mind was racing. "That means even your wife, Walt. You keep your mouth shut and tomorrow there will be a deposit of one hundred and twenty-five thousand dollars in your account. You can pay off your house and take Andrea for a nice vacation."

"You know my wife's name too?"

"Of course, I do, she just made dinner for us down at the store while we were busy talking to the owner."

"Why were you talking to the owner?"

"Walt, don't worry about what I'm doing, worry about what you need to do, it's simple and there's just one thing required of you. Keep your mouth shut, do that and you'll be fine, you'll own your home and have a little spending money to boot. Share any of this with one person and I'll be back with an arrest warrant and the rest of your life will be pure hell. Do you understand Walt?"

"I understand, can I ask a question?"

"Fair enough, Walt. What is your question?"

"What about Brandi Sloane, what if she tells somebody she saw a gunshot wound that wasn't there?"

Eastman smiled, "Don't worry about Brandi, Walt. I got her attention too, now do what I say, or you'll be seeing me again."

"Mister, I never want to see you again; believe me I'll be quiet."

"Good, exceptionally good. It was a pleasure talking to you Mr. Myers." With that, Eastman and the two men with him returned to their car; as they were pulling out, Walt's wife Andrea was returning home from work and passed them as they pulled onto the road.

Walt waited as she walked up to the porch. "What were those guys doing here?" She asked.

"Oh nothing, they were asking for directions to somebody's house I've never heard of." Walt said, doing his best to sound matter of fact.

"Did they tell you the deer lease was closed for the season?"

"No, you mean the big 400,000-acre lease on the mountain there?"

"Yes, they said the lease was closed for the upcoming season because the local deer have some type of a virus. They paid off, the store's owner to cover her losses for all the RV spots she has already reserved for the upcoming season, and that's not all, supposedly they paid off all the hunters who have already spent money on the lease to hunt here this year."

Walt's head was spinning as he closed the door behind him after Andrea entered the house. The television was on and tuned to a station out of Tulsa. The female anchor was telling the story of a tragic accident just North of Honobia and how a woman was killed when her car was struck by a boulder that had come loose, rolling down the side of the mountain and striking her vehicle. Andrea stopped and watched the story for a moment, then said, "I'm so sorry honey, I forgot you dealt with that today. That is so sad, I hear the lady was from Talihina, are you okay? Can I get anything for you?"

*If he is willing to spend money like this, he's certainly willing to do whatever it takes to keep you quiet.* "No, I'm okay," Walt suddenly felt the weight of the power Eastman possessed. "You know I was thinking, maybe we should get out of here for a while. How about a vacation, maybe Hawaii? We've always wanted to go there."

Andrea laughed, "Where are we going to get the money to go to Hawaii?"

"You let me worry about that, but we need to get away from here for a week or two." Walt said as he put the pistol back in its place; after a moment, he grabbed the weapon and stuck it back in his waistband. Then he made sure both his .308 hunting rifle and his AR-15 were both loaded and where he could get to them quickly.

## Friday, 25 November 2016 6:30 PM CST Saint Edwards Mercy Hospital Ft Smith, AR

Addison was feeling fatigued as he made his way into the hospital's emergency room. Loss and guilt weighed heavily on his heart; as he rounded a corner, he came face to face with Trent Simmons, "Addison one of the Police Officers from Talihina will ensure you get home okay. I need the keys to the truck; Nathan and I need to gear up and start scouting the mountains around Honobia." Addison quietly handed the keys to Trent. "Are you okay, Sir?" Trent asked. Sam just nodded his head and turned away to find his family. He immediately spotted Christa's mother, Diane Sanders, who had little Erin in tow.

"Am I glad to see you little one!" Addison said, kneeling before the small girl and hugging her.

"Grand Addy, we had a wreck and mommy has to stay here." The little girl said.

"I know sweetheart, we'll make sure she gets better." Addison said, rising.

"How is Christa?" He asked Diane Sanders, who grabbed him and hugged him, patting his back trying to comfort him. "She's okay, and it looks as if the baby is okay too."

Addison nearly collapsed even though the news was good; it was the first good news he'd had in a day that had been full of tragedy. "Thank God," he said, catching his breath.

"I'm so sorry to hear about Marsha Addison, do you need anything?" Diane asked

"No, seeing that Erin here is okay and hearing that Christa and the baby are too, was just what I needed. I don't think I could have taken any more bad news to be honest."

"Look, I'm taking Erin home to Sam and Christa's house. Derek and his family are coming over too. We'll get food out for you and Sam both, stop by and eat. Maybe you should even spend the night, their house is big enough. You shouldn't spend the night alone. They're just keeping Christa for 24 hours to make sure she doesn't have a concussion. She'll be home tomorrow. So please don't fret any more than you already have. Come by after you leave here and get some food in you."

"Thank you; I will, Diane," Addison said the words, even though he knew the last thing he was doing this night would be eating or resting. He leaned over and kissed Erin on the head and hugged Diane one more time, "I'd better go see Christa. As Addison walked into the ER cubical where Christa was located, he was glad to see she didn't look too banged up. There was a small bandage on her forehead, and her left arm was in a sling; other than that, she looked alert, but there was a sadness in her eyes.

"Addison, I'm so sorry," she said, sounding like her mother. She held up her good arm, and Addison walked over and hugged her lightly. Not wanting to cause her any pain. As he held her, she said lightly so people outside the cubical could not hear her." It was those Relic things again; you got to kill them before they kill all of us. Kill them Dad, kill them! I never want to see another one of them again, ever." Now she began sobbing into his shoulder.

"I will, sweetheart, I will."

"Marsha wasn't enough; they tried to kill me and my babies too!" She said as the sobbing increased. Holding her, Addison could only pat her back lightly and reassure her that he would take care of the problem. Suddenly the curtain was pulled back, and a nurse walked in,

"Okay, Mrs. Redstone, we've got a room for you and will be moving you in just a minute." Then looking at Addison and Sam, who he had just noticed sitting in the corner. "Her room number will be 217 gentlemen we'll have her ready in about twenty minutes, in the meantime I have to ask you to stay in the waiting room."

Addison and Sam each kissed Christa on the cheek and left the emergency room. The two men were walking down the hallway when suddenly Addison felt Sam grab his arm; he then whipped Addison around where he was facing him. "What the hell is wrong with you?" Sam demanded. "You let Marsha

186

drive them through Honobia after all that has been happening around us lately?

Addison pulled his arm away from Sam; "Calm down, Son."

"Don't call me son, fathers don't gamble with the lives of their children, or grandchildren for that matter. Have you lost your mind? You knew they were going through Honobia and you didn't tell me? You didn't tell Marsha what was going on down there? What is wrong with you?"

"You're right, I didn't think. I assumed they'd be okay in broad daylight. I'm sorry, I let them and you down. I won't make that mistake again."

"You assumed? You're sorry? Damned right you won't make that mistake again, because you're not going to be around my family. Take your Sasquatch and your friends and even your church for that matter and embrace it all. Because that is all you have, you're not part of this family anymore."

Sam wheeled away, storming down the hall just before he turned another corner Dale Thompkins ran into him. "Sam, how is Christa?" He asked.

"Fine" is all Dale got out of him before continuing his way around the corner.

Dale stood confused in the middle of the hall, looking at Addison. "So Christa is okay?" He asked. Addison nodded, "Is Sam, okay?" Addison shook his head. "Well how are you doing Addison, is there anything I can do? You know we all loved Marsha."

"Thank you," Addison said, "I think that is one of the reasons Sam is so upset. We all lost somebody special today."

"Well, I'm here to drive you home, Sir, Sam said you'd need a ride home."

"That must mean he's been stewing like that all evening. Well, okay, there's nothing I can do here but cause uneasiness, let's go.

"Do you remember that truck driver who was below Choctaw Vista the night the bikers were killed?"

"I never met or saw him, but I heard his story." Addison said his mind was preoccupied with his son.

"You'll never believe this, but I ran into him down the other hallway. He's a patient here; he is claiming he ran into a group of four of those Relics again on the road between Octavia and Honobia."

"Near Honobia you say?" Addison asked, his mind snapping back to their current predicament.

"Yeah, he says he saw four of them again."

"Was he sure?"

"I don't know if he's sure of anything Addison, as if seeing them wasn't enough, he said they came out of a flying saucer. Sounds crazy, doesn't it? I don't know if he's lost his mind, but I'm keep eyes in the back of my head. I got lucky two years ago, I'm not letting them sneak up on me again."

"That's probably a good idea, Dale, flying saucer huh?" What now? Addison thought to himself as he stepped out into the night air. He noticed Sam standing over against the hospital wall staring into the parking lot. He turned and headed in his direction, hoping to reconcile with him. When Sam noticed his approach, he simply turned his back and walked back into the hospital. Addison's heart sank, I've lost my wife, and now I'm about to lose my son as well. He thought as he became overwhelmed with the loss he hadn't felt in years. "Okay, Dale, I guess you'd better take me home," he said, tiredly.

# CHAPTER EIGHT

~~~~~WWWWW~~~~~

# Return of the Foo Fighters

*"I saw a disk up in the air, a silver disk that wasn't there. Two more weren't there again today, oh how I wish they'd go away."*
*- Graffiti on a men's room wall, White Sands Missile Range 1967*

**Monday, 17 June 1968, 12:05 AM, USS Enterprise, Yankee Station, ninety-five miles off the coast of North Vietnam.**

Commander Josh Nashoba sat at the small desk afforded him in his quarters afforded him aboard the carrier USS Enterprise. His eyes rested on a picture of his wife Kiyoshi, or "Kiyo," as Josh called her. The couple had met during the Korean War while Josh was serving as a fighter pilot with VF-111 aboard the USS Philippine Sea. One early fall morning in 1951, while his ship was in port at Yokosuka Naval Yard, Josh had decided to strike out alone to do some shopping in the surrounding community. He intended to purchase a silk Kimono for his mother and a nice knife for his father. As with the past two Christmas', Josh would not be home for the fast-approaching one. The sooner he got his parent's gifts shipped, the better.

He had been searching among the small shops on the crowded streets outside the naval yard for over an hour. When his eyes were attracted to a small shop window across the street from where he stood. Making his way across the road through the heavy traffic, which mainly consisted of US Naval vehicles and taxi's full of loud young sailors making the most of their shore leave, he arrived at the window. A neon sign boasted "Saito's Fine Gifts" in English. Above the lettering was a beautiful neon chrysanthemum, gold in color and the style the Imperial Japanese Navy had decorated the bows of their ships with, in honor of their Emperor. Through the window, Josh could see a treasure trove of beautiful handmade gifts. *This must be the place, he thought to himself as he opened the door entering the shop.*

A small bell above the door announced his entrance, the room was well lit, and the number of gifts arranged throughout the small shop was almost staggering; Josh could hardly focus his eyes on any single item before they were attracted to something else. Then a female voice that sounded as beautiful as any he'd ever heard said in perfect English, "May I help you, Sir?" Turning to his left, Josh saw a face that would be etched in his mind for the rest of his life. Twenty-four-year-old Kiyoshi Saito had entered quietly through a curtain that separated the shop from the back office and workshop. Josh stood dumbfounded by the beauty of the young petite Japanese woman before him. He could only stare at the lovely figure standing near the counter; her eyes were like brown diamonds that sparkled as if by some inner light.

"I need gifts," he stammered, then catching himself, he said, "Yes, miss, I'm looking for gifts I can send home for Christmas." The young woman stood looking at him, waiting for him to elaborate. Josh was back to being dumbstruck; she had the face of an angel, her long black hair was pulled back in a ponytail, and she wore an emerald, green dress that enhanced the image in his mind that he was standing before a human jewel.

Smiling, the young woman said, "Are you looking for gifts for a wife or sweetheart?" as she moved toward a counter with jewels and perfume.

Finally regaining his composure, Josh said, "Actually I am looking for something for my parents. I don't have a sweetheart," he said, blushing and then mentally kicking himself; for sounding so pathetic. "I mean, I just need Christmas gifts for my parents." Then taking a deep breath, he thought, *get it together, Josh, you're acting like you've never talked to a woman before.* It occurred to Josh that he really hadn't had much experience with women. Other than a woman he dated in New York while assigned to the Grumman Plant. That relationship never had a chance of going anywhere. Josh had been married to the Navy since 1944 and had concentrated on his duties exclusively the past six years. He figured he'd worry about women when he finally met one that he couldn't live without.

"Should we start with finding something for your mother or father first?" The young lady asked him, smiling politely.

"My mother first I suppose, you know your English is very good." He said, and then he noted the smile on her face diminished slightly. *She's probably heard that from every sailor that has come in here, think Josh. You've got one chance here; don't blow it by acting like a sailor looking for a good time.* Suddenly a fierce-looking man who appeared to be in his late 30s stepped out from behind the curtain into the shop. He looked at Josh with an intensity that said, "Walk Lightly" *That is an older brother or possibly a husband checking on her,* he thought. Josh knew the man was showing himself to let Josh know the young woman was protected; he also saw something else in the man's eyes. It was the look of a man of authority but also the look of a fellow warrior. Josh was dressed in his Service Dress Blues with ribbons. The man's eyes locked onto the gold Naval Aviator wings on Josh's left breast. Josh could see a look of recognition and possibly even a little respect come across the man's face. Standing ramrod straight, Josh said, "Good Morning, Sir," and nodded toward the fierce-looking man. The man bowed at the waist politely and then seemed to give instructions in gruff Japanese to the young woman before returning to the room behind the curtain.

The smile never left the young woman's face; it was obvious she was completely at ease with the man. "My older brother," she said, smiling. "He is very protective of me, especially when American sailors are in the store, and normally he won't leave the front of the store when sailors are here. However, since you are an officer, he trusts you."

"He didn't look trusting," Josh said, half laughing.

"He instructed me to be sure to you find the perfect gifts for your parents. He said you were a naval aviator; he too was a naval aviator during the war. So, he understands how important sending a gift home can be." She replied.

"Your brother flew for the Imperial Navy during the war?" Josh said, surprised for the first time being in the presence of one of the men he had desperately wanted to battle nearly ten years earlier.

"Yes, he flew in China and from one of the big carriers in the Pacific, before being wounded and becoming a flight instructor and home defense pilot for the rest of the war. Did you fly during the war too?" She asked.

"No, I missed that war; I have my hands full flying in the current one though." Josh replied.

"Yes, it's dreadful that once again fighting is taking the lives of so many again, and so soon."

"He knew who I was shopping for, so your brother speaks English too?"

"Yes, he learned it while serving in the Navy, for a couple of years he worked with the British Navy in some fashion before the war. He learned to speak it and taught me as well."

"Well, I would love to talk to him sometime and hear his story."

"He doesn't talk much about the war, he lost a lot of friends, not to mention our father and mother were killed in a bombing raid in 1945 on this very town. They took refuge in a shelter that was hit by a bomb, killing everyone in it. This shop belonged to our parents and somehow survived the attacks of 1945 with only a few broken windows. My brother's fiancée was also killed in one of the attacks. So now he only has me, he insists the war was unnecessary and a disaster for Japan."

"Yes, it was a disaster for a lot of countries." Josh replied. Looking into her eyes, he noted she looked back into his with no flinching or nervousness.

"I am Kiyoshi Saito," she said, holding her hand out. Josh took her small hand into his own; he had the sensation he was holding a beautiful flower.

"I am Joshua Nashoba, please call me Josh," he said, shaking her hand softly. He was impressed that she shook hands instead of bowing as many Japanese did. The handshake was a Western custom, not Japanese. Josh assumed the handshake was to put her American Navy customers at ease and make them feel at home in the shop. Good salesmanship. Josh thought to himself. "Nashoba, that sounds almost Asian, you're not white like most American sailors, so; If I'm not being too personal what kind of name is Nashoba?"

"Actually, it's American Indian, Choctaw, to be exact." Josh replied, impressed with the young woman's confidence, a trait rare among Japanese women who tended to be reserved and submissive.

"American Indian, how fascinating, I do not know much about these things so forgive me if my questions are awkward. Does your family live on a reservation, Josh?"

"No, actually we live in southeastern Oklahoma in what's known as the Choctaw Nation of Oklahoma. It isn't like the reservations you see in the movies."

"Is it dusty and dirty there, like the dust bowl?" Kiyoshi asked curiously.

"No, not at all, in fact the part of Oklahoma we live in is full of forest and mountains; it is a beautiful place to live." Josh replied, laughing. "You know a lot about what the dust bowl did to Oklahoma, I'm surprised."

"Well, I studied extensively on geography and one day I hope to have the chance to travel; maybe I will get to see your Choctaw Nation one day, Josh Nashoba," Kiyoshi said.

Josh normally was very reserved himself, but he had never encountered a woman that captured his whole being as the young Japanese woman in front of him. "It's beautiful Miss Saito, please forgive me for saying this, but it's not as beautiful as you," Josh winced again at his own words. *Are you trying to blow this?* he asked himself. To his surprise, the young lady again held his eye contact, never wavering. Silence fell over the two for a few moments before the young woman spoke again.

"What would you like to give your mother for a Christmas gift, Josh?"

"I was thinking a silk kimono would be nice for her to wear on the warm summer evenings in the mountains, but I'm also intrigued by the pearls in your jewelry case." Kiyoshi walked Josh through choosing a kimono that would be perfect for his mother. He settled for the "Yama," or mountain print which symbolized sacred places between heaven and earth. Then she assisted Josh as he looked through a collection of pearl pendant necklaces; a beautiful freshwater pearl pendant from Japan's Lake Biwa caught his attention.

"Would you like me to try it on, so you can how it looks?" Kiyoshi asked him.

"Yes, I would like that very much," Josh replied.

She produced a hair clip from the pocket of her dress; grabbing her long black hair, she clipped it into a bun allowing Josh to see her neck. Handing the necklace to Josh, she asked, "Would you mind attaching the clasp in the back?" She turned around, waiting for Josh to put the necklace on her. His hands were almost trembling as he noticed the delicate lines of her beautiful neck. As he closed the clasp on the necklace, he got a faint scent of her perfume, which was intoxicating to the young fighter pilot. *I'm a goner*, Josh thought as he became completely mesmerized with the grace and beauty of the young woman.

As she turned around, she said, "So do you think your mother would be pleased?"

Looking at the necklace against her skin, Josh's head almost began to spin. His breath quickened as he fought to control his emotions and actions. Trying very hard to sound calm and reserved, he replied, "Yes, she would think both the necklace and the woman wearing it looked beautiful." Kiyoshi smiled, and Josh noticed she was blushing slightly as her hands moved to the back of her neck to unfasten the clasp. "Let me do that," Josh said. As he removed the necklace, he let his fingers lightly brush against the skin of her neck. Even though the touch was so subtle, you would think neither person could actually feel it; a bolt of energy swept through both Josh and Kiyoshi.

She was still blushing as Josh handed the necklace back to her, setting it aside with the kimono; she asked Josh, "What do you have in mind for your father?"

"I was thinking possibly a good quality knife for him," Josh replied. "I think my brother, would be the best choice to help you with that." Before Josh could respond, Kiyoshi had summoned her brother from the back room. "Jiro-san, Lieutenant Nashoba would like to select a knife as a gift for his father. Lieutenant Nashoba's family is Choctaw Indian from the state of Oklahoma."

"Ah, I see, well we'll need something special for the father of the Lieutenant." The elder Saito said, approaching Josh. "I could not help but overhear your description of your home. Since you live in mountains and forest, does your father a hunt or fish Lieutenant?"

"Actually, he does both, Sir, I was thinking of a knife he could use for both as a gift," Josh responded.

"I see, perhaps your father would appreciate what we call a Kaiken, it fits the description of what those of you in the West call a knife. It is made in the same manner as our swords."

The man moved to a display case and gestured for Josh to examine the contents. Josh was amazed at the beauty of the knives and their scabbards. Some had ivory handles and scabbards, others with what looked to be a form of decorative rope around the handle, and others with beautiful colored wooden handles and scabbards. Both the ivory and wooden examples had beautifully carved animals, trees, or flowers. Josh's eyes fell on one of the wooden knives and scabbards, which appeared to have a wolf carved into both the handle and the scabbard.

"Is that a wolf, Mr. Saito? I didn't know there were wolves in Japan."

"Yes, Lieutenant, it is what we call Okami. They once lived in the mountainous regions of our islands. Sadly, most are thought to be extinct now, but people who live in those most remote areas still claim to see them occasionally."

"Sir, I would like to purchase that Kaiken for my father." "Ah, is your father fond of wolves?"

"Well, Sir, our family name, Nashoba, means wolf in the Choctaw language."

"Then your father must have it Lieutenant. Kiyoshi, would you wrap this for our friend here, along with the other items he wanted?"

"Yes, Jiro-san," Kiyoshi said, bowing slightly, before moving to her brother and taking the knife which now rested in its scabbard. She then took it along with the kimono and necklace to the back room.

"It will take my sister some time to wrap your items Lieutenant, if you have other tasks to do today, you could return in a couple of hours. Kiyoshi is most fastidious when it comes to wrapping gifts. You could say it is an art form for her."

"Mister Saito, I believe in speaking my mind, I find the contents of your entire shop, including your sister Kiyoshi are the most beautiful art I've ever been in the presence of. I mean this with the utmost respect, and I hope my American bluntness does not offend you Sir."

"No offense taken Lieutenant; I appreciate honesty. In fact, my own honesty compels me to inform you I am very protective of my sister and insist that she not be involved with American sailors. She will be a wonderful wife for the right man, but she will not serve as amusement for anyone."

"I completely understand, Sir, and I have no intention of dishonoring you or your sister, I will tell you though that I want to see her again, if it is her wish as well. It would honor me if she accompanied me to dinner tonight, and it would honor me even more if you would join us. That way we could all get to know each other better and you would know your sister is in the company of an honorable man."

The elder Saito quietly pondered Josh's words. Then he said, "If it is my sister's wish to accompany you tonight, I will gladly join the two of you." He then turned his head toward the back room and summoned Kiyoshi. When the young woman appeared from behind the curtain, he said, "Lieutenant Nashoba from Oklahoma has a question for you." She looked at Josh expectantly as Josh stood there speechless. After a few moments, Saito said, "Well, Lieutenant, she's waiting."

Fighting nervousness Josh asked Kiyoshi if she would be interested in joining both himself and her brother to dinner later in the evening. He was relieved to see a smile appear on her face as she looked to her brother, not knowing if he would approve. When he nodded slightly, her smile got even larger, and she replied,

"I would be very happy to have dinner with you Lieutenant." So it began; Josh decided his best bet for dinner would be the Officer's Club at Yokosuka Naval Yard. There would be less chance of encountering any of the young, enlisted sailors who had a tendency to get loud and drunk when out on the town at night. Plus, knowing the elder Saito was once himself a Naval Officer, Josh thought it might build a small bridge between the two men if they dined together as equals.

Josh arrived back at the shop at 6:00 PM sharp in his best dress uniform; he instructed the cab driver to wait as he rang a bell on a door next to the shop, which was the living quarters for the Saito's. Kiyoshi answered the door; Josh was struck once again by her beauty as she smiled at him in her sapphire blue evening gown. The elder Saito was looking very dapper himself in a black suit and tie. The Japanese taxicab was very small, and Josh didn't even try to pronounce the name of its manufacturer.

Josh decided to sit in the front seat next to the driver to avoid making anyone uncomfortable and show proper respect to both Kiyoshi and her father. It was a short drive from the Saito's residence to the gate of the naval yard. A young Marine Corporal stood guard at the gate; after confirming Josh's identity and giving both Kiyoshi and her father the usual stoic Marine stare, he waved his arm, allowing the taxi to proceed to the Officer's Club. Once inside the club, Kiyoshi was nearly breathless; she had never seen such a place. The men in their dress uniforms and the women all dressed in lovely evening gowns were like a scene out of a movie. Post-war Japan never offered this kind of experience to the local young woman. Immediately she felt out of place before noticing that she was not the only young Japanese woman in the club.

"The women are all dressed so beautifully," she said to Josh, who held her chair as she took her place at the table. "Their clothes are the most exquisite I have ever seen." Josh noticed her eyes were like those of a small child who had just stepped into a toy store. The look on her face completely stole Josh's heart, he knew he was in love, and he could think of nothing he wanted more than to ensure she had a lifetime of experiences like she was having now. A band on the stage played soft music; the combination of the music and Kiyoshi's charm even put Josh in a dream-like state. A Japanese waiter appeared at the table; he was a fairly young man just a few years older than Josh.

He was about to hand Josh a wine list when his eyes fell on Kiyoshi's brother. The waiter came to attention then said, "Good Evening, Saito-Sama, before bowing.

The elder Saito smiled and said, "Good evening, Hiroshi-san it is good to see you well. I have not seen you in years, I had no idea you were here." Even with his head bowed, the waiter's face beamed with pride at being recognized and addressed with admiration from Saito.

"Yes, Saito-Sama, I have been a waiter here for a few months now. Work like I did in the Navy is hard to find." He said, head still bowed.

"I'm sure it is, I would appreciate it if you could give me information on how to contact you before the night is over. I might find more suitable employment for a man with your skills."

"Yes, thank you, Saito-Sama," the waiter replied, head still down.

Hiroshi-san, please address me as your equal; we are no longer sailors, we are friends." Saito told the man.

The waiter's head rose, and he faced Saito with a smile. "Hai Jiro-san,' the man replied happily. Saito introduced the man to his sister as well as Josh, explaining that this man kept him alive the last year of the war.

"His name is Hiroshi Ito; he was one of our mechanics onboard the Kaga. I thought he had died when the carrier was sunk off Midway in 1942, then we were reunited when I get assigned to the 203rd Air Group at the end of the war, where he was my personal mechanic."

"Excuse me, Mister Saito, you flew from the Kaga?" Josh asked in awe.

"Please call me Jiro; yes, I flew from the Kaga. Until your carrier dive bombers sunk her off Midway. We had been fighting off torpedo plane attacks all morning; we slaughtered them in droves. We had always been told Americans had no will to fight. Those torpedo plane pilots from the American carriers and Midway Island proved that to be complete rubbish. The Americans attacked with a tenacity that surprised us all. They had no fighter escort; their planes were old, slow, and obsolete. Yet, they kept coming, even though they faced annihilation.

"So, you flew Zeros?" Josh asked.

"Yes, I flew the Zero exclusively during the Pacific war. I flew the early Model 21 from the beginning of the war through the Battle of Midway, I flew the Model 32 as a training instructor right from this very base in 1943 and early 1944. Then I was assigned to the 203rd Air Group and flew Home Defense in 1944 and 45 near Nagasaki, where I flew the Model 52."

"So, you flew Fleet Defense during the Battle of Midway?" Josh asked with a newfound interest in the man.

"Yes, it was a fateful day for our Navy and our nation. Like I said your American torpedo pilots and their crews sacrificed themselves valiantly. Even though they scored no hits on our fleet, our entire combat air patrol was pulled down low on the water where they were. When the dive bombers showed up fifteen thousand feet over our fleet, we had nobody up there to stop them. They dropped down on the fleet like avenging angels and within five minutes we had three carriers damaged and sinking."

"I could tell the Kaga was doomed, then suddenly I was fighting for my life as the American fighter planes put in their first appearance, dropping down to protect the dive bombers as they left the area. This was my first time to fight against American naval fighter pilots; they handled their Grumman F4Fs with much skill. I was alone with four at one point; I was able to bring one down, before being wounded. Luckily, I was able to escape the fight and land on the carrier Hiryu despite my wounds. I was taken to the ships medical facility and the doctors had just finished treating my wounds, when she too was hit by American dive bombers and became dead in the water."

"That is some day you had, your carrier destroyed, your plane damaged and you wounded. You manage to land on another carrier only to have it bombed too. How did you get off the Hiryu and get rescued?"

"Immediately after the attack I forced my way to the aft flight deck. While in the air, I had seen the fires on the carriers Kaga, Akagi, and Soryu, when they were struck and had no intention of staying below decks on the Hiryu. The whole front half of the flight deck seemed to be missing. When the order came to abandon ship, I leapt from the flight deck into the sea. I floundered for nearly an hour before I found a drop tank from a Zero floating in the water. I tied myself to it with my belt. Just before dark I was fished out of the water by the destroyer Arashi. From there we went to Sasebo naval base, where I was hospitalized until I was well enough for reassignment as a training pilot with the Tsukuba Flying Group."

"That is quite a story, so how many aerial victories did you have in your career Jiro?"

"Twenty I believe Lieutenant, although my recollection of it all is beginning to fade a bit. Not to mention I burned my logbooks prior to the Allies coming ashore after the surrender."

"Jiro, please call me Josh, were all your victories against American naval aircraft?" Josh asked.

"No, I had two victories in China before the Pacific war started. I shot a down a P-40 during the Pearl Harbor raid, an Australian Wirraway at Rabual, two Dutch Brewsters over Java, another P-40 over Darwin. That morning at Midway I got six, five torpedo planes and the one Grumman Wildcat. While serving with the 203rd Air Group in 1945, I downed a B-24, three Curtis dive bombers, two Grumman Hellcats and a Corsair."

"Pearl Harbor? My uncle was killed during the Pearl Harbor raid; he was killed at Hickman Field by a strafing aircraft." Josh said.

"I am most sorry for your loss. I must admit that it was my flight's job to attack Hickam Field during the raid. I could very well be responsible for the death of your uncle."

"He was doing his duty and you were doing yours Jiro, the sailors, soldiers, and airmen, don't make the wars. The politicians do. We're obligated to fight out what they can't resolve," Josh said.

"This is true Josh, but still the coincidence of my involvement in your uncle's death is most unfortunate." Saito said quietly.

"If he was here, he'd want us to be at peace and enjoy the evening, so what happened to you after the war?"

"I had attained the rank of Lieutenant Commander while in the Navy; of course, after the surrender, our Navy was disbanded, and there was no pension for us. I came home to find my sister alive, and my parents had died. As if our parents' shop and home were undamaged by some miracle, so Kiyoshi and I did our best to carry on with the business. There were some very hard years, but business continued to improve enough for us to make a living. Since the American Navy has started using the naval yard, business has been much better. "If I may ask you, Josh, what do you fly, and have you seen much aerial combat?"

"I fly the F-9 Panther, and yes sir I've had some aerial combat on my first cruise, this time not so much we're mainly attacking ground targets."

"Ah the Panther, it is also made by Grumman, like the Wildcats and Hellcats I fought against, correct?" Jiro asked.

"Yes, Sir, as a matter of fact I cut my teeth flying the F-8 Bearcat, Grumman's last piston engine fighter."

"Ah, remarkably interesting, two naval aviators from two different navies and two different wars connected by four different Grumman aircraft. So, tell me of your air-to-air experiences."

"I've got a three of victories under my belt, not much to tell, nothing like you accomplished," Josh replied.

"Nonsense, aerial combat is the last vestige of single man to man combat. If you're allowed, please tell me of your experiences." "Well, I've shot down two North Korean aircraft an IL-10 ground attack plane; the pilot never saw me, and a Yak-9 piston fighter near Sinuiju North Korea. A few days after the Yak kill, our flight was engaged by Chinese Mig-15s, I managed to get one of the Mig pilots into a turning contest and was able to bring him down. If he would have kept his speed up, I would never have gotten a shot at him."

"So, you have fought against the famed Russian jet?"

"Once, well I do have another aerial victory while flying my old Bearcat back in 1947 against a jet, but I'm not at liberty to discuss it."

"Hmm interesting, you know you say your victory against the Mig occurred because you were able to get the pilot into a slow speed turn fight, which is exactly how I was able to defeat the Corsair I fought in 1945. If he hadn't slowed and tried to maneuver with me, he'd still be alive. I found the Corsair the most troubling adversary I had during the war. I see them on the decks of the carriers entering port here. I've never had the opportunity to see one up close, maybe one day the chance will present itself. I am extremely interested in that aircraft type." Jiro Saito said, then quietly sat, appearing deep in thought.

*He's back in 1945 right now,* Josh assumed. "Good evening," a familiar voice said. Josh looked up to see Commander Brandt, Josh's old Squadron Commander from VF-10A, back in 1947, who was now the Commander Air Group, or 'CAG' onboard the USS Philippine Sea and in charge of all flight operations of the carrier.

Jumping to his feet, Josh said, "Good evening, Sir!"

"This looked like a wonderful party, and I just had to stop by." Brandt said, smiling.

"Sir, may I introduce you to Mister Jiro Saito, formerly Lieutenant Commander Saito of the Imperial Japanese Naval Air Force and his sister Miss Kiyoshi Saito. This is Commander Richard Brandt, the Commander of our air group aboard the USS Philippine Sea."

Jiro Saito stood at attention and bowed slightly; "It is an honor to meet you Commander Brandt."

"I'm honored to meet you and your lovely sister sir, please call me Dick;" he said, offering his hand. Saito shook Brandt's hand in the awkward way people from the orient do when first encountering the bluntness of American customs.

"Mister Saito has quite an interesting service record sir, he flew three different models of the A6M Zero and was serving on the carrier Kaga from Pearl Harbor until Midway." Josh said.

Commander Brandt was impressed and looked at Jiro with growing respect. "Josh, I wouldn't normally do this, but I would love to join your dinner party so I could talk to the Lieutenant Commander here, it isn't every day you meet an old enemy and make a new friend. I would love to chat with you, Sir," he said, smiling at Jiro.

"I have no objection sir as long as the Saitos don't," Josh replied.

Kiyoshi just nodded her approval while Jiro said, "I too would enjoy talking to you, Commander."

"It's settled then, saddle up, Sir," Josh said to the senior officer.

Brandt seated himself at an empty chair next to Saito and immediately began asking him questions. Josh was now free to turn his attention toward Kiyoshi, "Well now, I can devote my time talking to you Kiyoshi," Josh said, looking at the beautiful young woman.

"It's a good thing your superior officer arrived, or I would have had to turn myself into an airplane to get your attention." Kiyoshi said, just half-joking.

Josh laughed and said, "My apologies, Kiyoshi, but I thought it would be best to get to know your brother and give him a chance to know me before turning my attention to you." Then glancing at Brandt and Saito, he saw they were already deeply engrossed in talking of their shared experience as naval aviators. Josh smiled at Kiyoshi and said, "I think I'll be safe giving you my undivided attention the rest of the evening."

The meal and evening passed too quickly for Josh. He was fascinated with every word Kiyoshi spoke. He had never seen a woman as beautiful and delicate as her and found her stories of life as a young girl in wartime Japan the most interesting. Especially when compared to the relative luxury of his wartime experience in the United States. Toward the end of the evening, Josh was surprised when Kiyoshi asked him. "What do you want to do with your life Lieutenant Nashoba?"

Thinking for a minute, he said, "I want to take my career as a naval aviator as far as I can. I also want to marry the love of my life and know I have a loving wife and home to go to, when I'm not halfway around the world on a carrier. I want to retire from the Navy one day and move back to my home in the mountains above Honobia in Oklahoma. I devote my time to my wife and family while living in the beauty and peace of that area. How about you Kiyoshi, what do you want out of life?"

"I love my brother dearly and he is all that I have left of our old life. However, I don't want to be a drag on him, as you can see, like you flying is his life. I'd like to see him return to it one day, although I don't know how. I'd also love to see your dream come true and share it with you. As soon as you walked into our shop this afternoon, I knew you were the man I would fall in love with, if given half a chance. Please excuse my bluntness, but we may never see each other again and I believe you should know these things. If the war taught me anything, it was people can be taken away from you in an instant and you should always let them know how you feel before one of you is gone."

Josh was floored, he knew he was in love too, but he never expected her to feel the same way so soon. "Kiyoshi, we have a lot of obstacles ahead of us, but if you'll trust me, together we can have both our dreams come true."

Kiyoshi looked into his eyes unblinking; "Yes, we can, Josh."

The waiter reappeared at that moment, bowing, he said. "Regretfully it is time for the Officer's Club to close and I must ask you to bring your dinner to its conclusion."

Josh looked up, surprised to see that the four of them were the sole occupants of the room. Josh stood and said, "Thank you for such an enjoyable evening, Hiroshi." The waiter thanked him for his kindness, bowing uncomfortably once again. *I'm sure he's not used to being treated with respect here. How many times have I unwittingly behaved as a conqueror here instead of a guest?* he thought to himself.

"Nashoba, how are you taking the Saito's home?" Commander Brandt asked.

"I was going to use a taxi, Sir," Josh responded. "Nonsense we'll use my car, besides there is something I want to show Lieutenant Commander Saito." Commander Brandt said with just a hint of a slur. Both he and Saito had had a few scotches with their meal and throughout their long discussion. "By the way Nashoba, you're driving; the Lieutenant Commander and I order it."

Josh looked from Brandt to the smiling Saito, who was nodding his head in agreement. "Now take us to pier six Lieutenant." Brandt ordered.

"Yes, Sir." Josh said, smiling, knowing the USS Philippine Sea was berthed there. When they reached pier six, Josh parked the vehicle, and they exited, looking up at the huge form of the USS Philippine Sea.

"So, this is your ship?" Kiyoshi asked. "Yes," Josh replied as Commander Brandt walked over to the young sailor who guarded the gangway of the carrier. "Sailor, summon the officer of the deck," he growled.

The young sailor replied, "Yes, Sir," and scrambled up the gangway.

A few moments later, a young ensign appeared descending down the gangway." Ensign Bowman, Sir, may I help you?" The young man asked Brandt.

"I'm Commander Brandt, the CAG for this vessel. I am escorting Mister Saito and his sister up to the flight deck." "But, Sir, civilian visitors are not allowed on board after 1900 hours." The nervous young man said.

"They're not visitors, they are my guest. Now Ensign... Permission to come aboard, Sir?" Brandt growled.

"Permission granted, Sir," the young Ensign said nervously.

Once the group had made their way up to the flight deck, Kiyoshi was wide-eyed like a little girl, "I see these ships come into port, and they look gigantic. They are even bigger than they appear." Josh noticed Brandt and Saito had stopped for a few seconds by one of the F-9 Panthers parked on the deck. They looked at it momentarily before walking off in what Josh knew to be their real interest, a group of F4U Corsairs parked at the aft end of the deck. The World War Two vintage gull-winged; piston engine fighter still served as a potent ground attack aircraft supporting Marines on the ground in Korea. "Which type of plane do you fly Josh?" Kiyoshi asked.

"I fly these, the F-9 Panther." Josh said, moving her toward the group of jets from his squadron sitting on the deck. "In fact, this is the aircraft assigned to me." Josh said as they walked up to one of the dark blue jets with a large white 113 painted on the nose. Kiyoshi ran her hands along the aircraft's fuselage, stopping from time to time to ask a question concerning a part of the airplane or a particular marking. Stopping on the left side of the cockpit, she stopped looking at the white lettering that said "Lt Josh Nashoba." "So, they put your name on the plane?" She asked.

"Yes, my name as well as the Plane Captain's." Josh replied, pointing at another name painted on the PO3 James Franklin. "What is a Plane Captain and what is a PO3?" Kiyoshi asked.

"The plane captain is the mechanic assigned to this aircraft, he inspects it repairs it or oversees repairs made on it. Much the same as your brother's friend we met during dinner. PO3 is his rank Petty Officer 3rd Class."

"I see," Kiyoshi said, still looking at the area around the cockpit. "What are the three red stars under your name?" "Those represent the three enemy aircraft I've shot down."

"So, you keep track of the men you've killed?' She asked curiously." "Well not so much the man we kill, but the aircraft we shoot down, it's something that goes back to aerial warfare in the First World War. It is something fighter pilots of all Air Forces in the world have done, probably even your brother."

Kiyoshi looked at Josh and then glanced down the deck where her brother and Commander Brandt were intently discussing something. By the gestures they made with their hands, she could tell that it had something to do with flying in combat. "You men act as if this is a game, you must not end up as a mark on another man's airplane Josh Nashoba."

"I wouldn't say game, but it is a contest in the purest form. I will never be a victory mark on another man's aircraft, I promise," he replied. Looking forward, she came to a small silver square on the aircraft's nose. "What is this?"

"It's a patch," Josh replied.

"What do you mean by patch?" She asked.

"It's a small piece of metal covering a hole, my Plane Captain patched the hole but hasn't gotten around to painting the patch yet."

"Why did your plane have a hole in it, Josh?"

"It was a bullet hole, from ground fire on the last mission I flew."

"These patches are they part of the obstacles we face, Josh?"

"They could be, but I'll fight like hell to make sure they're not, Kiyoshi."

"No more patches Josh Nashoba; you fight hard and let no man harm you. Promise me."

"I promise Kiyoshi, I promise." Then glancing down the flight deck, he saw that both Brandt and Saito were busy looking over and discussing the Corsair. He took Kiyoshi in his arms and said, "Now you promise me, no matter where or how far the Navy sends me away, you'll be my wife and wait for me."

"I will love you, wait for you, and honor you always, Joshua-san."

"I will do the same, Kiyoshi," Josh said as he pulled her close for their first kiss.

Josh's mind drifted back to the present; he and Kiyoshi had now been married for 15 years, he had kept his promise to her and never allowed himself to be shot down during his next two cruises flying combat over Korea. They had married in 1953; their love for each other seemed to grow stronger even with the demands of the Navy constantly separating them. While Josh was at sea, Kiyoshi would stay with his parents Honobia Oklahoma; she'd join him at whatever base he was assigned when he was ashore. They were never able to have children, but that never affected their deep love and commitment for each other.

Kiyoshi excelled as a Navy wife; she took the separations with quiet dignity and never complained. She endured even the worst of the land base assignments and the occasional shunning by some of the other Officer's wives who had little to do with her because of her race. She never showed any reaction when she would hear the wife of another Naval Officer say things like, "There goes the Nip." while she was shopping in the base exchange or commissary.

Kiyoshi fell in love with Southeastern Oklahoma and the Nashoba family home in the mountains above Honobia. Her brother Jiro joined her and Joshua there once while Josh was taking a long leave away from the Navy. Jiro also fell in love with the area and had befriended Josh's father. The two men decided they would start on a home in the mountains for Josh and Kiyoshi to move into when he retired from the Navy. Josh's father insisted on giving a particularly beautiful spot on one of the ridges to Jiro so he, too, could have his own home. Jiro sold the family business in Yokosuka, Japan, to his old comrade Hiroshi Ito, whom he had hired to assist him after Josh and Kiyoshi had married. Jiro immersed himself in the surrounding mountains and became familiar with the traditions of the Choctaw people.

Jiro developed his own unique design on his personal cabin and later the home he finished for Josh and Kiyoshi after Josh's father passed away in 1959. The homes' style and the landscaping were a mix of the local log cabins built by the local Choctaw people, mixed with Japanese accents. Both homes were beautiful and mixed with the surrounding scenery in beautiful harmony. Once Jiro had finished the homes, he began to explore the local mountains in a constant study of the traditions and folklore of the Choctaw people and the tribes that had lived on and moved through the land before them, like the Caddo, Osage, and Wichita. When Josh and Kiyoshi would come home for visits, Jiro and Josh would talk for hours about the people of the Kiamichi Mountains and their ancient stories.

Josh's mind snapped back from the memories of his and Kiyoshi's love at first sight to the present. As the years had passed, he had made his mark in Naval Aviation. Besides his three aerial victories over Korea, he had also brought down a North Vietnamese Mig-17 in January of 1967 as the Executive Officer flying an older B model Phantom with the Naval Fighter Squadron VF-114. This had catapulted him to his current position as Commander of VF-96 and now off the coast of Vietnam aboard the USS Enterprise, the world's first nuclear-powered aircraft carrier. The squadron was on the final month of its deployment to "Yankee Station," a fixed area off the coast of Vietnam where US Navy carrier task forces conducted their airstrikes against North Vietnam. Josh had ensured his squadron Executive Officer scheduled him for the final nighttime "CAP" or Combat Air Patrol flight of the morning. The flight of four F-4 Phantoms would depart the USS Enterprise at 01:30 hours and fly a racetrack pattern between the Enterprise and the coast of Vietnam to defend the carrier against possible attack by the North Vietnamese Air Force. Josh knew the chances of an attack were very slim.

The Vietnam People's Air Force was strictly used as a defensive weapon against US Air Force, US Navy, and US Marine aircraft conducting operations over North Vietnam. They fought fiercely in the defensive role but had little to no offensive capability. It was unthinkable that they would attack the Enterprise or any of the other vessels in Task Force 77; still, the Navy never forgot Pearl Harbor and was not about to take any chances. There was also the specter of Hainan Island to the Northeast of the Task Force. The 13,100 square mile island was a province of Communist China, and the Chinese Air Force had Migs based there in several locations. Though it was unusual for aircraft from Task Force 77 and Migs from Hainan to encounter each other, there had been a few clashes that went back to 1965, when a USAF F-104 strayed into Hainan airspace and was shot down by Chinese Mig fighters. In 1967 two Navy A-6 Intruders were lost to Migs from Hainan and an A-1Skyraider from the USS Coral Sea just two months ago in April.

Operations for Josh's squadron were winding down, and he wanted his pilots to get as much rest as possible. So, he decided to take one of the CAP slots and sweat out the night carrier landing instead of thrusting it upon one of his younger pilots. It should be a quiet night, but when flying in an area with potential enemies on both sides, you could never let your guard down. Josh stepped from his quarters into the VF-96 Ready Room; the first face he saw was that of his Radar Intercept Officer or "RIO" Lieutenant Dan Freeman. Freeman sat in the backseat of the McDonald Douglas F-4J Phantom fighter, managing the radar and missile systems, as well as monitoring radio transmissions and electronic countermeasures. He also acted as a second pair of eyes and ears for the pilot. "Good morning, Dan, ready to stare at the darkness for a few hours?" Josh asked.

"Hell, Skipper if that is all we're going to do I could had stayed in my rack and studied my closed eyelids." Freeman replied.

"If I hear you snoring back there tonight, I'll buzz over the harbor at Hai Phong and you'll wakeup to Uncle Ho's fireworks," Josh said, smiling before turning to the other six men who made up the rest of the crews for the flight of four aircraft. "Good morning, gentlemen, as you can see, I've chosen the best, brightest, and biggest balls for this mission. Well, the biggest balls anyway..." The other aircrew laughed at Josh's joke. He proceeded to give them their area of operation for the evening and what other US Aircraft might be sharing the same airspace during their mission. He split the four aircraft into two separate flights. Josh and Freeman would have the call-sign Showtime Zero One; his wingman would be Lieutenant Tremble and his RIO Ensign Simmons and was designated Showtime Zero Two. The second flight Showtime Zero Three and Showtime Zero Four, would be manned by Lieutenants Self and Garcia, with Lieutenant JG Fields and Lieutenant Jefferies, respectively.

## Monday, 17 June 1968, 02:15 AM, USS Enterprise, Yankee Station, ninety-five miles off the coast of North Vietnam.

The Enterprise currently shared this piece of the ocean with three other U.S. aircraft carriers, the USS Kitty Hawk, USS Constellation, and the USS America. The air operations for all four of the big carriers were under the command of Vice Admiral Richard Brandt, who was the Commander of Task

Force 77. Throughout Josh's career as a naval aviator, he found himself fortunate enough to be in the command chain of his old squadron commander on the USS Philippine Sea back in 1947. Brandt had never forgotten Josh's performance that day against the unknown Foo Fighters that had attacked aircraft and ships of Operation High Jump off the coast of Antarctica. Little did Josh know, Brandt had monitored Josh's progress through his career, doing his best to keep him out of dead-end assignments that might jeopardize his chances for promotion.

However, the 1947 UFO engagement had left a mark on Josh's career path; his involvement in that incident, as well as his investigation into both Kenneth Arnold's sighting and the incident at Roswell in 1947, had retarded Josh's promotion chances. Although his flying and service record was stellar, the events caused some higher-ranking officers a moment of pause when considering Josh for promotion.

There was nearly a final nail in his promotion coffin when, in 1952, off the coast of Korea. Josh was witness to another UFO incident when a strange object buzzed the USS Philippine Sea in June of 1952. Unfortunately for Josh, he made a formal report of the incident, which was witnessed by numerous other personnel aboard the ship as well as Sailors on the USS Princeton another, aircraft carrier operating along with Josh's ship. Josh could not afford any more strange events if he were to advance in rank. Brandt knew if Josh survived this combat deployment, he was up for a position as Commander Air Group; this would catapult him to the rank of Captain and put him in a good position to make the rank of Admiral one day. Brandt was fond of this pilot from Oklahoma and wanted to see him with stars on his collar one day.

Brandt knew a fighter pilot and a leader when he saw one, and he ensured that Josh got an assignment at the point of the spear whenever there was conflict or the possibility of conflict. He also knew that Josh's aerial victory over the Foo Fighters off Antarctica in 1947 could be a career killer or worse if he weren't protected. Josh may not have known what the creature was that was pulled out of the wreckage he had shot down along with the remains of a long-missing German fighter pilot. Brandt, however, now knew exactly what it had been; he also knew the closely guarded secret went way past Washington. A secret so dark that it kept him in promotions and kept Josh's naval career alive if he wasn't asking questions or seeking answers to what happened that cold January afternoon in 1947.

Admiral Brandt was a notoriously light sleeper, and members of his staff were amazed at how little rest he functioned on. This, in turn, kept his staff on their feet because they knew he could appear at any moment, no matter the hour. Brandt made his way into The Enterprise' Combat Information Center "CIC" to check on the status of the fleet. He noticed a couple of sailors and the Watch Chief were crowded around the communication station designated to communicate with the USS Horne, a Belknap Class Guided Missile Cruiser, which served as the "PIRAZ" ship. PIRAZ am acronym for Positive Identification Radar Advisory Zone; within the ship, 35 to 40 officers and men manned radars and communication with aircraft and other ships to maintain command and control of air and sea assets conducting operations against North Vietnam; they also served as an early warning system for friendly aircraft and naval vessels should the Vietnam People's Air Force attempt offensive operations against American forces, they also kept an eye on the Chinese at Hainan Island. Ships assigned to this duty used the call-sign "Red Crown."

"What's all this? Do we have an issue?" Brandt asked as he approached the group of men.

"Sir, we have some strange activity upriver a few miles from Cua Viet." The Watch Chief informed him.

"What kind of activity, Chief?" Brandt demanded.

"Sir, one of our River Patrol Boats is being attacked by what they believe to be enemy helicopters. The boat in question is PCF-19; PCF-12 is rushing to their aid and should be on scene any minute now."

"Uncle Ho doesn't have helicopters Chief, are we sure it's not one of our choppers firing on them by mistake?"

"Sir we have no helicopters in the area, we occasionally get a radar hit on at least two aerial targets in that sector. They're vertical movement and ability to hover suggests helicopters except for one thing," the Chief said as if afraid to bring the one thing up.

"Well, I'm not getting any younger, Chief, what is the one thing?" Brandt asked with building frustration.

The conversation was interrupted as excited radio chatter from one of the river patrol boats came over the speaker. "Red Crown, this is Trident-12, Trident-19 has exploded, I repeat Trident One Nine is exploded and sunk." Gunfire and screaming could be heard in the background as the Captain of Trident-12 spoke.

"Trident-12, this is Red Crown, begin withdrawal back toward Cua Viet. We have two F-4s on the way, call-sign Rustic." After thirty seconds and no reply from Trident-12, the Red Crown controller was getting concerned.

"Trident-12 this is Red Crown, repeat this is Red Crown. Acknowledge my last transmission... Trident One Two this is Red Crown, come in over..." There was no reply.

Looking at the Chief, Brandt said, "Who the hell is Rustic?" Quickly grabbing a clipboard and running down the list, the Chief Petty officer replied, "Call-sign 'Rustic' is assigned to the 390th Tactical Fighter Squadron out of DaNang, Sir."

"Air Force pukes? Bullshit, I want sailors protecting sailors. This has a stench to it, he thought. "Who the hell has the CAP right now, Chief?"

"Our CAP just launched twenty minutes ago sir, to relieve the Kitty Hawk squadron, Sir."

"Good, which squadron, Chief?"

"VF-96, Sir, Commander Nashoba is the flight lead call-sign Showtime One."

*Damn*, was all Admiral Brandt could think of at the mentioning of Josh, something about this situation made him very uncomfortable. The North Vietnamese Air Force was not in the habit of offensive aerial activity, mainly because they possessed little aerial offensive power. He was keenly aware that Josh Nashoba had an uncanny ability to find himself encountering and even in combat with these dark secrets. Still, the Admiral could not think of anybody more qualified or blessed with the skill to counter these minions of the dark cabal that was behind every conflict that mankind involved itself in. The current administration had given itself over to the darkness. Political leaders of every party worldwide, save for a very few hard-liners, sought out the power and wealth that could be gained from this cabal. *Nashoba, you're going to end up knee-deep in this mess again, and I don't know that I can protect you,* he thought to himself.

The Admiral also knew Josh had the God-given ability to put down whatever was tormenting those sailors in the patrol boats. Brandt's thoughts were interrupted by a voice over the radio, "Red Crown, this is Trident One Two, the aircraft have moved off at an amazing speed to the north. They are heading toward the coast, we have taken hits but no casualties, and we are currently looking for survivors from Trident One Nine and will advise you of any progress."

"Are we receiving radar updates from Red Crown?" Brandt asked.

"Yes, Sir, the air speed on the two bandits that attacked the river patrol is indicating 1500 knots an hour, Sir."

"Helicopters my ass," Brandt barked.

"Tell Red Crown I want Showtime One and his wing man vectored to intercept the bandits, keep Showtime Three and Four on station. I also want a couple of Marine choppers out of Cua Viet sent to aid those river sailors and I want it RIGHT NOW, Chief."

"Aye, Sir, and what about Rustic Flight? It looks as if they've been vectored to intercept the bandits as well."

"Let Red Crown worry about the Air Force," Brandt growled as he moved over to the plotting map to study the building escalating engagement.

"Sir, the bandits are now feet wet off the coast, and closing on the Australian cruiser HMAS Hobart, just north of Tiger Island. Rustic flight has been vectored toward the Hobart. Sir, there is no way conventional aircraft could travel that far in this amount of time."

"Chief, the right man for the job is flying in Showtime One, get with Red Crown and get Nashoba's butt on scene now!"

## Monday, 17 June 1968, 02:50 AM, 21.000 feet over the South China Sea.

Josh Nashoba relaxed as he looked down at the ink-black ocean below him; Combat Air Patrol could be a very boring assignment. There was little action to be had protecting the fleet in this conflict. Taking a quick glance over his right shoulder, he could see the F-4J Phantom of his wingman, Lieutenant Michael Tremble, whose nickname was "Shakes" among his squadron-mates. He was formed up perfectly with Josh as they plowed through the dark sky some 45 miles off the coast of North Vietnam. The other two aircraft of his flight were lined up in a similar fashion off his left wing. Josh looked ahead in the darkness toward the coast of North Vietnam. He could see a few lights on the ground at his ten o'clock and two o'clock, these would be the small towns of Ha Tin and its southern neighbor Ba Don, and both sets of lights were dim and subdued, giving off little light when compared to Da Nang which Josh could clearly see over one hundred miles to his south, the American presence was vividly apparent as it looked like Las Vegas compared to the two North Vietnamese towns.

In two minutes, Josh would give the order for his flight to make a left turn heading south to stay just off the coast of North Vietnam and out of missile and gun range. *No need to get hurt this late in the game,* he thought. This could very well be the last combat flight Josh made as the commander of VF-96. Their ship was due to rotate off the line at the end of the month and soon head home to San Diego. Josh would be relieved of his command, and after a restful leave with his wife, he would be assuming a new assignment as the Commander Air Group of some yet-to-be-named aircraft carrier or naval airbase. Josh was anxious to see his wife Kiyoshi; he knew she worried excessively about him during these combat cruises. Almost done, baby, he mentally willed to her as if she would receive it back at their home in Oklahoma.

Freeman spoke up from the backseat of the fighter. "Skipper there is some weird crap going on out there tonight. I've been monitoring a separate tactical channel; Red Crown is about to call on us. I'm going to start warming up the magic box here," Freeman said, bringing the Westinghouse AN/APG-59 Pulse Doppler Radar to air search mode. The radar was the fangs of the Phantom's weapons system. Giving the aircrew beyond visual range tracking of enemy aircraft as well as look down shoot down capability against lower flying enemy aircraft that was unheard of in earlier radar-equipped fighters.

Seconds later, the speakers in Josh's helmet exploded with, "Showtime Zero One, Red Crown."

"Red Crown, Showtime Zero One," Josh replied.

"Roger, Showtime, we have some business for you. Expedite heading to 220 degrees. We have unknown aircraft that have fired on friendly units, current range from you is seven zero miles and tracking is 090. Heading of 220, is your intercept heading."

"Copy all Red Crown." Then looking over his shoulder to his number two, he said, "Okay, Shakes, come left to 220. Showtime Three and Four maintain station." Josh knew immediately that the other three pilots had received their orders, and they understood when each replied quickly with their flight number.

"Two"

"Three"

"Four"

Josh wrenched the large F-4 Phantom into a hard left turn leveling out on a compass heading of 220 degrees. Lieutenant Tremble copied his leader's maneuver giving the two aircraft roughly a half-mile spread where they could support each other if shooting started.

"Two, saddled up," Lieutenant Tremble said, letting Josh knew his wingman had completed the course correction and was in position. Josh simply clicked the microphone switch twice, which informed Tremble his message was received.

The voice of the Red Crown controller blasted into the earphones of Josh's helmet. "Showtime, come up on channel six," The controller ordered Josh to switch to a preset radio frequency that would allow him to communicate with the two Air Force F-4Cs already in pursuit of the hostile aircraft.

"Roger, Red Crown," Josh replied, then he ordered Tremble to do the same. "Okay, Shakes, push button six."

"Two," was the reply from Tremble; in the back seats of both aircraft, the RIOs made the frequency changes on their aircraft radios, allowing the pilots to keep focused on their flying. "We're up six!" Freeman said over the aircraft's intercom, letting Josh know the radio was tuned to the proper channel.

"Showtime, Check."

"Two," Shakes replied. Josh then alerted the Red Crown that his flight was on the correct frequency and ready to go to work.

"Red Crown, Showtime is squawking on 6.500" Josh gave the full transponder code to Red Crown to ensure there were no mistakes.

"Rustic, and Showtime, this is Red Crown, your target is stationary, Rustic your intercept heading is now 090."

"Rustic, to zero, nine, zero." The Air Force flight lead said, acknowledging his heading instructions.

"Showtime, maintain heading two, two, zero.", the Red Crown Controller said, keeping Josh on his current heading.

"Showtime, two, two, zero," Josh replied, acknowledging his own orders to maintain his current heading. "Dan, what are you seeing?" Josh asked his RIO.

"I'm searching out to a hundred and twenty miles Skipper, nothing yet." Freeman replied. The relative calm was shattered when the Red Crown controller's voice blasted over the frequency.

"Rustic, Showtime, your target has moved south standby."

There were twenty seconds of dead air over the radio; Josh was about to vent his disapproval when the controller's voice was heard again, "Rustic, make heading one, four, zero, degrees. Showtime, come to two, four, five, degrees."

"Rustic, one, two, zero," the Air Force flight lead responded.

Josh had already started his left turn while Rustic was transmitting, leveling out he replied. "Showtime is two, four, five." Then to Freeman, he asked, "Did that guy fall asleep or something that is a hell of a big course correction for both flights, wouldn't you say, Dan?"

"I would think so, Skipper, unless we're supposed to be chase planes for those NASA boys." The Air Force flight lead had questions too and didn't mind questioning Red Crown about it.

"Red Crown, Rustic confirm one, four, zero, for intercept. Say target speed."

The Red Crown controller replied, "Rustic, your heading is one, four, zero, target speed is zero." This caused the Air Force flight leader to lose all faith in the Red Crown.

"Red Crown, confirm target is in a hover."

"That is a roger Rustic, the target is hovering and we're now showing two separate bogies." The Red Crown controller replied.

"Red Crown, what was the target's speed before it began to hover?" Rustic asked.

"That would be 1,500 knots Rustic."

"Red Crown, did you say one, five, zero, zero, knots?"

"Roger that Rustic 1,500 knots," the controller said somewhat sheepishly.

"Now you're showing two bandits?" The Air Force pilot asked.

"Confirm, two contacts, in close formation."

"Rustic, is Feet Wet," the Air Force flight lead said, informing Red Crown that his flight was now over the waters of the South China Sea.

A voice with a heavy Australian accent came over the radio, "Red Crown, this is Royal Purple, we have unidentified aircraft that are two miles to our south hovering, they came in at high speed before stopping. No IFF code displayed by either target."

"Who the heck is Royal Purple Dan?" Josh asked his RIO in the back seat. The fact that whoever this was had radar contacts not responding with an (IFF) which stood for Identification Friend or Foe code, told Josh he was moments away from combat.

"That is the Australian Destroyer Hobart; they're operating off Tiger Island, to our South, roughly 45 miles just off our nose at 260 degrees." Dan replied over the intercom.

"You're positive on that bearing?" Josh asked.

"Roger, Skipper, two, six, zero, true," Freeman answered quickly.

Josh keyed his microphone and said over the radio, "Showtime come right to two six zero, ready, NOW!" Instantly both Josh's and Lt Tremble's F-4 Phantoms made a slight fifteen-degree course correction to the right. "Lock em up," Josh ordered not only his RIO but also Ensign Simmons in the back seat of Tremble's aircraft to attempt to get radar fixes on the two mysterious bandits.

The two Air Force F-4s out of DaNang were closer and had already acquired radar contacts on the two aircraft.

"Contact our two Air Force playmates, but no contact on the bandits yet, Skipper."

"Red Crown, Rustic is 'Judy' both bandits." The term Judy meant they were locked on and tracking the aircraft on their radar. "They're at Angels 15 and descending fast toward Royal Purple; we're turning to one, five, zero, for intercept and descending Angels 8."

The radar operators on Red Crown were doing their best to maintain control of a very confusing and potentially dangerous engagement. "Copy Rustic Flight we show you on a course of one, four, zero, degrees and now descending through Angels 8. You have the bandits and Royal Purple on your nose at 15 miles now. You also have Showtime Flight, two Navy F-4s at your ten o'clock, bearing One Six Zero, Angels 20, 40 miles out and closing."

"Roger that Red Crown, Showtime lead, this is Rustic. It looks like we'll get first crack at this, we will keep you advised." The leader of the Air Force F-4 flight was a pro. Even though he was keen to get to the enemy first and make the kill, he knew enough to keep Josh's flight of Navy F-4s informed of the situation, in case he needed mutual support as the engagement progressed, but also to keep the two groups of friendly aircraft from accidentally firing on each other.

Josh keyed the microphone and replied to the Air Force flight leader. "Rustic, Showtime Zero One, copy all, descending Angels 15, assuming high cover."

Although both the USAF and US Navy operated the F-4 Phantom, their aircraft were slightly different. The Air Force model was the F-4C, an older version compared to Josh's F-4J, the newest version of the Phantom designed for the Navy. It had updated AN/APG-59 Pulse Doppler Radar, coupled with the AN/AWD-10 Fire Control System, which allowed his aircraft to gain a missile lock on aircraft that were at much lower altitudes than his own. It denied the enemy his ability to hide his aircraft in the ground clutter that affected the older model radars on the earlier Phantoms that the Air Force flight was operating. Josh knew he could stay in high cover and still be in a position to shoot if needed.

"How about it, Dan, you got a bead on these guys yet?" he asked his RIO.

"Roger, Skipper, I've got the whole circus pulled up here. I'm putting scale on the scope at twenty miles, there are your two bandits close to center screen and Rustic flight now entering the screen from the northwest."

Josh took a quick glance down at his own radar display, then brought his eyes back up and looked through the windscreen into the darkness, straining to find visual clues of the impending battle. As if to confirm the mystery, the heavy accented voice of the Australian sailor onboard the HMAS Hobart came over the radio. "Bloody Ell Red Crown, the buggers are still overing alright, they look like a couple of Chinese lanterns about a mile off our starboard, and they don't have normal running lights." Before Red Crown could answer, the Air Force flight leader's voice boomed. "Rustic has visual; Bandits are stationary at Angels Two."

Onboard the Australian Destroyer Hobart, Able Seaman Nigel Styles watched the two mysterious craft through binoculars. The changing colors fascinated the young sailor, who was on his first cruise and a long way from his beloved Alice Springs, Australia, in the south-central part of the Northern Territories. The nearest large body of water was over 1500 miles from his home; now, as a sailor, he rarely saw anything but water. He still had not gotten used to the sea and how the waves and reflections on water could play tricks upon the eyes of those new to its mysteries. As he watched the two craft hover silently a mile away, the constant changing of colors had a hypnotic effect on his mind. He felt as if he were in a dream state; the rolling waves of the South China Sea caused the reflections of the lights from the craft to dance eerily from wave top to wave top.

The Hobart was steaming at a leisurely 15 knots. Her crew was at action stations, but nobody was expecting any trouble. The North Vietnamese Air Force never got their feet wet. Meaning they knew not to stray over the water, where they'd be sitting ducks for ships and aircraft of Task Force 77. These weren't enemy aircraft; they were probably some new American invention that was top secret. Everyone knew the Americans had exotic spy planes; he assumed these were something similar. As he continued to watch the two objects, the lower one gave off a brilliant whitish-blue flash, almost like a muzzle flash.

Able Seaman Styles saw a brilliant blue-white ball streaking toward his ship; it was upon him in a second and flashed past the ship with a resounding sonic boom that sounded like a thunderclap. Styles screamed into the intercom, "We're under fire, we're under fire." Immediately there was a loud bark as the forward five-inch gun turret fired a round toward one of the two objects; the aft gun turret followed suit a second later.

"Red Crown, Royal Purple, under attack, returning fire." The radio operator of the HMAS Hobart screamed into the radio.

"Roger, Royal Purple, Rustic, Showtime, cleared weapons free, EXPIDITE!" Red Crown ordered Josh's flight to engage now that the shooting had started.

"Showtime, go blowers," Josh gave the order for his flight to engage afterburners, increasing their speed. Vietnamese fishermen on boats far below the two aircraft were startled as the night sky above the South China Sea suddenly exploded in a fury from the sound and light as two J-79 engines in each aircraft spit orange-red cones of flame that quickly became bluish-white as the pilots brought the afterburners through their stages which would culminate in over 16,000 pounds of thrust from each engine. Along with the thrust came an enormous loss of fuel as the engines greedily drank the JP-4 fuel at an unbelievable rate.

As the two Navy fighter jets sped toward the developing battle, Josh quickly readied his weapons for battle. Muscle reflex took over; without glancing down to the Weapons Control Panel, he selected the power switch to "ON," then he toggled the Missile switch from "HEAT" to "RADAR," which brought his radar-guided Sparrow missiles to ready. Quickly he glanced up to the Missile Status Panel, which showed green lights for all four Sparrow missiles on his aircraft. Satisfied, he subconsciously removed his left hand from the throttles to the Gun Camera control panel just to the left of his throttles. Flipping the toggle switch to "ON," Josh turned on the KB-25/A Gun Camera which was mated to the optical display or gun sight as people tended to call the instrument. Any weapons firing Josh did would be filmed and recorded on a one-hundred-foot reel of film that was stored in what was called the "Dog Bone" because of its shape; Josh was now ready to do battle.

Josh held his flight in afterburner for just over a minute; the minute's increase of speed and fuel consumption paid off. Josh had brought Showtime Flight right to the spot he wanted them roughly fifteen miles away from and above the developing battle below and in front of them. Josh brought both throttles of the big fighter out of burner and back to mil power. His wingman seeing Josh's afterburners staging down, then cutting off, followed suit to maintain his position supporting Josh. "Let's go, Dan, get em locked!"

"We're locked, Skipper; range is set to twenty miles. Sparrows are still cold," he replied, letting Josh know the aircraft's radar was tracking the two

216

aircraft, and his radar-guided AIM-7 Sparrow missiles were now ready to shoot. "Skipper, the two bandits have a much smaller radar signature than the Phantoms. Careful we don't nail an Air Force guy by mistake."

Josh could look at his scope and see what his RIO was talking about, the two Air Force Phantoms looked bigger on the scope than the bandits, the transponders, or Identify Friend or Foe transmitters would help Josh keep track of the two Air Force aircraft allowing him to engaged the bandits safely if he needed to shoot.

"Showtime is Judy," Josh transmitted, letting both Rustic flight and Red Crown know his flight radar contact and in a position to fight. Both Air Force Phantoms were flying low, just a thousand feet above the waves of the South China Sea; Josh could clearly see the position and formation lights of both aircraft at his low two o'clock even at the fifteen-mile distance that separated them. Both the lead Air Force Phantom pilot and his wingman each had a radar lock on the bandits.

Rustic One had the nearest one, and Rustic Two had the one slightly left and closer to the Australian Destroyer. The screaming of the Australian sailor reporting the ship was under attack was punctuated by a spectacular light show as anti-aircraft guns from the ship erupted on the surface of the dark sea as the Hobart began to fight back against its attackers. The two objects began zigzagging left and right, throwing off the aim of the Australian gunners.

"Rustic Zero One, FOX ONE!" The lead Air Force pilot screamed into the radio. The term Fox One meant he had fired a radar-guided AIM-7 Sparrow Missile. His wingman replied, a split second later with his own, if somewhat less dramatic, Rustic "Zero Two, Fox One!"

Looking down, Josh caught the bright white flashes from the AIM-7 Sparrow missile's motors as they ignited and flew away from the two Air Force Phantoms that fired them. Their brilliant exhaust reflected off the waves of the South China Sea in a hypnotic shimmering effect that even the most seasoned fighter pilot had to fight hard to turn his eyes away from. Josh blinked his eyes hard twice, looking away from the speeding missiles in an attempt not to have his night vision completely ruined. He could now see the mysterious aircraft as well as the gunfire coming from the Australian destroyer. Something seemed off to Josh; the objects seemed to put little effort to avoid the gunfire from the destroyer, yet not a round seemed to be striking home. "Dan, remain focused, Rustic has two missiles in the air."

Josh heard two quick clicks of Freeman's microphone switch, indicating his RIO understood and was confirming his orders without verbally replying.

Good man, staying cool and focused, Josh thought of his RIO as he brought the aircraft's nose down slightly and banked the jet somewhat to the right, where he could get a better view of what was transpiring below. He could now clearly make out the two bandits and was awaiting the impact of the missiles fired by the Air Force when one of the objects vanished. "What happened?" Josh asked.

"He's gone," Freeman replied from the backseat.

"What do you mean he's gone; did he blow up?" Josh asked.

"No, Skipper, he just disappeared from radar there was no explosion that I could tell, I'm locking onto the second one... and I got him." In an instant, the remaining bandit went from two thousand feet to ten thousand feet in altitude." Did you see that he just went up eight thousand feet in less than a second?" Freeman screamed.

Josh now had a clear shot at the bandit since it was close to his own altitude. The two Air Force Phantoms were far below and now outside the range of his missiles. "Dan, keep this thing locked up," he said calmly. After a split second of once again confirming the sky was clear of any friendly combatants and seeing the "SHOOT" lights flashing on his canopy bow confirming he had a good firing solution, Josh fired two of his own AIM-7 Sparrow missiles. "Fox One...Fox One Again!" Josh said as he launched two AIM-7 Sparrow missiles at the strange aircraft now only five miles away and four thousand feet lower in altitude.

He dropped the nose of the big fighter sharply to help keep the radar locked onto his target as he watched the exhaust flame from the two five-hundred-pound missiles as they flew toward the target at over Mach-2. He watched with fascination as they closed with the large ring of light, now only three miles from his aircraft. Both missiles impacted the target with brilliant white flashes, and the craft fell toward the sea.

Following it down, Josh was too far inside the minimum launch range of his two remaining AIM-7 Sparrow missiles. He switched to one of the four AIM-9 Sidewinder heat-seeking missiles his aircraft carried. Two were mounted on the outboard pylons of each wing of his aircraft. He waited for the telltale growl in his headset as the missile locked onto a heat source of the fast-diving saucer-shaped craft he was following down. The growl never came; it was as if his missiles were pointed at an iceberg. "Lead I just saw two explosions on the water; I think that Aussie ship just took a hit." Lieutenant Tremble reported as he continued to cover Josh from a half-mile off and slightly behind his right wing.

"Copy that, Shakes," Josh replied.

Then from his RIO, "Skipper, we're blowing through six thousand feet, I really don't want to end up as fish food."

Josh had been watching his altimeter and was already pulling out of the dive as Freeman spoke. He watched with astonishment as the ring of light flew straight into the water; there was no huge splash; there were no pieces of debris flying, no explosions. He could see the ring of light continued to move swiftly under the water. Then the light began to fade as the craft obviously began to dive deeper away from the surface. There was pandemonium on the radio as the Australian destroyer called for assistance and the Air Force Phantoms called for the destroyer to check its fire. Evidently, some of the Australian anti-aircraft fire was getting dangerously close to their aircraft.

Josh keyed his microphone and transmitted to his flight and Red Crown. "Showtime, left Zero Five Zero, climb Angels 15… Red Crown Showtime is climbing east, possible splash on one bandit, advise if you have more contacts."

Red Crown replied, "Negative, Showtime, we show no bandits in the area now."

As the two F-4 Phantoms climbed back to the east and the patrol area, Freeman began talking from the backseat, "What the hell was that thing, Skipper? I watched it fly into and under the water. Did we shoot it down, or did somebody invent the flying submarine?"

Josh knew this incident did not bode well for him. For whatever reason, God once again had decided to place him among these mysterious aerial machines. This will probably get me more attention than I want, he thought to himself, thinking back on his experience with a similar engagement off the coast of Antarctica.

"Skipper, what are we going to tell the Intel Pukes during debriefing?"

"Dan, I think you'll find out during debrief, none of this crap happened tonight," Josh said, continuing the shallow climb toward the northeast and its faint glow that promised a new day; he had no idea what that new day held in store. All he knew for certain was that soon he'd be in the arms of his beloved wife. Kiyoshi, I'm coming home, baby, he thought.

Miles behind him, a small piece of sheet metal from the first AIM-7 Sparrow he had fired fluttered from two miles high in the air. It had been just a piece of random missile debris that had come apart when the missile's warhead detonated. It would come to haunt Josh as it lazily fell from the sky guided by a strong westerly wind only to splash and sink into the waters of the South China Sea. The small piece of missile held a small stencil on its side, which read… AIM-7D USN SER NO: R70010023, the piece of metal sank lazily down to the ocean floor some 350 feet, never to see the light of day again. Yet the very same serial number painted on the side of a similar piece of missile debris would haunt Josh the rest of his life.

On the deck of the HMAS Hobart, the Australian sailors were busy fighting fires and tending to the wounded following what they assumed was an attack by the strange aircraft. Nobody knew yet that the damage to the Hobart was from the AIM-7 Sparrow missiles fired from the Air Force Phantoms. As the missiles were fired, one UFO completely disappeared; the other had climbed eight thousand feet so quickly, it might as well have disappeared. There was nothing left for the two Air Force missiles to stay locked on. Both missiles had gone dumb flying unguided into the Hobart. One missile had exploded in the ship's forward funnel; the second hit the Ikara Missile Magazine. Both explosions started intense fires in small compartments that burned any identification of the missiles off completely.

Within a couple of hours, investigators could tell from the remains of the components that American AIM-7 Sparrow missiles had struck the Hobart. However, there were no identifying marks on the remains to confirm whose missiles struck the ship. The missiles Josh fired had nothing to do with the damage to the Hobart. Unfortunately for Josh, he had stomped on the tail of this particular snake one too many times.

# CHAPTER NINE

<the decorative divider>

# The Old Warrior

*"Cry havoc and let slip the dogs of war."*
*-William Shakespeare*

## Tuesday, 29 November 2016 3:30 PM CST, Kiamichi Mountains near Honobia, OK

Nathan and Trent had been lurking around the mountains just north of Honobia on and off since the previous Friday evening after Addison's wife, Marsha, had been killed. They had returned that evening after dark and had followed blood trails late into the night. Operating in the dark without proper equipment was difficult, and they knew they were in danger of losing the trail. Any further investigation at night in these mountains was a bad idea with their current limited resources. They backed out just before midnight and made the nearly two-hour drive back to Fort Smith, Arkansas, where they made their presence known to the local Arkansas Air National Guard unit stationed at the airport in Fort Smith. Initially, the young Staff Sergeant on duty didn't know what to make of the two men who presented their military identification cards and left paperwork demanding to speak to the ranking officer of the unit.

Nathan explained to the Staff Sergeant that he and Trent Simmons were both members of a Special Operations unit under the command of Major General Malcolm Henderson, and both men were on leave and needed to make immediate contact with the General. Nathan had been in the Arkansas National Guard prior to going active duty and joining General Henderson's Task Force Titan. When Nathan Parks had been a member of the National Guard, he knew the Air National Guard Unit in Fort Smith operated A-10 Warthogs and assumed they still did. Nathan had no idea the unit's mission had changed from Close Air Support with A-10s to their current mission as the 188th Intelligence, Surveillance, and Reconnaissance Group. They now operate the MQ-9 Reaper drone aircraft with a worldwide commitment. The unit had even supported Task Force Titan Missions several times, so when the young Staff Sergeant woke the 188th ISRG Commander from his holiday rest, mentioning both General Henderson and Task Force Titan, the Colonel couldn't have been more cooperative. Both Nathan and Trent were shown into the Operations Center and where they were linked into a face-to-face communication link with the General.

At first, the General was none too pleased to hear two of his most valuable assets were freelancing during what was supposed to be a time of rest and recuperation. "I told you two to get some rest and recover your strength, if I'd known you were going to go rouge, I would have kept your butts here," General Henderson growled, the scowl on his face very apparent over the computer screen.

"Sir, our intentions were to do just that, we were going to camp on Addison Redstone's property and do a little hunting and fishing. As it turned out things have gone bad here, Sir, in fact it appears as if the enemy we're fighting there is trying to open up shop here, Sir."

"So, what is it you need from me Gentleman?" Henderson asked.

Nathan began explaining the situation around Honobia, Oklahoma; he mentioned the missing boys being found on Addison's property, the couple who had the encounter on the bridge, and the death of Addison's wife. Then he told General Henderson about the remains of the missing Air Force pilot being found along the riverbed in Honobia and the message in Hebrew that scrawled on the rock, which was obviously intended for Nathan.

"Well, that's not good, Sergeant, in fact that is just the kind of crap I don't need to be hearing. It means you've been singled out and that is never good news," General Henderson replied.

"I'm afraid there's more bad news, Sir," Parks said.

"Go ahead," Henderson said tiredly.

"Addison Redstone's wife, Marsha, was killed by a Relic Friday afternoon."

"Oh no, are you sure, that is what killed her?" Henderson replied with apparent concern for his friend.

"Yes Sir, her vehicle was attacked on a mountain road about sixteen miles from Talihina. Sam's wife and daughter were in the car with her when it happened. A local man came to their rescue shooting all three creatures with a 308-caliber hunting rifle. The man said the three creatures fled the area, one of them had a head wound and one a shot to center mass, yet they still got to their feet and ran."

"Are Sam's wife and daughter, okay?"

"Yes Sir, the daughter was uninjured, Sam's wife was only slightly injured, but she is carrying a child and there was some concern about the baby, but it looks as if the three of them will be okay. There's one more thing Sir."

"Go ahead," Henderson replied, tiredly.

"Special Agent Paul Eastman is back as well, and he's been turned."

"Turned?"

"Yes, Sir, 'TURNED.' Black suit and tie with a couple of goons in tow. All three were hiding their eyes behind sunglasses," Nathan replied. Master Sergeant Simmons!" General Henderson snapped at the Air Force NCO.

"Sir!" Trent replied, snapping to attention even though the General was on the other side of the planet.

"Are you sure you want to be involved with this? Parks has managed to make himself a household name with our adversary, I'm not sure if you know what that means, but I can promise you that your involvement will change your life and not in a positive way."

"Sir, I see no reason to not be involved, I'm part of your team, just like Sergeant Parks, I'm here and I'm familiar with the area and the threat, Sir."

"This isn't like last time Simmons; this is an escalation for that area. You saw what Parks had to deal with just before I sent you two on leave; you could encounter something like that or even worse."

"If I wanted to fight mere humans, I would have joined the Seals, Sir. I'm in!"

"Alright then, I'm going to have the required weapons and gear flown to the Guard Unit there in Ft Smith. I will expedite it, so it gets there within twenty-four hours. How are you guys fixed for transportation?"

"Well, Sir, we rented a Jeep, and there are plenty of four-wheel drive vehicles available with the Redstone's."

"Okay, that's good news, get this done quick and clean, if it escalates and becomes a bigger issue, I'm not sure I'll be able to bail you out. Don't involve any of the locals other than the Redstone's if you can help it. Also, both of you find some decent clothes and attend the funeral for Mrs. Redstone and be sure to give Addison my sympathy."

In less than twenty-four hours, General Henderson had been true to his word, a C-130 arrived at Ft Smith, with a cache of weapons, ammunition, and equipment for the two men. The Air Force Loadmaster on the Hercules transport who handled the weight and balancing of the aircraft's cargo was very curious about the pallet he unloaded for the two men.

"Okay, gents, here you go. Two MK-14 Enhanced Battle Rifles, each with four magazines and 200 rounds of ammo, copper. Two M-4 Carbines, each with 4 magazines and 200 rounds of ammo, copper. One M1014 12-gauge shotgun 40 rounds of copper buckshot and 40 rounds of copper slugs. Two M45A1 Pistols 4 magazines each and 100 rounds, copper. Looking up at the two men quizzically, you also have fifty copper disks, what the hell is with all this copper?"

"We just like the way it shines, Sarge, Trent Simmons replied."

The LoadMaster just looked at him confused before going down the rest of the list, which included scopes for the rifles, borescope lasers for sighting in the weapons, and night vision gear. As fast as they could sign for it, they loaded the equipment in the Jeep, then thanking the confused Air Force Sergeant, the two men made their way off the flight line headed to Talihina.

The funeral for Marsha was held on Monday afternoon; the service was very crowded; Marsha had been a much-loved member of the community. Addison seemed to be in shock, and Nathan noticed Sam never approached his father to offer any comfort. Both Christa and her mother stayed near Addison during the funeral and at the post-funeral gathering at Marsha and Addison's house. At one point, Nathan noticed Sam standing alone in the kitchen area, approaching slowly. Nathan asked his friend, "So how is your dad holding up?"

"Well, he's on schedule to get us all killed if that's what you're asking?"

"What do you mean by that?" Nathan asked.

"I don't know how many times, I've told him to leave this stuff alone, yet he keeps getting pulled into it, it cost him his wife. He's pulled me into it, and it could have cost me my whole family."

"Sam, I don't think you're being fair," Nathan replied.

"It wasn't your wife and children in that car, Nathan. Plus, I dare say if you did have a family, your father wouldn't serve them up to a bunch of giant man-apes!"

Sam spoke so loudly that guests in the other room stopped talking and looked nervously at the two men in the kitchen. Catching himself, Sam used a lower tone as he continued, "We should have left this alone the last time it happened; those things would have moved along if we had."

"You don't know that, Sam."

"That's bullshit, Nathan; you know these things are seen all over the country, nobody else is losing loved ones to them, because nobody else is dumb enough to mess with them. Ignore them and they'll go away, but he can't ignore them, he had to start a war with them, and I don't think it will end until they kill him or all of us."

"Your father didn't start this, Sam, and I got news for you. He's right, you're going to have to fight them, or nobody will be safe, there's something bigger going on here. You're correct these things don't normally happen in other areas. Something else has moved in here and it's the root cause of the violence. These is not your average Sasquatch behavior Sam, there's more to this, much more. Trent, your father, and I are going to put a stop to it one way or the other. Your father could use your help, or at least your support."

Nathan walked away, leaving Sam alone in his thoughts; he went into the other room where he found Addison talking quietly to Christa. Addison, can I have a word with you?"

"Sure, Nathan, Christa would you excuse me a moment please?" Christa nodded and moved away toward another group of guests, "Okay, Nathan, what's on your mind?"

"Trent and I will be heading back up to Honobia in the morning, we've scouted the area a bit and I wanted to show you where we'll be." Unfolding a map he had printed, he pointed to the area he and Trent would start their operations.

"Dead Man's Hollow, that's appropriate," Addison said with no surprise in his voice."

"The blood trail pointed here sir, so this is where we'll open up shop," Nathan replied. "I have a few things to tie up here, and I'll be there Nathan, probably sometime Wednesday," Addison replied.

"We'll, have a spot saved for you at the fire sir." Nathan hugged Addison and gave him a healthy slap on the back. "See you soon, Sergeant Major."

Then nodding to Trent, they made their exit. Nathan's mind returned to his present situation; he shuddered slightly against the afternoon chill, whose cold, damp fingers began to probe his tired muscles. For hours, he and Trent Simmons had been lying in wait on a rocky outcrop above an area known as Dead Man's Hollow. They had positioned themselves roughly 1,200 feet from the hollow, which was a small canyon along Honobia creek where the river held a straight course running north to south, leaving a level area 5,000 feet long and 400 feet wide. It was bordered on all sides by steep, rugged hills. The two men were settled in on the edge of a tree line on the west side 600 feet up one of these hills. Their vantage point gave them a perfect kill zone in the canyon below. Nothing could enter or cross the hollow without being in the crosshairs of the two men.

Nathan heard Trent's stomach growl as the man lay next to him, scanning the eastern edge of the hollow below them with his spotter scope. "Man, you should have gotten yourself one of those Bigfoot burgers at the Honobia Creek Store while we were down there earlier, instead of flirting with the lady working there," Nathan whispered, teasing his companion.

"I wasn't flirting, I was just being friendly," Trent whispered, never moving his eyes from the spotting scope.

"Friendly is smiling and being polite. Asking her name and tipping her twenty dollars after buying a bottle of water and some jerky is flirting," Nathan countered.

"You've got to expand your thinking, Sarge, to an Army guy like you it was flirting. In the Air Force we call that Strategic Recon. Next time I do go into that store and I do want to eat, I'll get extra attention paid to my meal while it's being prepared and probably get my food way before you do," Trent replied confidently as he continued scanning the area below them.

"You're going to get special attention alright; she probably has a boyfriend that knows every rock, tree, and crevice in these mountains. He's probably watching us right now, waiting to split your wig once you drop your guard," Nathan said quietly.

"That will never happen," Trent countered confidently. "How can you be so sure?" Nathan asked. Removing his eyes from the spotting scope, Trent looked at Nathan with a sarcastic smile and said, "I've got the Army here to protect me," then, returning his eyes to the scope, he continued, "You have to admit; she's a cutie and obviously appreciates a cultured man like myself, but I'm not on the market anyway."

"Not in the market? I didn't realize you were married," Nathan said, his curiosity rising.

Trent sighed, "I'm not, well not anymore. My ex took off with a civilian a couple of tours ago. I haven't shaken off the bad vibes yet. There's nothing like coming home from war to an empty house and a note saying the woman you love left you for a car salesman. How about you, are you married Nathan?"

No, but I'm starting to get serious with a woman."

"What in the hell are you doing here man? Why are you spending time with your lady?" Trent asked, confused.

"My lady is back in Kandahar, she's a nurse at the base hospital. This leave was thrown onto me so fast and without warning, she couldn't get away too." Nathan replied.

226

"You're getting serious with an Officer? I didn't know I was in the presence of royalty. That sucks she couldn't get away. You should have told General Henderson, maybe he could have pulled some strings."

Pulling his face from the scope of the rifle and rubbing his eyes, Nathan said, "I didn't have time to ask, besides her tour is up in three weeks and she'll be going to San Antonio. Hopefully I'll have time left to go spend a few days with her."

"That's good, brother, so she's getting assigned to Brooke Army Medical Center?" Trent asked.

"Nathan paused a moment before answering because he knew Trent would never cease teasing him after he answered the question. "No, she's being assigned to Wilford Hall."

"Wilford Hall!" Trent asked. "That's an Air Force hospital, you're getting serious with an Air Force nurse?"

"That's right Simmons, I've invaded your beloved flying circus and am about to propose to an Air Force Officer." Nathan said, smirking.

"Well look at it this way Nathan, you're spending your leave time with me and dating an Air Force nurse. You're definitely starting to expand your social standing by hanging out with a better class of people. So does she speak Army?" Trent asked.

"What do you mean by that?"

"Does she know what you're saying when you grunt and click?" Trent said, trying to hide his smile.

Nathan picked up a small stone and threw it, hitting Trent in the forehead, which left a red mark and the promise of a small knot. Rubbing his forehead, Trent looked at his companion and said, "See, that's not going to work with an Air Force nurse, you need to learn how to use your words."

Nathan shook his head, stifled a laugh, and began to concentrate again on the task at hand. Nathan looked through the scope of the MK-14 Enhanced Battle Rifle, scanning the bank of Honobia Creek below them. Both men had MK-14s available, but for the moment, they thought one of them on a rifle and one of them using a spotting scope would work best as they were scouting the situation more than actively hunting the creatures.

An enormous crashing sound came from the woods along the opposite creek bank from the two men. Sound wasn't a proper term for the thundering crash of snapping limbs and breaking tree trunks. It was as if an unseen storm was ravaging the forest, although there was no wind. "I've got movement," Trent whispered as he peered through the spotting scope, as he watched the

227

tops of trees bend over, some snapping back into place and some simply disappearing as if the tree had been eaten.

Seeing nothing through his rifle scope, Nathan said, "I'm no joy, going Bull's-eye." Meaning he could not see what Trent was seeing, so he was putting his scope on the large boulder they had designated as the center of their kill zone. Trent would tell him which direction to adjust his view until he sighted the target. "Come South from Bull's-eye thirty, then up ten," Trent said.

Nathan moved his scope from the center of the large boulder thirty meters to the right and then slowly began to move the scope up. He could see a medium-sized pine tree moving back and forth violently as if something huge were shaking it. "Got it," he whispered.

He continued watching the tree shake and bend violently, it was positioned twenty feet or so into the tree line, then whatever was causing it to move stopped, and it swayed gently for a moment expending the last of the force that had been applied to it. Without warning, a large reddish-brown shape tumbled out of the tree line and landed hard on the rocks near the creek's bank. The thing was man-like and covered in hair; both men knew exactly what they were looking at. "Well, I'd say that's what we came here for." Trent whispered quietly under his breath.

"Yep," Nathan said as he clicked the selector on then rifle from safe to fire, holding the crosshairs on the creature. He noticed the creature seemed to be injured and dazed as his finger began to gently apply pressure to the trigger of the MK-14 rifle. It looked as if it was almost pleading with something still hidden in the tree line. Then another, larger creature and much darker, almost black in color, stepped into view out of the trees; it was holding a huge log that was so large it would take two strong men just to lift it. Yet this creature carried it as if it were a baseball bat. It walked calmly over to the first creature cowering on the creek bank and began beating it viciously with the log. Nathan and Trent suddenly experienced an overpowering stench that assaulted both of their senses. "Sheesh, what the hell did she put in that burger?" Trent asked in a whisper.

"Don't make me laugh when I'm about to do battle," Nathan growled back softly.

The smaller creature screamed in agony with each impact of the log on its body. Both men lay in silence, watching the drama unfold below them. It looked as if the larger creature would beat the smaller one to death when it suddenly stopped in mid-swing and turned, looking right at Nathan and

Trent. Although the two men were completely camouflaged and hidden nearly two hundred yards away. Looking through their scopes, they could clearly see that it was staring right into their eyes as displayed large sharp teeth and a look of pure hate, which burned into both men's souls. "Wow, that's one big spooky bastard, and he knows we're here." Trent whispered.

"Yep," Nathan said as he adjusted his aim to the center mass of the large creature and applied a little more pressure. The MK-14 barked loudly twice as the two copper bullets sped down from the outcrop at 3,200 feet per second, finding the chest of their intended target almost instantly. The 180-grain copper bullets ripped into the creature's chest; because of the creature's mass, they did not exit its body. Instead, the rounds bounced around in the chest cavity for a microsecond, turning the heart and lungs into a mass of pink and red chunks. The creature dropped to its knees swaying as if awaiting death.

The MK-14 barked again, and a third round hit the middle of the creature's forehead blowing the top of its head off. The smaller creature was in shock for a moment, then it scrambled up from its back and began running on all fours trying to get to the safety of the trees on the opposite side of the creek. Nathan calmly lined the creature in his sights, giving it the proper amount of lead; a moment before the pressure of his finger on the trigger met the sweet spot that would send another bullet home, a voice behind him said, "Don't shoot that one, let it go!"

Shocked by the unexpected sound of another human voice, both Nathan and Trent rolled quickly, facing the direction the voice came from. Nathan already had the barrel of the MK-14 pointed at the chest of the figure standing in the trees behind them; it took Trent a second longer to un-holster the M45A1 he was carrying, but he too had his weapon pointing at the figure in the trees.

"That isn't one of the creatures you're after; you can't kill every one of them you encounter," Josh Nashoba said, stepping from a group of trees behind the two men. Nathan and Trent lowered their weapons; both felt a little foolish, having been surprised by the elderly man's ability to move so close to them without their knowing it.

"What do you mean that isn't one of the creatures I'm after? I'm after all of them."

"Then you will start an even bigger fight than you have on your hands already. You'll end up fighting the good ones, the bad ones, and probably even some of the Choctaw people in these mountains. I know about what happened two years ago, we may be less than twenty miles from Talihina, but things are different in these mountains and this valley. We've had a peace with the Okla Chito for years; the only time there is a problem is when unsuspecting hunters from out of the area happen to run into one. Sometimes they'll panic and shoot, even when this happens, we've been able to keep the peace. You start shooting all you see and the problems you're trying to solve will only get worse."

Putting his eye back in the spotting scope, Trent saw a reddish-brown blur as the second creature disappeared into the wood-line below them. "Well, Sir, I hope you're right and the one that got away doesn't land in our lap in the next couple of minutes wanting some hand-to-hand combat."

"He'll head south until he can cross back over the creek out of sight from us," Josh responded confidently.

"Well, in case he doesn't and decides to leap up on this ledge and get some payback for his friend, you can have the honor of taking the first crack at him," Trent said, smiling, followed by, "I'm Master Sergeant Trent Simmons, U.S. Air Force, and this is Sergeant First Class Nathan Parks U.S. Army. He nodded toward the silent Parks before asking, "So who are you, if I may ask?"

I'm Joshua Nashoba, Commander, U.S. Navy Retired." Josh said, silently enjoying the first opportunity to state his rank in decades. He noticed the black Army Sergeant had been silently watching him and was ready to speak.

"A squid, huh? Now all we need is a Marine and we could form a color guard for the next Super Bowl. Commander, just how is it you know good ones from bad ones?" Nathan asked.

"Call me Josh, Sergeant, I'm retired."

"Call me Nathan, Commander, I'm on leave." Nathan replied with a smile before continuing, "You're the guy they call 'The Mad Footer' aren't you, Sir?"

Smiling, Josh replied, "Yes, they call me that, and a few other names up here."

"So, can you tell us the difference between the good ones and bad ones Commander?" "I have a feeling you know the difference between good and evil, I can tell by the gray hair on a man with your obvious youth that you have some experience fighting real evil. I would venture to say you have just as much experience if not more battling evil than I do."

"Yes, Sir, I've seen some things," Nathan admitted.

"You've done more than seen some things Nathan, you've sought it out. You gave up a comfortable life and have now traveled the world battling it. You made it your mission, your very reason for living; it is your calling. Sergeant Parks, you are a true Crusader." Then looking toward Trent

Simmons, he continued. "You, Sergeant Simmons, are an adventurer, a committed one I agree, but your heart and soul have been wounded so given up taking life serious so now you're living for thrill. You enjoy this kind of thing. You're bored with what you call the real world, you're unsettled in your soul because you lost something or someone and you're here for the adrenalin. Right now, you're getting away with it through pure talent and a lot of luck, despite your ignorance of the real danger. However, the day is going to come when the amusement of it all will no longer serve you, then you too must face your own calling."

Trent studied Josh's face for a moment. Deep inside, he knew that the older man had perfectly described his attitude toward life, especially since his wife left him. His constant seeking of duty assignments kept him in third-world countries or, at the very least, the fringes of twenty-first-century America, such as Honobia. He needed to exile himself away from that world and seek out life in extreme conditions; it was the only way he knew of to deal with the pain of being abandoned by his wife. "I'm serving my country, the best way I know how, Sir," Trent replied somewhat sheepishly.

"You know what's going on here, Sergeant Simmons; you can't keep hiding from it."

"I don't believe I'm hiding from anything; I'm here fighting these super monkeys for my friends and their loved ones," Trent said, becoming a bit angry. "Besides I don't recall asking for psychological help from a mountain man."

"You're here fighting pain Simmons. Face it, own up to it, and quit hiding from it. Ignoring it will get you killed."

"I'm doing alright." Trent responded.

"Yes, you're doing alright, but only because God has allowed you to get away with it so far. You need his protection; you need his full armor, not just luck. It wasn't luck that got you out of the woods near Talihina two years ago. The beasts you chased into the woods were about to take you and the horse you managed to capture and ride out on."

"How did you know about that?" Trent asked with growing confusion. "I was there; I distracted them long enough for you to escape."

"Bullshit, somebody told you about that night. Heck it's been talked about all over the Special Operations community."

"Sergeant Simmons, you made quite a name for yourself among Special Operators I'm sure, riding in out of the darkness like John Wayne on that horse."

231

"Yes, I did," Trent said, smiling.

"Did you forget to tell them about how you dropped your rifle, when you were overcome by seeing the UFO. You had to dismount to retrieve it? I'm sure you also failed to mention that while retrieving your rifle, you heard a loud crashing sound and you immediately jumped back on the horse and got out of the area as quickly as possible assuming one of the creatures was nearly on top of you."

Trent's jaw hung open as he recalled the night in 2014 after following two of the creatures into the woods. He and Sam Redstone had just rescued an armed teenager who had fallen off his horse and was about to be attacked by two creatures that had him flanked.

"Hey, Air Force, you dropped your weapon?" Nathan asked with obvious amusement.

Trent looked at Nathan for a moment, then Josh, then back to Nathan.

"Yeah, I dropped my rifle the lights from a helicopter or whatever that thing was had blinded me and I got dizzy. Who do I look like, Roy Rogers?"

"That was no helicopter Trent, you knew it then, and you know it now."

Still not believing this man was actually there, Trent said, "That kid had a go pro camera on him and was filming the whole video was broadcast at least once on the national news; that is how you knew about this."

"There was no camera in the woods that night when you dropped your rifle, was there, Sergeant?"

"No, I guess there wasn't, but why were you there?"

"I knew there were problems in Talihina. The night before the incident with you and the horse I slipped into the woods and was told to go to a certain spot and be still until I was needed." Josh replied.

"Who told you?" Trent asked.

"God told me."

"God told you to go spend twenty-four hours in one spot to rescue me?"

"No, God told me to go to a certain spot and be still until I was needed. When you dropped your rifle and had to dismount, two of the creatures were crawling to you just a few feet away and would have taken you. I told them to be still, this allowed you to grab your weapon, but you were slow to remount the horse. I pushed the boulder over which gave you incentive to remount and get out of the area."

"I have to admit, what you say is true, Commander."

"Again, call me Josh, and remember I was sent there by God for your benefit. He has plans for you Trent."

"So, you really dropped your weapon Air Force?" Nathan asked again, smiling.

Trent looked at Nathan, "Shut up." Then looking back at Josh, he asked. "How are you so good at all this sneaking around at your age? Plus, if you can command these things to be still, why not command them to go away for good?"

"They were not fully formed when we encountered them. Now they have nearly reached their full potential."

"Where did you learn all of this? What exactly did you do in the Navy?"

"I was a fighter pilot."

"Oh, I should have known, well, there goes the neighborhood," Trent said

"We'd better work our way down there and take care of the remains before dark sets in," Nathan said, rising from his shooting position. Then looking at Josh, he said, "Sir, there are a few things we need to do, and we'll be right back, unless of course you want to go down there too?"

"I'll stay here and keep an eye on your gear," Josh replied as Nathan dug through a hard plastic equipment case producing a large machete, which appeared to Josh to be made of copper. Seeing the blade, Josh nodded his approval and said, "Now I know you've been battling the very evil I suspected you had. Once you examine the remains of your victim down there, I'm sure you'll now know how to tell the good ones from bad ones by the way."

Confused, Nathan nodded back, saying, "Looks like we have a lot to discuss, do we need to leave a weapon with you?"

"I'll be fine," Josh replied. Then turning to Trent, Nathan said, "Trent, it might be a good idea if we both go down there heavy, we don't know what else is lurking in those trees."

"I agree," Trent said, retrieving his MK-14.

Nathan looked at Josh and winked before saying, "Trent, be careful you don't drop it."

The two men worked their way down the ridgeline to the creek; the water was still flowing strongly due to heavy rain the previous night. After finding a shallow place to cross, they came upon the body of the Relic, which had dropped like a pile of rocks after taking three rounds of 7.62x51mm from Nathan's MK-14. Nathan leaned down and inspected the remains, "Look at this, Trent," he said as he moved the head of the beast around with his foot.

"I see a big nasty foul-smelling corpse Nathan, what in particular are you try to point out?"

"The head wound, look at the head wound."

"I see it, not as big as I expected, but I see it," Trent said, unimpressed.

"There's a reason for that Trent, just as I suspected the wound is beginning to heal itself. You were looking through the spotting scope there was a piece as big as barn door blown off the top of this things head when I put the third round into it. These things are capable of regenerating their body after massive damage. Just like some of that creepy crap we've fought down range. Look at this, six fingers and toes, again just like a lot of the creepy crap we find in Afghanistan," Nathan replied.

"Are you saying this thing will heal itself?" Trent asked.

"Yes, this is some form of Nephilim. Possibly, the chest wounds are not healing, probably because the bullets didn't exit the body. The copper rounds are either stopping or delaying the body's ability to regenerate."

Trent looked at the wounds closer, suddenly taking more interest. "The copper bullet exited the back of the head, which is why there was so much tissue flying through the air. The copper is not there so the head is regenerating. The two rounds I put center mass did not exit, so they are still inside the chest cavity and disrupting, if not stopping the regeneration altogether," Nathan replied as he watched the head wound of the creature slowly regenerate right before his eyes.

"Sheesh, so copper to these things is like silver to a vampire? Do you know how crazy all this sounds?" Trent said, getting a bit concerned.

"I know, this may sound like an old horror movie, I'm not sure exactly why it works, but it does. I believe the conductivity of the copper interferes with the electrical impulses these BRENs use to regenerate." Nathan replied, still watching the head with a calm fascination.

Confused, Trent asked, "What do you mean BRENs?"

"BREN is an acronym for Biological Relic Entity.

Trent looked at Nathan for a moment, then shook his head in disgust at the thought of filing another, yet another military acronym in his brain.

"I wondered why you ordered all the copper. I thought you knew exactly why we needed copper rounds, copper blades and copper wafers. What the hell, you don't know for sure copper is going to keep these things down?" Trent exclaimed, suddenly becoming concerned about them standing next to the corpse. "What if that thing jumps up suddenly and starts to kick our asses? Did you bring copper brass knuckles to fist fight it with too?"

"Relax Trent," Nathan said calmly. "Remember every BREN our unit killed down range was immediately flown out by chopper and handed over to the

CIA. To be honest we assumed the copper rounds and weapons we had been issued had something more to do with their genetic makeup and being able to bring them down. I didn't know they would regenerate. We were told to fill them full of copper rounds and behead them. We thought it was to ensure they were dead, not to keep them dead. Here Trent, hold this and don't drop it," Nathan said, holding his rifle out. Trent took the rifle, placing the sling over his left shoulder as Nathan removed a copper wafer the size of a hockey puck and the copper-bladed machete from his pack.

"Am I'm to assume the 'Don't Drop It' remark is going to become a regular thing in our daily conversations now?" Trent asked annoyed.

Nathan stopped momentarily standing above the corpse, then looking at Trent with a grin, he said, "That's right, butter fingers." Then he leaned over and pried the mouth of the creature open and inserted the copper wafer into its mouth, pushing it in as far as he could with the blade of the machete. Then he began to use the machete to hack away at the creature's thick neck to remove the head from the rest of the body. With every swing of the machete made a wet meaty sound and dark red blood splattered about the ground.

Trent winced with every swing of the blade, "I don't know what is worse the stench or the sound the blade makes when it hits the flesh."

"This is one thick neck; I'll need a rest soon and you can take a few hacks at it," Nathan answered.

"Not me, I might drop the machete," Trent said, enjoying his moment of payback.

"Well played, Air Farce," Nathan said sarcastically, never looking up from his task. "You know there is something we don't have we're going to need, diesel. We need to burn these things as we kill them."

"Why not just call your buddies at the CIA?" Trent asked.

"I'm not real sure General Henderson wants what we're doing here to get out to other agencies."

"Why would he not want others to know we're here? That doesn't make any sense, Nathan."

"There are Special Ops, and then you have Black Ops, which is basically what we've been doing overseas. Finally, you have Ultra Black Ops; I think that is who has been taking possession of the specimens we've been killing down range. I can't be sure, but I get the feeling we're not all on the same page, maybe not even the same team."

"What makes you think that?"

"Just a feeling I get, sometimes General Henderson doesn't give them the whole story, I think he holds information back for good reason."

"What would possibly be a good reason to hold information back from another agency further up the food chain?" Trent asked, now thoroughly confused.

"I'm not sure, but it may be some of these critters are more than just your average bogyman."

"I'd say that brute you killed just before we left Afghanistan was not your average bogyman, that thing had to be fifteen feet tall," Trent said, wincing as he heard the blade of Nathan's Machete starting to make a loud cracking noise with each swing as he began chopping through bone. After much effort, the blade was finally through the bone, and Nathan doubled his efforts as his task was nearing completion, "How the hell do you call any of this average, Nathan?"

With a final heavy swing, Nathan cut through the last bit of flesh holding the creature's head to its body. He straightened up, taking heavy breaths of air; the muscles in his arms were burning from the effort he had just expended. Looking at Trent, he said, "Have you ever heard of a Satyr?"

"Is that one of those four legged things that has a horse's body, and the torso of a man?" Trent replied.

"Close enough, actually they're two-legged. The lower body is like that of a goat, complete with hooves for feet." Nathan said as he used his foot to roll the detached head of the creature away from the body. Leaning over, he inspected his handy work. "Just as I expected, the original head wound has not healed anymore, nor is the neck healing. It has to be that copper wafer I put in the mouth. Then he looked back at Trent. "Back to my story, one of the first operations I was on with Task Force Titan, we were in the Kunar Province of Afghanistan this time. Women in a nearby settlement were regularly disappearing; they would be found days later raped and murdered. It was assumed we had a Taliban faction or something similar coming in and abducting young women for their personal pleasure, then killing them when they had no more use for them."

"We sent out patrols hoping to intercept them, we had nothing else going on at the time, the strange happenings we were usually sent into counter had been quiet for a while. The General thought it would be a good idea for us to be out doing conventional soldiering. We were an eight-man team patrolling an area between the village and the border with Pakistan; we had an Afghan national with us as an interpreter. The area had been quiet with no action for a couple of weeks. The team leader thought the area was safe enough for us to spread out into two-man groups with a couple of hundred yards between us. It was Staff Sergeant Bennett and I, with the Afghan tagging along."

"Bennett, isn't that the guy I flew in and picked up a couple of months ago? It looked like something just bit a chunk out of his rear end." Trent asked.

"Yeah, that's him and something did bite a chunk out of him, but anyway on this day we were working our way through a small canyon, actually it was similar to a deep creek bed back in the states, but of course there was no water. I'm walking point and I hear what sounds like a struggle on the other side of a bend in the canyon wall. I signal the other guys to freeze, and I ease my gun and shoulder around the turn in this wall to see what is going on. At first, I see what appears to be a man accosting a young girl, so I yell stop. He stops and looks right at me; the bastard had little horns growing out the side of his head. Even worse it had hair covered legs, and a tail, not to mention its knees is positioned backwards from ours. It's extremely pissed that I interrupted it and stands to his full height which was a little over six foot and screams at me barring these enormous fangs."

"Wow, what did you do?" Trent asked.

"I shot it in the face."

"I guess that did the trick huh?" Trent chuckled.

"Yeah, it dropped like a shot putt in a swimming pool. I wasn't too impressed with it, whatever he was, he never twitched again."

"Did the thing harm the girl?"

"No, she was okay for the moment, until the Afghan National starts dragging her by the hair and tying her hands together. I ask him what the hell he's doing, and he tells me she must be returned to her village so the elders can restore honor. I didn't like the sound of that."

"What did he mean, by restore honor?"

"Trent you've been there, you know exactly what he meant."

"That's what I was afraid of." Trent replied.

"I tried to explain to him the young girl was still clothed and obviously hadn't been raped yet. He didn't care he said she had been defiled merely by being touched by this evil creature and the honor of the village was at stake. He stated that this girl was absolutely going back to her village to be properly cleansed for the sake of the tribe's honor, and then he pointed toward the sky and tells me, Allah wills it."

"What did you do?"

"I shot him in the face too." Nathan said without remorse.

"How the hell did you explain that to General Henderson?"

"Bennett and I buried his ass right there in that canyon. Then I told General Henderson exactly what I had done. He swore us both to secrecy unless the three of us wanted to be spending the rest of our days in Leavenworth together. Our report didn't mention a thing about the girl, we said the Afghan panicked and ran off into the desert when encountered the entity, never to be seen again. The General pulled some strings and got the girl out on a C-17 that was headed to Wright-Patterson AFB. The best part was, the aircraft had an all-female crew, so she was in good hands, and they understood what would happen to her if we didn't get her out of Afghanistan."

"Wow, do you know what became of her?"

"The General told me she was only thirteen and that she ended up living with a family on a ranch in Wyoming of all places."

"So that is why the General sometimes holds back information from the Spooks at Central Intelligence?" Trent asked.

"Oh no, I'm just getting to that part, so an unnamed agency helicopter lands to pick up the remains of this horny bastard I schwhacked, and a guy in a black suit with sunglasses on gets off the chopper to sign for the remains. He had blue skin, as I live and breathe this guy had blue skin, light blue, but still blue. He had weird body movements and strange features. It was like he was human but not human. He seemed to be upset that I had killed this goat boy, and he wants to question me further. General Henderson is not going to let this happen, I believe he was afraid the guy will figure out the truth. The guy was as arrogant as they come and gave us this weird smile as he boarded his chopper to leave. After it took off, I told the General that the guy didn't seem very pleased that I had capped that thing, he told me... 'Hell that guy probably is one of those things.' So, if you think this stuff was weird is now, something tells me it gets a whole lot weirder upstream, so weird we may not even have a clue of who or what is actually running the country."

The sound of dry leaves crackling in the trees alerted both men that something was moving along the ground. Trent brought his rifle up to the ready. Then he dropped his left arm slightly, allowing Nathan to slide his rifle off Trent's shoulder. "See anything?" Nathan asked.

"I see some brush moving at two o'clock twenty meters in."

Once he had retrieved his rifle, Nathan brought it to ready as well and began looking through his scope to the area Trent told him. He picked up low brush moving and thought it was possibly just a deer or some other wildlife. Then he saw an almost human hand covered in hair reach up out of the brush to grab a limb on a small pine tree. The hand gripped the tree limb, and a Sasquatch pulled itself up from the forest floor. Using the scope on his rifle, Nathan could tell it was the creature Josh had warned him not to kill earlier. It had blood in its hair, and its facial expression showed fear and pain. Nathan was shocked to see it carried the limp body of a smaller creature over its shoulder.

The smaller Sasquatch was obviously dead, and Nathan guessed it was the child of the one who carried it. He could sense the reverence and love in how it carried the smaller body.

Trent was using open sights, and although he could see the creature, he didn't have the magnified view Nathan did. "Well, is it good or bad, do we shoot, or not?" he asked Nathan.

As Nathan watched, the creature looked at him and held its hand up, and spread its fingers wide as if saying, I mean you no harm. Removing his finger from the trigger of his weapon and raising his own hand, Nathan said, "No, let it go. It's the one this ugly bastard was tuning up earlier." He could see the expression on the creature's face soften as if it knew the men had no intention of harming it. It limped quietly into the woods carrying its sad burden and disappeared out of sight of the two men. "I never thought I'd say something like this, but I nearly feel sorry for it. We'd better get back up to our nest, since you got to rest while I did all the dirty work... I'll carry your rifle and you can lug this damn head up the hill, don't drop it our it will roll all the way back down here."

"Yeah, yeah, wise ass," Trent said, grabbing a hand full of hair and lifting the head off the ground with a large amount of grunting. "I never knew a head weighed so much."

As Nathan and Trent made their way back up to their sniper's nest overlooking Dead Man's Hollow, they found Joshua Nashoba sitting quietly on a large rock. "We saw the one you told us not to shoot, and just like you said it had crossed back over to the other side of the creek and was retreating into the forest. One thing though, it carried the dead body of a smaller one with it."

Josh's face turned grim, "The Shampe are attacking and killing the Okla Chito in this area. They are looking to breed, and they will kill every male Okla Chito they find, young and old. This particular group of four have been terrorizing all the mountains for a thirty-mile radius the past two years."

"If you're correct about there being good ones and bad ones, again; how do we tell the difference?" Nathan asked Josh.

"You're going to have to trust your instincts first," Josh replied.

"That may pose a problem Josh, two years ago around Talihina, they were all bad. My instincts are to shoot first and not worry about having to figure out if they're good or bad." Nathan said, becoming a little frustrated with the elderly man.

"There are physical signs," Josh replied calmly.

"What signs, do they have a certain appearance?"

"You have served in combat against humans, I assume? Josh asked him. "Yes, Sir, I have, both in Iran and Afghanistan," Nathan answered.

Josh continued, "I'm sure while serving in both of those countries, you just didn't shoot every local you saw?"

"No, of course I didn't." Nathan said, becoming a little impatient.

"Of course, you did not, you trained yourself to watch for certain behavior and signals from the people you encountered as to what their intent was. The same rules apply to the Okla Chito, in fact you'll rarely encounter one, and even rarer still, have a reason to harm it."

Starting to feel frustrated, Nathan said," No disrespect intended Sir, but I keep asking questions and I'm not getting any straight answers, so once again… How do I tell the difference?"

"The creatures you seek are not what is known as Okla Chito, Sasquatch, or Bigfoot, they are a hybrid. In fact, the name Relics you and your friends have been calling them is probably the best description for them. Only they are not relic humans, or relic hominids. They are relic Nephilim. A sure give away will be six fingers and toes and a double row of teeth."

"I've heard that term." Nathan said. "General Henderson has used it many times referring to some of the biological entities we've come across. I've run across the six fingers, toes, and double row of teeth as well, but it isn't always the case. Some seem to be more advanced. We usually find the extra digits and teeth on what we call BRENS, which is short for Biological Relic Entity. However, we have another classification, RENU, Relic Entity Unknown, these things are the same type of nasty life form but even worse. They don't seem to follow the rules about six fingers or toes or teeth, they have their own rules and could care less about ours. I've read the Bible. To be honest I recall the term Nephilim and I realize it's explained in the Old Testament in Genesis somewhere, but I've been too busy fighting things to go wading through Genesis. I've barely had time to pray while down range to be honest."

"That is okay, Nathan, I believe that is why we have been brought together, you need to know more than you've been taught. I had the same problem during my time in the military, I too fought the Nephilim, but they were in another form and my fight was aerial. Like you I had a wonderful commanding officer, but he never told me the full truth. He probably thought he was keeping me safe from political and military leaders in high positions that have made a pact with the enemy. I had the good fortune to be guided through my career by a man you might call a modern-day Crusader. He was an Admiral when they finally killed him. Your General Henderson seems to be cut from the same cloth."

"Why would General Henderson keep such knowledge away from the me or any of the other men doing the fighting?" Nathan asked.

"I'm sure he doesn't want to put you at any more risk than you already are. Up until recently you weren't on the radar of the enemy. You have appeared to be nothing more than a soldier doing his duty, if that is the extent of your knowledge, you're not in anymore danger than any other average soldier in combat. However once aware of the true enemy and the true nature of the war you're involved in… You're in much more danger than you ever imagined, not only is your life in danger, but your soul is as well. You must learn exactly who you're fighting, and you must not blatantly kill the innocent of any species, man or beast. You must know the difference between a Okla Chito and a Shampe, as well as a Man and a Nephilim. The same as you learned the difference between a Merchant and a Jihadist. The Nephilim appear in human form too, not just giants and monsters. Nathan and you must become aware of that, I intend to teach you how, so you don't become lost in blood lust." Josh said.

"Well, I don't consider it a bad idea. Had this one not stopped and looked right into my eyes, I would have let him finish beating the other one to death and then whacked him. Never interrupt your enemy when he is busy making mistakes, I always say. By the way, exactly how did he know we were here? He was fully committed to the task at hand, then suddenly he looks right into our eyes… What's up with that?"

"He sensed you Nathan, that is why I'm here to help you. You are no longer just a soldier to the enemy, you have become a threat, and enemy of flesh and spirit."

"So, did it not sense me, do I have some kind of Bigfoot stealth ability?" Trent asked sarcastically.

"Absolutely not Trent, in fact you're probably in more spiritual danger than either of us are." Josh said softly. "You're not a Christian, you do not have the blood of Jesus as a shield. You could have his protection this very moment, all you have to do is ask."

"No thanks, Sailor; I'm not the church type, do you have any idea of the weird stuff we've seen around the world? Creatures of every kind, strange things in the sky, there is just too much paranormal activity in the world for me to believe in a lone supreme being. If there was an Almighty Father that loves us, why would he allow all these other beings to torment us? I've done some Bible reading none of it makes sense, a global flood and ordering the murder of whole tribes including women, children, and animal. None of it sounds like a loving deity to me, but your mileage may vary," Trent said, shrugging his shoulders.

"If you'll allow me, I may have the answers you need for your understanding and ultimate salvation Trent. The fact that you are aware of these events in the Bible tells me you're more in tune with our Father God and Lord Jesus, than you realize. We're all going to need to be covered in the Blood of the Lamb to survive this, spiritually and physically." Josh replied.

"See, there you go with the church speak. 'Blood of the Lamb' I don't even know what that means." Trent exclaimed.

Nathan interrupted the two men. "Gentlemen, we have some immediate work to do before you two engage in a theological discussion. We need to make sure this brute can't recover, or else it might re-animate, and we'll all learn the secrets of heaven and hell the hard way. Josh, I have some four-foot-long copper rods that are used as grounding spikes for telephone boxes. I know it's a medieval thing to do, but I think I'd better keep this head spiked on one until we totally destroy the remains with fire."

"Yes, Nathan that would be the wise thing to do," Josh answered, "Before you do, let me show you something." Nathan removed a large hunting knife from the sheath on his belt; he used the knife to open the mouth of the creature Nathan had just killed. "Look at this and tell me what you see," he instructed the men.

Peering into the mouth and trying not to wretch from the smell, Trent was the first to notice. "It has two rows of teeth!" He remarked.

"That's right, and if you go back down and take a closer look at the body, you'll find it has six fingers on each hand and six toes on each foot," Josh replied.

"I didn't notice the hands having six fingers or the toes for that matter. I should have though," Nathan replied.

"Of course, you didn't, the creature itself is already strange enough, even a person of your experience is going to miss things like this, especially right after a fight. You expect this sort of thing while you're in Afghanistan. You're not expecting it here, you have got to understand, you're fighting the same evil. You also have to understand, you are a marked man."

"The ones we fought and killed near Talihina a couple of years ago had human like hands four fingers and a thumb, I remember. Also, the ones at the crash site of the F-16, in Queen Wilhelmina State Park just had five fingers, I distinctly remember that. These guys were killers and definitely bullet worthy, so I'm confused." Nathan said.

"This is one of the beasts you fought near Talihina. At the time they were juveniles, but not like normal Okla Chito. As I was saying they carry a Nephilim gene, and they are controlled by the spirit of a dead Nephilim. The longer they walk with the evil spirit in them, the more of the traits of the Nephilim they take on."

Nathan was trying to make sense of what the older man was telling him, "So, this is either one of the two we thought we killed or one of the two that were allowed to leave, they're back and now they're fully evolved into a Nephilim creature, or BREN, am I following you?"

"The explanation isn't as hard as it seems Nathan, look back to the aircraft crash where you first got involved in this. When that F-16 crashed it came down on a clan of normal Sasquatch. The clan had a large concentration of young females. This one and his three comrades were stalking this group for no other reason than to take possession of the females and mate with them. They must mate, not only to reproduce more of their kind but to also bring on their own maturity as an oppressive creature of Nephilim lineage. This act for the Nephilim strain is one of the two factors that brings on their final change to a true unholy hybrid being blended from the earthly and celestial union. The other act is the taking of life. The killing and the sexual activity serve as an evil communion or covenant with the enemies of God. It brings on the final transformation as a dark spiritual being that walks the earth in physical form. The acts of violence and domination, along with the hybrid bloodline forms an unholy trinity that mocks God's laws of creation."

"Simply put, Satan cannot create life, like our Heavenly Father, so to build his army he has found a way to corrupt God's creation, by mixing the genetics of God's heavenly creations and earthly creations. Remember a third of the angels fell with Satan, he's outnumbered, other than deceiving humans, this is the only way he can increase his army."

Nathan was quiet for a moment; then he nodded his head in understanding, "Like I said earlier, I've been aware for a while about the Nephilim, but I always assumed they took only the form of giants as in the Old Testament, but now it is starting to make sense to me. Nephilim don't have to be giants, they can be in the form of any creature that has the genetic lineage of the fallen angels, and those genetics are being used as a weapon against God and man. Is that correct?"

Josh was relieved and excited to see the lights were coming on for Nathan. "Yes, you're getting it, we're involved in a cosmic Seed War. All the strange creatures you have been fighting are in fact Nephilim, just not the classic Biblical giant version."

Nathan rose, putting an end to the current conversation. "I'm going to need some diesel to burn this thing, which means one of us is going to have to go to town. I'll go to Talihina and get it unless you want to go, Trent?"

Trent shook his head, "No, I'd rather not, and I've been up and down that mountain road a hundred times the past few days. Besides, I want Josh here to enlighten me on Biblical history; we can discuss it while you're running errands."

"Okay, but keep your guard up, don't get so involved in your discussion that something sneaks up on you," Nathan warned.

"No worries, we'll hold down the fort, but bring back something with sugar in it. I'm getting a sweet tooth sitting up here with no other forms of entertainment."

"Josh, if you're hungry we have some MREs and canned food in the back of the jeep, or I can pick you up something from town?" Nathan asked.

"I'm getting hungry, I would love to try one of your MREs. Tell me, you wouldn't happen to have some coffee too, would you?" Josh asked.

"Trent, grab the cooler out of the jeep and fix this man up with a meal and some coffee; you're a lousy hostess." I'll be back as soon as I can."

# CHAPTER TEN

# The Cabal

*"The Cabal mocks the natural order. For its minions, death is just a pause between duties."~ Kamahl*

## Monday, 17 June 1968, 07:25 AM, USS Enterprise

Josh Nashoba sat in the Officer's Mess aboard the USS Enterprise, eating slowly and thinking about the mission he had been involved in just a few hours earlier. He was tired and looking forward to catching a couple hours of sleep before his duties as Squadron Commander would require his attention again. The mission the night before had an eerie similarity to his first combat mission twenty-one years earlier off the coast of Antarctica, when as a much younger Lieutenant Junior Grade, he had also engaged unknown aircraft and managed to bring one down. Back then, just like now, the hostile aircraft possessed a higher level of performance and technical advancement than the aircraft he was flying. It didn't matter that during both engagements Josh was flying the hottest fighter the Navy possessed at the time. Just like in 1947 when his F-8F Bearcat was totally outclassed by bat like aircraft he engaged off the coast of Antarctica, the unknown aircraft he'd engaged in the darkness just hours before also displayed performance his F-4J Phantom could not hope to match. Josh knew there wasn't another jet fighter in the world that could out speed and out power his Phantom, *So, what the hell was that thing?*

Once his flight had landed, Josh along with his RIO, and his wingman Lieutenant Tremble, along with Tremble's RIO, Ensign Simmons had been through a rigorous debrief. The Air Group Commander, (CAG) had even sat in at one point asking questions. Everything looked to be cut and dried; the flight recorders and gun camera footage all confirmed the four men's statements during the debriefing. Two unknown hostile aircraft had attacked an Allied warship, both US Air Force F-4 Phantoms and US Navy F-4 Phantoms had been ordered and vectored by radar to the scene, the Air Force took the first swing and missed, Josh and Dan Freeman took the second swing and brought one of the aircraft down. The whole engagement seemed cut and dried other than the fact that the hostile aircraft could not be associated with any known aircraft in the Soviet or American arsenals. There was talk of a

Soviet Super Mig that was under development, but it was still some years from becoming operational and surely it would not be able to match the performance of what they had encountered over the HMAS Hobart. One thing that made Josh uneasy was the lack of excitement over the aerial victory. Air to air kills, were not as common during the current conflict as they were in wars past. As aircraft became more advanced and expensive, air forces naturally got smaller. The sky above Vietnam didn't offer the same target rich environment of World War II, or even the Korean conflict where nearly 800 Migs were downed in the course of just over three years. In the same amount of time during the current war less than 70 enemy aircraft had been brought down.

An aerial victory was usually a call for celebration in any squadron during this conflict, what seemed to be happening now was far from celebrating. This would be Josh's sixth aerial victory but only his fifth officially since the record of his first off Antarctica remained buried deep in secret government beau acracy. Five aerial victories would make Josh the first new American fighter ace since the Korean War. Nobody was saying anything, much less congratulating him. Not that Josh needed the attention, he'd been living with the fact for over a year that he was a fighter ace, and nobody was aware of it. It wasn't the lack of attention, it was the type of attention Josh was getting, that had him uneasy.

The Chief of Intelligence aboard the Enterprise had watched the debriefing silently taking notes at one point the Captain of the Enterprise himself made an appearance during the process, whispering to the Intelligence Chief and watching the proceedings quietly before his duties called him back to the bridge of the aircraft carrier. Something wasn't right and Josh knew it. After the debriefing he's told the other three aviators of his flight, to go get some food and rest. They had not hesitated in taking his advice, even with their limited amount of time in the Navy, they too knew something was off center and were anxious to be away from the brass and intelligence guys. Josh had tried to speak with the Air Group Commander, who was direct supervisor an hour earlier, only to be told that the CAG was in a meeting with the brass. So, Josh had made his way to the Officer's Mess where he sat alone staring at, more than eating his breakfast. As he was looking down, he noticed a pair of blue trousers with the red or more commonly known "Blood Stripe", down the leg. Looking up he saw the tan shirt with three green stripes denoting a Marine Sergeant standing next to his table.

"Sir, I have been ordered to escort you to the Air Group Commander's quarters immediately." The young sergeant spoke in the clipped and to the point manner that Marines NCOs are known for. The sergeant's uniform was topped off with a white peaked hat, which told Josh, he was armed. As Josh rose to his feet, he never said a word. Looking at the sergeant's belt Josh did indeed see a polished holster which held a Colt Government 1911 .45 caliber pistol.

*Not quite the day I was expecting,* Josh thought to himself and he followed the young Marine sergeant out into the ship's passageways. It took nearly ten minutes to reach the CAG's quarters through the cavernous super carrier. Josh stopped in front of the door which had the following title painted on it, 'Captain Henry Starnes, Commander Carrier Air Wing Nine'. Josh made a single hard knock on the door and heard Captain Starnes reply, "Enter".

Josh opened the door and came to the position of attention; Captain Starnes looked at the Marine and said, "Thank you Sergeant that will be all." The Marine saluted, then made a precise about face and left the room closing the door behind him. Looking at the door for a moment, Captain Starnes chuckled and said, 'If I made facing moments that precise, I'd throw my back out." Then noticing Josh was standing at attention, he said. "At ease Nashoba."

Josh relaxed from the position of attention saying, "It's not every day I'm summoned to the bosses' office by an armed Marine sir."

Josh had reason to be cautious. Captain Starnes was a fast burner, who had climbed through the ranks quickly in naval aviation. His father was a retired Admiral, and now a Senator representing one of the districts from California. He had served four years less than Josh, and never flown a combat mission in his life, yet here he was Josh's senior officer and in command of all the flying squadrons aboard the Enterprise. Although he was friendly to Josh and maintained an outward appearance of professionalism, there was something Josh didn't trust about the man. He was a politician, not the warrior most aviators were. Josh at times could feel the man's silent resentment, not only of himself, but also the other aviators the man was commanding. The man had connections and Josh had no doubt that Starnes' pen was mightier than Josh's own sword.

"Sorry about that, Commander, I tried finding you in your squadron ready room, and your quarters. I asked the young Sergeant to look for you in Officer's Mess, how was the chow?"

"I didn't eat much sir, I'm not very hungry this morning."

"Well, let me see if I can give you something better to chew on. I called you in to congratulate you on your successful mission last night. I also want to be the first to congratulate you on your fifth kill and becoming the first Navy Fighter Ace since 1953, and only the second since World War II, that is quite an achievement Nashoba."

"So, our kill was confirmed, sir?" Josh asked feeling a little relieved, he used the word "our" wanting to ensure his boss knew it was a team effort between himself his RIO and the other Phantom crew that had covered them during the engagement.

That's right, Commander, you have three victories flying the Panther in Korea, and now two flying the Phantom, you're also the Navy's first Jet Ace."

"Well, Sir, I had a lot of help from my RIO, Dan Freeman out there last night. Has anyone been able to identify what type of aircraft we brought down?"

"The hostile type of aircraft, Commander," Captain Starnes replied. "After reviewing the radar data and gun camera footage intelligence believes you guys tangled with a couple of Soviet built Yak-36s last night."

"Never heard of it, but if they're making them in large numbers, we'd better get something to counter them, and damn fast." Josh replied.

Captain Starnes through a manila envelope on the table in front of Josh, "Take a gander at the info there Josh. Evidently the Soviets have been working on V/STOL technology since the late 40s."

"V/STOL technology sir, you're talking about vertical takeoff and landing I assume? I don't know much about it; the British seem to be big on it I hear." Josh said opening the folder and viewing the contents. The first thing he saw was a photo of a rather ugly aircraft, like many Soviet designs the high swept back tail gave the aircraft the appearance of a fish more than an aircraft. The fat body and massive mouth-like intake at the front of the aircraft reminded Josh of the catfish he would catch in Honobia Creek back home as a kid. The appearance of the aircraft suggested it would be more at home sucking mud at the bottom of a river, than it would flying and fighting in the sky.

"Yes, that is correct, Commander, the Brits are big on V/STOL, and it appears our vodka drinking friends over in Russia are just as enthusiastic if not more. They had this thing flying in early 1966 and started production before the British got the Harrier off the ground in 1967. Our shadowy friends in the CIA are extremely interested in your engagement last night. With the damage to the Australian warship this whole episode has gotten a lot of attention."

"How much attention, Sir?" Josh asked.

"Well, we've heard from CIA, NSA, Commander 7th Fleet, and last but not least the White House."

As Captain Starnes spoke, Josh was reading the suspected performance and armament of the Yak-36," Sir this is not what we fought against last night." Josh said flatly.

"I can assure you it is Commander Nashoba; the CIA has confirmed that four of these types of aircraft have been snuck into North Vietnam by the Soviet Union for testing and evaluation under combat conditions. The North Vietnamese have a rough airfield outside Ban Hai, just a few miles from the Demilitarized Zone. Not only is it perfect for testing an aircraft of this type, but it is works out precisely to the radar tracks last night. Remember before they engaged the Hobart, they engaged two Navy Riverboats just inland from that area, moving out to sea. Then you and your flight came along upset the graduation ceremony by bringing one of them down."

"What about the other one sir, the one that disappeared?" Josh asked.

"We think it either crashed or was able to get low on the water and make its way back to Ban Hai once the shooting started."

"Sir, we did not engage a fixed wing aircraft, and the performance reports on this chubby hanger queen does not match up at all to what we were up against last night. What we witnessed was a large ring of light that was able to climb from two thousand feet to ten thousand feet in the blink of an eye. That should have also shown on the radar data."

"Commander, we have had our best people going over this since you landed this morning, the weather conditions near the Hobart were ideal for what is called a superior mirage, there was a cool easterly flow of air that is unusual for this part of the world. That boundary of cool air was clashing with the hot humid air coming off from the hot humid jungles inland, causing light to appear to bend. Between the missiles flying, tracer rounds and explosions from the Hobart, after burners from your aircraft as well as the two Air Force birds, it's a wonder you didn't see Neptune riding on Pegasus last night. Plus add to the fact the aircraft you were flying against had the ability to hover. You brought down a Yak-36 last night Commander, no two ways about it."

"The radar data, Sir, what about that?" Josh asked.

"Electronic Countermeasures, Commander, we have ECM pods to fool radar, what makes you think the Soviets don't have them too." Starnes countered.

"Sir, the fact that both our radar and missiles had solid locks on the target, and we got two hits kind of blows the ECM theory out of the water."

"Not exactly, Josh, we believe the ECM activates as the aircraft moves, and once in a hover it loses its ability to spoof our radar. By the way Josh, you flew Balls Five last night, correct?"

Balls Five was slang meaning the serial number of Josh's aircraft ended in zero, zero, five. "Yes Sir, that is correct," Josh replied.

"I have an armament report sheet here I need you to sign confirming your aircraft number and missile data numbers."

Suddenly Josh felt like something wasn't right. "What do you mean by armament report?"

"It's a report we have to send in on which aircraft the missiles were fired from as well as which missiles were fired," Captain Starnes replied.

"I didn't load the damn missiles, so I'm not signing for them," Josh said suspiciously.

Captain Starnes sighed heavily, "Josh, you're not signing for the damn missiles, you're signing for the damn aircraft. The sailor in charge of arming the aircraft has already signed for the damn missiles. Now did you fly zero, zero, five, last night or not?"

"Yes Sir, I did, but this is unusual," Josh said.

"Better get used to it Josh, the bean counters want to track every missile now, so will you please sign the damn paperwork Commander? I've got a whole Air Wing on hold for this crap." Josh took the pen and signed on the line stating aircraft number and pilot name. "Thank you, Commander, you need to report to Admiral Brandt's cabin at twelve hundred hours, I don't know what has you spooked but get some rest and a shower before you report and Josh, try to relax, you made history last night and good things are coming your way."

Josh came to attention and saluted, "Aye-Aye, Sir." Then, he executed an about face that would have made any Marine envious and exited Captain Starnes cabin. Once in the gangway outside he leaned against a bulkhead for a moment, his mind was racing. Something isn't right about all this, he thought to himself. At least I'll have a chance to talk to Admiral Brandt about this goat rope; the thought of his old Squadron Commander gave him a much-needed boost of relief.

## Monday, 17 June 1968, 12:15 AM, USS Enterprise

Josh Nashoba sat in a small chair inside the Admiral's Quarters on the USS Enterprise. Admiral Brandt sat at his desk, three other men, one a Navy Captain, one an Air Force Colonel, and the last a civilian dressed in a black suit sat opposite of Josh at a long conference table situated in the middle of the room. Josh had no idea who the man was, but his appearance was strange to say the least his head had a funny shape that almost came to a cone that tapered down to a pointed chin. His eyes didn't look real, they looked almost as if they were painted into the sockets instead of positioned there, his skin complexion was also strange. The man seemed to be a shade of blue. No doubt this strange man was a member of the CIA, NSA, or some other intelligence wing of the federal government. The three men had been flown aboard the carrier three hours earlier, by helicopter. They had already interviewed Josh's RIO Dan Freeman, as well as the crew of the second Navy F-4 Lieutenant Tremble and Ensign Simmons. Each man was interviewed separately, and each man had come out of the interview looking shaken, Josh had noticed.

"Commander Nashoba, the purpose of this interview is together as much information from you as possible on the aircraft you engaged last night off Tiger Island, we're also conducting an informal evaluation of your performance into what has become a sticky situation with our Aussie allies."

Looking at both the Navy and Air Force Officer's uniforms, Josh noted neither wore pilot's wings or any other aviation badges. Damn shoe clerks, he thought to himself. "So just how are a couple of guys who have no experience operating aircraft, much less any actual aerial combat experience going to evaluate my performance defending the Hobart from aerial attack? Exactly what part of my flights performance makes this situation sticky with our Australian Allies?" Josh asked sarcastically.

"We were hoping for cooperation, Commander. It would be a shame if this interview took a downward slide and we had to make a judgment call on the evidence only." The Air Force Colonel replied.

"Exactly what evidence are you looking at? I was told a few hours ago I had shot down a Soviet built Yak-36, which doesn't make any sense at all. What our missiles hit last night was no Yak-36, Colonel."

"You mean your missiles, don't you Commander?" The Navy Captain asked.

"Come again sir?" Josh asked, not knowing exactly the point was the Navy Captain was making.

"You said, 'OUR MISSILES', exactly who fired the missiles commander, you, your RIO, or your wingman?"

"Well, Sir, if you were sent to investigate this incident, I would think you'd have some understanding of how a two-ship formation of fighter planes work together in combat. Or did they not cover that in shoe clerk school?"

"Easy, Commander," Admiral Brandt cautioned Josh, trying to keep things from getting out of hand.

"I think you will find Commander, they taught us a lot more than you'd expect at shoe clerk school. We also covered flight suits and boots we're experts at getting hot shot aviators out of them and dressing them in khakis and low quarters. It's the standard uniform for smart ass flyboys on the verge of becoming civilians," the Naval Captain replied, coolly.

"Okay, that is enough of this mutual admiration crap. Let's keep the discussion on topic, and that goes for everybody," Admiral Brandt said, making it clear he was not going to allow anymore insults, from either side.

"Commander, you will answer the questions to the best of your ability, and gentlemen, if you're here to conduct an investigation, then conduct it. If you have a point to make, then make it. Nobody who flies combat in my chain of command will be exposed to a half assed Spanish Inquisition. I want everyone clear on this before we proceed further."

Josh and the two officers replied with a "Yes Sir", the civilian sat quietly never taking his eyes off Josh. Whatever was going on with the investigation, Josh felt it was somehow personal with this guy. "Yes Captain, you are correct. I fired both missiles, when I used the word 'WE' I was referring to my flight as a team. My wingman and his RIO were covering my RIO, Lieutenant Freeman, and I. Lieutenant Freeman, achieved the initial radar lock on the enemy aircraft allowing me to get a missile solution and fire both AIM-7 Sparrow missiles. The answer is 'YES' I fired both missiles, Sir." Josh said doing his best to be respectful, even though he could sense there was a hidden agenda with the three men across from him.

"Commander, you stated what you hit with your missiles was not a Yak-36, even though our intelligence agencies believe that is exactly what encountered. Can you explain this?" The Air Force Colonel asked.

"Yes, Sir, first off, I am no expert on this Yak-36, in fact I'd never heard of or seen a photo of one until just a few hours ago. What I base my statement on is, what we engaged last night could not have been a Yak-36 according to the intelligence I was shown earlier this morning by Captain Starnes the Air Group Commander."

"Why not, Commander?" The civilian asked finally joining the conversation. His voice was as strange as his appearance, it seemed to slither off his tongue in an almost hissing manner.

"For one thing, size. The Yak is reported to be nearly 56 feet long with a 33-foot wingspan. What we tangled with was over twice that size. Also, if you base the reported performance of the Yak, compared to what we were up against last night... The Yak isn't in the same league with the thing we flew against. What we encountered last night was round or saucer shaped, the edge was lined in light giving it the appearance of a glowing ring, would be my best description." Josh replied.

"You encountered a Yak-36, Commander", the civilian said flatly.

"No Sir, I encountered a ring of light, I hit the ring of light with two missiles and then it plunged into the surface of the sea. We followed to down to below six thousand feet before pulling up. The thing made contact with the sea and then continued submerged for some distance until we could no longer see it."

"Captain, it would be in your best interest to accept and sign off on the fact you shot down a Yak-36." The civilian responded, pushing two sets of papers toward the center of the table staring at Josh.

Josh held the man's stare, never allowing his eyes to fall on the papers, "No Sir, it is always in my best interest to tell the truth."

"Take the Yak-36 kill, Commander; enjoy the accolades of your fellow fighter pilots by achieving Ace status, get your name in history books and magazines. Then you can continue with your career, but no more talk of rings of light or flying saucers," the civilian said calmly.

"I will admit I shot down an unidentified enemy aircraft, but I will not say I shot down this mystery Yak, Sir," Josh said defiantly.

"Oh, I think different, Commander." The civilian said with a slight smirk beginning to show, and then looking at the Naval Captain he said, "Please make it clear to the Commander here that he will sign one of these documents if he wishes to stay in the Navy."

"Commander Nashoba, have you ever heard of the weather phenomenon called a Superior Mirage?" The Navy Captain asked.

"Why yes, I heard of it just a few hours ago, in Captain Starnes office. I just love how well you all have prepped for this dog and pony show." Josh replied, suddenly regretting he had tried to cooperate with the three men in front of him. "It's caused when a boundary layer of cold air collides with warm humid air, it appears to almost bend light, so you're trying..." Josh was cut off suddenly by the Naval Captain.

"Your newfound meteorological expertise is very impressive Commander. However, the point we're making is, one or both of your missiles struck the HMAS Hobart in the early morning hours this morning. This ring of light you saw was nothing more than reflections of the ships lights on the surface and bouncing off ice crystals just below the altitude of your aircraft. You were never locked onto this mysterious aircraft; you were in fact locked on to the Hobart. There was never another aircraft, there was a lot of confusion and a lot of mistakes made. The two biggest mistakes were your two AIM-7 missiles that struck the HMAS Hobart killing one Sailor and wounding two more. I will also add, that in your haste to get that all important fifth aerial kill of your career, you did not ensure your radar was locked onto a credible aerial target. Your haste and eagerness to become a jet ace caused you to make mistakes at key points of this engagement. I would also remind you that anything you say now could be used against you as evidence later under the rules of the Uniform Code of Military Justice."

"If you're saying that two AIM-7s struck the Hobart, you're talking to the wrong people. You should be in DaNang, talking to his guys." Josh said nodding toward the Air Force Colonel.

"Unfortunately, the evidence doesn't point to the two Air Force F-4s, Commander." The Air Force Colonel responded quickly.

"You weren't there, Colonel, have you interviewed the Air Force crews already? Or are you here just to cover the Air Force's ass?" Josh questioned the men with rising anger in his voice.

"At least one if not both of your missiles hit the Hobart," the Air Force Colonel said flatly.

"Bullshit," Josh responded sternly. "We had a good lock-on and I watched both missiles ride the beam right into the bandit. No question, we scored two hits on the thing. Our radar tape footage and gun camera prove it."

"Once again, Commander, what was this 'Bandit', you were shooting at?" The Navy Captain asked, "You can't seem to identify it as anything but a ring of light, you sure don't want to identify it as the Yak-36 intelligence seems to think it is. So, the only conclusion was you took a half assed pot shot at an aerial anomaly and some poor Aussie sailor paid for it with his life."

"Are we discussing the same incident here? The Hobart was not only taking fire, but also returning it and the two Air Force Phantoms already had missiles in the air before I fired. You're acting like I flew into San Francisco Bay on a sleepy morning and went crazy. The fight was on when we arrived," Josh said barely holding his temper.

The strange looking civilian spoke up again, "Commander, in January 1947, we have a report stating that you engaged and shot down an unidentified aircraft off Antarctica, in of June 1947, you spent days in the company of an Air Force Captain in a P-82, repeatedly flying sorties around Mount Rainier Washington trying to establish the speed of flying saucers reported by a Mister Kenneth Arnold. Then in July of 1947, you and this very same Army Air Force Captain find a downed flying saucer on the desert floor, near Roswell New Mexico, June 1952; you were one of several personnel reporting a UFO buzzing the USS Philippine Sea off the coast of Japan---Commander we have your signature on each of these reports, what do you think that tells us?"

"May I have your name sir and what agency you work for?" Josh asked, taking another close look at the civilian. The more he looked at him the more his appearance seemed wrong; his build was tall but slight, almost wispy, the cone toward the rear of his head almost appeared to be swelling.

"My name and agency is not of importance to you, what is important is we have a Naval Officer operating a multi-million-dollar aircraft with a long history of seeing little green men." The man replied with a self-satisfied smirk on his face.

"Little gray men," Josh replied, flatly.

"Excuse me?" The man replied.

"You said little green men, they're little gray men at least the one I saw was gray," Josh said, with his own smirk.

"Thank you for proving my point, Commander, I don't believe it is in the best interest of the United States or of the Navy for that matter to continue allowing a man of your, let's say experience to operate Phantoms from the deck of the USS Enterprise. You asked me who I am; I'm the guy that is going to decide if you continue flying Commander."

"Every report from every incident that my name appears on also has the names of at least three other Naval Officers reporting the same thing. So, the only reason I am a concern is because you're afraid I know something you don't, or maybe you're afraid I'll say something people like you don't want said. Also, my RIO as well as wingman and his RIO watched both my missiles impact on the bandit we had locked up. I think you're scratching fleas and howling at the moon, Mister."

"Didn't your wingman Lieutenant Tremble report explosions on the surface indication the HMAS Hobart had been hit?"

"Yes, he did, but by that time I had already fired on and hit the target we were engaging." Josh replied, feeling a tingle of concern on where he sensed the questioning was heading.

"Are you sure you saw your missiles impact the target you fired on? Are you sure with all the excitement and strange lights in the sky, you were mistaken about the two explosions? Commander, is it possible you lost track of your missiles?"

"Absolutely not, I saw two explosions on the target."

"Commander, what if I told you an investigation of the HMAS Hobart reviled wreckage of two AIM-7 Sparrow Missiles indicating the Hobart was hit by friendly fire? What would your answer to that be?"

"My answer would be, you're barking up the wrong branch, go talk to the Air Force crews, I heard two separate Fox One calls from their flight, I even saw the missiles in flight." Josh said as his anger began to rise.

"We've talked to the Air Force crew; they all stated their missiles went dumb and straight into the water once the two bandits retreated from the area."

"The bandits didn't retreat!" Josh said angrily, "one simply disappeared and the other shot up to eight thousand feet in an instant and that is the one I engaged. The Air Force missiles had nowhere to go except into the water or the Hobart. Both of my missiles tracked true and impacted the target. Again, our radar tape and gun camera film confirm that."

"Commander, I have here the armament report for your aircraft. You were loaded with four Aim-7 Sparrow Missiles, four AIM-9 Sidewinder Missiles and one six-hundred-gallon centerline fuel tank."

"That is correct," Josh replied.

"Was your aircraft at a slight nose down altitude when you made your attack Commander?"

"That is also correct." Josh replied.

The civilian pulled out another piece of paper, this one Josh recognized immediately as the very same document he had signed earlier in captain Starnes office. "According to this armament document, signed by you just this morning, you fired two of the four AIM-7s you carried. The two you fired were serial numbers R70010023 and R70010110, is this correct Commander?"

"Yes, that is correct; I fired two missiles from my aircraft, as far as the serial numbers you will have to get a statement from the armament man who signed for the missiles." Josh replied.

"Oh yes we have his name right here", the civilian said pointing at the signature on the document. The civilian then reached down next to his chair and brought up medium sized leather bag and placed it on the table. Reaching into it he removed a small piece of white metal which he placed on the table, then with a slight pause for drama, he slid the piece of metal to Josh. "This was found on the deck of the Hobart this morning Commander. Any idea how it could have been on the Hobart if your missiles struck the intended target as you say they did?"

Looking down at the piece of metal, Josh saw the familiar stencil script applied to everything in the military. The black lettering read; AIM-7D USN SER NO: R70010023. "Would you care to comment on this Commander?" The man in the suit asked smugly.

"I have no reason to believe any weapon fired by myself impacted the Hobart." Josh replied coldly. Josh knew his missiles did not hit the Hobart; he also knew that his flying days were in serious jeopardy. If he could not fly, there was no reason to stay in the Navy, and Josh understood that he had been expertly setup. He tried to think of anything that would prove his point and give him leverage. "Watch the film, during the post flight debrief all four of us in the flight reviewed the film from my aircraft on which you could clearly see the target and the impact of the missiles." Josh said.

"Was there any film from your wingman?" The civilian asked.

"No for some reason he forgot to turn on his camera, but the dog bone containing my film is down below in the Squadron Ready Room gear locker. Have a look for yourself."

Smirking, the civilian said, "Oh we don't have to do that Commander." He opened and oversized metallic brief case that sat near him, first he pulled out a copy of the film log, which contained the number of the dog bone shaped film canister, along with the aircraft tail number and signature of the pilot who last used it in flight."

"Well, if you've seen the film, why are we having this Kangaroo Court?" Josh asked angrily.

The civilian loaded the canister into a projector and pointed it at the one bulkhead in the cabin that was bare. Then looking at Admiral Brandt he asked. "Sir may I dim the lights?"

Brandt nodded gruffly, not sure himself what was going on. Once the room darkened the civilian turned on the projector. The film seemed a bit grainy and dark, but Josh immediately recognized it as the beginning of his encounter with the object. He could clearly see, the UFO as it appeared as a whitish ring of light. He could also hear the exchanges between himself and Freeman. *Well, this should cut the crust off this turd sandwich,* Josh thought to himself, as he watched the film.

As the film progressed, Josh heard his voice say, Fox One… Fox One," as he expected the film went white as the flash of the fiery exhaust from the two missiles caused the film to go completely white for a couple of seconds before the image would come back. The problem was the image would not come back, the film continued but with a blinded white image, to make matters worse any communications recorded on the film were also gone now as a high-pitched static scream was the only audio generated from the film. Josh knew the setup was complete and anger began to rise in him at a surprising rate. "Bullshit, you people have tampered with that film, I don't know what this is about or why, but I'm going to fight this, and I'm not going to stop fighting this until you three are sitting in a court martial getting your own rear ends hammered for tampering with evidence."

"What this is about is the death of an Australian Sailor and the wounding of two others because of your own ineptness Commander." The civilian said with a satisfied smirk on his face. Josh returned the man's stare, determined to not back down, he would fight him until hell froze over if need be. The two men continued to stare at each other; the other occupants in the room could feel the rage and hate growing between the two with each passing second. As Josh stared into the man's dark eyes something happened, the pupils of the man's eyes suddenly went from round circles to vertical slits. The face of the man turned from a stoic stare to a grin consisting of fangs and a forked tongue which for the merest of moments darted out of the man's mouth like that of a serpent. As quick as the appearance of the man took on a reptilian look, it changed back to that of a normal man. The man continued to stare at Josh, but now with an amused and confident smile, assured that lifting the veil ever so slightly would terrify the mortal in front of him.

"You don't want to force judicial action Commander, you'll lose. Now you can sign a document stating you shot down a Yak-36 which we can blame for the damage to the Hobart, and you can continue your career unblemished, or you can sign a document requesting your immediate retirement from the U.S. Navy, and you can go on and lead a peaceful life as a civilian. You will sign one or the other, or you will be reprimanded and possibly put on trial by Court Martial, which will end your flying career. The choice is yours."

Admiral Brandt interrupted the conversation. "I know who and what you are," he said calmly and confidently. "In fact, I know who's name to mention, and when I do, you'll shit your pants and slither out of here like the snake you are." The Admiral said rising from the table slowly, facing the man.

"I wouldn't advise you do that," the civilian said with concern in his voice for the first time entering the room, "Your boy here is in enough trouble already… Almost as much as you Admiral" The man stammered.

"Oh, we're not in trouble, you are, we may not have any film, but I have something better, don't I?" Brandt said, as a smile came over his face.

The other men in the room noticed an immediate change in temperature; it was as if somebody opened the door to a freezer and a fan was blowing the cold air about them. The civilian was becoming more nervous and unsure of himself. He began to give off an odor that reeked of feces and sulfur. The Navy Captain began to feel sick from the stench and was about to vomit.

"Now tell me your name, before I call upon the all-powerful, and force you to tell me," the Admiral continued as the tension in the room became oppressive. The civilian's eyes seemed to change from human looking to something reptilian. His mouth opened to speak, then he was suddenly cutoff.

"Enough!" the voice of Admiral Brandt boomed, cutting through the thick oppressive atmosphere and returning things to a condition that was almost normal, the room seemed to warm slightly, and the stench was beginning to recede. "I want you three out of my quarters, and I'm going to ensure the captain of this vessel has you removed immediately." With that he pushed a button on the intercom box that rested at his desk.

A voice was heard coming from the box that said "Bridge!"

"This is Admiral Brandt; I want a security detail to my quarters now! Make sure they're ready to kill and break things."

"Aye-Aye, Admiral," the confused voice replied.

The civilian looked at Admiral Brandt with surprise, "Careful Admiral, you wouldn't want to make a mistake." The Navy and Air Force officers, who had accompanied the civilian, now looked nervous and confused.

"I'm not making a mistake", Brandt growled, as he picked up the piece of missile debris that was lying on the table. "Funny thing about gloss paint," he said as he pressed his thumb against the white part of the metal." After a day or so you can touch it and not blemish the paint," he held up the metal for all to see. "However, fresh paint, gives away all your secrets", he said pressing his thumb against the black stenciled numbers on the panel reveling his large thumb print. "You wormy piece of shit, do you think the ship's Captain and I haven't been aware of your location since you've been aboard? Do you think we don't know about your visit with Captain Starnes, or the little trip this hunk of metal made to the ship's paint shop?"

There was a knock at the door, a young Marine Lieutenant, dressed in tan shirt and blue slacks with his .45 caliber pistol drawn but pointing upwards entered the room, four Marine Privates in Battle Dress and armed with M-16s at the ready were just outside the doorway. "How can we assist you Admiral?" The Lieutenant asked.

"I want these three escorted to the flight deck, put on a chopper and off this ship immediately," Brandt barked.

"Aye-Aye, Sir!" the Lieutenant said motioning for the three men to rise and proceed out of the room.

"Oh, and Lieutenant…" Brandt said motioning toward the civilian, "If that Ichabod Crane looking bastard gives you any trouble, you're free to use as much force as necessary to throw his ass into the sea. Something tells me, he'll be just fine if you do."

Confused, the Marine Lieutenant replied simply, "Aye Sir."

It took less than twenty seconds to remove the three men from the room, once the door closed Brandt turned to Josh, "Well that went over like a turd in a punchbowl."

"Sorry for the trouble, Sir, but I'm going to fight this no matter what it takes." Josh said.

Brandt sighed and walked out over to the lone port hole in his cabin, staring out quietly he collected his thoughts. "Nashoba, you and I have been through a lot in the past twenty-one years. Has it ever occurred to you why we have been in the same command consistently since the old days aboard the Philippine Sea?"

"I always looked upon it as good fortune for me, Sir," Josh responded quietly.

"No doubt it was good fortune shining on both of us for the most part. Josh, I'm looking out at the USS Ranger in the distance right now, as she's launching her aircraft. Are you familiar with her?" Brandt asked.

"I can't say that I am sir I've never been aboard her, I know she's one of four carriers of the Forrestal class sir." Josh replied.

"Exactly the Forrestal class, named for the very first carrier of the class the USS Forrestal. Which is named for a past Secretary of the Navy and very first Secretary of Defense, James Forrestal, correct?"

"Yes Sir," Josh responded somewhat confused by the direction the conversation was going. "What became of the honorable James Forrestal for which these ship's class are named? Can you tell me that?" Brandt asked.

"Well Admiral, as far as I know he committed suicide, jumping out of his window at Bethesda Naval Hospital back in 1949 sir." Josh answered, still unsure where all of this was leading.

"Suicide, brought on by psychiatric problems, not your usual choice of a person to honor with the naming of a warship. Or especially an entire class of warships, is it?" Brandt said looking away from the porthole and focusing on Josh.

"I've never thought about it that way sir, but I suppose you have a point."

"I do have a point to make Josh, I want you to do yourself a favor and listen closely." Brandt's eyes focused hard on Josh. "Josh you have some things in common with the late Secretary Forrestal and if you're not careful you could end up just like him."

"How is that sir? I don't understand." Josh replied confused.

"He knew more about these craft than he should of, for that matter so did President Kennedy and look what happened to him."

"So, you're saying Kennedy and Forrestal were killed because of flying saucers?" Josh asked the Admiral trying to stifle a laugh.

"I'm saying they knew more about who and what controls these things than they should have, and they both tried to interfere. Forrestal directly attacked the presence and existence of these things. The late President Kennedy went after the people and entities that run the show, now they're both dead with aircraft carriers named after them. Let me show you something Josh," Brandt walked over to his desk and retrieved a folder. "This was sent to me by my counterpart in the submarine fleet. Now the Silent Service, is just that SILENT. The only reason I have this information is because like me, the Admiral who provided this info also participated in Operation High Jump off the Antarctic right along beside us back in 1947. At the time he was an executive officer onboard the submarine USS Sennet, unfortunately they too had adventures with unknown craft. You may not know this, but we have American submarines all around our fleet monitoring any underwater threats and protecting the fleet from Soviet or North Vietnamese submarines.

Four different subs picked up the craft you engaged last night. Once it went into the drink it preceded east staying submerged at an astounding rate of speed. It seemed to be bouncing off the ocean floor as if it were damaged and the subs were picking up tearing noises as if something were coming apart. It traveled a little over 513 miles to a point about 50 miles northeast of the Paracel Islands, where if stopped abruptly and began breaking up as it sunk into the deeper waters, finally exploding or imploding between the Paracel Islands and the Philippines. At times, the thing was moving at over 125 miles an hour under water. They began tracking it at the exact moment the thing you fired on went into the drink. Luckily, our subs happened to be staged where four different ones were able to monitor it with their equipment as it passed." Brandt then quietly watched Josh giving him time to process the information.

"Well, there you go sir that should get me off the hook." Josh said feeling hopeful.

"No, Josh, you've always been on the hook since you shot that thing down back in 1947. Now you've shot another one down. Those clowns were not here to accuse you of hitting the Hobart, they were here to warn you that you've gotten too close, and you need to go away. That crazy looking bastard in the suit is one of them. What he was telling you was, go away or die. You're not going to be allowed to fly combat anymore or much less lead an air group in combat. There is more to this than you know, you're not running into aliens when you encounter these things Josh, you're running into devils or demons. They're not extraterrestrial, they're inner dimensional and for some reason you have a God given gift to not only encounter them but defeat them. You're in danger Commander, so is everyone and everything you care about."

Josh stared blankly at the Admiral; his mind was racing trying to process all the information he's just heard. "How do we fight them?" Josh asked, finally said breaking the silence.

"You don't, Commander, not like you think anyway." Brandt replied. "Josh this thing goes deep, this goes all the way back to Hitler, basically he made a pact with the devil that is how he got a jump on technology. Do you think those Nazi bastards were smarter than the rest of the world? No, they had help."

"So how did we win the war if we fought against them?" Josh asked. "We won because our people started making deals with the devil too. A sell out here, a sell out there, next thing you know you have the atomic bomb, sell out a little more and you have a nuclear-powered aircraft carrier. The more you sell out, the more money and power you have and the more money and power you have the more you're allowed to lord over the rest of humanity. Do you recall Eisenhower talking about the Military Industrial Complex and what a danger it was to humanity when he left office?"

Josh nodded, feeling more confused than informed. "This is what he was talking about Josh. Except it isn't a Military Industrial Complex, it's an International Cabal, run by the devil himself and its most powerful human members are not completely human."

"What do you mean not completely human?"

"Just what I said, Josh, do you read the bible?"

"Yes, Sir, I do, my father always insisted."

"Do you recall Genesis chapter six?" Brandt asked. "You mean the part about the sons of God taking wives from the daughters of man?"

"Exactly, the Nephilim Josh, we're dealing with modern day Nephilim."

"The Nephilim were giants, and they all died out in the great flood," Josh said.

"Yes, and then they reappeared in the time of Moses, remember when Moses sent the spies into the promise land they came back with reports of giants, only Joshua and Caleb were willing to fight? The rest wanted nothing to do with them. Well, you're the modern-day Joshua and you're willing to fight, but you cannot fight them up front."

"So, you're saying modern day Nephilim are piloting these flying saucers people see, or like the ones I've shot down?" Josh asked incredulously.

"Maybe, but I really think it's the fallen angels possibly, or at least their technology. It could be demons in these machines. I think the modern-day Nephilim is a bit more subdued than the giants of old. I believe some families have somehow mixed their bloodlines with these fallen ones and they are working to control mankind and the entire world. They've gotten control through wealth and politics and are working vigorously to get in a position to control mankind and if possible, delay or even prevent the second coming of Christ."

"I don't understand aren't fallen angels and demons the same thing? How can they possibly think they can defeat God?" Josh asked, he couldn't believe he was sitting in the Admiral's quarters aboard the most powerful warship on the planet talking of such things. He was getting bewildered.

"The way the devil has always tried to win, through a seed war. The Nephilim bloodline was taking over mankind in the time of Noah. Had it not been for the flood with Noah and his family which was untainted by the Nephilim bloodline we may not be here now. Jesus could not be born into a Nephilim bloodline; his mother had to have a direct bloodline back to Adam with no interference. That was the main reason for the flood, maintain Adam's bloodline and get rid of the Nephilim bloodline, making a path for the future

263

Messiah. So, God brought the flood and preserved the line of Adam. There is a huge difference between fallen angels and demons Josh, I don't have time to explain the difference at this moment. I hope you get far enough away from this, so you don't learn the difference."

"So, what's to be accomplished by this cabal you speak of? I mean if giants couldn't do the trick, how could mere men?" Josh aske

"These are not mere men and women Josh, don't be fooled, like I said, we just had one of them in this very cabin. They have somehow mixed their blood with Satan himself. Their internal physical makeup has changed; they have no love or sympathy for humanity. They continue to prosper becoming wealthier and more powerful every year. They enrich and bring power to others that help them, I believe your Air Group Commander, Captain Starnes is in on it with them. They use mankind to destroy mankind."

"Admiral, how are they going to do that without also destroying themselves?" Josh asked.

"I don't have the answer to that Josh, and I may not live long enough to see it. Hopefully you will though, so even if you survive a court martial I'm going to pressure every Admiral in your chain of command to steer you away from a combat flying command,"

Josh started to interrupt but was cut off. "Quiet Commander and listen to me, get out now. You can't do a damn thing to fight this while you're in the Navy. They want you gone, you're too much of a threat here and they'll get you one way or the other. Arrestor gear failure on landing, an engine flameout, or even friendly fire. They will find a way to get rid of you Josh. So, sign that damn paper saying you shot down a Yak-36, if you don't, they'll kill you, and your family. Take the retirement; get as far away from military flying and the government as you can. You won't see another promotion, and I won't be around long enough to protect your career or your life. Get out Josh, if I can't force you out, they'll kill you. Get out now, I'm not giving you any choice."

Josh was stunned; his whole world had just come crashing down around him, he thought for a few moments of that September afternoon back in 1942, at the movie theater in Talihina Oklahoma. His whole life had been devoted to being a Naval Aviator since that day. Now everything had changed, his whole identity was being taken away he felt. Something told him he should be angry at Admiral Brandt, but he could not. Deep down inside he knew his career was ruined because of his multiple encounters with other worldly aircraft. He knew there was a black mark hanging over his service record, fair or not it was there, and he couldn't deny it. Looking Admiral Brandt in the eye, Josh knew the man was trying to save his life.

"I believe you; I have no reason not to, I trust you too much. It was an honor to serve under you sir." He said offering the Admiral his hand.

"The pleasure was all mine Josh, and you're the best damn fighter pilot I ever served with, and you're doing the right thing. Besides, Nashoba is a lousy name for an aircraft carrier kid." Brandt said shaking his hand, Josh smiled at the joke, then came to attention and saluted the Admiral before doing an about face and walking out the door. After flying together in combat and serving on the same ship through two different wars, the two men would never see each other again. *Best choice you ever made kid; wish I had that choice,* Brandt thought to himself.

Josh would retire his commission in the United States Navy, a little over a month later in July of 1968. He returned to Honobia and settled into a life with his wife Kiyoshi, her brother Jiro and Josh's parents. In September of 1968, news reached Josh that Admiral Brandt had died in a helicopter crash off Pearl Harbor Hawaii while riding as a passenger in transit from 7th Fleet Headquarters back to the USS Enterprise. He also heard that Captain Henry Starnes had been promoted to Rear Admiral, the promotion was a surprise as he was selected well ahead of other Captains that were senior to him. Josh grieved for his mentor and made a vow to continue the fight and even the score with Starnes, even if he had to do it from a place as remote as Honobia Oklahoma.

## Friday, 27 March 1970 3:30 PM CST, Kiamichi Mountains near Honobia OK

It was a warm afternoon in March of 1970, Josh was planting some flowers for Kiyoshi, he started thinking about his old friend Admiral Brandt, Josh heard an approaching vehicle and assumed it was his brother-in-law Jiro Saito who had a house on the same dirt road. Looking up Josh saw an unfamiliar tan late model Ford Galaxy sedan pulling off the road into his drive. Red Oklahoma dust from the dry road swirled around the vehicle as it came to a stop in front of Josh. The driver a young man who appeared to be in his twenties exited the vehicle and approached Josh.

"Would you be Commander Joshua Nashoba?" the young man asked.

"That would be me, but you can add retired to the end of that title," Josh responded.

"Sir, I work for a courier service, and I have a package for you from an Admiral Brandt."

"I don't know how that could be young man, the Admiral has been dead for over a year now."

"Sir, when the Admiral was alive, he made arrangements with our company to have this delivered to you exactly eighteen months after his death."

"Why would he do that?"

"I don't know, Sir, but those were his instructions. I'll need you to sign here, Sir." The young man held out a cheap Bic pen and a clipboard.

Josh took both the pen and the clipboard and signed his signature on the line the young courier pointed to. "Seems a bit strange to me." Josh replied.

The young man handed the package to Josh and said, "Not really, Sir, a lot of people have packages scheduled to be sent after they die. Many times, they want to give people time to recover from their loss before they give them something. Occasionally it's something to do with an issue or a problem that they want somebody to think died with them before they let the cat out of the bag to somebody else." The man bid his farewell, returned to his car and sped back the way he had come from, once again kicking up a cloud of red dust.

Josh looked at the swirling dust for a moment knowing it would upset Kiyoshi who waged a constant war against dust in the house. The first thing she did every day was dust the wooded furniture in their home she took so much pride in. Josh walked into the house with the mystery package in hand. As he entered the home he shared with his wife, Simon and Garfunkel's 'Bridge Over Troubled Water' was playing on the radio. As expected, Kiyoshi was watching the dust cloud through the large bay window in the living room, her brow furrowed as she watched the progress of the red cloud approaching ever closer to the house.

"Would you like something cold to drink?" She asked.

"I'm okay my dear," Josh replied.

"I brewed some tea about an hour ago and I just sliced some lemons, how about a nice glass of iced tea?"

Josh had moved into the small office the house had that was just off the kitchen. He was concentrating on the package and his curiosity was running on overdrive. What could this be? He wondered to himself, then he heard his name.

"Joshua!" He heard his wife's voice call out. "I asked you if you would like some iced tea?"

"Yeah, that sounds good," His voice trailed off as he surrendered, knowing Kiyoshi would attempt to serve him some form of cold liquid until he relinquished his objections. In her mind, an honorable Japanese wife would never allow her husband to dehydrate.

"You must replace your liquids after working out in the sun." He heard her say in the background. Also, in the background the music had ended, and the radio channel based in Fort Smith Arkansas began broadcasting the top of the hour news. Josh could hear Richard Nixon's deep baritone voice promising peace with honor in Vietnam. The sounds of the house began to disappear as Josh opened the package. Once the paper wrapping was removed Josh was looking at a none descript cardboard box. He lifted the lid from the box, to see it contained numerous file folders. There looked to be at least ten folders stacked neatly in the box, on top of the very first folder was an envelope with the name Joshua neatly typed on it. He opened the envelope, the contents contained two sheets of paper, Josh began reading the first page.

"Joshua, I assume it's been roughly eighteen months since my death as you read this letter. I also assume if this letter did in fact make it to you, that you are safely tucked away in your beloved Oklahoma mountains with your lovely wife. This is the exact scenario I planned for when I put this package together. I am gone and you are feeling forgotten by the Navy and the government and are now happily living in peace. This letter is to warn you that you will never be forgotten by the same dark forces in our government that took my life. My destiny and yours were sealed off Antarctica in 1947. I never shared this with you, but you and I were the only surviving aviators that took place in that strange battle that afternoon. All the other pilots that flew with us on that mission were dead when we last spoke to each other aboard the Enterprise. They all died in flying accidents or by strange illness over the years. So now there is only one of us left, and that one is you. For whatever reason you are the last one standing, that is fitting since you were the only one with the ability to defeat them twice." Curious Josh glanced at the second page and saw...

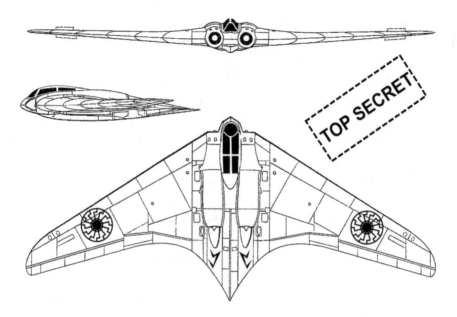

Type: Fighter
Origin: Unknown
Manufacturer: Unknown
Length: 27 Ft
Wingspan: 60 Ft
Crew: Two, 1 Human, 1 Unknown Entity
Propulsion: Two advanced jet engines. Type and origin unknown
Armament: One 20mm Gatling syle cannon, with a rate of fire
at 6000 rounds per minute (Estimated)
Speed: 650 MPH (Estimated)
Avionics: Advanced solid state and unknown

Conclusion: Design is based on the German Horton 229, with highly
advanced technical improvements of unknown origen. Markings seem
Germanic in nature, but also of unknown origen. Possibly connected to
what is known as the Vril Society a Nazi Occult Group that formed through
their belief of life forms visiting earth from other planets. The groups beliefs
are based on a novel written in 1871 titled 'The Coming Rance). Written by
Edward Lytton.

Wing Marking          Fin Flash

Josh was stunned the events of that cold afternoon off Antarctica in 1947
came rushing back to him. *Why are they keeping all of this secret?* he thought
before returning to the letter, "The files contained in this box will give you

answers to questions I'm sure you had for years. It will also give you answers to why I was so adamant about your retirement and separation from the Navy. For now, you are safe, and only if you stay away from going public on the issue of UFOs or any other paranormal manifestations. I urge you to keep to yourself and go on with your life quietly and attract no attention to yourself. This will ensure both you and your wife can live a long healthy life. However, knowing you as I do and knowing the warrior you are, I'm keenly aware of the fact that sooner or later, you will find a way to battle these forces. As much as I pray you heed my warning, I know better than to assume you will, so I am sending you my personal files on all events involving these strange craft from even before we had our encounter in 1947. We were right about some things.

As the body of the German fighter pilot found in the wreckage of that strange craft, you shot down in 1947 suggested... The Nazis were in league with these beings; you may be surprised to know our own government was too, and still is. Joshua, they play both sides against each other. They helped the Germans with rockets and jet aircraft; they helped the Americans with atomic weapons. We made a huge mistake assuming they came from another planet. They are not extraterrestrial Josh; they are interdimensional. This is not alien technology we've been witnessing; it is angel technology. In fact, it is fallen angel technology, and you'll need more than stick and rudder skill to fight them - you'll need the full armor of God. If you proceed, Josh, do so with open eyes and a heart that belongs to the Almighty God. Anything less will be folly.' The letter was signed, "Your comrade in life and afterlife, Richard Brandt."

Josh was stunned, he knew Brandt had been more informed on the strange encounters and craft than he was, but he had no idea to the extent. A quick glance at just the first folder told him his old boss had given him one hot potato; there were signatures on documents as well as photos of well-known politicians and military brass around strange craft and even stranger-looking entities. Josh felt an ancient fear forming in the pit of his stomach, a fear he'd never known before. The sudden appearance of Kiyoshi in the room made him flinch. She walked very softly and many times would enter a room Josh was in, and he was not aware of her presence.

"I'm sorry to startle you, Joshua-san." She produced a warm wet towel that had been run under hot water and wrung out." Here, this will make you feel better," she said, wiping his face with the towel. "You look pale, Joshua-san, you'd better drink your tea and get some liquid in you."

He looked at Kiyoshi's face; she was still as beautiful as the first time he saw her. The warm damp towel, the cold iced tea, and the beautiful woman tending to him relaxed him and made the subject of Brandt's package seem a million miles away. Josh wondered what the effect would be on this pleasant life he had if he pursued the contents of the package. He also knew, for better or worse, he would end up finding out; this was something he couldn't ignore.

# CHAPTER ELEVEN

## Reinforcements

*The wicked, envy and hate, it is their way of admiring."*
*-Victor Hugo*

### Tuesday, 29 November 2016, 7:30 PM CST, Sam and Christa Redstone residence, Talihina, OK

The house seemed particularly quiet this evening. Christa, having recovered for the most part from the vehicle crash that took the life of her friend and mother-in-law, Marsha, was trying to return the home to some sort of normalcy. She had spent the previous Friday night in the hospital as a precaution. Christa was thankful to be home and thinking back on how amazed the doctors at the hospital in Ft Smith had been that neither she, her daughter Erin, or her unborn son suffered any serious injury or complications after the accident. *'It was no accident; it was an attack,'* she reminded herself. The entire family was hurting from the loss of Marsha, most of all her father-in-law. Addison had managed to remain stoic during the funeral the afternoon before, but having known the man for years, Christa knew he was hurting. The pain he felt wasn't just for the loss of his wife. Sam was displaying unusual anger toward Addison; in fact, Christa felt as if her husband was on the verge of disowning his father.

Christa had approached Sam several times since coming home from the hospital, urging her husband to make peace with his father as much for his own sake as that of Addison's. Sam wouldn't hear of it. "My whole life he drilled into my head duty before everything else." Her husband would say in an angry tone, "I'm not doing that ever again. I put duty before you once and lost you to that moron Fletcher, I swore if I ever got you back, I'd never do it again. Damned if I didn't do it again Friday and nearly got you killed. No more of my father's duty before all and no more of his monster hunting, you would think by now he would have learned his lesson. He's probably sitting out at the ranch scheming on a way to fight these things instead of mourning his dead wife. She may have been my stepmother for just two years, but she was also a lifelong friend. I think I'm grieving her loss more than he is."

"Don't say that!" Christa had scolded him, "You have no idea how your father is feeling, he's having to deal with the loss of his wife, and you're adding to it by taking the rest of his family away." She remembered Sam looking at her, his eyes filled with anger and worry.

"Yes, and if I do things his way, my family will be taken away from me, I'm not losing you again, or our children. For anybody, or anything," Sam told her sternly.

His words had haunted Christa the rest of the afternoon and evening. *What exactly is he worrying about? She kept asking herself. He's by no means a cowardly or overly cautious man. He's been a soldier and a police officer; he fought this evil two years ago when it first appeared shattering the usually peaceful community. He went to war in Iraq twice; he didn't even have to go the second time, he could have stayed home and...* Suddenly, it dawned on Christa why Sam would not support his father and why the thought of leaving his own family to fight the dark forces that seemed to be against them was so repugnant to him. *It's me; I'm the reason. He lost me when he volunteered to go to Iraq for the second time; that's why he doesn't want to fight now. He's scared I'll go away again and take his family with me this time.*

A sudden feeling of relief, along with a small twinge of guilt, swept over Christa. She now realized Sam's biggest fear was that she would leave him. She knew her husband had a reason to harbor such fears. She had, in fact, left him in 2006 when he volunteered to go on a second deployment to Iraq, even though his enlistment was nearly up. She remembered how broken they had both been at the time, but she could not have suffered through another fifteen-month deployment waiting and worrying every day. As for Sam, he couldn't do anything but his duty. She had the sudden urge to rush to Sam and reassure him that no matter what he was called on to do now, she would never leave him again. She turned toward the spacious living room, where he had been sitting quietly watching young Erin going through a box of Christmas decorations in anticipation of every child's favorite holiday. She noticed a strange bluish glow was coming from the room. *Had he gotten a string of Christmas lights out?* she wondered; she also became aware of a strong unpleasant smell as she turned the corner from the kitchen where she had a full view into the room, and her heart stopped.

Before her was what could only be called a scene of unspeakable horror, the blue glow was coming from outside the house and had enveloped the living room because of the large windows. Her husband stood frozen, unable to move. In his hand was a pistol of some type; she only knew the square-shaped weapon as one of his favorites. He held it in his right hand, his right arm frozen at a forty-five-degree angle, leaving the pistol pointing at the floor. Three beings were across the room from Sam; two of them had their hands, or what passed as hands on young Erin. The hands did not grasp the small girl; instead, they just touched her. More terrifying than the fact they were touching her was that she was levitating, her feet at least a foot off the ground.

Her face was frozen in a mask of fear, her body unable to move because of whatever spell or power the beings were using on her. As if the situation couldn't get any more horrifying, a fourth creature moved, or perhaps a better description would be glided through the heavy wood cabin wall from the outside as if it were spirit and not flesh. The four beings looked at Christa; there was no sign of surprise or concern. It was as if Christa was just another small inconvenience to deal with as they proceeded with whatever sinister plan they had for the family. Obviously, they had never encountered Christa; without hesitation, her voice thundered, "I take authority over you in the mighty name of Jesus! I command you to get your hands off my child, to get away from my husband and to get out of this house right now! The boundary lines have fallen for me in pleasant places, and you are trespassing! Leave now and don't you Ever Return!"

The room seemed to explode in spiritual power; the blue glow rose to a blinding flash. Christa blinked her eyes as they adjusted back to the normal lighting of the room. All evidence of the beings was gone except a strong, unpleasant, sulfur-like smell that hung heavily in the room, yet it too seemed to be dissipating quickly. Erin was now standing, her feet on the ground; she was clutching a small stuffed reindeer in her hands, a look of confusion on her face. "Mommy?" she said as Christa ran to her and scooped her up in her arms. Sam, too, had come out of the hypnotic spell he had been under; he brought the gun in his hand to the ready and bolted outside through the front door of the house. Christa knew her husband would find nothing. They were gone; she knew they had no choice once she spoke the name of her Lord and Savior.

"Who were they mommy, were they bad elves?"

Christa hugged her daughter fiercely and comforted her, "No, baby, they were nothing special and they can never come back."

"Are you sure, Mommy, I don't like them, they scare me."

Sam came back into the house; to say he looked confused was an understatement. "How did you do that?" He asked.

"If you'd go to church and Bible study, you'd know how."

Erin was shivering, "Are you sure they won't come back Mommy?"

"I promise you they will never come back, honey; Jesus won't let them."

"Is Jesus their boss?" Christa smiled at her daughter.

"He certainly is, sweetheart." Clutching Erin tightly, she looked at Sam. "You and I need to talk."

## Tuesday, 29 November 2016 7:30 PM CST, Kiamichi Mountains near Honobia, OK

The Beast was furious; the humans had killed one of his own as easily as if were any other creature in the forest. He knew he was in the presence of the most dangerous of enemies; this one man's death was a priority. The creature knew this through a genetic instinct as well as through its own experience. He had dealt with this human before; it was the same night he had battled the elder and his son near here. He had this human in his grasp, flinging him into the night when he lost his grip, launching the human into some trees. He should have died in those trees. Two years ago, at that time, human was weak, slow, and ignorant. Now he was different; he had a strength and aptitude not possessed by normal humans. He had given himself to his own master, and his master had strengthened him, he was now not just a mere human but a warrior of his God, and each day he gained in faith and strength. He posed a huge danger, not only to the beast and his kind but to the whole collective and overlords he served. The Beast knew this one's name as well. Nathaniel… The name had been carved in rock and laid in the creek for this human to find. It was a warning to strike fear in the heart of this human. Yet the human fought on without fear.

The Beast had watched earlier how this human had taken down his brother with comparative ease. The Beast understood, not only had this human grown in power since their last battle, but now he possessed the knowledge to take them down and prevent any of them from rising again. It was much harder to sense this human now; it was as if a protective force hid him from detection. His brother should have detected this human much earlier than he did. His failure allowed the human to take him down, and now he would be gone forever.

The presence of an unfamiliar elder was troubling as well. Though old and physically weakened by age, his life force was strong, and he was covered in the spiritual amour of his protector. This one, too, could prove to be even more troubling than the elder Redstone or Nathaniel. The Beast feared the protector of these humans. He feared their protector's presence even more than he feared his own overlords. He knew this was the ultimate enemy of his kind. This was the force his kind and his overlords were in a constant battle with. He also knew that he must overcome his fear and dispatch these humans, as they were all becoming stronger with every encounter.

Earlier, the warrior Nathaniel had left the area in one of the steel machines, the Beast closed silently on the two humans he had left behind. They were sitting in the dark forest near a fire; they prepared food and talked quietly in their strange thin voices and language. The Beast had to be cautious; otherwise, the elder human would detect him. The Beast closed his eyes and took in silent deep breaths; he must let the rage and hate that normally drove his actions and behavior dissipate before moving closer. If not, the elder human would surely detect him. The Beast became as still as any of the large rocks and boulders that littered the pine needle-covered forest floor. His focus became the focus of a hunter, not the rage of an avenger.

The Beast knew by controlling his rage; his spiritual presence would be harder to detect. Time was of no consequence to the Beast; he remained still and quiet in the darkness. He would stay that way however long it took to mask his presence; three white-tailed deer moved between the humans and the Beast. The fact that they didn't detect the Beast assured him he was nearly prepared to move in and attack the two humans. His attack would have to be fast; if the elder detected him, the younger human might have time to use one of his weapons against the Beast. Although the elder was a larger danger, the younger one with his weapons and knowledge of how to kill was the biggest immediate threat. He would die first the Beast decided.

The Beast had regained control over its blood lust. The wind had changed direction; the beast could now smell the burning wood of the fire the humans were sitting by. With its emotions and scent now masked by a breeze and the smoke from the fire, it began to move slowly and stealthily toward the two men. As quickly as it had decided to attack the two men, the creature stopped abruptly. There was sudden chaos in the collective's system of communication. The Beast and the other entities in their territorial battle zone were suddenly thrown into a state of confusion and fear. Fear was an emotion the Beast rarely felt; it looked about cautiously to see if one of the servants the human's master's servants had manifested.

The beast had seen one of these celestial beings before; his own master was one of these beings. The difference was his master was one that had rebelled, and he too lived in fear of the pure ones. The Beasts' muscles relaxed slightly; it sensed no other beings in its immediate area. The Beast knew of only one more event that could cause this much confusion in the collective. Somewhere out in the night, one of the humans had cried out to their own Master for protection against the collective. The Beast had experienced this kind of event before; he knew the other beings in the collective, as well as his Master, would have to regroup. It was one of the most effective weapons humans had, but very few ever used it. He and his kind could sometimes hold up against this tactic, but some of the lesser smaller beings in the collective could not.

## Tuesday, 29 November 2016 8:00 PM CST, Sam and Christa Redstone residence, Talihina, OK

The events of the evening had shaken Sam to his core. He sat at the kitchen table as Christa prepared a cup of coffee for him. He was amazed at her calm demeanor after their home had just been invaded by what he could only describe as aliens from another planet. He was amazed even more by how young Erin was already tucked into bed and apparently sleeping soundly. *How does a little girl that age process everything she'd been through the last four days and find the peace of mind to fall asleep without fussing or fear? How is it that both females in the home have recovered from the evening as if it had been nothing more than a wild bird or rodent invading their home?*

Christa placed a cup of coffee in front of Sam and sat down across from him, "I added a shot of Woodford Reserve to your coffee, to ease your nerves a bit." She said, smiling and gripping his left hand in both of hers.

"Maybe you should have put a shot of coffee into a cup of the bourbon," he replied.

"How are you doing, Sam?" she asked, looking into his eyes.

"I'm wondering how my wife and daughter seem to be perfectly fine, and I'm sitting here trying not to lose my mind. Christa how did you know what to do? I went for my gun, my body froze, and there was nothing I could do. I could not force my body to function. How did you know what to do to get the aliens out of our house?"

"Sam, those were not aliens, well not in the sense you think."

Sam shook his head, "No, Christa, that is exactly what they were, I've seen their spaceship before. I saw one two years ago the night my father, Nathan, and I fought the Relics. Plus, the people in Honobia we went to help last week claimed to see two different spaceships the night they were attacked. As if I don't have enough to deal with, now I have to keep little saucer people out of my house too?" He shook his head once again; Christa could see the pain and turmoil in her husband. She knew what she needed to do for his own good, and she knew what she needed to do to help him do it.

"Sam, look at me," she said. Sam knew there was something she needed to say, and he needed to hear it. He looked at her, then nodded, giving her the lead in the conversation. "Sam what is your biggest fear in life?"

"That's easy, losing my family and especially losing you," he replied.

"When you say losing me, do you mean because of something that might happen to me, or are you afraid that I might leave you?"

Sam looked stunned; he wasn't ready for this question. His unease with it was hard to hide. "Well, I...," he stammered in confusion.

Reaching up, she put her right hand against his cheek, "I won't leave you again Sam, ever," she said softly. "I can't be sure of that Christa, I lost you once and I never want to lose you again."

"This is different Sam; this isn't like last time."

"There's really little difference, Christa, to do what I need to do means leaving you home to go fight a battle and this time I'm not sure exactly what I'm fighting. At least in Iraq, I knew exactly who the enemy was and how to defeat them. Now I'm not so sure what they are, or how to kill them. I do know I don't want to come home to an empty house only to find you've left me because of the uncertainty of what could happen to me."

"You're wrong, Sam, there is a huge difference now. Number one, you're my husband now, and number two if you don't defeat these things, they'll keep coming. I want you to fight them Sam, I need you to fight and defeat them. I know what happened to us back in 2006 still worries you. Sam, you, your father and my father, when he was still alive carry a heavy sense of duty. It's not even that you carry this sense of duty it's a part of your very fiber. There is a huge difference now, we have no choice in this battle, it has to be fought, it must be fought. The enemy is seeking us out, you're not running off halfway around the world to possibly be killed because some politician needs more money in his bank account. Let's face it Sam, we should not have been in Iraq. I believe the war in Afghanistan was righteous because of 911, but the war in Iraq was never something we should have gotten involved in. You couldn't see it then because you had your duty to do, but looking back now, do you think the war Iraq was worth the American lives lost or the innocent Iraqi civilian lives lost?"

"Well, not really, Christa, but hindsight is twenty-twenty."

"Sam, it was unnecessary, and I took second place to it. I needed you safe, and you needed a crusade, your crusade was a false one, Sam."

He nodded slightly; he knew his own view of Operation Iraqi Freedom had changed over the years, he'd lost too many good friends, and he'd lost Christa.

"Sam, this crusade is a real one, you're fighting for us and now I need you to fight it with the same dedication you gave this country in Iraq. Sam, fight for your children, fight for the woman you love, fight for our peace and safety. Sam, I know this is partly on me because of what I did when you re-enlisted, but now, Sam, I need you to fight, and fight like you never have before."

Sam looked at his wife; her words were like a guard turning a key on a cell door to release a prisoner. "You know the fight isn't just in Oklahoma don't you Christa?" he asked.

"I realize that, Sam, but I need you to fight and fight wherever its necessary, even if that means doing what Nathan did by going back into the Army and joining Special Forces. Sam what you saw tonight is our real enemy, the eternal enemy. I need you to be a soldier again, but this time a soldier of God. Be my soldier of God, Sam, go assist your father in defeating them here. Then go and defeat them wherever you find them. I will be here Sam; I will love and honor you and keep your home and children safe. Sam fight for me, fight for your children, fight for your father, fight for your home. Destroy them all, then come home to me."

"From how you handled the situation, maybe you should do the fighting and I stay home with the children," Sam said, trying to bring some levity into the situation. "Seriously, Chrissy, how did you know what to do."

Christa smiled, and her heart warmed when she heard him use his pet name for her. It's been a long time since he called me Chrissy, she thought. "Ever since those things came onto the property and grabbed Jeri two years ago, I've been on guard against something like that happening again. I believe Howard's personality, his crimes, and even his death left a dark stain over the property. That is why I insisted we bulldoze down the old house and build our own brand new one."

"I assumed getting rid of the old house had something to do with Howard, but what I'm asking is. How did you know you could rebuke space aliens, and why are they here in the first place?"

Christa sighed slightly, "Sam since we've married you haven't taken my faith or your father's faith seriously. Even worse you've neglected your own faith; you're missing so much Sam. Not just your own salvation, but your attitude has put all of us at risk. Those Sasquatch, or Relics as you call them would not have come on this property two years ago had Howard not had an evil heart. These impish little demonic runts would have never dared entering this house had there been a Mighty Man of God in the room."

Sam sighed, Christa's words made sense, but he couldn't grasp what his relationship with the Almighty had to do with Sasquatch and Aliens. "Christa, those were space aliens, and the Relics are just some left over form of early man. It's like I'm having to fight prehistoric beings and futuristic beings at the same time. All of this is hard enough to believe and I want to protect my family, I know my faith is lacking as well as my knowledge of the Bible, but I'm not making the connection between cavemen, space men, and God."

"Sam, these are not cavemen and space men, they are Nephilim and demons. The spaceship you claimed you saw two years ago wasn't alien technology, it was angel technology, or better yet, fallen angel technology. They don't come from another star system, they come from another dimension."

Sam sat back in the chair and pondered his wife's words. He knew he had been less than enthusiastic about church and studying the Bible. He wondered if Christa's ideas came from the books she read. He looked at the stack of books that were resting on a countertop in the kitchen; there were at least six sitting there. He knew there were dozens more stacked away in the guest bedroom. He had scanned the titles before; they were usually biblically based, but the subject matter seemed to be more science fiction than religious. He'd seen the covers of many of the books with what looked like UFOs, aliens, giants, as well as others on subjects like quantum physics. There were other books with a more biblical flare he'd seen in the stacks, like The Book of Enoch and The Book of Jasher; he'd also seen one titled Spiritual Warfare Bible. It was all confusing to Sam, and he assumed his wife just had a quirky interest in the paranormal. He'd chalked it up to a childlike cuteness and just one of the little things he didn't understand about her, but somehow it made him love her more.

Sam's mind was racing, *Have I been this blind, has my lack of confidence in being able to hold on to her kept me from being the man she needed me to be, to be the man everyone I love needs me to be? What about God? Surely, I haven't been the man he needs me to be,* he thought to himself. He looked back into Christa's eyes; it was as if she was trying to see into his soul to see if the lights were coming on. "Okay Chrissy, I think I'm beginning to understand, or at least for once I'm trying to understand. If I do join in on the fight against all these things, how will you Erin, and the baby be safe without me?"

Christa smiled and said, "The same way we were safe earlier tonight. Only now we'll be even safer, because every night you will pray for our safety as we pray for yours. I want you to call your father, and ask him to forgive you for your anger, and tell him you're beginning to understand. I want you to help him fight these things and give him the honor and respect he deserves. I want you to find Jesus and to come to know him. If you'll do these things Sam, we will remain safe here."

"Chrissy, there's so much I don't understand, I need a crash course in scripture and praying. I've been so ignorant to so much. Now when I need to pick your brain for knowledge, there seems to be no time. How will I learn what I need to learn in time?"

Christa smiled at her husband; Sam could see her love and confidence in him. He almost felt guilty for his attitude toward her faith since they'd been married. "Sam, what happened tonight may not seem like it, but it was an answer to my prayers."

"How so?" Sam asked, not understanding how what seemed like an alien abduction attempt could be an answer to prayer.

"Sam I've prayed so hard for your eyes to be opened, encountering those beings tonight did just that for you. God opened your eyes in a spectacular fashion did he not?"

Sam gave a quick chuckle, "I guess he did at that, Chrissy; I'm still going to be operating on a lot of self-inflicted ignorance though."

"No, Sam, you won't, I've also prayed that a teacher and messenger be sent to you and your father."

"Well, I hope he gets here in time," Josh responded.

"He's already here, Josh, you just haven't recognized him yet."

"Chrissy, forgive me for asking but how do you know?"

Christa just smiled at her husband and said, "I know that I know that I know."

## Tuesday, 29 November 2016 8:15 PM CST, Kiamichi Mountains near Honobia, OK

Josh Nashoba sipped his coffee quietly, contemplating the stories of Trent Simmons; the fire they shared gave off pleasant warmth as the young man described some of the adventures he and Nathan had shared. The two men had no idea the danger that had been lurking just yards from them in the dark. The stories of adventures in Afghanistan, as well as two years ago less than twenty miles from where the two men now sat, had taken their focus away from the night.

"Tell me again, what is the secret to knowing the difference between the evil ones or Relics and the average Sasquatch."

"Well, as I said before, extra digits, a second row of teeth and the smell is a dead giveaway also. They seem to go to a dark grey or black once turned as well." Josh replied.

"You know, I didn't smell the ones near Talihina two years ago, but they were definitely out to kill me, that's evil in my book."

"Trent, the oppressive smell is in reality the stench of hell," Josh said as he took a last sip of coffee.

"You mean they actually come from hell? How, is there an elevator or something?" Trent asked, not sure whether to believe the old man.

"You're not far off, there is a method of transport or teleportation. If they are not coming from hell, they are coming from close contact with the fallen."

"You mean fallen angels, like demons?" Trent said more, stating than asking.

"It is a common misconception that demons are fallen angels. Nothing could be further from the truth. Fallen angels are far superior and extremely more powerful than demons. Demons are nothing more than the disembodied spirits of the dead Nephilim. They were an abomination, their souls cannot go to heaven or hell, they walk in the fringes of our dimension, always hungry, always thirsty, always lusting for the carnal pleasures of the life they enjoyed on earth before the flood."

"Wait, wait, wait, somebody is going to have to explain all this to me. Demons are the spirits of dead Nephilim; they are not the same as a fallen angel? It doesn't make sense." Trent said.

"As I said, you are not alone in your belief that fallen angels and demons are the same thing. Fortunately for me I had the difference explained to me in a letter from a long dead Admiral. So, bear with me young man, I will have to take you on a little trip through Genesis, Chapter Six," Trent nodded, so Josh continued, "In chapter six we are told of the fallen angels that came down on Mount Hermon, there two hundred of the fallen came down to earth. They were dispatched to earth by Satan. Once on earth, their primary mission was cohabiting with human females to create a race which would corrupt the bloodline that the savior was to come through. Satan assumed his minions could breed out any possibility of the birth of a redeemer by taking away the pureness of the bloodline God created with Adam."

"The offspring of these unholy unions between humans and angels were what is known as Nephilim. The Bible describes them as giants and men of renown. Demons are not fallen angels; nothing could be further from the truth. Fallen angels are far superior and extremely more powerful than demons. Demons are nothing more than the disembodied spirits of the dead Nephilim. They were an abomination; their souls cannot go to heaven or hell. They walk in the fringes of our dimension, always hungry, always thirsty, always lusting for the carnal pleasures of the life they enjoyed on earth before the flood. Josh was interrupted by Trent.

"This is where the Greek and Roman Mythology came from, young Sergeant, these creatures had the blood of man and angel flowing through them, and to normal men, they appeared as gods. They were huge and were mighty warriors. They set about upon all areas of the earth. As you mentioned, the Greeks called them Titans; they were, in fact, the Nephilim of the Bible. These are not the only two civilizations that dealt with these giants. Brythonic and Gallic civilizations in the British Isles also had them. In fact, London was supposedly founded by the giant Magog. The Romans had them, the Egyptians, the Hindus, the Norse, the Shinto in Japan, and even the Native American tribes have tales of giants. These giant offspring were ravenous. Their hunger could not be sated; no matter how hard men tried to produce enough food to feed them, it was of no use.

Soon these giants began to devour man himself; humanity was on the verge of disappearing altogether from the sins of the fallen angels and the curse of their abominable offspring. Very few humans remained with the original bloodline back to Adam intact. God put Noah, his wife, and sons and their wives in the ark, as their bloodlines were pure and flooded the world. He had the two hundred fallen angels imprisoned in the pit. The souls of the dead Nephilim are not souls of man or angel, so they roam the earth as evil spirits. These are your demons, in my opinion, Trent."

"So, what does all of this have to do with Sasquatch, and why are there evil ones and ones that stay to themselves?" Trent asked.

"The fallen angels didn't just molest human women Trent; they defiled every creature they could. They detested God's creations and were responsible for many of the freakish and monstrous creatures you read about in ancient myths from around the world. They defiled every animal, bird, reptile, even fish and insects they could. This is where the legendary creatures like the dragon, griffin, minotaur, and centaur come from. If it's a monster of any type you can rest assured it wasn't God's doing, it came about because of

282

the devil and his follower's rebellion against our Heavenly Father. They also defiled the great apes and like many species over time."

"The Nephilim gene has been diluted in most of the species but still strong in small number of them. That small number keeps the gene alive by forced procreation and violence. Just as do the remnant of some human-Nephilim hybrids. Okla Chito, or Sasquatch as you know them are natural creatures of God's creation. The Shampe or Relics are a Nephilim hybrid made originally from the union of fallen angels defiling female Sasquatch. Now the Shampe itself can carry on the strain by defiling a female Sasquatch. That explains why they're bigger, stronger, and faster possess powers a normal Sasquatch doesn't. It's just like human hybrids have abilities and strengths normal humans don't."

"You mean like that fifteen-footer Nathan whacked in Afghanistan?" "Yes, like that one, but there are others that appear normal in size and appearance."

"So, I could be walking down the street, and pass one and not know it?"

"That's correct, to be honest, Trent, you may have worked for one at some point or even voted for one in an election. Like the Relics as you guys call the creatures we fight here, the human ones also use sex and violence to advance their gene pool." Trent went silent, staring at the fire. Josh could tell his mind was working hard to make sense of all he had just heard.

"If the flood killed all the Nephilim, then why do we have sasquatch, giants, and some of the other weird crap our friend Nathan has had to dispatch?"

"There was a second incursion, Trent. I don't know exactly how it was accomplished, but Satan seems to think he can somehow win a seed war where his vile mutants can deceive and corrupt mankind as much as possible before the second coming of Christ." Joshua's words were interrupted by a voice coming from a tree line just downslope from where they sat.

A voice with a thick Southeast Oklahoma accent, yelled, "Hello in the camp!" Trent reached for his rifle; Joshua lifted his arm slightly to reassure him they were not in danger.

"I know that voice," he said, "You're going to love this guy, you're two of a kind."

## Tuesday, 29 November 2016, 8:35 PM CST, Redstone Ranch, two miles North of Talihina, OK

Addison had been feeling lonely and disconnected. He had prayed for strength to overcome the recent tragedy of the loss of his wife. He knew

Marsha was in heaven and happily in the company of her Lord Jesus as well as reunited with her daughter and other loved ones. He prayed hardest for his son Sam and his young family. He begged God for his son's forgiveness and understanding. Usually, prayer helped soothe Addison and give him some respite from his troubles. However, tonight seemed darker than normal, and Addison was lonelier than he could ever remember. So, he welcomed the unexpected arrival of Nathan Parks, who had stopped by to check on him, as well as update him on the events earlier in the evening. He was pleased to hear one of the Relics had been taken down and would be disposed of in a manner that would prevent it from returning ever again. He was curious but not completely surprised by the sudden appearance of Joshua Nashoba at Nathan and Trent's camp.

"He's in good shape for his age," Nathan commented on the elderly man.

"Yes, he sure has a knack for showing up where you wouldn't expect him," Addison replied.

"He seems to know you Addison," Nathan said.

"Yes, he does, but I just can't seem to ever remember meeting him, he must have been a friend of my father. Nathan, I think I'm ready to join you and Trent in Honobia."

"Are you sure, Sir? Marsha's funeral was just yesterday, don't you think you need more time?"

"I'll have plenty of time to mourn Marsha later, Nathan, right now I need to avenge her."

"Is vengeance an emotion you should use to hunt these things, Sir?" Nathan asked.

"I can't think of a better one, besides it's the only emotion I got when it comes to these things," Addison replied.

"Maybe we should get in touch with, Sam, he might want to weigh in on your decision," Nathan said, hoping to change Addison's mind.

"Sam has his own family to care for in his own way. I'm not too sure he would approve of me calling him anyway."

"Well, I have to admit I'd like Sam to know you're joining us and don't think I'm implying you're over the hill, Sir, I certainly wouldn't look forward to having you or this Josh Nashoba guy hunting me. I just wonder if it would be better to wait until your son can be there too."

Addison smiled to himself, thinking, *I guess I'm old enough to be considered a liability by these younger men now.* The thought didn't help his feeling of being disconnected. He wasn't too surprised to hear his phone ring, but when the display said the call was from Sam, he was surprised. "Excuse me one moment," he told Nathan and stepped out on his front porch. "Hello?" He answered, praying he didn't encounter an angry Sam on the other end of the line.

"Hi, Pop," replied the familiar voice of his son.

"Sam? Is everything okay?" Addison asked, unsure of why his son would be calling after the anger he had displayed toward his father the last few days.

"Well yes and no, Pop. Yes, in that we're all okay here, and yes in that I realize I've been wrong in the way I've treated you lately, I apologize for how I've acted, Pop."

"It's okay, Son, we've been through a lot more than most people. You're allowed some confusion and anger."

"Pop, a lot of the confusion is being lifted, don't ask me how. I'll tell you when you arrive."

"Arrive?" Addison asked his son.

"Yes, I need you to come by and pick me up Pop, like I said... Yes, most everything is okay, but there is still the no on something that's not okay."

"Can you tell me what's not, okay?" Addison asked.

"What's not okay is that we've got some oversized hairy creatures and their keepers we need to get rid of, wouldn't you agree, Pop?"

Addison felt as if a huge burden had been lifted from him. "Are you sure, Son?" He was almost afraid to allow himself to believe his son was returning to him.

"I've never been more sure, Pop; I love you and I'm sorry for my behavior. What's more, I need your advice and strength to fight these things. Please come get me Dad and let's do this."

"I'll be there shortly, Son," Addison said before disconnecting the phone. He walked back into the house and walked straight to his desktop computer. Bringing up Google Earth, he zeroed in on the Mountains around Honobia. Then he turned toward his guest. "Nathan, please show me where your camp is."

## Tuesday, 29 November 2016 8:15 PM CST, Kiamichi Mountains near Honobia, OK

Trent was hesitant to allow anyone to approach the camp, the amount and types of weapons they carried as well as the head of the dead Relic impaled on a copper spike might not be well received by some casual local that would arrive thinking of joining an innocent evening of sitting around a campfire. A large, strong-looking man who appeared to be in his late 40s to early 50s eased into camp with an AR-15 slung over his shoulder. He was accompanied by a much younger man, who Trent guessed to be in his early twenties.

"Evening," the older man said, squinting toward Trent and Joshua.

"Good evening, Boomer," Josh replied.

The man had to shield his eyes a bit with his right hand, then recognizing Josh, he smiled." "Hey, Josh, good to see you. I hate to bust in on your campfire here, but you boys have some kind of law enforcement about to move in on you. The glow from your fire is visible from the road, and these guys have been pretty active around here, running people out of the hills and especially people on this deer lease."

"How is it, you got past them and up here?" Trent asked with some suspicion.

"Tell ya what, lets introduce ourselves and show our hold cards and then maybe that way we'll all have a good reason to relax."

"Good idea, Boomer Jefferson, this is Trent Simmons of the U.S. Air Force."

"Nice to meet you, Trent, a fly boy huh? My daddy did some flying back in World War Two," Boomer said, extending his hand.

"I'm more of what you might call a combat medic and occasional trigger puller," Trent said, shaking hands with Boomer, who nodded toward the younger man with him and said,

"This is my cousin, Levi."

Trent then turned and shook hands with the younger man. Levi nodded at the head impaled on the spike and asked. "Looks like somebody pulled a trigger and then some on this ugly devil."

Trent still wasn't quite sure if he could trust the two men. Boomer took wasted no time in easing his concerns, "Hey man, like I said, we wouldn't have busted in on ya like this, but I think you may have trouble with the law.

There's two vehicles and six guys total pulled over on the side by at the overlook just down the road; they're all armed and dressed in tactical gear. We passed them heading to my house a while ago. I have a suspicion it may have to do you two, or with this feller, you got dressed out here," he said, nodding toward the severed head. "I'm thinking if they're after you, they'll wait until your friend is back, and they think you're all asleep."

Trent knew he didn't have many options; he'd have to truthful and share why he was here and that he had a teammate do back any minute. "Boomer, my buddy went to Talihina for some supplies, if he comes back and runs into these men you're talking about, and if they try to impede him in any way, it will go ugly quick. So, if you have any ideas, I'd love to hear them."

Boomer thought for a moment, then said, "My side by side is about three hundred yards down that game trail parked on the other side of the fence on my property. Let's get as much of your gear to the fence as we can right now, then I'm going to drive you to my house, where you and Levi can take my truck and try to head off your friend. Cell signal up here is lousy and I doubt you'll get a signal long enough to warn him if he's on the road back. Have your friend follow Levi back to my house, you guys can put up there for the night."

"Why would we be any safer at your place than here?" Trent asked.

"Because somebody is running everyone off this lease and it has to do with those things," he said, nodding once again at the impaled head. "They can probably get away with just about anything on this lease, but if they get on my property, I'll make em wish they hadn't. In the meantime, I'll get all your gear out of the camp site hopefully before those these mystery cops move in. It will look like nothing more than an abandoned campsite and they won't be onto you fellers."

Trent considered Boomer's plan better than any other option he had; the four men began grabbing gear as quickly as they could. One thing, Josh said before the men left to go down the mountain, "Trent, you Nathan, Sam, and Addison need to turn off your cell phones and pull out the batteries before coming back. Or else you'll be tracked and come right to Boomer's house looking for us".

## Tuesday, 29 November 2016 9:30 PM CST, Indian Trail Highway between Honobia and Talihina, OK

Trent recognized the headlights of the rented Jeep he and Nathan had been using as the vehicle turned off Highway 217 just south of Talihina and onto Indian Trail Highway. He asked Levi to quickly flash the pickup's lights they were sitting in on the side of the road. Fortunately, he had been able to catch Nathan on his cell phone while both men had a signal. Nathan was expecting to meet the two men at this location. He quickly pulled over and exited the Jeep.

"So, what's the scoop, Brother?" Nathan asked as he approached.

Trent quickly introduced Nathan to Levi and then related the events in detail to Nathan. "So, they're probably watching for this Jeep, I'm not sure we can avoid them seeing it no matter what we do," Nathan remarked.

287

Hearing Nathan's concerns, Levi offered a solution. "We can all head back toward Talihina, then take Highway 63 to Big Cedar, from there we can run North on Highway 259 to Octavia and come in from the Southeast. Just before Honobia, we jump on Cline Rd and drive to my folk's place. There's a private road from our property up the mountain to Boomer's house. the back way. They'll never know we came that way and will never guess you're anywhere near Honobia."

Trent and Nathan both thought this plan was a much better option than driving right past the mysterious team of men lurking near where they had been camped. Nathan was not quite sure yet of what to think of the young man Levi. The young man seemed courteous, confident, and intelligent beyond his years. He was tall and strong-looking, and his eyes were alert and determined. His hair was long and dark, hanging nearly to his shoulders; he was dressed in jeans boots and wore a tan Carhart jacket. On his head, he wore a trucker's cap complete with a confederate flag on the front of it. Nathan decided there was no time better than now to mention the elephant in the room.

"Levi, I'm not going to lie to you, what we're involved in could be dangerous, extremely dangerous. I don't want to make assumptions, but I need to ask you. Would your father and cousin approve of what you're getting involved in here? I mean, it's not every day a guy that looks like you is going to put their life in jeopardy for a guy that looks like me."

Levi broke into a large smile, "You mean because you're black and I'm a hillbilly? Nathan, your skin could be Texas Longhorn burnt orange, but if Josh Nashoba says you're good people, then you're good people, that goes for my cousin and father too. Just do us a favor and not scream Hook Em Horns."

Nathan laughed, "No chance of that, I'm a Razorback fan."

Levi, not missing a beat, shot back with, "Well, there goes the neighborhood."

Laughter broke out among the three men taking any tension with it. On a more serious note, Nathan said, "I need to get with Addison and Sam, they're coming in tonight as well. Do you think your cousin would mind having two tents on his property?"

"Boomer has a huge game room in the back of his house, there's a wood stove in there to keep it warm and plenty of room for all of you to spread out and put your sleeping bags on the floor," Levi said.

"That's very generous, you're sure that your cousin won't mind?"

"Boomer loves adventure and after what we saw this morning, he's happier than a puppy with two peters to do anything that helps you guys. Besides, once he saw that feller bully that man and his son off the lease, you couldn't drag him away from this fight."

Trent watched the conversation and decided there was a still a particularly cold bucket of water yet to pour over the proceedings. "You know General Henderson is going to be pissed, one of the last things he said was don't involve any civilians other than the Redstone's."

Looking at Trent, Nathan said, "Yeah, well, what's the worst thing he can do, drag us back to Afghanistan when our leave is over."

"Good point," Trent admitted.

## Tuesday, 29 November 2016 9:50 PM CST, Sam and Christa Redstone residence, Talihina, OK

Addison had made the trip to the home of their son and daughter-in-law in record time. The weapons and gear he'd need for Honobia had been packed since before Marsha's funeral. He knew he would be going there to set things right since the evening of her death. Regardless of what his son had said over the phone, he still had been apprehensive on the drive to their home. Sam had been so angry for so long, and it had all come to a head after the attack that had taken the life of his wife Marsha and threatened the lives of his son's wife, stepdaughter, and unborn son.

He prayed that when he arrived his son had not suffered a relapse of his anger. Sam's confusion and anger toward his father had been an issue ever since the cold November night in 2014 when he, Sam, and Nathan Parks had battled the Relics in the very mountains whose dark outline he could see against the night sky out of the window of his truck. *Please God, bless Sam, bless all of us with the clarity we need to fight this incursion and bring it to an end.* He prayed silently as he drove in the darkness. He had been surprised by a phone call from Nathan, they had just spoken, and he hoped that nothing had happened, or anyone had been injured or worse. He was relieved to hear that a couple of Honobia locals had appeared and offered not only their assistance but much-needed information about a group of suspicious men gathering near their camp.

*No doubt some of Eastman's goons,* he thought to himself. He knew this meant things were ramping up in seriousness and danger. He also knew that the more cards Eastman played, the better. *Go ahead and put all your cards on the table, Eastman,* he silently willed his enemy. If what Nathan said about the

289

offers of assistance and the location of the two Honobia locals was true. There was an incredibly good chance they could surprise Paul Eastman by coming from a direction he'd never think of. Addison took another precaution before arriving at Sam and Christa's house. He called Jimmy and Jeri Chula as well a Dale Thompkins; he gave them a quick rundown on where he and Sam would be and asked them to keep an eye on Christa and Erin. *It would be just like Eastman to attempt another attack on the Redstone women. That was what cowards do;* the thought brought anger bordering on rage to Addison. *You're not going to be allowed to walk away this time, Eastman; I'll make sure of it,* Addison vowed angrily.

When Addison arrived at the large stylish cabin of Sam and Christa's, he was a bit surprised to see the outside lights were on, brightly illuminating well into the forest that surrounded the house. His fears that they may have just had an unexpected visit or attack from Relics were quickly put to ease when he saw both Sam and Christa on the porch, and both smiled and waved as he pulled up to the house. He was equally surprised when Sam came off the porch and greeted him as soon as he exited his truck.

"Glad you're here, Dad; thank you for coming so fast," he said as he hugged his father, followed by a strong slap on the shoulder. The three of them sat on the porch as Sam and Christa related the evenings' events. At one point, Christa went into the house to check on Erin and make coffee to help the two men stay alert for their drive to Honobia.

"Dad, I'm sorry for how I've behaved since we fought those things, honestly I was afraid I'd lose Christa, and after I've gotten so attached to Erin and now that Christa is carrying our child, I just could not stand the thought of losing them," Sam confided.

"You never have to apologize to me because you're trying to protect your family, Sam." Addison reassured his son. As Christa returned, the three of them talked some more about what had happened and what lay ahead. "Christa, I had never considered that what people report as UFOs or aliens could be something demonic instead of something from outer space, but there is a point to be made there. Maybe we'll find some answers soon. I agree with you, I believe the messenger you've prayed for is among us in the form of this Joshua Nashoba fella, at least I pray he is."

Sam excused himself to kiss sleeping Erin goodnight and grab his gear for loading in his father's truck. Christa took the opportunity to hug Addison, "Thank you, Dad, thank you for not giving up on Sam."

Addison held his daughter-in-law tightly and said, "I couldn't give up on him anymore than you could darlin, you stay safe and take care of my grandchildren. If you have any problems go to your mom's or call Jimmy, Jeri, and Dale."

She gave him a peck on the cheek, "I will, Sam called them to let them know he'd be away with you, and they said you had already called and told them to keep an eye on me."

Addison blushed a bit, "Nobody can keep a secret nowadays. All the same, you be careful and be on guard."

"I will," she said as Sam came out of the door. Looking at her husband, Christa said, "I want one more thing tonight, Sam, I want to pray over you two before you leave."

"Okay," Sam replied with some discomfort, he had never put much effort into prayer, and he almost felt guilty asking for God's protection now. However, he felt he was at a crossroad, and it was time to surrender his pride, fear, and lack of faith. He wanted the relationship his father and wife had with the Almighty; he agreed to the prayer, saying, "Okay, but I don't feel worthy of God's blessings Christa."

His wife smiled, her eyes beginning to tear, "Sam, none of us are worthy, all of us require God's grace and forgiveness which was paid for by the blood of Jesus. Now give me your hand."

Sam set down his gear and took his wife's hand, he also took his father's hand, and the three of them formed a small circle, each of them holding a hand of the other two. Sam opened his heart and listened intently to the prayer his wife offered. She began with thanks for all the blessings the three of them enjoyed each day. Their lives, family, freedom, their homes and provisions, their church, their friends, and community. Her words touched Sam; it occurred to him for the first time how blessed he really was. He'd always been aware of how fortunate he was to enjoy these very things Christa was thanking God for, especially after his two tours in Iraq. However, this was the first time it really occurred to him the blessing was from God. Before, he had assumed it was just luck of the draw by being born in the United States. The more Christa prayed, the more awareness Sam had of just how blind he had been his whole life, assuming everything was provided by the power of the country he lived in, not the power of his Creator. Christa finished her prayer, asking God to bless and protect his two soldiers, his two Soldiers of God. When she had finished, all three said Amen, Sam with more sincerity than he had ever felt before.

"I'll load your gear so you can kiss this one goodnight." Addison said as he took a military-style flight bag and two long gun cases from his son. Sam turned to his wife, and taking her into his arms, he said, "I always hate leaving you, even if it's only for an hour. Somehow you always manage to make me miss you."

"You'd better miss me and don't get tied up with any of them mountain girls," she teased.

"No worries there, you're the daughter of Mike Sanders, no way am I going to give you a reason to be mad at me."

Christa grabbed him tightly; she kissed him once more, then pulled away. "Sam, I love you, I need you. Now go send all of these things straight to hell where they belong and come back home to me."

"I promise," Sam said, kissing her one more time before walking to his father's truck.

As he entered the truck and closed the door, he thought about how blessed he was to have a wife to pray for him and see him off. It occurred to him that his father had just buried his wife the day before and had no one waiting at home for him. A sudden wave of guilt and sadness washed over Sam. *How could I have treated this man so callously?* he thought, he started to say something, but his father cut him off with a knowing smile. "It's okay, Son, now let's go make these hairballs pay."

"Amen," Sam replied as the truck headed down the drive taking the two men to battle an enemy that had haunted them both for over two years. Neither man knew if the enemy would take the form of man, beast, or spirit, or all three. They were certain of only one thing. There would be no quarter given by either side. When the dust settled, there would be no enemy, or there would be no Redstone's.

# CHAPTER TWELVE

~~~∿∿∿∿~~~

# The Revelation

*"Sometimes God doesn't send you to battle to win it; he sends you to end it."*
*~ Shannon L Alder*

## Tuesday, 29 November 2016 11:30 PM CST, Jefferson Residence Kiamichi Mountains Honobia, OK

Addison and Sam were the last to arrive at Boomer Jefferson's cabin which rested on the Southern slope of the North range of mountains overlooking Honobia. Cabin would be a misleading description of Boomer's home. It was in fact a full-sized house built of logs on the very edge of the mountain. The front of the house rested firmly on the hard rock of the mountain top, while the rear of the house was supported by beams that went fifteen feet down the slope supporting the back third of the building. A spacious room took up the rear quarter of the house and was attached to a large balcony that looked down on the small valley in which Honobia rested, all the way to the South range of the Kiamichi Mountains a mile away on the valley's opposite side. Boomer was a generous host and made food and drink available to his guest. "I know we got a job ahead of us, and there's a lot of information some of us need to hear about. I think it would be a good idea if we all just relaxed and got to know each other for a bit, then get some rest. Tomorrow we can get down to business, those boys out in the woods aint gonna figure out where you guys are anyway."

"Boomer, if they do go into the campsite, don't you don't think they'll search around here looking for Nathan and Trent? They've probably been watching the area for days without anybody knowing." Sam asked.

"If they've been spying on me, that's even better, there's always a crowd up here having a good time, it'll just look like a normal night at this place."

"Even for a Tuesday?" Sam asked.

"It's Tuesday?" Boomer asked in mock seriousness before winking at Sam. "Hey y'all, have some moonshine." He said offering Sam a mason jar half full, a clear liquid sloshed around inside as Boomer extended the jar toward Sam. Looking at the jar Sam struggled to come up with an excuse, he didn't want to insult his host. Sam was on his second beer, and he knew if he took a shot of Boomer's homemade whiskey, he'd more than likely get ill. Sam's honesty prevailed and he told Boomer,

"If I drink that on top of this beer, I'll spew my guts out." Boomer laughed loudly,

"Well, there you go, Sam, if they are watching and they see somebody go outside and throw up, they'll be convinced everything's normal here."

Everyone in the room erupted in laughter, even Josh who had setup his sleeping bag nearest the wood burning stove sat on a small stool enjoying the fire and laughter. He was impressed how quickly all the men in the room were bonding, most had vastly different life experiences, some had known each other for years, some hadn't seen each other in years, and some just a few hours ago were complete strangers. Yet here they were, all enjoying the camaraderie of each other. It reminded Josh of the years he spent in naval fighter squadrons, where the threat of a mutual enemy and mutual danger would form a bond quicker than any words, previous experiences, or manufactured narrative, ever could. He had particularly enjoyed talking aircraft and flying with Levi. The young man had been bitten hard by the airplane bug and had developed a vast knowledge of aircraft and flying.

At the tender age of twenty the young man already owned his own aircraft, using money he saved from working in the oil fields of West Texas, he purchased a 1946 Piper J-3 Cub. His small yellow aircraft buzzing through the valley was a regular sight in Honobia, when Levi wasn't working or attending college classes. Joshua hoped that once the dust cleared from the current turmoil, he could spend time with Levi and encourage him to pursue his aviation interest. Josh wondered if he had squandered his life having been a recluse since the passing of his wife. He quickly pushed the thought away and decided to enjoy what time he had with this group of men no matter what was to come. I may never get another chance. He thought to himself.

Nathan voiced a question asking if he and Trent should sneak close to their abandoned campsite to see if the mysterious men in tactical gear had gone into the camp yet. "When they find the camp abandoned, they may start looking around Honobia and surrounding properties, they may even decide to investigate your property as well.

Boomer set him at ease, "I have a buddy just down the hill in Ho-nubby," he said reminding Nathan of the correct pronunciation of the community.

"He drives a log truck and goes up and down that mountain road a few times a day starting about three in the morning. I told him to keep an eye out for those guys, plus he's called his other friends in the area to warn them about these guys. Nathan there's quite a few folks up in these hills and down in the valley that like to make their own whiskey and some even grow a little weed for themselves. Them fellers down there staking out the road don't realize it, but they're on Hillbilly Radar now. Everybody up here is watching them, now they may scare a couple of folks, but there's quite a few of these ole boys up here that would be their worst nightmare. They'll find out soon enough, not to go farting around too much on other people's property."

After a while, the group seemed to fully relax. More brisket was eaten more beverages were consumed, more laughs and stories were shared. After another two hours it was obvious most were ready to turn in.

Before everyone broke for their beds or sleeping bags Addison said, "I'm happy and honored to be here with you men, I can't thank our host enough. Tomorrow we'll need to get down to business." Then nodding toward Josh, he said. "I believe Mister Nashoba has a lot of information to share with us concerning why we're here and what we're up against. Most of us probably have no idea why all this is happening and exactly who or what our opponents are, we'll need Mister Nashoba's knowledge and experience, so be ready to learn in the morning gents, and after that you'll each have to decide for yourself how far you want to get involved in this thing. All the men agreed, said their goodnights and settled in. After getting into his sleeping bag, Sam's thoughts went to Christa. *I'm settled in for the night, we're in a warm, safe, place. Don't worry about us, sleep tight, I Love You.* Little did Sam know that at the exact same moment, his wife was sending him the same thoughts after her nightly prayers.

## Wednesday, 30 November 2016 9:30 AM CST, Jefferson Residence Kiamichi Mountains Honobia, OK

The men started stirring early, by 6:30 in the morning all were up and moving. Most had little to say until they'd had a cup of coffee or two, as was the case with Trent who had sampled a bit too much of the local moonshine the night before. "Man, that stuff will sneak up on you!"

He said to Nathan who seemed to be fully alert with no aftereffects from the previous evening, "You're just not cut out for this lifestyle is all. Maybe you should see if General Henderson will let you go back to the regular Air Force. After a couple of days of sitting around in the air conditioning and dropping your pencil instead of a weapon, you'll feel better." Nathan said grinning.

Overhearing the banter of the two men, Sam smiled. He had to admit he missed the military and knew no matter how much grief Nathan dished out to Trent, they had a bond that nothing could break. Not hardships, not danger, not skin color, and especially not the uniform color of their respective branches of the military. He sipped his coffee and for the first time in years, entertained the idea of going back into the Army, and nearly blew his coffee through his nose when he heard Trent reply, "I tried to get in the Army and the Marines," Trent exclaimed.

"So, what happened?" Nathan asked.

"I kept getting high scores on the IQ test so the Army wouldn't touch me, and I'm allergic to wax and can't eat crayons, so the Marines didn't want me either."

Trent and Nathan soon tired of their game and started checking their gear and weapons. Boomer and Levi were busy in the kitchen cooking breakfast. Levi was frying venison sausage and chopping up the patties before handing them over to Boomer who added the sausage into a large frying pan in which he was scrambling eggs, peppers and onions. Once ready Levi took the ingredients and rolled them into flour tortillas along with some cheese, by the time the two men were done there were two dozen breakfast burritos on a platter complete with a jar of home-made salsa. Both men had learned this skill from Levi's father, who fell in love with breakfast burritos and making his own salsa after years of working in the West Texas oil fields. The men sat quietly making small talk during breakfast, afterward they all pitched in to help their host clean up.

Once the domestic duties were done Addison began to speak, "I don't know exactly why we've all been drawn together, this feels a lot like two years ago when Nathan and I were drawn together. My son Sam and Trent also ended up together in the same weird situation during that time. Now it seems our group has grown once again, and once again we're in a strange situation, thrown together with perfect strangers that we somehow, we are able to effectively mesh with in a team setting. I suppose the best thing to do, is to let everyone give us a quick introduction and how we came to be together in this spot. That way we all know, what each of us have seen or encountered, and take it from there. I don't have an answer for why we're here, I'm hoping... I'm praying Mister Nashoba here can take all our experiences and tie them together into some explanation that will make sense to all of us. I feel like maybe we should start with the two gentlemen here that have graciously fed and given us a safe place to operate for the time being. Boomer, would you and Levi lead off and tell us what drew you to us and our situation?"

Boomer stood up, obviously feeling put on the spot but at the same time willing to share he and his cousins recent experience." Well, to be honest with you fellas, until last Friday I thought all this Bigfoot stuff was a joke. I've lived in these mountains for years and the only time I seen anything to do with Bigfoot was in the store do there in Ho-Nubby, or when they have the Bigfoot Festival in the fall. To me all these Bigfoot folks were a joke, Levi and I would make fake calls and mess with them at night and scare them for fun. That was before last Friday morning."

Boomer proceeded to share the experience he and Levi had early the previous Friday. "Now I'm not comfortable sharing all this with you, even though from what little I've heard most of you have gone through much weirder stuff than I can imagine. To be honest if it wasn't for these government men bullying local folks and hunters, I would be trying to forget what I saw last Friday. That government big shot pissed me off though, I could probably go the rest of my life and make peace with the fact that there are big hairy cavemen running around up here, but I won't accept federal boys coming in and pushing me or my neighbors around. I'm just not going to let that go."

Addison nodded and thanked Boomer, and asked Levi if he added anything to add. "Nope, Boomer covered what I saw and how I feel pretty well," the young man said.

Next, Sam and Addison proceeded with their own stories from the autumn of 2014, the battles in the mountains surrounding Talihina. He covered their experiences up until the recent events that had occurred on Addison's property, the encounter with the Relic, the encounter with the strange looking man dressed in the black suit, the missing boys from Arkansas being found on his property, as well as the sasquatch and UFO encounter of Jim and Melinda Vaughn, he and Sam had investigated. Josh who was listening quietly seemed to stir when told of the remains of the USAF pilot who went missing in the mountains near Mena Arkansas in 2014 and the message to Nathan in Hebrew carved into a large rock found there at the same time, where Honobia Creek empties into the Little River, less than two miles from where the men now sat. Addison finished with the attack on Marsha's car which took her life and came close to taking the lives of Sam's young family. Sam added in details of his own personal experiences up until the attempted abduction of his daughter in his own home by what he could only describe as aliens.

Next, was Trent followed by Nathan, they didn't elaborate much on their shared experiences in Talihina in 2014, mainly because Addison and Sam had already covered those incidents in their own words. Both men told of their encounters with strange creatures in Afghanistan to a point, but there was much they couldn't disclose as many of their operations were classified and they were both subject to the Uniform Code of Military Justice or "UCMJ". They could be punished under those laws by disclosure of classified information. Josh quietly took in the stories from all six men. Noting how so many different men had come together from different walks of life and now were engaged in a battle with forces they did not understand.

Boomer and Levi were involved almost by chance, they just happened to be in the right spot when the whole phenomenon fell basically in Boomer's back yard. The same could also be said of Addison and Sam, the phenomenon had fallen in their laps as well. However, their own personal revelation had now become a fight for survival. Their lives and fortunes had been changed because they had chosen to fight the enemy. They had both lost friends and loved ones in the struggle, and they were both determined to see the fight through to the bitter end. Joshua wondered if either of them were aware of how bitter the end could be. Boomer, Levi, Addison, and Sam all had one thing in common, location. Josh knew the evil they were battling had chosen this geographical region to curse and spread its dark spiritual plague. Nathan and Trent were a different case altogether both had basically stumbled upon their part of this battle solely because of their military service.

The only difference being Nathan pursued the fight going back into the regular Army after being involved in the situation in Talihina two years ago, even to the point of managing to pass through Special Forces Training and getting assigned to General Malcom Henderson's Titan unit that hunted down and destroyed these paranormal enemies of God. Trent was still a bit of a mystery, he seemed to be just along for the ride. Josh wasn't sure if it was just a fool's need for adventure, or if the young sergeant looked upon it as his patriotic duty. Josh could only trust that God had the combat medic involved for a reason that would be apparent in good time.

Josh stood to talk; the other six men sat quietly in anticipation, "What I have to say is going to take a while. I suggest we take a ten-minute break, so you can relieve yourselves, or get something to drink as I will probably take longer than the six of you together to share my story and my opinion of why we're here and what we're fighting. So please take a quick break so I can have your full attention."

The men got up and stretched and proceeded to tend to whatever needs they had, all were back in less than five minutes, and all seemed to be in eager anticipation of his words. Joshua looked at their faces, and it hit him that whatever lay ahead in the next hours or days would depend on what he was able to communicate to them now at this time. Yes, they were all skilled men, any could handle themselves in a fight and all of them could endure things most average men couldn't. Yet he knew that none of them had yet been told the true nature of their enemy, they were still assuming for the most part their fight was an earthly fight. Only Addison seemed to have a true grasp of what they were up against, but Josh doubted if he knew to what extent the manifestation of evil was in this time and in this place. Silently he prayed before talking. *Dear Heavenly Father, use my words, to share my experiences and knowledge of your enemies to these men. Don't let me fail them or you my God, my creator. Amen.*

Josh took a deep breath and began, "Trent, I started sharing this with you while we waited on Nathan, yesterday evening. At the time I had no idea we would be blessed with the company of Boomer and Levi, so You'll hear a little of what I was talking about last night again, but we'll go a bit deeper into the discussion, each of you men need to hear this information, so you can effectively deal with what we're up against. I've come to this point in my life and your lives for one reason and one reason only. Because God put me here in this place and this time, he put me in similar challenges and mysteries before, long before most of you were born."

"I'm here by his grace to do one thing, educate you on the identity of your enemy. My experiences are different in some ways from yours, but I'm here to tell you we're fighting the same enemy no matter in what form they manifest themselves. If you want to know why you've encountered the things you've encountered, fought the things you've fought, and lost the loved ones and friends you've lost...I can tell you right now where all of this started." Josh could tell, Addison, Sam, and Nathan were following him down the path and were anticipating his answer to be what they too knew it was."

"As for the other three men, all looked a bit confused but none the less excited to have revealed to them when and where this strangeness had first begun. It didn't start in Roswell, New Mexico in 1947 at the UFO crash site, it didn't start at Bluff Creek California in 1967 when those two cowboys filmed a Sasquatch. It started here." He said holding up Boomer's Bible that had been laying on a nearby table. "It started in Genesis Chapter Three, after Adam and Eve had both eaten the forbidden fruit. The serpent had deceived Eve into eating the fruit and she in turn gave it to Adam to eat. When God confronted the serpent, he said. **'Because thou hast done this, thou art cursed above all cattle, and above every beast of the field; upon thy belly shalt thou go, and dust shalt thou eat all the days of thy life. And I will put enmity between thee and the woman, and between thy seed and her seed; it shall crush they head and thou shalt bruise his heel.'** God declared a war on Satan at this moment. It would manifest into a seed war later in Genesis, Chapter Six"

"What do you mean by seed war?" Trent asked, interrupting Josh.

"Let me read to you from Chapter Six and we can discuss it. 'The Nephilim were on the earth in those days, and also after, when the sons of God came into the daughters of men, and they bore children to them. Those were the mighty men who were of old, men of renown.' Most of you probably have never been exposed to a serious study of the meaning of Chapter Six in the Old Testament, and those who have studied it were probably taught the Sethite view as opposed to the Angel view. Many graduates of Seminary Schools have no idea that there are two schools of thought when it comes to Genesis Chapter 6. I'll cover the Sethite view first. In the Sethite view the Sons of God are portrayed as Godly men from the line of Seth, and the Daughters of Man are portrayed as women from the wicked line of Caine."

"The original Hebrew text does not support this theory. Celsus and Julian the Apostate used the traditional "angel" belief to attack Christianity. Julius Africanus resorted to the Sethite interpretation as a more comfortable ground, rather than defending the Word of God, and what had been taught for centuries. Cyril of Alexandria also repudiated the orthodox "angel" position with the "line of Seth" interpretation. Augustine also embraced the Sethite theory and thus it prevailed into the Middle Ages. It is still widely taught today among many churches who find the literal "angel" view a bit disturbing. The Sethite view came along some five centuries after the resurrection of Christ. Which you can take to mean even Jesus Christ when reading or speaking from the Torah, what we now call the Old Testament, He was aware of and speaking of the Angel Theory."

Trent held his hand up somewhat sheepishly. "Go ahead, Trent," Josh replied, a bit amused.

"Sir, I'm not trying to be the class clown and the Good Lord knows I've neglected any serious study of the bible, but I just don't get where this is going, much less what this has to do with what we're dealing with."

300

"I understand, Trent, and I'm trying to get there, be patient and relax. You won't be ready to be a television evangelist when I'm done, but you will have a fundamental knowledge of why we're here and what we're up against. Do you recall stories of Noah and the Great Flood?" Josh asked.

Trent nodded his head, and Josh continued, "According to what most of us are taught, the Lord saw how great the wickedness of the human race had become on the earth, and that every inclination of the thoughts of the human heart was only evil all the time. The level of sin and corruption among the human population was staggering people thought about doing evil all the time. So according to the Sethite view the Great Flood came about only because of the sin of man, which I might remind you, has never been extinguished."

"Man still sins to this day. In fact, our sin is just as wicked as it was in the days of Noah. Take for example The Holocaust, and the millions of people murdered by the likes of Hitler, Stalin, and Mao. Think about the murdering of millions of innocent babies through what could be described as nothing more than an abortion industry, the pornography industry, the child pornography industry, human trafficking, the lawful rape, murder and mutilation of women in some societies, unchecked criminal activity in governments across the planet, including our own. There are world leaders that torture and starve their own citizens to hold onto their power. You've got preachers on television who are only interested in money, stealing and lying to their viewers just to keep the dollars flowing, you've got priests that are molesting young children and going unpunished. If God were going to destroy mankind simply over sin, we would be under water now, instead we have a way out we have a savior in Jesus. The Sethite view doesn't allow for the difference between humanity at this point and humanity at the time of Noah though, but even it is subject to change."

"Okay, gentlemen, now that I have you all looking confused, all of you except for Addison and Nathan, I'll try and explain the difference between our civilization and civilization in the time of Noah and the difference between the two. The difference gentlemen is simple, it's called DNA. So far, our gene pool has not become the abomination that it was in the time of Noah. To explain this, we will once again go back to Chapter Six of Genesis, so once again let me read to you, **'The Nephilim were on the earth in those days, and also afterward, when the sons of God came into the daughters of men, and they bore children to them. Those were the mighty men who were of old, men of renown.'** The Nephilim the Torah speaks of were the offspring of

Fallen Angels and Human Women. They were an abomination, a mixture of angel DNA and human DNA. Demigods, small g gods. They were larger, stronger, and possessed angelic properties normal humans did not. This was not a union of the human men of the line of Seth and human women from the line of Caine. As most seminary schools would have you believe as they promote the Sethite view. This was a deliberate attack on the human genome by Satan himself. He knew a Messiah could not come in human flesh if the human flesh were corrupted by angelic DNA. That is why I say what happened in Chapter Four developed into a seed war."

"In the ancient Hebrew Text of Genesis Six uses, the Hebrew term for sons of God which is Bene HaElohim and is consistently used in the Old Testament to mean angels or heavenly beings. It literally means a "direct creation of God." In our natural state, we are not sons of God, but instead, sons of Adam. Adam was a direct creation of God, and besides Jesus Himself, Adam is the only man referred to as a "son of God. The term used for "daughters of men in the text is "Benoth Adam" or daughters of Adam. This is not a segment of family branch such as the line of Caine, but rather humanity period, when referring to the women."

"The Torah does not say. Bene Seth and Benoth Caine. It says what it means which is Sons of God, (Angels), and Daughters of Men, (Human Females). These Nephilim as they became known were savage giants who pillaged the earth and endangered humanity. Along with their leader, they became corrupt, teaching humans to make metal weapons, cosmetics, and other necessities of civilization that had been kept secret. They continued to take human women to the point where humanity as God intended was close to disappearing. If you read in Genesis Six Chapter Nine you will see it says, Noah was perfect in his generations. This doesn't mean Noah was perfect, yes, he was a Godly man. However, he was perfect in his generations. His bloodline was not tainted by the blood of the Nephilim. Neither was the blood of his wife, or the wives of his sons."

"God sends Archangel Uriel to warn Noah of a great flood to rid the earth of the Nephilim. God was saving humanity from becoming a genetic sewer. He flooded the earth save for Noah and his family and the animals carried within the arc. Of course, this didn't stop Satan, he tried again, he had four hundred years to fill the promise land with giants once again hoping to thwart God's promise to his chosen people. This is one of the reason's God instructs Joshua and Caleb to destroy every man, woman, and child, in some of the tribes of Canaan. It wasn't because our God is a blood thirsty God, it was because the devil was trying to deny the promise that God had made to his chosen people."

Josh paused for a moment looking at the men, "How are we doing is everyone following me so far?"

The men nodded, and once again, Trent raised his hand and Josh nodded his direction." This is interesting stuff and I think I'm keeping up, but I still don't know how this relates to what we're doing. I can understand the giants, heck I've seen one that Nathan here dispatched personally. What does this have to do with what we're facing? What does this have to do with hairy monsters, and aliens in UFOs. I'd venture to say none of us in here are Jewish and this information would be fitting were back in the middle east, but it isn't clicking in my mind for what we're facing here in Oklahoma."

"Great question, Trent, and I'm glad you asked it, because it serves as a great transition to our current problem. Just a couple of last words on the Nephilim. Not only did these fallen angels corrupt human flesh, but they also corrupted the flesh of almost every creation God put on this planet. The strange beings you hear about such as Sasquatch, Loch Ness monster, Jersey Devil, Mothman, Demons, these are all entities brought on by the fallen angels tampering with God's creations. The stories you've read or hear about, concerning gods and demigods from many of the post flood cultures can be traced back to the Nephilim," Josh said.

"Wait, you said these fallen angels are responsible for many of these other entities, like demons. I thought demons were fallen angels," Boomer said looking a bit confused.

"I did too, Josh was just explaining the difference to me about the time you two showed up last night," Trent said.

"Great question, Boomer, and I'll be glad to explain the difference." Josh said excitedly, the other men were impressed with the elder man's energy and excitement. "Angels are a direct creation of God, and enormously powerful, even the fallen ones. Demons are nothing more than evil spirits, in fact a lot of Christians, me included believe that demons are the spirits of the dead Nephilim. They are an abomination, they can't go to heaven, and God for his own reasons has not yet cast them into hell. They walk the earth in constant hunger and thirst, they are always looking for a body to possess so they can quench their hunger and thirst as well as their other physical desires. Okay, we're starting to come to how we arrived in our current situation."

"We're all involved in this battle, but we came here along different paths. A few of us have paid a heavy price to get here, there's a good chance we'll

303

pay even more before it is over. Addison and I grew up with a large Choctaw influence in our lives. Through listening to spoken tribal histories and the stories of our fathers, creatures like the Shampe, or what you call Sasquatch, Bigfoot, or Relics were always a reality to us. Through our tribal upbringing and oral traditions. So, when things like the troubles in Honobia started happening in this area back in 2000, and what occurred around Talihina in 2014, I doubt either of us were too surprised. What was surprising was the violence and the shear dedication to that violence the creatures possessed. I can't speak for Addison, but for me it was a surprise."

"It was for me as well," Addison added.

Josh smiled at Addison saying, "I thought as much, according to the legends I grew up hearing other than occasionally encountering a Okla Chito, that was hungry, mad, or injured, they were rarely a problem. A simple offering such as dropping part of the meat or fruit you were carrying was enough to stop any aggressive behavior, which was rare anyway. Usually if Okla Chito were encountered, they went on their way intent on avoiding any further contact. Then I joined the Navy and became a fighter pilot, no I didn't encounter any flying Okla Chito."

"What I did encounter was the same evil force that seems to be in control of your Relics. I won't refer to the ones we're up against as Okla Chito, or Sasquatch, or Bigfoot. These are something entirely different in my book. I believe the Relics we are facing are in fact Nephilim hybrids made by fallen angels sexually assaulting female Sasquatch. The hybrid is always male, and the hybrid race is kept going by repetition of this same process by the hybrids themselves. They move into an area and proceed to kill or chase off the local males in the clan and breed with the females. Just as they do with any species God created, even man. My people refer to these creatures as Shampe, their created the same as any Nephilim type creature, through unnatural breeding."

"Believe it or not, my first brush with this evil was while flying air combat against advanced aircraft, what were referred to as Flying Saucers back in 1947 above the Antarctic Ocean during what the Navy called Operation High Jump. I won't go into detail, but through the grace of God I was allowed to survive the encounter. I also managed, again with God's grace to bring down one of the strange aircraft which was able to be salvaged from the ocean by one of the ships in the task force."

"You shot down a flying saucer?" Levi asked with a newfound excitement now that the story was focused on flying and aircraft. "What were you flying when you shot it down, he persisted.

"I was flying an F-8F Bearcat, Levi, I would not describe the aircraft we were fighting as flying saucers. They were shaped more like a flying wing, like the B-2 bomber our Air Force has now."

This time Nathan asked a question, "You say it was salvaged; did you guys have to get it off the ocean floor?"

"No, Nathan when I shot the thing down it flopped, for lack of a better description onto the water near a seaplane tender that had a huge crane. The captain of the vessel was very sharp and immediately had the plane connected to the cable of one of the ship's large cranes and lifted it and its occupants onto the deck of the ship."

"Were the occupants as you call them, alive?" Nathan asked.

"No, unfortunately they were dead, well the human was dead, the other occupant looked dead, but now I believe the body was not an alien corpse, I believe it was a suit of some kind, like a space suit, or biological suit. The suit contained organs as well as a circulatory system, but not in the way life on earth has those things."

Nathan's curiosity was now peaking as well, because of the numerous encounters with strange creatures he had been subject to in Afghanistan. "What was the difference other than the shape and size?"

"It wasn't a carbon-based life form, Nathan."

Before Josh could finish, Nathan said, "Let me guess, it was silicon based, wasn't it?"

"That's right, how did you know?" Josh asked.

"We have these little turds we call Sand Fairies in Afghanistan; they play games against both sides. They do things like move IEDs around, or sneak into an area and sabotage vehicles and steal gear. Like I said they have no loyalty to either side, they screw around with everyone and everything over there. They especially love to do anything possible to get people to start shooting at each other, even friendlies will pour fire down on other friendlies because these little bastards will get everyone confused. I've found if you shoot them with a copper round, they spark and fizzle. It's one of the little joys I get from time to time."

"Okay, y'all hold on a minute," Boomer said looking as if he was running out of patience. "Five days ago, I didn't even believe in Bigfoot. To be honest since I saw what I saw Friday morning, I'm not even sure my eyes weren't

305

playing tricks on me. That was until last night when I saw the head of that thing Nathan and Trent had on a spike. Now I'm supposed to believe there's more than those out here? There's these Nephilim, flying saucers, aliens and now fairies, we gonna be fighting them too? I'm not sure I can believe in all this stuff at one time."

Josh understood Boomer's confusion and tried to slow down to ease him into a world that was suddenly much different form the one he'd known for over fifty years. "Boomer, no matter what we discuss here, be it what you saw, or aliens, giants, UFOs, or the creatures Nathan just described. They're all feathers off the same bird, and they're all meant to cause confusion and test our faith."

"It all sounds so crazy," Boomer continued, "I have friends and family that would laugh me out of these mountains if they heard what we're talking about in here." He looked toward Levi who could only smile and give a shoulder shrug in agreement. "Hell, most people up here would run you out of their house and call you crazy for talking about this stuff."

Josh allowed Boomer to finish voicing his concerns then continued, "Boomer that is exactly how most people would react, that is why I've lived as an outcast for so many years. It wasn't so much I wanted to be alone, but what else could I do? People have thought me crazy for years and called me names like 'The Mad Footer' simply because I kept track of the Okla Chito activity. Yet the same people that make fun of somebody who claims to see one will do anything they can to make a buck off it. You can't go into a town for fifty miles around here and not see something to do with Bigfoot., so Boomer in their own way, they believe too. Your question allows me to point out something else as well. There's an old saying that goes. 'Making you think he doesn't exist is the devil's greatest trick.' There is a lot of truth in that statement Boomer."

"It goes right back to the Sethite theory being accepted and taught in most seminary schools. Blame it on the daughters of Caine, not the devil. That way the devil can hide in plain sight. The devil uses our own arrogance to stay hidden. You're thought a fool for believing in the supernatural, so the devil hides there. As I said earlier this all goes back to the Bible, and it starts with the fallen angels defiling human women and other earthly creatures."

"Mankind enables the devil to hide because of our own arrogance when it comes to the supernatural. Look how the evil of the fallen angels has been covered up by the introduction of the Sethite view in Genesis Six. That simple change in scripture could in fact be called the beginning of the coverup of evil.

Think about this, our Lord Jesus Christ walked the earth and taught from the Torah, or Old Testament during his life on earth. If there was something not correct about the written word, don't you think he would have warned us? We didn't need Julius Africanus to correct something Jesus himself seemed not to have a problem with."

Next it was Addison that had questions, "You said the human was dead, Josh. Who was this human and where did he come from?"

"Great question Addison, yes as I said earlier, there were two occupants in the aircraft I downed. One was a human and for lack of a better word, one non-human. The human we identified as Major Rudolph Moritz, of the German Luftwaffe. This guy had somehow gone missing during the war. He was thought to have died flying the German ME-262 jet in combat in early 1945. It was quite a shock for this young Navy Lieutenant to find out I had shot down a high scoring German flying ace and what appeared to be a space man off the coast of Antarctica in 1947."

"A German pilot?" Addison asked, "How did he get there?"

"That was the same question I had at the time Addison, and I didn't get the answer until two decades later." Josh replied.

"Well, you going to share or make us wait two decades?" Trent asked, causing chuckles to break out in the group.

"I don't have two decades to spare," Josh replied causing even more chuckles. "I doubt that any of you will find this hard to believe, but Hitler made a pact with the devil. That is how he rose to absolute power so quickly it also helps to explain the leap in technology the German's enjoyed for a lot of the war. Look at some of the weapons Nazi Germany fielded during the war. The first operational jet fighter, the Me-262, the first operational rocket fighter, the Me-163, The first operational jet bomber, the Ar-234. As if that wasn't enough, they also introduced the world's first cruise missile in the form of the V-1, as well as the world's first long range guided ballistic missile the V-2."

"They also had the first television guided bomb, and another operational jet fighter the He-162. In total they had at least 60 jet and rocket aircraft on the drawing board by the end of the war, many of those were close to becoming operational. What I shot down off Antarctica I believed to had been an operational version of the Ho-229 flying wing jet fighter."

"Okay, if Germany received all this technological help from the devil, why didn't they get the atomic bomb? Did God decide to give us the bomb to counter their advanced weapons." Sam asked.

"Actually, it seems our government made its own deal with the devil for that one, Sam." Josh replied. "I'm confused, why would the devil help both sides?"

"The real question is why wouldn't he, Sam? The devil despises mankind, he's never happier than when we're destroying ourselves. Also don't forget we didn't use the bomb against Germany, we dropped two of them on Japan, a country that by 1945 could only attack our homeland with balloon bombs and had resigned its military to suicide attacks. Basically, we nuked a country who was hell bent on killing itself. I'm not saying the dropping of the bombs wasn't warranted to bring the war to a end quicker, in the long run it may have been more humane. However, I don't think Japan had any idea of how much technology was stacked against them. We were profiting quickly from the technology we captured in Germany along with what we possessed."

"I'm trying to follow you, Mister Nashoba, but what you're describing reflects a global struggle, I don't get what any of this has to do with Talihina two years ago, or Honobia now," Sam added.

"Two years ago, was a fluke, Sam. If that F-16 had not crashed where it did when it did, we probably wouldn't be sitting here right now, our world and our lives would have remained unaffected. Once it did however, it caused a chain of events that opened the door for the enemy to take advantage of the situation and set up shop in the local area. The crash and fire that caused those four juvenile Relics to blunder into the group of bikers they slaughtered just north of town set off a chain reaction of violent events, and the enemy swooped in and took advantage of it."

"The government knew those things were there because the government has its own dark side and not everyone with their hands on controls of the government are human. There are Nephilim walking the earth right now and not just in the form of giants, the angelic DNA isn't just flowing in human hybrids, but Sasquatch as well. Their supernatural side is extraordinarily strong, and they have powers we don't. The ones you were fighting two years ago were Nephilim, though they had not yet matured completely. You thought you killed them, but they're back and they're out for revenge."

"Well, the type we're fighting can't be that bad, Nathan and Trent have already killed one of them. No offense Nathan, I'm just saying we had four to fight and you've already cut them down to three." Sam said.

"Don't let that lull you into a false sense of security, Sam. The one Nathan killed was probably the weakest mentally and physically of the four and Nathan got lucky it was busy beating on a member of the local clan. Also,

Nathan will tell you just before he shot it the creature made eye contact with him. Correct, Nathan?"

"Yes, it made eye contact with me even though I was in a concealed position over 150 yards away looking through a scope. There was no way it could have just spotted me; it was like it knew right where I was, it was one of the creepiest things I've ever seen," Nathan, replied.

Josh paused for a moment to let Nathan's words sink in, then said, "I'm not knocking your ability as a soldier Nathan, but I will say you were blessed it was distracted, the other three won't be as easy. You're here for a reason Nathan, they want you, they want Addison, they want Sam, and they want me. There's reason your name was found carved in the stone next to the remains of the missing pilot. They want you to know, that they saw you were there that night, they want to unnerve you, not only for what you did two years ago, but also for what you've been doing since. You've gone back into the military and have been serving under General Henderson. You've made enemies of some very vile personalities, I'm afraid. I'm not just talking about the dark spirits and Nephilim either. The worst part is you are now becoming an enemy to some of the humans under their control."

"Well, I knew the job was dangerous when I took it." Nathan said smiling. Causing the room to erupt in laughter. After a few moments Addison asked.

"Josh, you're doing a great job of tying all of this together, there is something about this I don't understand. Why here, why Southeast Oklahoma of all places?" Sam asked.

"I have a suspicion it may be the spirit of revival in this area and the enemy intends to squash it Churches are popping up everywhere and I believe a spiritual awakening is coming. I also think that what happened two years ago in Talihina caught the eye of the devil. The four creatures that blundered into the Talihina area fleeing the plane crash and resulting forest fire attracted a lot of energy here, both good and evil. I believe had they not encountered humans they would have milled around and eventually made their way back deeper into the mountains and eventually found another clan to terrorize."

"Instead, they ran into a group of bikers, not just any bikers but a group of actual one percenter types, not pretenders, not wannabes, but the actual apex of real outlaws. One or more of the bikers could have been infested with their own demon or at least under the influence. If the devil can use this violence to put a curse upon the land he will. Don't forget this area was the end of the Trail of Tears for the ancestors of all the Choctaw people here. You could say because of this the area has already suffered a curse. The fact that the locals especially the Choctaw are overcoming that old curse and finding Christ is not something the devil is happy about. The people aren't just overcoming they're thriving."

"Josh, I've always thought that every book in the Bible is important, from Genesis to Revelation. I believe that things will play out just as the Bible says it will, so why fight over this place? Jesus will return and God will win in the end. The war is already won, why fight a battle we don't need to?" Addison asked.

"Great question, Addison. Imagine if we allow the evil here to fester, if we don't fight it, we'll probably be killed by it. Unless of course we all leave behind our homes and never come back. Even that may not be enough, we may be hunted and haunted wherever we go in the world for the rest of our lives. It's not so much about us, it's about the area and the people living here. We're being called to serve them, to serve their futures, not our own. I pointed out the churches and the spiritual revival, but what else do you see?"

"I see people with gambling problems, people with drinking problems, people with drug problems, prostitution, broken homes, hungry children. Our biggest industry in the local area isn't tourism, it's vice. Gambling, drinking, marijuana sales, and all that goes with it. I'm not judging people for any of these activities, but I do feel the vice needs to be balanced with legitimate business and activity. If not, the vice will push everything else out and the area will become a cesspool. I condemn no man or woman for their leisure activity that is between them and God. I do however believe in moderation. The future of the families and children in the area needs more industry than vice."

"If we don't fight, souls that could one day rejoice in heaven will suffer in hell. That is why the devil doesn't want you here. He knows he's going to lose the war, and he's determined to take as many souls with him as possible. He doesn't want a man to come home from working at a job he loves to a happy home and life with his wife and children. He'd much prefer a man come home drunk after toiling at a job he hates. Then proceed to slap his wife around and his children go hungry because he blew his paycheck at a casino. He doesn't want happiness for the people, he wants misery. He wants to drag as many souls as possible into the torment of hell. We're in his way, and we have to be removed."

"So, all we have to do is kill these three Relics, we'll save the area and things will be peachy in the Choctaw Nation?" Sam asked.

Josh replied, "It's not that easy, Sam, I wish it was, but we will always struggle against the evil, against the lie. People have made gods out of everything but God. People are looking to make a god out of Sasquatch. How many people do you see at these local festivals that tell you Sasquatch is a guardian spirit of the forest, and that he speaks to them through mental telepathy? They try and get other people to buy a lie that has been sold to them by devil. I have no doubt they think they're having a communion of some kind with a Sasquatch, but what they're communing with is one of these Relics. The truth they think they are hearing is nothing but a whisper of lies to get them to forget or never know the one true God. The same can be said for the people who think the UFOs are operated by our space brothers. They believe we were seeded here by aliens and that they are our creators, and that Jesus was himself a space alien. They repeat this over and over to anyone who will listen. When the fact is the UFOs, they see are not the technology of a race of people from another star, they are the technology of the Angels. They are operated by fallen angels, or their demonic underlings. The aliens they see are not star people, they're nothing more than demons in disguise. I would not be the least bit surprised if the anti-Christ arrived one day in a flying saucer claiming to be our savior from another star. Its these kinds of lies the devil spreads trying to confuse mankind. Yet again, his biggest lie, is that he himself doesn't exist."

The seven men sat in silence for a few moments, before Trent broke their silence. "You know lately we've been up against worse things than men down range. It's been things like this or worse, you wouldn't believe the last thing Nathan dispatched before we were sent home to get some rest. Funny thing too, how both Nathan and I were in Talihina two years ago and ended up running into each other down range. Now here we are together again in Oklahoma, I sometimes wonder how things happen like that. I mean we're both sent home by the same General and told to get rested, we bump into each other waiting on a plane and here we are again."

"There's a reason for this Trent," Josh said.

"If you mean General Henderson, I'm not sure this was what he had in mind when he sent us home to rest and recover. I'm not even sure if he knew before we got here, we were even aware of each other. I doubt his plan was for us to hookup and come to Oklahoma for a monster hunt."

"Maybe consciously that wasn't his plan, yet something compelled him to send both of you back at the same time." Josh said.

"You mean God then?" Trent asked.

311

"Either God or his Holy Spirit moved your General to make the decisions he did, especially if you guys are fighting the same evil there, we are here. I believe you are."

"Well, only the General or Nathan could tell you that for sure sir. I'm not privy to the actual operations in the field they're doing, I'm a pararescue man, we usually show up after the fact to tend to any wounded and get them out. Of course, we've come in under fire from insurgents to get guys out, but I've never been around when Nathan has dispatched one. Normally all I see is that there's been a fight and we need to get some wounded guys out. Except just before we came home, I saw what Nathan had killed, and these things doesn't hold a candle to it. I'm not really sure why I'm even here."

"God doesn't deal in coincidence Trent, you were put here for a purpose, the same as Nathan, Addison, and Sam. The same as I was when God told me to go to that spot in the forest and be still two years ago. I didn't know why God wanted me there. I simply obeyed his command and did what he led me to do. That is why I was there to distract the creatures when you were most in danger, even though you had no idea I was there, God knew you would be there, and he knew you would need a guardian that evening. I didn't know you, and you had no idea I was there. In fact, I never thought I'd see you again, I assumed I had completed whatever task God had for me concerning you. Now you need a spiritual mentor and once again God has brought us together, not by chance, by design."

"Well, I suppose God has his reasons, we sure came together after some vastly different experiences. Tell us more about your path to this point," Trent replied.

"My first encounter was in 1947 about 15,000 feet above the Antarctic Ocean when I shot down what we called Foo Fighters in those days. My flight engaged and fought these craft that were posing a threat to a Navy Taskforce under the command of Admiral Richard Byrd."

"This foo fighter you shot down was actually a flying saucer?" Trent asked. "Yes, but like I mentioned earlier it wasn't so much a saucer, it was more of a boomerang shape, but yes I slapped his butt down on the water like a pancake on a griddle. I splashed another one off the coast of Vietnam back in 1968. This was more of saucer shape, although it looked like a ring of light."

"So, these things have an Air Force?" Trent said, concerned.

Josh chuckled a bit before continuing, "I guess you could put it that way, but once again I want to make clear to you these things are not from outer space like everyone thinks, they're actually Fallen Angel Technology, and are inter-dimensional, not inter-planetary."

"So, you kicked their butts, in the air and now you're going to kick their butts on the ground?" Trent said jokingly.

"My first encounter I was flying a Grumman F8F Bearcat in nineteen forty-seven, in sixty-eight off Vietnam I was flying an F-4 Phantom. I won the air battles; the enemy won the war so I'm not sure you could say I kicked their butts. The last fight ended my Navy career."

"How did it end your career; did you get labeled as crazy for claiming to shoot down a saucer?" Trent asked.

"The bigger problem was, there was too much proof of what I shot down, it couldn't be denied and in case you didn't know... Our enemy has had a grip on Washington for decades, in fact since the 1940s. I could retire, or die, those were my only two options. So, I came back home and laid low, just minded my own business and lived my life with my wife and family. My boss, an Admiral, who was much like your General Henderson ended up paying the price for my two aerial victories against the enemy. He was killed in a suspicious helicopter crash just a few weeks after I retired. The enemy wanted his pound of flesh and got it."

"I'm sorry to hear that, so why did you pick up the fight again?" Trent asked.

"Because the enemy came here, I don't know if it was to draw me out or to spite me, but they setup shop in this little valley."

"Here? You mean UFOs started showing up here."

"No, not UFOs, aggressive Sasquatch activity began in this area. Have you heard of the Siege of Honobia?" Josh asked.

"Yes, in fact, I listened to the story on a podcast just a couple of days ago. Were you involved in that?"

"No, not officially, but I did get suspicious when I first heard about and it and would work my up the riverbank to the property where the activity was reported. I had to be stealthy, I stayed mostly along the riverbank after dark and watch for activity in the area."

"Did you witness anything?"

"Yes, they had a problem alright, again though it wasn't normal Sasquatch, they were young Nephilim like you guys faced two years ago. The night the people who owned the property killed one, I had crept up close to the house, a little too close. At one point I was between the property owners and the sasquatch themselves, I barely got myself to a safe spot before the shooting started."

"So, they killed one, like they reported."

"Yeah, they killed one, everything happened pretty much like they said. What they didn't realize were these weren't your average Sasquatch; the one they killed just reanimated later, as the ones you guys dealt with two years ago."

"So why did they leave then, yet they're still sticking around this time?" Trent asked.

"I'm afraid I may be part of the problem here." Josh began, little did I know that when I downed the UFOs during my Navy career, that I had made some powerful enemies. Especially one named Nergal. He is a powerful enemy; he is the true power behind all the bad things befalling your families and this entire area. He is in fact a fallen angel, once worshipped as a god during the Nergal he was the Mesopotamian god of death, war, and destruction. He began as a regional, probably agricultural, god of the Babylonian city of Kutha in the Early Dynastic Period 2900-2700 BC. He was still associated with death even at this early period as he represented the high summer sun which scorched the earth, and the afternoon sun of most intense heat, which hindered crop production. The destructive power of the sun was thought to be a manifestation of Meslamtaea's intense fury, and he became associated with war, pestilence, and death, transforming into the universal god known as Nergal by the time of the Ur III Period 2047-1750 BC. He is ancient, since we're using the term Relic, he is perfect description that."

"The UFOs I downed were his. My actions caused investigations by honest government and military officials, who had no idea our government and many others around the planet were being manipulated and controlled by officials that worshipped Nergal and other fallen angels like him all across the world. Their great plan is to corrupt and destroy mankind by any and every means necessary to destroy God's creations and thwart the second coming. For whatever reason gentlemen, my actions against the UFOs interrupted their plans."

"Nergal has his sights set on Southeastern Oklahoma. Trent when I intervened on your behalf two years ago, I came up on his radar and now he wants to destroy me. The F-16 crash two years ago destroyed any chance the four Relics as you refer to them had for breeding with the Sasquatch females local for that area, so they started moving this direction. Addison you and your son fought and defeated them in 2014, so now you're on Nergal's list.

Nathan, Trent you've been fighting the same evil as members of Team Titan. "The Relics we're facing have matured, they're not the same juveniles you faced then. They own this valley and probably every mountain and valley for a fifty-mile radius."

"The natural Okla Chito clans have been in hiding from these four creatures. The smart ones have left the area entirely, other clans have sent away the females and young to safer areas, and the males are sticking around in hopes of defeating the Relics. What is left of the clan in Honobia is a mere remnant of what was here two years ago."

"Why don't these natural Sasquatch fight the Relics and destroy them?" Boomer asked.

"They're powerless because of the presence of Nergal, they can't even defend themselves much less destroy them. They're as much of a victim of these beings as we are. The fact is we have to find a way to not only defeat, the Relics, and Eastman and his men, but ultimately find a way to defeat Nergal as well."

Once again, the men fell silent each lost in his own thoughts. It was Levi, the youngest of the group that broke the silence. "Well, it seems what we need is a battle plan. From what I've hearing and what I've seen the last few days, the world is a scarier place than I ever imagined. This isn't going to come down to simply guts and guns, we're in a serious situation here."

"We have to be fluid and ready to counter any enemies we face, all of them," Josh said.

"Yes, we have the Nephilim Sasquatch, or Relics and that is bad enough. However, we have more than that I'm afraid, we have UFO activity, we also have humans in the area under the control of a territorial spirit."

"You mean they're possessed by demons?" Levi asked.

"Either possessed by demons or under control by something worse. They could be under the control of a territorial spirit, or a living full blooded Nephilim just like out of the Old Testament... A fallen angel/human hybrid just like back in the days of Noah. I've noticed there seems to be some bad blood between you Redstone's and the Forestry Service Agent, am I correct?" Josh asked looking toward Addison.

"Eastman is your biggest threat; I witnessed the venom in his voice and his hatred for your entire family. He has to go, one way or the other. He cannot be allowed to leave this battle in his current condition."

"By current condition, you mean possessed, right?" Levi asked.

"No, young man, by current condition I mean breathing." Josh replied flatly. "Don't be fooled gentlemen, this isn't a school yard fight, this isn't a barroom brawl. This is a life-or-death battle, and you're going to get dirty, by dirty I mean you will be a marked man, if you survive. If you don't kill the threats that are flesh and blood, you won't survive, and make no mistake anything or anybody you kill will absolutely mark you for destruction by the enemy."

"By enemy, who are you referring to, this Nergal character?" Boomer asked. "Yes, Nergal and his minions, both spiritual and physical. You may very well have elements of the federal government after you as well."

"Just whose side is the federal government on?" Boomer asked.

"It's not on our side, I can tell you for sure. Maybe things will change in January when the new administration takes over, but I don't know if the new president can offer any of us protection. I realize he has declared war on the swamp as he calls it, but I don't think he has any idea just how deep the swamp is and even less aware of the fact that the swamp extends out from Washington DC. It is in fact, a worldwide cabal of human and non-human entities that inhabit this swamp. There are good people in government that are working for your benefit, but they are outnumbered and out maneuvered at every turn. Some of the people you trust are part of the cabal and you'll be surprised in the coming years by their treachery. I believe you're going to start witnessing unimaginable political corruption unveiled soon. Once this starts happening the new administration will be under siege like never seen before."

"The seeds planted the past couple of decades by the other administrations have taken root and the fruit will be poisonous lies and behavior spilling into the streets and glorified by the media, celebrities, and followers of Satan who hold high political office and influence. You will be hated, scorned and hunted for what happens here gentlemen, make no mistake. Addison, Sam, Nathan, Trent, and I are already on their radar. Boomer, you and Levi are still in the clear, however just giving us shelter so far is enough to bring down the wraith of the Cabal. So, if you have any qualms about getting involved, now is the time for us to part company so we don't involve you any further."

Boomer looked thoughtful for a moment, then said, "No, I'm not running from these turds. This valley is my home and I'll fight tooth and nail for it. I'm not real sure I want to get my young cousin here involved." Looking toward Levi.

"Well, my dad didn't raise me to run from trouble, and I'm way more afraid of disappointing him than I am of any man, or boogeyman. I'm staying," Levi said without hesitation.

"Well, you two are unknown right now and that makes you our aces in the hole. We need to keep it that way for absolutely as long as possible." Josh stopped speaking when Levi snorted.

"Well, this isn't the first time Boomer and I have been called Ace Holes."

The room erupted in laughter again, which seemed to fill Nathan with optimism. *I'll fight beside a man with a sense of humor any day. A man with no sense of humor is a man that will get you killed*, he thought. Boomer spoke up suddenly, "Levi and I ran across something the other day, you guys need to see. I'm not sure what it is, but it must be important."

Josh, looked at Boomer, then nodded toward Nathan, "Do you think you two could sneak in close enough for photos and not be seen?" Both men nodded confidently that they could.

"Good get photos, and any information you can. Levi, I have a special mission for you. We need secure communications with Sam and Addison's people in Talihina. Do you think if I gave you the money you could get your father to purchase some prepaid cell phones? Once they figure out, they can't find any of us, they'll start tracking phones if they haven't already. Plus, we can use everyone's regular phones later to draw them out to a location of our choosing."

"My dad will be thrilled to help," Levi replied.

Nathan thought about the plan for the phones and said to Boomer. "I love the way this guy thinks, let's not screwup this recon, this is one guy I don't want to disappoint."

"Yeah, no kidding, I'd feel like a turd in a punch bowl if I let this man down." Boomer said before walking over and whispering something to Levi.

Nathan watched as Levi look quizzically at Boomer and said, "You want what?"

Boomer, once again leaned in and whispered but his body language was much more forcible this time. Levi grinned and nodded, Boomer turned back and said to Nathan, "Cousins… Come on Nathan, you can teach me some of that Army sneaking and I'll teach you some hillbilly sneaking."

"You got a deal!" Nathan said.

# CHAPTER THIRTEEN

# Soul of Darkness

*"While there remains one dark soul without the light of God, I'll fight."*
*-William Booth*

## Wednesday, 30 November 2016 11:00 AM CST, Kiamichi Mountains Honobia OK

Paul Eastman looked down on the headless corpse of the beast. He could feel his anger rising over the handiwork of Nathan Parks. *How did they do this? How do these morons beat me to the punch time after time?* he asked himself. He didn't ask long because his anger quickly gave way to fear, the fear of what his superior would do when he became aware of this failure.

"How do you think they killed this Bigfoot, Boss?"

One of his underlings asked, mouth hanging agape. Eastman viciously backhanded the man sending him sprawling to the hard rocky ground.

"Idiot, you will call them biologicals and nothing else. This isn't a Finding Bigfoot episode; this is a war, and these biologicals are hard to come by. The real question is how did I get saddled with mentally challenged subordinates like you? This is your fault; you and these other idiots were supposed to come in here last night and take the two men that were here out. Now I have a dead biological and the men you were supposed to dispose of have escaped to God knows where, and you're asking stupid questions!" Eastman suddenly flinched at his own referral to the almighty. He knew if his superior heard him, he would suffer his own chastisement. The man he struck sat on the ground, rubbing his jaw, looking at Eastman full of menace.

"Is that the dirtiest look you've got? It's not scaring me, maybe if I kick your teeth in, you'll manage an even dirtier look." The man removed his hand from his face, then, using both arms, pushed himself up onto his feet, careful to stay out of the reach of his angry boss. His face pointed toward the ground, fearful of Eastman's gaze. Eastman felt a twinge of pleasure, almost sexual in nature, at the apparent fear the man had of him.

Eastman slapped him again, sending him to the ground once again. Two weeks ago, in the same situation, Paul Eastman would be the one who had been backhanded and now standing cowed and gelded. However, since his pact with Nergal, he now had power over men and women he'd never dreamed of before. It had been years since he'd been with a woman; last night, he'd had two. He had found them in a bar in Hochatown some thirty miles South. He'd never met them before, and they had never met each other. Yet somehow, last night, he knew he could have them both, and for the whole night or however long as he wanted. Just like he knew the blonde's boyfriend would not dare object to his leaving the bar with his woman. He'd left the two women standing half-dressed and bewildered standing outside the expensive cabin he was renting with state money while working in the area.

He remembered how the two women stood there, not knowing what to do; the blonde was crying and exclaimed, "What happened, where is my fiancée?"

"Evidently your fiancée didn't think you were worth fighting for, maybe he'll take you back... Then again, maybe he won't." Eastman felt pure joy when the blonde woman broke down, sobbing furiously.

She held her hands over her face repeating, "What happened? What happened?" The brunette was made of stronger stuff; at first, she assumed that Eastman had slipped them both a date rape drunk of some kind. Then there was a tender voice in her heart, it soothed her and told her she had succumbed to an evil force, and now she had nothing more to fear. "Hey, jerk, if you're going to leave us stranded, at least point us in the direction of Hochatown." Eastman pointed south, "Keep walking about five miles and you'll come to 259. Take a right from there you have another twenty-five miles or so. Maybe a lonely log truck driver will give you a ride. You can pay for the ride by taking it out in trade. Tramps always find a way to pay their way." Eastman laughed as he saw the flash of anger in the brunette woman's brown eyes. Then the woman looked at him strangely, as if she could see something he didn't.

"You're not going to make it," she said in a matter-of-fact manner as she reached to comfort the blonde.

"What did you say?" Eastman demanded.

The woman turned around, facing him once again. She looked at him without fear and said, "You're not going to make it, your ticket is going to get punched soon." Then she turned to the blonde, saying, "Come on, honey, walk with me, we'll get you back to your man. This wasn't your fault; everything is going to be okay."

"That's right, young tramps always have a resource, and they always find a way." Eastman sneered. The brunette turned around, only this time there was no anger in her expression, just a look of peaceful determination.

"Our resource isn't in our bodies; our resource is in the Lord. He'll guide us through this."

"Of course, he will, just like he did last night?" Eastman shouted, laughing as the women were beginning to put distance between them and himself. Once again, the brunette turned around. "He never left me; it was me that turned my back on him. It was me that put myself in the lair of the enemy, I'm forgiven, she's forgiven," she said, nodding to the blonde who was starting to regain her strength and composure, "You're not, somehow you've cast your allegiance to enemy, the bill will come due soon and..."

The sound of an approaching vehicle cut off the woman's words; a white dual cab Chevrolet pickup came to a stop near the women. It carried an insignia on the door of one of the many timber contractors in the area. A large young man exited the truck and talked with the women. Eastman could tell he was of Native American descent. The man's strong jaw, jet-black hair, and dark eyes gave him the look of a Hollywood actor. The man's face displayed concern and empathy as he helped the two women into the truck's rear cab. The man's handsome face had a comforting expression of compassion as he reached into a cooler that rested in the bed of the truck grabbing two bottles of water, and handed them to the brunette before closing the door.

He glanced at Eastman after he closed the rear door of the truck. The man's expression never wavered, but Eastman now saw the face of a warrior. The compassion was still there, but now there was also strength, courage, and determination in the face. Along with something else, something he had seen in the face of the Redstone's, Nathan Parks, and the Joshua Nashoba. The man said nothing; he merely climbed back into the truck and sped down the road. The face haunted Eastman for a short time, but only a short time. By the time he had arrived at Honobia, he was feeling quite pleased with himself until, of course, he was taken to the headless corpse of one of Nergal's beasts.

Looking down at the man he'd just backhanded, the moment of weakness he'd felt looking into the eyes of the good Samaritan had passed. He was feeling better than he had ever remembered. I lord over men and women both, he thought to himself. I am a deity walking the earth. His moment of self-actualization was short-lived, however, as he felt a tingling in his right forearm. Turning his hand over, he could see a white glow under his skin; it was the implant Nergal had inserted the night he first encountered him. For a moment, he felt sick; his newfound self-importance flushed away instantly like so much waste down a toilet. He walked away a few yards, separating himself from the men milling around the corpse.

Quickly he pulled out his cell phone, and pulling up the contacts list, he went to the first contact. There was no name, just an asterisk. He hit the *, there was no ring or any hint of a cellular connection, just the high-toned snakelike hiss of the voice of Nergal.

**Nergal:** You are failing me, Paul.

**Eastman:** No, Master, my men have failed. I am here to set this right and rid the area of your enemies.

**Nergal:** One of my minions is lying dead at your feet. Is that your idea of setting this right? Maybe I put too much faith in you as I did, Mason. Maybe I should allow my creatures to consume your life the way they did Mason's.

**Eastman:** No, Master, please. This is a setback, nothing more. I will accomplish your instructions; I will destroy your enemies, Master. Your enemies are mine, and I will see that they are all dead and rotting in these mountains, just as I ensured the wife of the elder Redstone was destroyed.

**Nergal:** Yes, Paul, you have one minor victory to your credit. One, my instructions were to kill all the Redstone women. There are still two left, the wife of Samuel and her daughter; why are they not dead?

**Eastman:** A fluke Master, a local man happened to be in a position to interfere before the other two could be finished off.

**Nergal:** Yes, your choice of an ambush site was questionable, Paul. My minions were damaged and scattered; you're not exactly the Field General I hoped you would be. Now, one is dead and cannot be reanimated. There was a witness; not only did he see the creatures, but he also damaged them. Not even Mason screwed up that bad. Why should I trust you to carry out my plans after a failure like this?

**Eastman:** There will be no more mistakes, Master. I will not allow any. I will accomplish the mission you put before me.

**Nergal:** I chose Mason because he was a man who lived to kill and terrorize people. However, I learned that wasn't enough. I chose you for the same reason; although killing isn't your first choice, you have a need to lord over others and impose your will upon them. You like that, don't you, Paul? You love having power over people? I saw in it you when you demanded your position with the Forestry Service. I saw it when you terrorized the man and his son and the way you took the two women last night and imposed your wicked carnal desires upon them. I saw it just now as you slapped the agent to the ground as if he was no more than a whimpering dog begging for your favor. You love it, don't you, Paul? WELL, DON'T YOU, PAUL?

**Eastman:** Yes, Master, yes! God help me; I love it.

**Nergal:** SILENCE! Never use that word again. God isn't giving you your current bounty of power, I am. If you speak that word again, you will suffer the same fate as Mason. There are millions of quivering human wretches like yourself who would do anything for the power you now enjoy.

Eastman: Yes, Master, forgive me. It was an expression, nothing more.

**Nergal:** Fortunately for you, I still have much work that needs human hands to accomplish. The remaining Redstone wife seems to be more of a spiritual warrior than the men in the family. Last night she thwarted an attempt to do away with her and the child and the Redstone men. I'll need you and your men to finish the task. If your targets have disappeared. Find them, and when you do, kill the soldier Nathan Parks first. The corpse you see on the ground is his handiwork; he is much more dangerous than before.

**Eastman:** Master, I will begin searching immediately. I have no idea where they are. I have made a call to have their cell phones tracked. I should have some idea of their whereabouts soon.

**Nergal:** You want to draw them out, find their women, bait them in, then kill their women before their eyes. I have no more minions to send you like the one they killed. Of the three left, one is the Alpha; he is stronger and smarter than the other two. When you find our enemy, attack them with a fury they can't stand against, use the men I have given you and the three minions. Make sure the Alpha is in place, and in the attack, he will be the most dangerous to them. I am sending you more soldiers for your battle. They will come from the sky, and they will operate alongside the three minions. Keep your human soldiers in reserve; only use a few of them to finish off the Redstone women. Do not let the humans you command near my minions or the beings coming to assist them, or they will be destroyed. Make this happen, Paul, and you'll be rewarded. Fail, and I will destroy you, and you'll burn in the pit forever. You made your choice which side you're on; victory or agony are your only choices.

The phone went dead in Eastman's hand. The glow of the implant under his skin died as well. For a moment, he felt as if he was going to have a stroke; his body was weakening and wanting to fail him. Then quickly, he started recovering his strength and determination were coming back stronger than before. Looking back toward the corpse of the beast, he saw the man he'd slapped still sitting on the ground, still rubbing his jaw. He walked over, and the man looked up at him, fear in his eyes. Eastman reached out to offer his hand.

"Get up," he said. The man warily took his hand, not sure if he would be slapped down a third time. "What is your name again?"

"Waters." The man replied. "Well Waters, I've got a job for you, get it done right and you'll get off my shit list and you'll be rewarded handsomely. Screw it up, and it will be the last thing you screwup, understand?"

The man nodded his head, "Good, you're in luck, you don't have to worry about these things anymore. Surely you can handle a woman and child can't you Waters?"

The man nodded his head, "Good, I love confidence. Get this done and I'll pay you a bonus equal to a year's pay and I can get you a week anywhere you want with all the women you want. Does that sound like something you'd be interested in, Waters?"

"Absolutely sir."

"I need you to be a killer Waters, a stone-cold killer, a killer of women and children." Eastman was a little surprised to see a smile come over the man's face.

"That's my specialty, Sir," Waters replied as a sinister smile spread across his bruised face.

## Wednesday, 30 November 2016 11:30 PM CST, Kiamichi Mountains Honobia, OK

Boomer and Nathan lay prone on the forest floor; they were well hidden by the tall wild grass and small brush covering the local mountains. The grass had turned an orange-tan color over the past two weeks; most of the leaves on the scrub brush had not yet given up its green hues to the chill of Autumn. Nathan was busy peering through his binoculars at the object Boomer had told him about back at the cabin.

"Can you see it?" Boomer asked in a whisper.

"Yes, I see it," Came the calm reply from Nathan.

"Well, what is it?"

"It's an Obelisk," Nathan replied.

"What is an Obelisk?"

"It's a four-sided tower with a pyramid on top."

"Well, I aint been to no Army Special Forces Commando School but I got that much figured out. I mean what's it for?" Boomer hissed softly.

Nathan smiled, keeping the object in view through his binoculars, he replied, "Sorry, Boom, I wasn't trying to be a wise guy. I don't know what it is for, hopefully Joshua can help us figure it out. I do know the Romans and Ancient Greeks were big on them. I need to get a picture of this, so we can show it to Joshua."

Putting down the binoculars, he reached into his pack and extracted what looked to Boomer like a tiny toy helicopter.

"What the hell is that?" Boomer asked.

"It's called a Black Nano, it's a small drone with three cameras in it. I'm going to fly it over to the Obelisk and take photos of it that we can show to Josh."

"It looks like a toy helicopter Levi would have had when he was a little boy."

"Basically, it is, don't tell Trent about this or he'll try and steal it. Those Air Force boys get jealous if you have something that flies, and they don't."

Boomer watched, fascinated as Nathan dug another object out of his pack. This object looked like a cell phone but slightly larger and protected in an olive drab case.

Nathan looked skyward for a moment, and a smirk came across his face. "Something funny?" Boomer asked.

"I was just thinking, First Sergeant Briggs whose still back in Afghanistan used to give me a hard time when we were training to use these things. I have a habit of looking up in the air when I go to make the satellite linkup with the controller," Nathan said, holding the device up where Boomer could see it. "He'd always say, you aint going to see that satellite wink at you Parks. Get the connection and get that little bastard airborne before something takes a chunk outta your butt."

"Looks like you still got the habit," Boomer whispered in a chuckle.

"Yeah, I wish he and General Henderson were here now, we could use them and a few more troops. This whole thing is getting a lot more complicated than I expected."

"You have doubts we can handle this?" Boomer asked.

"We'll handle it, we've got no choice. Failure isn't an option," Nathan said as the small drone came to life with a light purring sound.

The drone rose to a height of about four feet off the ground then buzzed away in the direction of the Obelisk. It buzzed between the upper and second wire of the barb wire fence that separated Boomer's property and the hunting lease. As it came to Obelisk, it stopped and hovered in front of it. It descended to the base and then rose to the top of the object before moving to one side to repeat the process on each of the four sides of the object. As it hovered and photographed the fourth and final section of the object, Nathan heard Boomer say, "Vehicle coming you'd better bring that thing back."

Nathan lifted his head, and he too could hear the vehicle lumbering over the rough and rocky into the area of the Obelisk. Boomer was impressed when instead of retrieving the tiny drone, Nathan flew it over twenty feet and had it land deftly on the damaged branch the young boy had shot the preceding Friday morning when his buck fever had caused him to take a not so accurate or safe shot.

"What if they see it?" Boomer asked.

"They won't," Nathan replied confidently. "Plus, if they get out, we'll get some great videos and voice recordings. Let's get behind those trees and just below that rise. They won't be able to see us don't raise your head or expose anything of yourself. With any luck we'll get more info than we expected."

The two men backed out slowly in a slow reverse crawl until they were concealed behind a slight rise with a group of trees between them and the fence line. Nathan motioned to Boomer to look at the display on the device he held in his hand. Although the drone sat quietly on the tree branch, it was positioned where its three small cameras covered a wide arc. Even on the small screen, Boomer could clearly see the Obelisk and the black Hummer H3 approaching; the vehicle looked brand new and came to a stop about twenty feet from the Obelisk. The doors opened, and four men exited the vehicle and walked to the Obelisk, and began to inspect it.

"Who are they?" Boomer whispered.

"Men in Black, and the guy in the lead is Paul Eastman, I'm not even sure he's human anymore."

"Men in Black, are you serious?"

Nathan nodded and brought his index finger to his lips giving Boomer the sign for silence. Three of the men were armed. Nathan easily identified the M-4 carbines strapped to their shoulders; Eastman did not carry any weapons

Nathan could see. Probably too important to get his own hands dirty. Nathan thought as he listened to the conversation of the four men.

"I'm not exactly excited about where this is placed, too close to that fence line. What do we know about the property owner on that side of the fence?" Eastman asked one of his men.

"Just your usual hillbilly boss, we've done extensive investigations into the locals. This guy doesn't wander the property too much as far as we can tell. He's usually working, out on his motorcycle, or hanging out at the house he has on the far side of the property. He has a lot of guests from time to time, but they seem to hangout around the house usually sitting around the fire, drinking and raising hell. He's known as a nice guy, but he has a reputation of being somebody you don't want to push too far. One of those guys you don't want to anger, because he'll spare no expense putting right anything he thinks is wrong. Also, he's known to have quite a collection of guns, so we don't want to antagonize him if possible."

Eastman shook his head in disgust. "So basically, we have another Redstone type personality, this whole part of the country is full of these people. Has anyone been monitoring his whereabouts?"

"We've had a helicopter overfly his place just like everywhere else bordering this area. Nothing unusual his house seems to have a lot of visitors like I said earlier, but nothing out of the ordinary for this time of the year. Just mountain people enjoying the cooler weather."

"Any chance he's friends with the Redstone's?"

"None that we can tell, he rarely goes into Talihina, maybe just to get gas or supplies of some type. Most of the time, he heads South to Hochatown or Broken Bow, other than that he hangs out at a cousin's house down along the river to the East."

"Well, the Redstone's, Nathan Parks, and his sidekick as well as this character Joshua Nashoba have all disappeared off the radar. Something stinks, let me know as soon as Waters checks in from Talihina. I'm still not comfortable with this device so close to the fence line."

"Couldn't we move it, Sir?" Eastman's assistant asked.

"No, that damn tower disrupts the signal," he said, nodding toward a cell tower a few peaks away. "The best possible position for this is right here, otherwise communication with the biologicals and the aerials could be disrupted causing them to manifest in the wrong area or not at all. This will have to do, somehow, I must draw the Redstone's and their group back to where they destroyed the biological. They have to be destroyed here on this mountain."

"What does it matter, Sir, as long as they are dead?" the aid asked.

"Dead isn't good enough, there needs to be a blood sacrifice, and atoning for what they've done against my Master, and it must be done here, so his rule of this region can begin."

The aid looked around the area, confused, "I don't understand, why here?"

"No better place, every year more and more people are coming here from Texas, the area feeds their need for what they call freedom. They start out simply enjoying the forests, lakes, mountains and rivers. Many of them get sidetracked, they start leaving their families at home. They return alone for the gambling, drunkenness, drugs, and adultery. The casinos ruin lives and marriages, the drunkenness and drugs take lives in the way of auto wrecks, boating accidents, ATV accidents, and drownings in the rivers and lakes. Do you have any idea how many married men bored with their wives claim they're coming up here to hunt and fish? Instead, they bring their mistress to some cabin for a weekend of debauchery. It's perfect, the cabins are hard to find, tucked away in remote areas, their wives would never dream of coming to snoop around even if they suspected something. It's perfect and it keeps bringing more people every year."

"They come up here and poison their souls, then carry the poison back home to their wives and families. Not to mention the bodies tucked away in these mountains, there are a lot of problems buried in these hills. Most will never be found, you kill them in Dallas, then dump them in a rock crevasse in the Kiamichi's. Even those that don't get pulled all the way in, are here almost every weekend. They spend their money and their time on trinkets, overpriced food, booze, and personal satisfaction. They save nothing, give nothing to charity, they don't waste time helping others, and they don't take time to worship their God. They're too busy worshipping Oklahoma. In another decade or two this area will be as self-destructive as Las Vegas, or New Orleans, only all the ugliness will be hidden by tress and mountains. Those that burn out here, won't leave here. They'll be tramps living on the streets of these small towns causing even more squalor and unhappiness. The locals that profit from all of this will have their own problems, they'll become riddled with greed, worshipping money over their God. Family members with more money in the bank then they know what to do with will fight each other over mere coins. In the end they too, will be swallowed up in their own ruin. Local churches and missions will be overwhelmed with people needing help, as their own coffers dry up from a lack giving since their congregation has departed for their own pursuit of greed and self-indulgence. It's perfect!" Eastman said, smiling.

"I guess I don't visualize the big picture," Eastman's aid said, looking blankly across the tree and grass-covered terrain."

"If you don't find the Redstone's, you won't be seeing anything, you won't even be breathing. Now get in touch with Waters, if he can't find the male Redstone's, he will bring us the lone surviving Redstone wife, then we'll use her to bring them here."

"What about the dead Sasq… err Biological down near the creek, you want us to burn it?"

"No, leave it, I want it to look like nothing has happened since they left the area. You and the others meet me at the little store in Honobia at 5:00 PM sharp, we'll eat and be seen by the locals. I want them to know we're here, maybe it will keep them in their homes at night and out of our business so we can…" Eastman's words trailed off; he began looking around as if he knew he was being watched. Looking into the display on his device, Nathan could tell Eastman was looking right at the clump of trees between Eastman and the slight depression he and Boomer lay in. Then confused, he looked in the opposite direction from Nathan and Boomer; he was looking directly at the branch the tiny drone rested on. To Nathan, it appeared as if Eastman was looking right into the camera lens. Damn it, Eastman, look another direction! Nathan thought to himself, then as if on que, Eastman looked away from the branch and back in the direction they had come from.

"They're here somewhere, I feel them," Eastman told his aid, the followed up with. Come on, let's get back to the others. The men climbed back into the Hummer and drove slowly down the path in the direction they'd come from.

As soon as the Hummer was out of sight, Nathan flew the small drone back to the spot where he and Boomer were still lying prone behind the trees. "Here, use your head," he said as the small drone landed deftly on Boomer's camouflaged hat.

"Very funny," Boomer said, removing the small drone from the top of his hat and handing it to Nathan. Smiling, Nathan gave a nod of his head, and the men began slowly crawling down the shallow slope until it was safe to walk upright back to Boomer's cabin. "We'd better get word to Sam; we're going to need to counter any moves on his family."

Waters stood alongside the highway North of Talihina, wearing an orange high visibility vest and hardhat. He looked through the surveyor's scope at the house Eastman had told him to monitor. His assistant held a grade staff about two hundred feet past the house to give the appearance that the two men were nothing more than surveyors taking measurements for upcoming road construction. The two men were operating out of a decoy vehicle with a magnetic sign reading Daemon Construction and Survey Company in large black letters on the door. There was even a small orange bulldozer under the text. A similarly marked van sat alongside the road 50 yards to the south toward Talihina. Both vehicles had yellow flashing warning lights for added authenticity. Two men milled around the outside the van, one with a measurement wheel and another with a clipboard. They stood around aimlessly unless there was oncoming traffic, then they would act busy as if measuring and recording distances. Their eyes never strayed too long from the home of Sam and Christa Redstone.

Inside the van, two more men were in the back; both wore black tactical dress. Two men were in the van, which also contained weapons, both long guns, and sidearms for all the men in the group. One man peered out the dark tinted windows armed with an M-4 style carbine as the other monitored a laptop on which he was running cell phone tracking software. So far, the phones of Sam and Addison Redstone had been silent. In fact, they were either turned off completely, Christa Redstone's phone was on and active. She had been using it to chat on Facebook as well as ordering items from Amazon. Both men sat quietly, neither interested in small talk. Neither wanted to fail Eastman. It wasn't so much Eastman they feared; it was who Eastman answered to that they really worried about.

Though Eastman was the only man on this operation who had laid eyes on their true leader. The other men in the operation had seen and heard enough to know they did not want to draw any attention to themselves, especially through failure. All the men had started as federal employees, most of them as security of some type. A few were technicians with skills in communications or networking. They all had one thing in common, they had been caught committing various felonies while employed by the federal government. The crimes ranged from theft to sexual assault and even murder.

Each man on the team should be facing years of incarceration in federal prisons for their crimes. Yet, just when things looked the darkest for each of these individuals, a savior appeared. To their amazement, the savior was always a government official. Many times, these saviors would claim they had been sent by some high-ranking member of the house or senate; some were sent by an even higher office. One thing the men all had in common, they either took their current positions or were promised they would not survive their prison terms. Each man knew they were in the employment of the deep state branch of the government for the rest of their lives. They were also aware that failure was not an option; failure meant termination. They also knew that termination in their case was complete, there were no tomorrows. As far as their employment went, few had any complaints. When they were on an operation, they were on it until it was completed. One more thing each man was aware of to their core, they didn't exist on any government employment records, and they were completely expendable. When not on an operation, they were well taken care of. They were rewarded in their downtime to enjoy pretty much anything their hearts desired, from the simple to the sadistic. Whatever they wanted was made available. Since the election earlier in the month, all of them had been on duty. Leadership was stressed, and projects, even small ones, were being pushed with the utmost urgency. A different kind of man had been elected as leader of the country. His campaign promises meant their very existence was in jeopardy. The calls by the public for the new president to drain the swamp meant they had to dig the swamp much deeper. The man monitoring the laptop was shaken away from his boredom when a message box appeared on the screen of his laptop, saying, "Call in Progress." He watched as an incoming call to the Redstone woman's cell phone was receiving a call from Diane Sanders, the woman's mother.

**Christa:** Hello?

**Diane:** Hi, baby, how are you doing?

**Christa:** I'm okay, Mom; just waiting to hear from Sam.

**Diane:** Well, where is he?

**Christa:** Hunting, Mom, you know how men are when they're hunting?

**Diane:** Well, that would depend on what they're hunting, wouldn't it, dear?

**Christa:** Mom! You know Sam's not like that; besides, he is with Addison. They're just hunting to help Addison get over his loss.

**Diane:** Whatever you say, dear, I was thinking maybe you and Erin would like to come spend the night with me so you're not out there all alone.

The man monitoring the phone winced; they were setup to strike the Redstone home. Although they knew the address of Diane Sanders, they had not even thought to give it a proper recon in case they had to move the operation to that location.

**Christa:** Mom, I want to be here in case Sam comes home.

**Diane:** Well, how about Erin, maybe she would like to spend some time with her grandmother?

**Christa:** I don't know, Mom; I'd kind of like to have her with me while Sam's away.

**Diane:** Oh, come on, Christa, don't deny an old woman a night with her Granddaughter!

Christa was confused. What is with Mom this afternoon? She never acts this way? Something about her mother's behavior was off. Must be the holidays. She thought, calling out to her daughter. "Erin, do you want to spend the night with Grandma tonight?" "Okay." The man monitoring the call heard the tiny voice reply in the background.

**Christa:** Okay, Mom, Erin wants to stay with you tonight.

**Diane:** Good darling, wonderful, meet me at Saint Catherine of Siena Catholic Church in about twenty minutes. You can drop her off with me there.

**Christa:** What? Why there?

**Diane:** I'm unloading my car there now; the Police Department is having a Toys for Tots collection there.

**Christa:** Why can't you just come pick her up, or I'll drop her off later?

**Diane:** No, that won't do dear, there's a Santa here, and I want to get our photos taken together, so please hurry and get here before Santa puts his police uniform back on.

**Christa:** Okay, Mom, let me gather her some clothes and be down there as quick as I can.

**Diane:** Wonderful, dear, see you in a few minutes, oh and don't tell Erin. I want her to be surprised.

Christa ended the call and placed her phone on the countertop. She sighed deeply. Why was her mother acting so strange? She shook her head in surrender and went to Erin's room to pack her clothes for her visit.

Water's saw the movement of the corner of his eye; he watched as an obviously pregnant woman with shoulder-length blonde hair walked out of the house, holding a small girl by the arms as she approached the white Escalade. Waters became aware of a vehicle slowing down in front of him. With his eyes focused on the woman and child, he didn't notice the white Talihina Police Cruiser easing up next to him. The window rolled down, and Waters looked into the smiling face of Jimmy Chula.

"Good afternoon, Sir," The police officer said.

"Good afternoon, Officer, I mean, Sergeant," Waters said, noticing the three chevrons on the police officer's shoulder. The police officer was young and fit. Waters could tell by his mannerism that he was professional and not the cliché small-town cop.

"So, when is the state going to work on this road again?" The officer asked waters.

"You know, I really couldn't tell you officer, we just get told where to go and what to survey. For all I know they'll take our measurements and never show up. Sometimes they just want the grade check for erosion and so on."

The police sergeant nodded his head as if considering what Waters had just told him. By now, the woman Waters was supposed to be monitoring was pulling out onto the highway. She waved at Waters and the police officer as she passed.

"People sure seem nice around here." Waters said, trying to make innocent-sounding small talk.

"Yes, lots of good people around here," the officer said, looking down the road toward the van.

Waters didn't like the fact the cop was so curious. Just go! He willed the police officer on silently. Finally, the police officer looked back at Waters and smiled.

"You fellas be careful; it gets dark early now and a lot of people come barreling down this road at high speed in a hurry to get home in the evenings. So, keep your guard up and stay safe."

"We certainly will, Officer," Waters said, waving as the cop pulled away, then muttered under his breath, "Keep moving, moron."

## Wednesday, 30 November 2016, 3:05 PM CST, Saint Catherine of Siena Catholic Church, Talihina, OK

Christa entered the church, and her confusion grew even more. Her mother was there alright, and so were Jeri Chula in her Oklahoma Highway Patrol uniform and Talihina Police Chief Dale Thompkins. There was no Santa Claus, and everyone looked tense.

"What's going on?" Christa asked, "Is Sam okay?" She nervously pulled Erin close to her. She also noticed two other men, one in his mid to late 50s and another younger man, both looked familiar. She didn't know their names but had seen them around town before.

"He's fine, dear, here let me take Erin into the main cathedral. I want to show her the Christmas decorations." Diane said, taking young Erin by the hand and leading her out of the room. The young man she didn't know spoke next.

"Mrs. Redstone my name is Levi Taylor, this is my father George, we live in Ho-nubby, your husband and father-in-law are safe. They're actually at my cousin's cabin just above Ho-nubby in the mountains."

"Okay, so what is this all about?" Christa asked, not sure if it was safe to let her breath escape.

"Sam and Addison shared with the group…"

"The group? What group?" Christa asked.

"Excuse me, let me start from the beginning," the young man said. "Your husband, and father-in-law, along with Nathan, Trent, and Josh are all safe at my cousin's cabin. We all know what happened at your house last night. We're convinced from what Sam described about your encounter that you're more than capable of handling any type of spiritual attacks. However, we got wind of a different kind of threat."

# CHAPTER FOURTEEN

## The High Noon of Midnight

*"A man's duty? Be ready with rifle or rood to defend his home when the showdown comes."*
*~ Edward Abbey*

### Wednesday, 30 November 2016, 3:50 PM CST, Sam and Christa Redstone residence, Talihina, OK

Waters sat in the pickup, looking at his cell phone. He had moved the truck slightly, giving himself a clear view of the driveway into the large cabin-like home of the Redstone's. The woman had returned to her home a few minutes earlier, without the child. *That's okay, the woman is enough,* he thought to himself. His assistant leaned his head against the passenger and fell asleep. His soft snoring began to irritate Waters; he nudged the man. "Wake up!" The man's eyes opened suddenly, surprise registering on his face. "Keep alert, we can't screw this up."

"What's to screwup?" The man said gruffly,

"We're just going to take out a pregnant woman. Piece of cake."

"This could turn out to be one stale cake if we're not careful. Eastman warned me about the last time a team like ours operated in this area. Not one of them is still around to operate. We don't know where the men are in this woman's family. For all we know we could be in somebody's cross hairs right now. That cop that stopped and talked to me earlier. His name is Chula, he's one of the bastards that was involved two years ago when the last team was taken out. So, you'd better stay alert."

"Calm down, Waters, these people aren't anything special. Just your usual Oklahoma rednecks and Indians. It's not like we're up against Marines or something." Waters had no intention of relaxing, at least not until he heard from Eastman instructing him to move on the woman.

## Wednesday, 30 November 2016 4:30 PM CST, Kiamichi Mountains Honobia, OK

Levi had returned to Boomer's cabin a few minutes earlier and confirmed that he had met with Dale Thompkins of the Talihina Police Department and Jeri Chula of the Oklahoma Highway Patrol. He also mentioned to Sam that he had met his wife and daughter, and both were safe. "My dad and I didn't stick around much longer after that but I'm pretty sure Chief Thompkins is going to get help from the Leflore County Sheriff as well." He said,

"That's good news," Sam replied. "The Sheriff can arrest, and hold them, even if they have Federal title. He can deputize the Talihina Police Officers if needed as well."

"What if there's a shootout?" Asked Boomer.

"I know our Sheriff and he's not going to allow FBI, or anybody like that point guns at him or his deputies." Joshua said.

"These will be goons, Eastman's men in black for the most part. Eastman may be the only one with government credentials." Addison replied.

"If they pull guns, they'll wish they hadn't, a lot of people don't realize the powers of a County Sheriff, and we've got a good one. You don't come into Leflore County and endanger the people or his deputies."

Joshua cleared his throat and nodded to the Redstone's, Nathan, and Trent, "Okay men we've managed to throw Eastman off the trail of you four. He seems oblivious to Boomer and Levi, but we can't relax or think we've got the upper hand. Never forget Eastman may be employed by people in Washington, but he answers to a powerful non-human entity. His master has powers we don't understand and can bring in other entities that none of us have ever seen, except maybe for Nathan here."

"How powerful is this thing?" Addison asked Josh.

"I'd say extremely powerful, it could be a territorial spirit as powerful as a fallen angel, or it could be a Nephilim type entity, which will still be very dangerous and very powerful."

"So, a giant?" Boomer asked.

"Possibly, but not for sure. I was in presence of a Nephilim or possibly a fallen angel once in of all places an Admiral's cabin onboard an aircraft carrier in the Gulf of Tonkin back during Vietnam. This one was no giant, but he did manifest physical traits that convinced me he wasn't human. For all I know it could be something like that, in fact for all I know it could be the same entity. I had made quite an enemy the evening before."

335

"Now, thanks to Nathan and his small drone we know Eastman is up to something tonight, we think he is going to attack Sam's family to draw us out into the open. We're certain that this won't happens until he knows for sure his guys can get to Sam's family without fear also know Sam or any of his friends being around. Eastman and some of his henchmen will be meeting down at the Honobia Creek Store around 5:00. Boomer and Levi, I'd like you two to go down there and interrupt them a little bit. Whatever you do, don't start a fight. Just throw them off their game a little. If you can annoy them and cause Eastman to make a mental blunder or two before we reveal our location that would be perfect. Just don't get in an altercation or get yourself hurt. Then get back up here to your cabin."

Boomer looked at Levi and smiled, then turning to Josh, he said confidently, "We can do that, Levi did you get what I asked?"

Levi held up an average-looking bottle of water you would find at any convenience store. "Got it."

Josh turned back to the other men, "Okay at 7:30 this evening we're going to move out of here and setup near the Obelisk while Eastman and his goons are waiting to make their moves, we're going to take up positions on the high ground surrounding the object. Sam you and Nathan set up the Tannerite bombs you're making in the area around the Obelisk, try to conceal them the best you can, but not so much you can target them. Boomer, I want you down by your main gate where you can keep an eye on Eastman and his men, warn us when they move. Especially if they decide to move onto the lease before we kick things off. Once they start moving into the lease you will use this radio, just say the word Showtime once over the radio and then join Levi near the Obelisk on your side of the fence. I want you two on your property when things kick off, that way your participation is as little as possible."

"If we lose this fight, you two will be on your own, and I'd just as soon your participation goes without notice. At 11:45 pm sharp Sam will turn his cell phone on so he can be tracked, in fact Sam, I want you to call your wife's number and carry on a conversation with Jeri Chula as if she's Christa."

"Does this mean I get to talk dirty to her?" Sam asked, receiving chuckles from everyone but Addison and Josh. Seeing the frown on Josh's face, Sam said, "Sorry just trying to lighten the mood."

Josh continued, "In the meantime, here's a disposable cell phone if you'd like to call your wife right now and ensure everything is okay. The number to the disposable she was given to use its number is already programed in. You can call her now if you'd like Sam, I'm sure you'd both love to hear each other's voices, but if you're going to talk dirty make it fast. We've got work to do." Sam looked at Josh with surprise, then noticed the wry expression on his face and smiled.

"Well played, Sir," he said smiling.

Josh gave a slight nod and continued. "Addison at 11:50 PM sharp, I want you to call Dale Thompkins cell. He'll be waiting for your call at his office in Talihina. Tell him you have something you want to show him, and you'll come into his office in the morning. I want them all confident that they know where everyone is. After both you and Sam make your diversion calls, leave your cell phones on, you can lay them on a rock or in a tree wherever, but I want Eastman and his men to know you're in the vicinity of the Obelisk. Levi at 11:55 I want you to sneak up the Obelisk, twist the top of it counterclockwise that should activate it. I'm not sure what that thing does yet, so once it turns on get your butt back across the fence and join your cousin. I suspect it may be some kind of portal or summoning device for the creatures, but we just don't know what will manifest once it's activated."

"Nathan and Trent seem to be the only ones armed with copper rounds for their weapons, any of the rest of you may find your firearms have little or effect. If you can knock them down long enough to get away or even to give Nathan and Trent time to dispatch them permanently…That too will work, if you down one with a gun, get away from it even if it looks dead, it may not be."

"What about Eastman and his men?" Sam asked. "I don't think Eastman's men are anything more than human monsters, but don't by any means turn your back on Eastman. I don't care what happened two years ago, he's not that man anymore. Also, don't be afraid to call on the name of Jesus, it just may save your life. Any questions?" None of the men said a thing. "Good, Boomer, after Eastman and his men are on the move get join Levi where you two first saw the Obelisk set up from. Bring the heaviest caliber rifle you have. I may need you to take it out somehow. Any of you have questions?"

The men sat silently, shaking their heads to indicate they understood the plan. "Okay, we'd better get geared up, get some water and food in you. Hopefully, we'll run these things out of here tonight."

"I do have one question." Sam as everyone stood up. "I can see us getting rid of Eastman and his goons, and I can see us going as far as getting rid of the Relics… What about these UFOs and the creatures they bring to the party? I know my wife was able to make them flee through rebuking. That was in the home of a devote Christian woman. She was able to run them out of her home,

337

we're talking a whole mountain here, heck we're talking a whole mountain range if you think about it."

"One thing at a time, Sam, these beings are not operating independently, even the humans are tied to these entities. In the case of this Paul Eastman, I doubt he's still fully human. I think he's a transhuman in the process of becoming something else. These things are not magic, supernatural maybe, but not completely immune to physics. They're abominations and they have their weaknesses. Well, find those weaknesses."

Sam nodded, then said. "Well, we've got the team to do it with. We got four veterans of ground combat in Nathan, Trent, my father and me. I have no doubt in the capabilities of Boomer and Levi here. The other side seems to have UFOs, and we don't have an Air Force, no offense Josh, I'm not sure if you're up to flying combat anymore at your age."

Josh smiled, "I shot down the first flying saucer I ever saw."

## Wednesday, 30 November 2016 5:25 PM CST, Honobia Creek Store, Honobia, OK

Boomer and Levi entered the store. Boomer came through the door first and greeted the ladies behind the counter in his usual deep Texoma accent. "Hey Kim, hey Sarah! Is it too late to get a couple of burgers?" "Five more minutes and the grill would be closed." Sarah replied, busily working on other orders.

"That's why I brought your bouncing baby boy, just in case I was late." Sarah looked up, smiling at Boomer and Levi. She winked then said, "If Levi knew what was good for him, he'd go home and cook for me."

Boomer spun the cap off the water bottle he carried, took a sip, and looked around the store. There were seven men crowded around a table that was designed for six. All were busy discussing a map and speaking in hushed tones, and all were dressed in tactical gear. Boomer approached the table and made his presence known in his booming voice, "You fellers in a swat team or something?"

The men all looked at him, seemingly shocked that he had the audacity to speak to them. Eastman was the only one to speak, "What we are is no concern of yours."

"Oh, I'm not concerned, just trying to be neighborly." Boomer said, taking another swig from his water bottle while leaning confidently against an ice maker. "We're not your neighbors bumkin, now move along."

A slight grin formed on Boomer's lips; Levi, having seen this expression before, eased around the two short grocery aisles. If it was going to be seven vs. two, he at least wanted to outflank them. Sarah had known Boomer much longer than her son and knew a confrontation was imminent. Grabbing as many of the prepared plates of food motioning for Kim to grab the others, she quickly moved toward the table, placing herself between Boomer and the men seated at the table. Seeing the food was being served, Eastman began rolling off the sleaves of his black battle dress shirt, never taking his eyes off Boomer. As his right sleeve was rolled up, Boomer happened to notice a small white glow just under the skin on the inner side of Eastman's forearm. Watching this, he continued to prod Eastman.

"You're right, Mister, we're not neighbors and it's a good thing. I wouldn't be comfortable with a bunch of ninja campfire girls for neighbors."

Eastman's face turned to a fiery red. He began to rise from his seat. Boomer could see the glow under his skin becoming brighter and changing to a fiery red color. Eastman began to curse Boomer; spittle flew from his mouth and collected on his lips. Jabbing his right index finger in Boomer's face, he said, "You're lucky I have other business Hillbilly, or you'd be dead right now."

Levi was uncomfortable; things seemed to be going south in a hurry. Slowly he took a large can of beans from the shelf next to him. It was the only thing even close to a weapon he could reach. He was mad at himself for coming in unarmed and mentally started picking who he would hit first.

Boomer wasn't backing down with a sweeping gesture. He opened both arms wide, saying, "I'll oblige you and your girlfriends, missy."

As he opened his arms, he squeezed the water bottle drenching Eastman and two of his men that had been sitting to his left. A large splash of water struck Eastman's left hand, with a few smaller drops landing on his face. Where the water struck Eastman, small puffs of smoke rose from Eastman's bare skin. He screamed in pain and confusion and ran for the door; his men hurriedly ran behind him, confused and concerned.

"What the hell did you just do Boomer?" Sarah asked. Her expression was one of both anger and fear. Kim had retreated behind the counter and was now fearfully clutching the phone, ready to call 911. She looked at Sarah in confusion as if waiting to know if she should. Sarah nodded and said, "Make the call."

Kim quickly dialed 911 and began speaking to the operator. Boomer looking pleased with the results, noticed the men had left their map on the table. Looking at Levi, he said, "Quick grab that."

Levi followed the instructions of his cousin, quickly grabbing the map and stuffing it into the pocket of his jacket.

"Boomer, what did you do to that man?" Sarah demanded.

"I didn't do anything; I accidentally spilled some water on him. He said innocently, taking another swig. Then looking at Levi, he said, "We'd better get out of here."

Sarah put herself between Boomer and her son, "You're getting my boy beat up or killed Boomer, he stays here!"

"It's okay Mom, we know what we're doing." Levi said.

"I doubt that very seriously," Sarah replied before adding, "If you're going to leave than leave fast, we just called the law."

Boomer and Levi made their way out of the store. Eastman and his men were gathered around two black Humvees. One of the men was busily applying some type of medical cream to Eastman's hand. Seeing this, Boomer pointed to a picnic table that sat just outside the door of the building under the overhanging roof, "Hey man, if yawl got blisters or something there's an aloe plant on that table. You can't beat aloe for burns or blisters."

Eastman was livid; his hand went to his belt where he had a holstered Glock 9mm. "I'm going to kill you Hillbilly," he spat viciously, then stopped short, seeing Boomer already had a Model 1911 .45 caliber up and ready. "I wouldn't do that slick; it won't end well."

For a moment, Eastman hesitated, experiencing unexpected pain he'd forgotten the gift of his Master, Nergal. He knew the .45 might hurt him, but he would survive. Still, he was confused. Why did the water burn me? Why would my Master allow that?

Three of Eastman's men also had their hands on pistols, "You won't get us all Hillbilly, the best you'll do is tickle me a little."

"All right that's enough, out of all of you!" A female voice called from the door of the building. Sarah stood there defiantly holding a .38 Special revolver. "Aint nobody shooting a gun anywhere near my boy, unless they want to get shot themselves. Boomer you and Levi get out of here right now, GIT!" She yelled forcibly. Then looking at Eastman, "Mister I don't know who you are, and I don't care, but the sheriff's department is on the way, and so is the husband of the lady that owns this place. He's bringing a lot of friends, Mister, and every damn one of them carries a gun and knows how to use it. So, take my advice and get out of here."

Boomer, already in his truck, started the engine. He revved the diesel engine, which made a large black cloud that floated over Eastman and his men, adding more insult to injury. Once Levi was in the truck, Boomer backed out slightly then turned the wheel so he would drive by Eastman. Once he was alongside them, he whipped the steering wheel to the right and hit the accelerator, causing the tires to throw loose gravel all over Eastman and his men as well as their vehicles. Once out of the parking lot, Boomer made a left turn and sped away, heading south.

Levi looked at Boomer, laughing, "You do know Josh asked you not to start a fight don't you."

Boomer snorted, "That weren't no fight, plus he seemed upset him enough to take him off his game. I reckon I did just that."

"You did more than that, not only did you get him off his game, but you also got him off his rocker."

Boomer looked in the mirror and saw that Eastman and his men had taken Sarah's advice and were pulling out of the parking lot. He let a sigh of relief escape when they turned right, heading in the opposite direction from him. "Hey man, get that map out and tell me what's on it."

Levi pulled the map from his pocket and unfolded it. "Looks like they plan on setting an ambush of their own. I think they're planning to lure the guys over to where Nathan and Trent killed that big ugly Sasquatch. I think we'd better hustle this to Josh and Addison."

"Well, hang on, man!" Boomer said as he made a hard left turn onto Highway 144, speeding to the access to his property from the east.

## Wednesday, 30 November 2016 5:55 PM CST, Honobia Creek Store, Honobia, OK

Darkness was fast enveloping the mountain as Eastman and most of his men sat in their vehicles on the mountain overlook above Honobia. Eastman was still stewing over the incident at the store. From the overlook, they could just make out the roof of the store and part of the parking lot. One of Eastman's men watched the activity through a set of binoculars. Three pickup trucks and two Sheriff's Department vehicles could be seen along with a sizable group of men who looked to be in a heated discussion. A large man seemed particularly upset and kept making gestures toward the overlook where Eastman and his men were parked. Both Sheriff Deputies climbed back into their vehicles, drove out of the parking lot, turning right to make the mile-long drive up to the overlook. "They're coming," the man said to Eastman.

"Okay get back in and relax I'll handle this."

It took only two minutes for the two Leflore County Sheriff Department vehicles to arrive at the overlook. Eastman noted both vehicles took up blocking positions, but he also noticed the deputies seemed casual in exiting the vehicles. Eastman slowly exited the vehicle, as did his men. One deputy approached Eastman, and his group as another remained near his vehicle, close to an AR-15 which was stored on a rack in the front seat. Eastman and his men kept their hands out away from their bodies to show they were not armed.

"Good evening, Deputy," Eastman said, displaying his badge and identification, "I'm Special Agent Paul Eastman with the Bureau of Land Management."

Seeing the badge from a distance, the Deputy stopped for a moment, assessing the group of men. It was now apparent that all the men were wearing holsters and sidearms. "Sir, I'm Deputy Pollard with the Leflore County Sheriff's Department. Would you kindly approach me slowly, so we can sort this out. You other gentlemen please stay where you are and please keep your hands where I can see them."

Upon hearing the conversation and seeing the side arms, the second deputy removed the AR-15 from its rack and held it with the barrel pointed up, and took position behind his SUV, using it both for cover and a gun rest.

"Of course, Deputy." Eastman said, following the man's instructions, making sure not to cause any alarm. He handed his identification holder to Deputy Pollard.

"Bureau of Land Management, huh? We don't see too much of you guys in the Choctaw Nation."

"Well, the Choctaw were considered one of the civilized tribes," Eastman, said trying to ease the man's tension; he could see Deputy's facial muscles were tight with stress.

The Deputy looked up at Eastman after his remark about the Choctaw and said, "My mother is full blooded Choctaw, and I can tell you for a fact we can be as uncivilized as a situation calls for."

"I meant no offense, Deputy."

"None taken," the man said, closing Eastman's identity case and handing it back to him. "Would the rest of you gentlemen please step forward and show me your identification?"

The other six men came approached, and each one displayed their credentials, satisfied they were who they claimed to be. Pollard relaxed and said, "So can you tell me what happened down at the little store earlier?"

"I believe we just got off on the wrong foot with one of the locals, I'm afraid I let his intrusiveness get the better of me. I said words, he said words and things got a little tense."

"Sounded as if they got a little more than tense Agent Eastman."

"Well, he did interrupt our working meal, we haven't had much time for relaxing or even eating. In fact, none of us have had a meal since yesterday and now we've missed our chance for this evening."

"Well, the lady that works there bagged your food up and it's in the back of the other deputy's Blazer. So, you boys will at least get your food. What was this about Mr. Jefferson burning you? What was that all about?"

Eastman didn't hesitate, "I have a certain skin disorder, I must use a sodium-based creme when outdoors. It is designed to slowly soak into my skin. I had foolishly applied some it before going into the store. When the water from his bottle hit my skin, there were places where I had applied the creme too thick, and the water caused a reaction. I should have taken more caution; the crème can react dramatically when in contact with pure water. Although it can look fairly spectacular when it happens, it's a short-lived effect. In fact, I'm fine now, I wish no ill will on this Mister. Jefferson and am interested only in putting the matter behind me so we can resume our duties."

Deputy Pollard nodded, "Well, Sir, I'm glad to hear it, the locals have had more excitement than they're used to the past week or so. May I ask what duties, you and your men are performing up here, Agent Eastwood."

"Certainly, Deputy, some of the deer in this particular area of the Kiamichi Mountains have developed a rare viral fungus. Though not particularly dangerous, it could taint their meat causing illness in some people who may ingest the meat. The good news is the cooler temperatures will cause the fungus to dissipate so we won't have to close off hunting for long. Our job is to ensure there's no hunting in this area until the temperatures drop off making the fungus less of a threat."

Pollard nodded his head then asked, "Fair enough, but why Bureau of Land Management? Shouldn't fish and game officials be doing this?"

"I wish they were, Deputy, but it is the beginning of deer season and I'm afraid the game wardens are being kept busy with other duties," Eastman replied.

Deputy Pollard nodded his head once more, "Yes, I guess they are at that." Then he turned and looked at the other Deputy still holding his position behind his SUV. "Jeff, let's give these fellers their food. Thank you, Agent Eastman."

"Thank you, Deputy."

The men retrieved their meals, and the deputies said their goodbyes and drove back down the mountain. Eastman turned and looked at the other men. "Eat up; I've got a chopper coming; I'll be coordinating from it. We're putting an end to this tonight.

## Wednesday, 30 November 2016 7:10 PM CST, Honobia, OK

The seven men milled about around the large table in Boomer's cabin. Tension was building in all of the men; they were all aware of what the night could bring. Levi standing over to the table, watched, fascinated as Sam and Addison filled plastic coffee creamer containers with Tannerite and small chunks of copper broken and cut from the supply of copper disks Nathan had. They filled five containers with these contents. Once filled, the red lids were screwed back on the containers, and both men began busily wrapping the containers in a heavy layer of camouflaged duct tape.

"I've done a little Tannerite shooting in my day but what the hell is that for?" Levi asked.

"It's a little trick we used two years ago, only then we used PVC pipe instead of these containers. You shoot the container, and it blows sending shrapnel in all directions," Sam answered busily wrapping one of the containers in duct tape.

"So how well did it work?" Levi asked.

"It worked pretty good, but there's a couple of concerns this time. We're up against the same Relics we fought last time and I have a feeling they'll be more wary of this kind of thing now. The white PVC pipe we used last time might just look familiar and they might avoid it. Hopefully they won't notice these containers."

You said a couple of concerns," Levi prodded.

Finishing with the wrap on one of the containers, Sam said, "These things can be just as dangerous to us as them. We need to have distance and cover when one of us shoots these things. So we're probably going to have to designate a kill zone for these and only use them if a worthwhile target presents itself."

Sam now took the same container and began applying several strips of black colored tape to the container; noticing Levi's curious expression, he said, "IR reflective tape, my AR-15 as well as Nathan and Trent's weapons have IR scopes with IR illuminators. We'll be able to pick these out in the dark through our scopes. We can't shoot them if we can't see them."

Boomer had been on his phone in the kitchen area; he walked in with a grim look on his face. "Just got a call from a buddy of mine, he said that a helicopter just landed in the field between the store and the bridge, He said it was a UH-60 type."

"There's nothing we can do about that now." Josh said calmly, "If it interferes, we'll just have to deal with it. We've got to be ready for anything tonight, if a helicopter is the worst thing that drops out of the sky on us, consider yourselves blessed."

"So exactly what could be worse than a helicopter?" Levi asked.

"Well like I mentioned earlier I believe Nergal is close, he could bring in anything, including his UFOs or their occupants. What I'm saying is don't be surprised by anything tonight, man, beast, or machine."

Trent looked at Nathan and said, "Remind me never let you pick where we spend our leave from now on. This is as bad as Kandahar."

Josh spoke up, "Gentlemen, we might as well get setup, I haven't been in combat in decades, and I've never been in ground combat. So with your permission before we leave I'd like to offer a quick prayer."

The men nodded in agreement and closed in a circle around Josh, each man's arms on the shoulder of the men to the left and right of him. Josh began, "Dear Father We are not alone, you are by our side. Hold us, guide us, as we seek you and serve you. You have called us to rescue, to protect, and to make peace. We are not alone; you are by our side. Amen," The men all stood up, looking at each other.

Addison broke the silence. "Sam and I have suffered a lot of personal loss to this evil over the past two years. We are honored to have you men with us, we could not have done this alone. This is a unique group of men and our coming together has to be because God deemed it so. The way I see it, he has a job for us to do, we even have a new leader among us who shares the name of one of the mightiest of God's warriors. Joshua before we go I'd like to remind everyone that Joshua of the Bible did not vanquish all of his enemies in the manner God ordered him, he allowed some to live, and because of it, mankind is still cursed today by an evil presence. I don't want us to make that same mistake. So, I'm thinking, tonight we destroy them all, no quarter given, and none asked."

Joshua nodded and said, "Addison's words are true; kill every evil man or creature we encounter tonight."

Nathan replied, "Sounds better every time I hear it, there's no other way to fight evil. Let's go." The men headed out the door into the night.

## Wednesday, 30 November 2016 11:40 PM CST, Honobia, OK

Paul Eastman's frustration had him at the breaking point as he stood outside the side cargo door of the black-colored UH-60 helicopter sitting in the dark field in Honobia. His master expected results, and the results were expected soon. He knew the issue with the Redstone's had to be settled tonight. Yet somehow, the Redstone men had disappeared entirely. It was beginning to look as if his only option was to abduct and kill the wife and children of Sam Redstone. However, according to his men lurking in Talihina, the wife was alone in her home; her child had been taken on a trip with a grandparent. He had a six-man team led by Waters on the scene just off the Redstone property, waiting to move. All of them sadists that had been appointed by his own master for just such an operation.

The men were itching to move in on the woman; her impending fate was an ugly one. These men would not be satisfied with an easy execution; they had horrific games to play with her first. A month ago, Eastman would have been terrified to be in the company of such men. Now he ruled them with an iron fist. A warm electric current moved through his right arm; looking down, he could see a red glow under his skin. His master's impatience was showing as the implant delivered a steady warm energy through his arm to his brain. It gave him unusual abilities, strength, and power. It also served to remind him his very existence was allowed only by the whim or pleasure of his new deity. He was never sure if his master was man or devil; all he knew was he could not fail to provide results soon.

He had no idea why this section of the world was so important to his master, and he dared not question him. His thoughts were interrupted by the specialist in the helicopter that monitored the cell phone tracking system. "Sir, we're getting a ping on one of the Redstone cell phones." Which one?"

"The younger one, Sam."

"Sir, its pinging from the tower on the mountain just above us. He's on that mountain," the man said, pointing to the very place the Redstone's had disappeared from. Eastman was curious but not overly concerned at least he knew where the Redstone's were now. Eastman quickly picked up his own cell phone and dialed Waters in Talihina.

**Waters:** "Yes, Sir?"

**Eastman:** "Heads up, the husbands cell phone just went active."

**Waters:** "Yes, Sir we see the wife has just answered hers. Should we monitor the call?"

**Eastman:** "Put your plan in motion start moving in, but don't strike until I give you the go ahead."

**Waters:** Roger that, my guy has it on his monitor too, it looks as if the cell calling her is within a mile or so of you."

**Eastman:** "Let me worry about that. Just get ready to move on her. I'll call you when I'm ready.

Eastman disconnected from the call; his breathing became heavy as he began to anticipate his success being achieved within the next hour or two. Once again, his thoughts were interrupted by a systems specialist.

"Sir, we have a ping on the other Redstone phone now as well. It is also making a call to Talihina, and just like the other phone, it is also being operated from the very same mountain. I'm trying to get a location fix on both right now, Sir. Okay, the first phone has disconnected from its call but is still on and able to be tracked.

"Is the number it's calling on our threat list?" Eastman asked excitedly.

"Yes, Sir, it's calling the cell phone of Dale Thompkins, the Police Chief of Talihina."

This concerned Eastman, Do the Redstone's know of my plan? He wondered, "Can you Jam it?"

"I can, Sir, but the other party never answered." Excellent, he thought as he picked up his own cell again, dialing Waters.

**Waters:** Yes, Sir?

**Eastman:** Do it!

Eastman quickly disconnected and looked back at the systems specialist. "Are both phones still on?"

"Yes, Sir."

"Then jam them both. He grabbed a secured portable radio and contacted his team that was stationed on the overlook a mile up the mountain road from him. "We have locations on both phones; they're on the property. We're sending the info to you. You should be able to detect them on your portable trackers. Move in and position yourself close, but don't blunder into an ambush. I know they have at least one man assisting them, and I know he's a trained combat soldier. Drive to the lease gate, then go in on foot, use stealth."

"Roger that," was the reply he received from the man on the overlook.

## Wednesday, 30 November 2016, 11:50 PM CST, Sam and Christa Redstone residence, Talihina, OK

Waters looked through the living window of the house. He could see the Redstone woman was standing in the kitchen near the sink, looking at a television in the living room. She was oblivious to everything but the television. His excitement was heightened by the thought of what was about to happen. He had three men positioned at the back of the house and two more at the front porch. He moved quietly toward the two at the front of the house. As he joined them, he noticed one of the men was totally nude and in an obvious state of arousal, armed with a large Bowie knife. He gave the man a look of disgust.

"You'll wait your turn," he said disgustedly as if he was of superior moral character.

The man just smiled and whispered, "It's a party brother, and I plan on beating you to the punch bowl."

Jimmy Chula crouched in the dark, watching three men approach the back of Sam and Christa Redstone's house. He and four other officers were ready and waiting to intercept Eastman's men. All of the peace officers participating in this operation were facing a moral dilemma. They were ready to kill them all even the men surrendered; they had to be put down. The evil these men were capable of knew no bounds, and they could not be allowed to live. If they were arrested, no doubt Eastman's government connections would have them free and back on the streets in a short time.

Dale Thompkins covered the front of the house. He was backed up by two Leflore County Sheriff Deputies as well as two Oklahoma State Troopers. As the men approached the back of the house, Jimmy eased up to a standing position, ready to fire. Jimmy looked through open sights; the half-moon supplied sufficient light to pick out his targets.

As Jimmy waited for the best moment to squeeze the trigger when a large swift shadow swept across his vision. It seemed to engulf the men, and then it was gone. Jimmy could hear the sound of weapons and equipment hitting the ground, but the men had disappeared, vanished into thin air. He lowered his weapon and looked at the officer to his right,

"What happened?" He asked in a whisper.

The man just stood speechless, shaking his head. In his earpiece, he heard Dale Thompkins' voice softly say, "Jimmy, our suspects just vanished."

"Same here, Chief," Jimmy replied.

"Screw it lets light up and see where they are." Dale said before loudly speaking over the radio, "GO!" Once the command was given, all the law enforcement officers turned on flashlights and illuminated the property. Jeri Chula ripped the blonde wig off her head; the need to disguise herself at Christa Redstone had now passed. She ran to a row of light switches in the kitchen, turning on all the outside floodlights. The area outside the house was immediately bathed in bright white light, which momentarily blinded all the peace officers.

As Jeri exited the house through the front door, she could see Dale and the other officers blinking their eyes and looking around the immediate area. A few seconds later, her husband Jimmy came around to the front of the house and hugged her.

"You guys okay?" She asked, confused.

"Yeah, we're fine, I don't know what the hell happened to Eastman's men though. I saw a big shadow and then they were gone."

Dale confirmed the same strange occurrence had befallen the men at the front of the house as well. Weapons and equipment littered the ground everywhere the six men had been. Closer inspection revealed drops and small splatters of blood at both the front and back of the property. What blood there was led off in a hard-to-follow trail to the East into the larger mountains. Everyone looked around the scene in confusion. Laying alongside a Glock pistol on the ground near the front of the house, Jeri spotted a cell phone. Picking it up, she noticed the last call on it had happened just a few minutes earlier. There was a name on the display; it said, Eastman.

"What do you think happened?" Jimmy asked Dale.

Picking up the phone, Jeri said, "I'll tell you what happened, we're not the only ones living in these mountains that are tired of this crap." She pushed the display, dialing Eastman.

Answering the phone in Honobia, Eastman heard a female voice say, "You should have never come back." Then the phone went silent. Eastman felt his stomach go into a knot, and then things got suddenly worse. The system specialist spoke again before he could.

"Sir, the device has been activated?"

"What device?" Eastman asked angrily.

"The Obelisk, Sir."

# CHAPTER FIFTEEN

## The Remnant Rises

*"Fire is the test of gold; adversity, of strong men."*
*~ Martha Graham*

### Thursday, 1 December 2016 12:01 AM CST, Kiamichi Mountains Honobia, OK

Boomer crouched near the trees next to the gate of his property. He knew the men were coming; he was close enough to hear the engines of their SUVs come to life. Stepping back into the shadows, he let them pass before keying the microphone of the radio; he simply said, "Showtime."

Then he turned and jogged back toward the area near the fence where he knew Levi would be waiting for him. He could feel the energy of the device Levi had been charged with turning on. An uncomfortable buzzing and electricity moved through his body. He hoped Levi was able to make it back to the reverse slope where he could get some relief from the effects. As he jogged along the familiar trail of his property, he was suddenly snatched off his feet. He kicked his feet and flailed his arms, trying to free himself. His rifle was forcibly jerked from his hands; he reached for his sidearm in a holster on his hip. A large leathery hand grasped him before he could get to the gun.

The grip was firm but gentle. Boomer ceased struggling and looked into the face of his captor. The face was massive, with large dark eyes and a massive jaw. The shoulders of his captor were huge, muscled mountains that seemed to taper to the head without a neck. The creature reached out with its left hand and patted Boomer's shoulder. It seemed to be trying to calm Boomer's fear. Slowly his heart rate came down from the jackhammer speed it had reached when he was first lifted off his feet.

He felt himself being lowered to his feet, and once on the ground, he looked once again into the face of his captor. The large eyes had softened, and the creature held up its massive right hand displaying four fingers and a thumb. The creature then took Boomer by the wrist and opened his hand to display his fingers and thumbs. The creature then put his hand on Boomer's chest for a moment, then removed it and lightly pounded its own chest over where Boomer assumed its heart would be as if to show they were similar.

Boomer became aware of another creature to his right. It was holding his rifle; the first creature touched the rifle, then its chest again, and shook its head as if to say know. Once again, it held out its right hand displaying its four fingers and thumb. Boomer understood the gesture that the creature was making. He was not in the grip of the enemy he had first assumed. These meant him no harm. *Joshua and Addison are right*, he thought in amazement. *A few days ago, I didn't believe in these things, and now I'm making friends with one.* Boomer thought, feeling slightly lightheaded as if in a dream state. The second creature handed Boomer his rifle. The first stood to its full height and pointed in the direction down the trail Boomer was heading.

"Thank you," Boomer said as he continued down the trail. *I'm thanking King Kong for allowing me to walk on my own property,* he thought as he ran down the trail, then it occurred to him. *He wanted me to know he was here, and he let me see him, why? These damn things may have been out here watching me for years. How long have we been sharing this land?* It occurred to Boomer suddenly why the creature allowed itself to be seen. He stopped for a moment and grabbed the radio, and said, "Boys, we may have some help tonight, some big hairy help."

## Thursday, 1 December 2016 12:10 AM CST, Kiamichi Mountains Honobia, OK

Addison and Sam had positioned themselves two hundred yards from the gate they expected Eastman and his men to come in from. Sam had saved one of his Tannerite bombs to use here. The rest were positioned in the area around the Obelisk. He had put the device just slightly off-center of the trail in hopes of bringing down as many of Eastman's men as possible with one shot. Although they had heard no sounds, they knew the men were coming because of the warning given by Boomer.

"What do you think Boomer meant with that last transmission?" Sam whispered to his father.

"I'm not quite sure, but I'll take any help we can get."

Sam continued to watch through his IR scope on his AR-15 for any approaching figures. Pulling his head away for a moment, he looked at his father's choice of weapon for the night, an M1 Garand. "Why don't you get yourself an AR-15 for crying out loud?"

"Just keep looking through your fancy scope on your fancy rifle. This gun was good enough for your grandfather, its good enough for me."

"You can't see crap, Pop!"

"I'll see plenty when the shooting starts, Sam," Addison whispered, grateful to be beside his son when they were about to fight a battle."

"You know, Pop, this is like 2014 all over again, I hope we manage to do as well as we did two years go."

"We're going to do better," Addison replied, giving his son a reassuring pat on the shoulder.

Sam felt the vibration of his cell phone alerting him to a text message. It was from Jimmy Chula, it simply said, (All Clear). Sam leaned over and whispered to his father. "Everything seems to be good in Talihina."

Addison just nodded, wondering if any lives had to be taken by Dale and the law enforcement officers who aided him. Addison wondered how long any of them could stay out of legal trouble with the government. *Killing government agents, even crooked ones, is not going to sit well with folks.* His thoughts were quietly interrupted.

"I got movement," Sam whispered. Addison heard the slight click as Sam clicked the selector from safety to fire. He slowly rolled to his right two rotations then quietly crawled along the forest floor, taking a position behind the trunk of a large tree. Sliding his finger inside the trigger guard, he pushed the safety lock forward, making his weapon ready to fire.

Sam could now make out six figures silently moving in his and his father's direction. He allowed his breathing to calm down and waited for the men to move closer to the Tannerite device. *I'll give them about ten more yards, and then I'm going to punch their ticket,* Sam thought.

Addison could make out three of the figures as they moved slowly and stealthily through the shadows cast by the half-moon. He eased his cheek down in the stock of the Garand rifle and lined the nearest man to him in the ring sight of the weapon. He studied the man's movement and tried to anticipate which way he would dive for cover if he and Sam were detected before the shooting started. Like his son, Addison allowed his breathing to slow and his pulse rate to drop. Other than his battle with the Relics two years ago, his last combat against men had been 45 years earlier in the jungles of Vietnam. At age 67, he could still soldier and was a very lethal adversary in the situation he now found himself in.

These men were part of the reason he'd just buried his wife. They were also part of the reason for his community's misery and anguish. The bill had come due. His finger tightened on the trigger slightly, not quite reaching the five pounds per square inch trigger pull necessary for the rifle to fire. As he concentrated on his target, the man instantly went straight into the air as if launched by a slingshot.

Confused, Addison pulled his eyes away from the sight of the rifle and looked at his son. To his surprise, he could see Sam had his left arm in the air high above his shoulder as if greeting somebody. He was even more surprised as Sam stood up and held his rifle casually with the barrel pointed down. Rising to a crouch, Addison joined his son, "What just happened?" he asked.

"You didn't see that, Pop?" Sam whispered.

"I saw the guy I had targeted suddenly come off the ground straight up."

"The Okla Chito took them."

"The Okla Chito? Are you sure the damn Relics didn't take them?"

"I am sure, Pop; I was about to shoot the Tannerite and then all of the sudden I saw huge fast moving shadows and the men all disappeared it was over in a split second."

"All of the men are gone?" Addison asked incredulously.

"All of them are gone, Pop."

"Are you sure they were Okla Chito and not the Relics?"

"Yes, I saw five altogether, four were carrying off six men. One walked out into the clearing, it looked right at me and held up five fingers. Pop, if I remember tribal oral histories you've shared, showing you have only five digits was the signal to show you were not of a hybrid race. When I held my hand up and spread my fingers it nodded in recognition and moved off into the same direction as the ones carrying Eastman's men."

"Well, I'm glad to hear some of the First Nations customs are starting to have an effect on you. I take it you didn't see Eastman in that group of men?"

"I couldn't tell, Pop, but I wouldn't think our troubles are over that easy." The words no sooner left his mouth when a helicopter overflew the two men at low altitude.

"I'll bet that's Eastman and he's in a big damn hurry. We'd better join the others at the Obelisk," Addison said.

## Thursday, 1 December 2016 12:17 AM CST, Kiamichi Mountains Honobia, OK

Nathan and Trent watched the Obelisk closely, hoping for the Relics to manifest the device so they would have clean shots at the creatures. The Obelisk gave off a strange energy that generated sounds the two men had never heard before. The waves caused uncomfortable side effects for the men; both were suffering from impaired vision and dizziness. Trent's teeth seemed

353

to be vibrating from the energy, and the discomfort it was causing him had put him in a foul mood. "I swear if something doesn't happen soon I'm going to blast that damn thing to Mars or wherever the hell else it's from."

"Hang in there, flyboy, it has to be signaling something." Nathan said, barely hiding his own discomfort. A sound that was familiar to both men was becoming apparent over the energized torture that the Obelisk was transmitting; it was a thump of rotor blades accompanied by the whine of two General Electric T700 turboshaft engines. The helicopter came into view, circling the area once before coming to a hover near the Obelisk.

"They must not be running any infra-red or they would have seen us," Trent remarked.

"Don't get too comfortable they may have spotted us and just waiting on us to do something stupid, like relax." Nathan growled back.

The helicopter began to slowly descend from its hover. It touched down, and its engines came to idle. A lone figure jumped out of the left side cargo door of the aircraft and ran to the Obelisk. "That's Eastman," Nathan said, tracking the man through his rifle scope.

"Drop his ass," Trent said

"Wait, let me see what he's doing first," Nathan replied.

The man was clearly armed, carrying an M-4 or AR-15 type weapon, which he slung over his shoulder as he approached the Obelisk. The figure manipulated something on the object, and the surrounding area became bathed in a brilliant white light, blinding both Nathan and Trent as well as Boomer and Levi, who were positioned on Boomer's property overlooking the Obelisk some three hundred yards to the left and south of Nathan and Trent's position. Its glow was so intense Sam and Addison could see it through the trees as they approached the area from the northwest. The helicopter's engines could be heard revving up, and the aircraft lifted off and sped from the area to the north. After two minutes, the white light went out, and the Obelisk began to send a softer white pulsating light straight into the night sky. The pulses came every 18 seconds, and with each pulse, a loud sound like somebody pounding a bass drum would echo across the forest.

"Where's the guy that turned it on? Did he get back on the chopper?" Trent asked.

"How the hell should I know. I don't have welder's goggles," Nathan said, looking through his scope at the device.

"This thing is a beacon for something, we better get ready for anything," Nathan said. Trent grabbed his MK-14 rifle and positioned himself fifty feet to the right of Nathan. The pulsating on the Obelisk began to speed up, peaking at a pulse every two seconds. Then there was one massive pulse of light and sound that stunned all of the men watching it. Looking through his scope, Nathan could make out four small figures standing around the Obelisk.

"What in the hell are those?" He asked Trent.

"I don't know but I have a better question, what the hell is Josh doing? Look at that silly bastard."

Nathan now saw Josh slowly walking toward the figures near the Obelisk. This isn't good. Nathan thought, adjusting his aim to the closest of the small figures to Joshua. Nathan was startled by the sound of Trent's weapon firing.

"Get it, get it, get!" He heard Trent screaming as he fired.

Now Nathan saw why Trent was firing. One of the Relics was running on all fours at an incredible speed toward Josh. When it slammed into Josh, it looked as if he'd been hit by a bus. The elderly man flew 30 feet through the air slamming into a tall tree at the edge of the clearing.

"Kill them all!" Nathan screamed as he started firing. His first shot connected in the shoulder of the Relic and sent it tumbling along the ground.

Trent decided that a still target was his best option; he sighted in on one of the Tannerite bombs and squeezed the trigger. The explosion sent copper shrapnel flying for a hundred yards in all directions and knocking down two of the smaller figures wrestling with the Obelisk.

"Trent don't shoot those damn things anymore Josh is still down there, plus you may hit Boomer and Levi with the shrapnel. Shoot that damn device those two midgets were after. Put it out of commission before causes anything else to appear."

No sooner had Nathan got the words out of his mouth, then he spotted the two missing Relics. One was running toward the Obelisk; the other was running south out of the killing zone. Nathan targeted the one heading toward the Obelisk putting two rounds in it, watching with satisfaction as it dropped like a rock. He began looking for the first Relic Trent had shot. He knew it was hurt and lurking somewhere, making it even more dangerous by his estimation. He could hear Trent firing steadily, and he could also hear metallic thuds as his rounds made contact with the Obelisk.

Laying prone just below the lip of a small rise on his property, Boomer and Levi both had their guns up and ready. They had been told to stay out of the fight if at all possible so they would be safe from any investigations should everything go bad. In Boomer's mind, everything had gone bad. He watched as two of what appeared to be small alien creatures and one of the Relics approached his fence a mere thirty yards from where he and Levi were positioned.

"Levi, I think that's far enough; I'll take the big one. Both men rose to a crouch and began firing into the fast-approaching creatures. Levi was surprised when the two small grey aliens looking creatures dropped with no problem. Boomer was surprised his target was eating one bullet after another with little or effect. Levi also joined in firing at the Relic, and the combined firepower was enough to turn the creature and send it running back into the direction it had come from.

When the shooting started, Sam and Addison ran toward the sound of the battle, hoping to be there in time to help. The multitude of gunshots and the sound of the exploding Tannerite was enough to cause them to throw caution to the wind. As they approached the clearing, they could see the glow of the Obelisk and figures moving around it as gunshots came from two directions. Addison was just about to warn Sam to slow down so they wouldn't be hit by mistake when a figure stepped out behind a tree twenty feet in front of him. Addison's mind registered a hint of a muzzle flash before darkness took him. Sam saw the figure an instant before Addison. He knew none of the others in their group would be at this spot. His gun came up at the same instant the figure fired his own. Sam put two rounds center mass into the figure, and it dropped. Then looking to his left, he saw his father lying still on the ground. Rushing over, he checked his father for vital signs - there were none. Sam could tell the bullet had hit him in the heart by inspecting his closer. Tears welled up in Sam's eyes as he looked at his father's lifeless body. He heard a noise to his right and looked up to see the figure he had shot was pulling himself up with the aid of the tree next to him.

Sam heard laughter coming from the figure; it was Eastman. Not bothering to pick up his weapon, Sam ran and tackled the figure and began viciously beating him. Eastman laughed harder with each strike of Sam's fist. Sam suddenly felt his strength leaving his body; he was weakening to the point where he couldn't throw another punch. He put his hands on Eastman's throat in an effort to choke him; he couldn't even do that. He was becoming so weak he could hardly see or even breathe. He sensed himself flying through the air as Eastman hurled from where they lay on the ground.

What is this? Sam's mind was racing, trying to understand. Eastman's sarcastic laugh belted out above the sound of rifle fire in the background.

"You answer to man, Redstone; I answer to a god." Eastman walked over and viciously kicked Sam in the ribs, followed by another kick in the face. "I'm going to kill you soon, Redstone, but first, I'm going to find your wife, and I'll cut your child out of her while she bellows like a cow being carved up alive. I'm going to make you watch as I do it. You can't run far enough, and you can't hide her anywhere. I have all the time in the world. Eastman's wounds had healed completely. Sam watched as he stood motionless, staring at the sky. Then he turned to Sam and said, "My Master comes." Then he casually turned and walked toward the clearing.

Nathan saw a lone figure come out of the tree line to the North casually walking in the direction of the Obelisk, at first he assumed it was Addison or Sam; he'd heard the rifle shots from that area a few minutes earlier and hoped his two friends had not run afoul of the missing Relic.

"Nathan, I don't see the Relic I hit earlier that attacked Josh, but there's another one coming from where Boomer and Levi were." Nathan swung his gun to his left and could clearly see the creature walking slowly toward the device. He lined up on the creature's chest and fired two shots center mass, and sent a third round into its head. The creature dropped from the impact of the copper rounds and didn't move again.

"Nathan, I think that's Eastman walking in the open. That means the shots we heard were him... You don't think he killed Addison and Sam, do you?"

"If he did, he's going to pay for it right now," Nathan said, taking aim. At first, he thought it was adrenalin. He tried slowing his breathing, looking through his scope, it dawned on him something else was happening. His vision was blurring, and his strength was fading; even his hearing was impaired. A strong vibration was once again returning. It didn't seem to be coming from the Obelisk. Looking up, Nathan saw a large triangular UFO was hovering over the clearing. He returned to his scope and tried to shoot Eastman even though he couldn't keep a sight picture on him. Allowing his rifle to drift across the target, he pulled the trigger. Nothing happened; his rifle wouldn't function. He saw one of the small alien-like creatures was approaching him. He pulled his sidearm, took aim, and squeezed the trigger... Again nothing.

The vibrations and sounds were too much to ignore, the triangle in the sky was the source, but there was nothing any of the men could do about it. He knew it was affecting Boomer and Levi, just like it was affecting him and Trent. He hoped Addison and Sam were alive and merely suffering through this like them instead of the alternative. The helicopter was back; it came in and landed near the Obelisk. It and its crew, like Eastman, seemed to be immune to the effects of the triangle.

Through the intense pain, Nathan watched Eastman pickup up the Obelisk and carry it to the waiting chopper. The lone gray alien continued to approach Nathan. It carried a large, tapered spike as it approached. Now Nathan could no longer move the pain was so intense he screamed in agony, as did Trent just a few feet away. He rolled over on his side and laid looking off into the distance. The alien approached and took his arm. It occurred to Nathan what it held in its hand was some type of syringe. It was going to place an implant in Nathan, and he was helpless to resist.

As he laid on his side, he waited for the inevitable, will I become a goon like Eastman? He thought as he stared blankly into the distance. His eyes were attracted to the movement beyond. The helicopter was making good its escape with Eastman and the damaged Obelisk. Just as it seemed all hope was lost Nathan saw a lone figure in the distance.

It was Josh, who had somehow survived the collision with the Relic. He was on his knees and seemed to be in prayer. There was a sudden change in the atmosphere. The sky beyond the clearing began to glow a faint bluish tint, then became a patch of brilliant cobalt blue rippling like waves in the water; there was a discharge of blue energy. Not like lightning, something with more mass than electricity. The thought of plasma entered Nathan's mind, and that's when something began to part the waves in the sky, moving through it as a person might walk through a curtain. It was a blue-white sphere; it looked to be at least two hundred feet in circumference. It had the appearance of a giant pearl hanging in the sky.

It seemed the area had become a vacuum; there was no sound, no smell, no air to breath. Trees and grass blew as if there were a huge storm, yet Nathan felt nothing or heard anything. The helicopter containing Eastman's rotor blades no longer had air to bite into to gain lift. The machine fell straight down two hundred feet into the clearing. It crushed, warped, and bent upon contact with the earth, but no noise indicated a crash. The triangle began to shake and vibrate; it seemed to explode in a brilliant blue flash that expanded then quickly sucked back into a small dot that dissipated.

The giant pearl slowly moved back to the rippling cobalt-colored patch of sky. It stopped for a moment, then moved back into the rippling waves, then it too was gone. Suddenly, there was air to breathe again, sound to hear again, smell and taste returned. The small grey alien creature had been looking at the pearl, now found itself left behind; it seemed confused. It turned at looked into Nathan's eyes. Nathan jerked his arm free from the creature's grasp and raised his .45 pistol. Before he could fire, the creature flew through the air as

358

it took a round in the face from Trent's MK-14 rifle, then it floated slowly to the ground bobbing back and forth the way a dead leaf falls from a tree.

"How's that for dropping it?" Trent yelled to Nathan as he ran toward Josh, who was just on the other side of the helicopter. The smoldering wreckage of the aircraft suddenly burst into flames now that oxygen was returned to the atmosphere. By the time they got to Josh, he had fallen over and was lying on his side. Boomer and Levi arrived shortly after them. Nathan held Josh in his arms; the old man smiled up at him. Trent asked, "Josh, what was that thing?" as he glanced skyward, looking for the pearl-like UFO.

Josh smiled and said, "Good angels have their technology too. It looks as if Nergal got sent to the pit." Josh grimaced and caught his breath before continuing. "Nathan, there's a wooden chest in the den of my house. Get it and give its contents to your General Henderson, tell him he will find answers there and to pay attention to the Black Sun."

"Hang on, Josh, you're going to be okay," Nathan said.

Josh smiled and said, "I'm an old man and I want to go be with my wife, I'm not dying on this mountain Nathan, I'm going home to my loved ones."

Then Josh looked at Levi, "You, young man, I need you to do something for me."

"Anything, Josh," Levi said.

Josh looked Levi in the eye and said, "I have no family left, when they bury me I want you to accept my flag from the color guard. Then I want you to Fly!"

The men were all silent for a moment, then Trent said, "Oh no." Looking across the field, Sam was hobbling slowly along, carrying his father in his arms.

Trent and Boomer ran to Sam and helped him carry Addison's lifeless body, and they laid him gently next to Joshua. Sam was broken; he couldn't stand, he couldn't sit all he could do was kneel over his father.

"Samuel, listen to me," Joshua said.

Sam broke his gaze away from his father's lifeless body and faced the dying Choctaw elder.

"Your father is not in that body; he is standing next to me. He is waiting for me to accompany him on the path to our Great Father. He says you should not morn him, instead honor the life he led. He says you are to also honor the life he and his mother gave you, by finishing tonight's battle, then continue the war. He says don't make the same mistake the Ancient Israelites did. Finish the war and take your promise land. You are loved and well able."

Then Josh went silent, his eyes shut, and his breathing stopped. Like Addison, Joshua Nashoba was gone.

A moan came from some high grass near the helicopter; Levi went to investigate. "It's Eastman," he yelled to the other men. Eastman had been thrown clear of the wreckage on impact and was not caught in the fire that consumed the aircraft.

Nathan and Trent walked over to see Eastman crawling along the ground. Nathan raised his .45 pistol, prepared to put an end to this scourge. Looking up at Nathan, Eastman just smiled and said, "Go ahead, crusader. You can't kill me."

"We'll see about that," Nathan said, applying pressure to the trigger.

"Wait!" Sam screamed.

Nathan lowered his weapon and waited for Sam to walk over to where Eastman lay. He was already healing from his wounds, his connection to Nergal still not broken.

"You're too weak to kill me, Redstone," Eastman spat.

Sam calmly reached over and took the copper-bladed machete off Nathan's belt. In one vicious swing, he severed Eastman's right forearm from the rest of his body. Eastman screamed in agony, and the night air was filled with his curses. Sam handed Nathan back his machete calmly picked up Eastman's severed forearm. Taking a knife from his pocket, he made an incision in the skin of the forearm and removed the implant. Eastman was screaming in pain and oblivious to Sam's actions. Once Sam had the implant out, he threw Eastman's severed forearm into the burning wreckage of the helicopter.

He then handed the implant to Trent and said, "When you guys get back make sure General Henderson gets that. It may be something of value to his effort."

"Nathan, will you grab his legs?" He said, nodding toward Eastman. Nathan picked Eastman up by the legs as Sam took him under the arms.

"Paul you're going to burn in hell anyway, might as well get an early start." They threw Eastman into the burning wreckage; all of the men walked away from the screaming spectacle, save for Sam, who stayed there until Eastman's last whimper. Finally, Sam joined the other men where his father and Josh lay.

Nathan looked at Sam, "We got a hell of a mess here. A downed helicopter with a dead crew and two dead civilians, one with gunshot wounds. Not to mention one big pissed-off Relic still running loose. Sam grabbed his cell phone and dialed the Leflore County Sheriff's private cell phone. "I got the legal stuff covered, don't know what to do about the Relic."

## Thursday, 1 December 2016 03:40 AM CST, Kiamichi Mountains Honobia, OK

For the first time in its existence, the beast was running for its life. Its whole reality had changed. It no longer was the apex hunter; it was the hunted. Its Master was dead or had abandoned it, and the collective, as well as its brothers, were no more. The local clan that he and its brothers had terrorized the past two years was now hunting him. As it ran down the middle of the shallow creek, it could hear the others in pursuit of him.

They whooped and growled and knocked down small trees in an effort to chase him down. It had to get out of this valley and get to a place with fewer of the clan types and more humans. It had kept running at a steady pace so far, able to stay just out of the grasp of the pursuing clan. As it came to a deep, narrow part of the creek, it stopped abruptly before standing in the creek bed with eight male clan members. He started to climb one of the sheer rock-strewn canyon walls to safety.

Then it heard a loud whoop; looking up, it saw the top of the canyon wall was lined with more male clan members from other parts of the valley. A quick look at the opposite side of the creek showed the same situation. Sounds of splashing feet could be heard behind him. He saw nothing but angry feral eyes and barred large flat teeth as he turned. Some held rocks some small trees to use as clubs. All were armed, all had hatred in their eyes, and all were letting out low primal growls.

The beast knew it was his time; he straightened to every inch of his height and expanded his chest and muscles as wide as they would go. Letting out a massive roar, he charged ahead toward the seven clan members blocking his path. A river rock the size of a basketball slammed into his massive head, causing him to slow slightly, but he was somehow able to remain conscious and continue his charge. Next, a log that was twelve inches in diameter whipped viciously into his legs, causing him to lose his balance and fall into the shallow creek. In an instant, twenty of the Kiamichi mountains clan members were upon him. The last thing he saw was an avalanche of teeth, fur, and eyes burning with hatred as the night air became a storm of animalistic screams and howls.

## Thursday, 1 December 2016 04:50 AM CST, Kiamichi Mountains Honobia, OK

Sam sat next to his father's body, quietly reflecting. Nathan, Trent, Boomer, and Levi had set up a defensive perimeter in case the missing Relic returned. The Sheriff's Department had units on the way, and they should be arriving at any moment. The dark morning stillness was broken by a loud smack of wood hitting wood. It came from the direction of Boomer's house. Then another smack came across from the other side of the field. Sam rose to his feet; all of the men were now on alert. There was a loud whoop to the east. Nathan shined his flashlight expecting to see eyeshine and the face of the Relic. Instead, what he saw were ten sets of eyes and ten Sasquatch standing shoulder just outside the wood line. Each had its right hand in the air displaying five fingers. A large, bloodstained male stepped forward into the illumination of the still-burning helicopter. In its left hand, it carried a grisly trophy—the severed head of the missing Relic.

It raised the head for all to see, then it looked at Nathan and nodded toward the fire. Nathan returned the nod and stepped back. The Sasquatch threw the head of the dead Relic into the fire, then turned and walked calmly back into the forest, disappearing into the dark along with the others. The men all looked at each other silently as red and blue flashes of light became visible as first responders from Leflore County arrived on the scene.

# EPILOGUE

*"Now this is not the end. It is not even the beginning of the end. But it is, perhaps, the end of the beginning."*
*-Winston Churchill*

## Monday, 5 December 2016, 12:30 PM CST, Talihina, OK

Christa Redstone clutched her husband's arm closely and watched his eyes as the two flag draped coffins of Addison Redstone and Joshua Nashoba were quietly carried by the two groups of honor Guard s to their positions for the graveside ceremony. Addison's was carried by three soldiers from the US Army's 1st Cavalry Division, each wore the black Stetson trooper's hat topping off their dress blues. Joining them were three members of the local Choctaw Veteran's Honor Guard. Another three Choctaw Veteran's carried Josh Nashoba's coffin along with three US Navy Sailors, dressed in the dark blue Navy crackerjack uniform. Christa knew the look she saw in her husband's eyes.

The grief for his father was there of course, but there was something else in his eyes. She'd seen it before. She knew Sam struggled with decisions of duty and always would. He seemed to think he could not devote himself to two families, his wife and children or the Army. She could see the look in his eyes as he watched the soldiers carrying the casket of his father. She also saw the same look when he glanced at Nathan Parks who was dressed in his Army dress blues, standing next to Trent Simmons who wore his Air Force dress blues and red Pararescue Beret, as both men rendered salutes when the caskets passed them where they stood about fifty feet away from the group of chairs setup by the funeral home for family and mourners.

Addison would be buried here in Talihina; Joshua's remains would be taken another twenty-four miles into the Kiamichi mountains to a cemetery on the Rock Creek Church grounds in Honobia. Members of the local Choctaw people there were waiting to set him in his final resting spot next to his wife Kiyoshi.

Because Joshua Nashoba had no living relatives, Christa mentioned to Sam that his father would want Joshua to be treated as part of the Redstone family and suggested a dual service. Sam agreed, Addison would not want a lonely ceremony for Josh. Christa suggested to Josh an added way to honor both men. The baby boy she was carrying inside her would be named Addison Joshua Redstone. The deaths of both men were ruled accidental caused by being in the wrong place at the wrong time when a U.S. Forest Service helicopter suffered a catastrophic rotor failure and crashed into their campsite. Local and state law enforcement cooperated in keeping the true nature of what had happened from getting out. It would be the last time the Federal Government got a free pass in Leflore County Oklahoma.

When Federal officials began snooping around the crash site and asking questions about what had taken place there. The Leflore County Sheriff reminded them of who the law really in these mountains. He also reminded them that this was the second incident involving government agents that ended in deaths in the past two years. The officials also asked questions about missing agents in the area. The Sheriff had no knowledge of the whereabouts of the agents, but once again mentioned this was the second incident like that in two years.

The investigation became suddenly less intense when the Sheriff said, "From now on I'll just start arresting federal agents that are operating in my county without checking through me first. "That way they won't go missing and when you're looking for them... You can find them in my county jail, safe and sound. Plus, the media parked outside asking what they were doing here in the first place."

When the Forestry agent smirked, the Sheriff looked him in the eyes and said coldly. "Bring this crap to Leflore County again, and the whole world is going to be seeing your stained underwear. Whoever the bigwig is sitting on his throne in Washington, won't like what we'll have to show the press. So go away and don't come back."

Sam watched as the Chaplin began to wind down the ceremony, as he stepped aside and motioned for the family and mourners to stand. An Army Major moved to the head of Addison's coffin and a Naval Lt Commander moved to the head of Joshua's. Many of the people flinched as the first volley from the seven member Choctaw Veterans Rifle squad fired their first of three volleys. Followed by a Choctaw Veteran bugler playing Taps. Once Taps had been played, the mourners took their seats as the flags on each coffin were folded by the respective honor Guard s and given to the two officers. They stepped in unison, the Army Major to Sam, and the Navy Lt. Commander to Levi.

Both quietly recited the same words as they handed the flags to the two men. "On behalf of the President of the United States, and a grateful nation."

As the two officers backed away a four-ship formation of USAF F-16s appeared suddenly from the east heading west. Just before they were over the cemetery the number three plane broke from formation rocketing straight into the cool cloudless Oklahoma sky performing an impressive missing man formation. The roar of their engines thundered over the area then faded quickly as the proceeded west.

"Wow, I wonder who paid for that?" Trent asked.

Nathan replied, "General Henderson called in some markers. He found an Air Force unit that would be flying in the vicinity on a training mission. He talked an Air Force General into having them take a short detour, no wasted fuel, no wasted mission, but a damn fine show of respect."

Watching the dots disappear into the west Trent shared a thought with Nathan, "Pretty ironic, this whole mess started with an F-16 crash two years ago. Now it ends with an F-16 flyby."

"Yeah, you Air Force boys are more trouble than you're worth." Replied Nathan continuing the nearly seventy-year rivalry.

"I should have let that little grey guy inject you with the cosmic jungle juice in his syringe." Trent replied, before quietly pondering a thought. "You know Nathan, even though we've been in the front lines fighting all this weird stuff for a couple of years now. It feels like we lost two of our best with Addison and Joshua. I mean for a couple of old guys; they really made a difference. If it wasn't for Addison in 2014 and Joshua this time, I have to wonder if we would have won."

"I don't know if we've won anything Trent. I'm not even sure you could call what we've accomplished as any kind of victory at all. I have a feeling we're looking at the very tip of a huge iceberg and we can't even fathom what's below the visible surface of this thing. We've lost two very wise leaders; they can't be replaced. We've got to step up now and carry the fight on without their wisdom. I wonder if we have it in us?" Nathan said looking at Sam, then to Levi.

Trent caught his gaze and said, "Guys like those two would be a huge help. Maybe Sam will come back to active duty, and hopefully there's more young guys like Levi there that will catch on and eventually help us. The problem is civilians like Levi there are not able to help us when we're half a world away."

Levi sat mesmerized by the departing jets. Their speed power and noise caused his heart to skip. He thought about Joshua's last word to him and now it hit home. Fly… He was right I need to fly, really fly. Fly fighters like he did. Suddenly Levi knew he had outgrown Honobia and flying his own Piper Cub.

As he watched the lone F-16 in the distance that had become separated from the other three during the missing man formation rolled from its inverted attitude, then banked left and quickly positioned itself to intercept the other three jets. It rejoined the formation so smoothly, it looked effortless. Levi knew better though; he knew there was remarkable skill and experience in the maneuver he'd just witnessed. Levi wanted this and was determined to have it. Although not consciously aware of it, Levi just grabbed the torch Joshua had held out to him with his last words,

Christa could not stand to see the turmoil in her husband's eyes any longer. "Do it!" She said.

Looking at her confused, "Do what?" Sam asked. "Go back into the Army, go finish this so it never comes to our home again."

"Christa, I know you're being supportive, but believe me, you don't want to be an Army wife."

Christa looked at her husband and shook her head. "No Sam, that's not me talking, that's you. It's always been you. You never trusted me enough to be an Army wife, that is why our life together has suffered so many detours. It's time to trust me Sam, it's time to put your fears away. I've proved my strength and faith in you as a wife, now prove yours as a husband."

Sam looked into her determined green eyes, and knew she spoke the truth. "You're right darlin'," he said as he pulled her close in an embrace and thought. Lord please, never let me lose this woman.

## Friday, 9 December 2016, 1:30 AM CST, Kiamichi Mountains Honobia OK

The large male stood at the top of a peak of the north range of mountains overlooking Honobia. His neck and chest bore the scars of battle with the dark ones. The night air, laced with the scent of pine and distant campfires was delicious to its senses. The putrid smell of evil from the dark ones was no longer present. The stars in the chilled autumn sky seemed to shine brighter, the faint glow of man-made lights in the small village below held no threats. His massive chest took in air then expelled it in an explosive whoop lasting fifteen seconds. He did it three more times; he listened as the similar whoops of his brethren came from the mountains in all directions.

From Honobia west to Nashoba, and Clayton, east to Octavia, and Smithville. North to Big Cedar, and Talihina, and south to Bethel, and Batiste. The whoops reverberated loudly through the mountains and valleys. As males from the various clans in the Kiamichi, Winding Stair, and Ouachita Mountains whooped and roared into the crisp night air.

Deer hunters in their tents burrowed just a bit deeper into their sleeping bags, campers around their fires became quietly nervous, worried that their scary campfire tales were coming true. Couples in their beds throughout the various valleys held each other just a bit closer as the thundering vocalizations struck a primal chord in their psyches. A few knew what it was, others could only speculate as to what fearful creature could shatter the silence of the night with such terrific power. The nocturnal forest creatures understood. They stopped their foraging, their hunting, and their mating. They scurried for cover or froze as motionless as boulders. For they knew, it was the song of the Mountain Kings who had returned to reclaim their realm.

THE END

# THE AUTHOR

# JOHN VANDEVENTER

John Vandeventer is originally from Plano, Texas. He is a sixteen-year veteran of the United States Air Force. His lifelong love of military aviation history and interest in UFOs has made him an avid reader. His other hobbies include target shooting, and more recently, writing has become an enjoyable pastime for him. The author's first novel, RELICS, was first published in 2017 after he spent a little over two years writing the novel and researching the topic of Sasquatch as he wrote. In 2018 the author and his wife moved to Honobia,

Oklahoma, in the heart of Oklahoma Sasquatch Country. John has been a guest on several Bigfoot Podcasts as well as a guest speaker at The Honobia Bigfoot Festival in 2018, and he also served as the MC for the 2021 Honobia Bigfoot Festival. RELICS II: The Honobia Remnant is the second book in a planned trilogy. Once the RELICS series is complete, John hopes to continue his writing with more novels and hopefully some Non-Fiction work as well.

# BIBLIOGRAPHY

It would be impossible to mention every book, podcast, or YouTube Channel that has planted creative seeds in my mind, enabling me to write the books in the Relics Series. I've lost track of the hundreds of podcasts I've listened to, trying to get a whiff of an idea that would stimulate my mind to help write the novels, especially this second novel. Besides the obvious inspirations such as Sasquatch Chronicles or Coast to Coast Radio, I ran across numerous other programs, such as Now You See TV. There are ancient non-Biblical texts such as the Book of Enoch and the Book of Jasher. The authors I mention below, I have either read their books or listened to them on podcasts. Their stories and opinions have greatly inspired me while writing this novel. If you are interested in my novels' subject matter, I would suggest doing a google search for any podcasts they're on or, even better, reading their books.

**Frank Edwards:** Flying Saucers Serious Business

**Thomas Horn:** The Invisible Invasion, Petrus Romanus, Exo-Vaticana, Nephilim Stargates

**Frank Joseph:** Military Encounters with Extraterrestrials.

**John Keel:** The Mothman Prophecies

**Donald Keyhoe:** Flying Saucers Are Real, The Flying Saucer Conspiracy, Flying Saucers: Top Secret

**LA Marzulli:** The Cosmic Chess Match, Counter Move, On the Trail of The Nephilim, On the Trail of The Nephilim II

**David Paulides:** Tribal Bigfoot, The Hoopa Project, Missing 411 Series

**Ronald Morehead:** The Quantum Bigfoot

**David Paulides:** Tribal Bigfoot, The Hoopa Project, Missing 411 Series

**Steve Quayle:** Empire Beneath the Ice, Genesis 6 Giants, Aliens and Fallen Angels, Trye Legends, Angel Wars, Long Walkers

**Dr. I.D.E. Thomas:** The Omega Conspiracy

Printed in the USA
CPSIA information can be obtained
at www.ICGtesting.com
LVHW081554181223
766791LV00007B/61